"Donna Gordon has written a true adventure story, and created one of the most unlikely, lovable couples I've ever met: one tiny, one tall, both very scarred and very wise. Lee and Tomas will break your heart and put it back together again."

—Anna Solomon, author of *The Book of V*

WHAT BEN FRANKLIN WOULD HAVE TOLD ME

Donna Gordon

Regal House Publishing

Copyright © 2022 Donna Gordon. All rights reserved.

 Published by
Regal House Publishing, LLC
Raleigh, NC 27587
All rights reserved

ISBN -13 (paperback): 9781646032303
ISBN -13 (epub): 9781646032310
Library of Congress Control Number: 2021943778

Interior layout by C.B. Royal Designs
Cover images © by C.B. Royal
Author photo by Margaret Lampert

Regal House Publishing, LLC
https://regalhousepublishing.com

For Phil, Ben, Jack

"There's a quality of legend about freaks.
Like a person in a fairy tale who stops you and demands that you answer a riddle. Most people go through life dreading they'll have a traumatic experience. Freaks were born with their trauma. They've already passed their test in life. They're aristocrats."

— Diane Arbus

"Sometimes even to live is an act of courage."

— Lucius Annaeus Seneca

PART I

1

Lee knew for a fact that his obituary was already written, by the same reporter who interviewed President Ronald Reagan last fall, shortly after his election. He hoped the headline would be dignified. *Lee Foster Adams, conqueror, explorer, detective—dies at thirteen from rare illness.*

Sometimes he forgot that he looked like a 102-year-old man trapped in a kid's body. But then he would catch a glimpse of his reflection or, worse, see how his appearance frightened others. Bony beyond belief, he looked like an *Outer Limits* alien, his profile as old and cracked as the dead presidents on Mount Rushmore, insides as decrepit as *Night of the Living Dead.* That's what Hutchinson-Gilford progeria syndrome did: decayed you from the moment you were born—causing the cells in your body to age at a super accelerated rate. About the same as a cat, but half as quickly as a zebra, and not nearly as fast as a fruit fly or mouse.

He was three feet eight and weighed thirty-five pounds. He had false teeth, heart disease, arthritis, a defibrillator, and was as bald as the bird on the back of a dollar bill.

He was forbidden to chew gum. Dr. Bream at Children's said he chewed it anyway because he liked to tempt fate and was already living on borrowed time. Dr. Bream said the whole thing, meaning his condition, came about on account of his father's faulty Y chromosome. You can pinpoint things like that in the lab.

In the whole history of modern times, there'd been only about a hundred freaks like him, with an average life expectancy of twelve. Going on thirteen, he was an anomaly. Like the 50 Foot Woman, or Jesus Christ, or Frankenstein.

Lee's favorite thing to eat was strawberries, and his favorite book was *Shane.* He liked westerns, but his favorite character of all time was James Bond. If he had to live his life over, he'd be a spy with a capital *S*, but work for America, not Britain. His favorite gadgets were the spy pen with the ammunition inside and the shoe-phone that Agent 86 had hidden in his heel on *Get Smart*.

Patrick was Lee's pet Vietnamese potbellied pig. Lee and his mother, Cass, adopted him from Little Orphan Hammie's when Lee was five. Patrick was distinctive in his pink-and-white coloring, well-defined snout, and split hooves that made his hip-wide stance both princely and humble. Most people didn't realize what good pets pigs make. How they are smart and clean and look almost identical to humans in the embryonic stage. Then the porcine features kick in at about the fourth month, the tail and snout and bacon in between.

Tomás was splayed out on the couch in the next room. He was Lee's personal Jack-and-the-Beanstalk giant who could carry Lee wherever he wanted when he pretended he couldn't move. He'd been with Lee's family for less than two weeks and was a sorry replacement for their old friend Z, who had been with them since Lee was five, but who couldn't do the job anymore on account of arthritis so bad it locked his elbows and knees.

You'd think Tomás would feel sorry for Lee, but no such luck. Lee could hear Tomás's heavy breathing against the couch cushions, revving loudly and then quieter, like an old airplane engine too heavy for its weight. This was the end of his two-week trial period. Now it was up to Cass and Lee to decide whether or not to let him stay. Lee was sure Tomás had some horrible secret. If he could find out what it was, he'd be able to expose him and convince Cass to send him on his way.

Lee's naps had been running longer and longer as daylight saving time approached and the October light flattened everything into gray. From his room at the far end of a long hall, Lee heard the *ric rac* sound of TV voices and staggered crookedly, like some geriatric version of Bruce Lee in smelly socks, toward the living room, where Tomás was splayed out like a beached whale watching *Who Wants to Make a Deal?*

Tomás saw Lee coming, switched off the TV. He looked away quickly, then looked back, having tucked some raw emptiness behind his eyes. Lee blinked and adjusted his glasses, which day by day appeared thicker and more opaque from degenerative cataracts. "Hey, little man." Tomás stood, then checked his watch. "Two hours. Quite a nap." He slapped the couch cushion next to him, beckoning Lee closer.

"¿Cómo te sientes? How are you feeling?"

At six feet five, with size-sixteen shoes, Tomás Concepción was intimidatingly king-sized—way beyond tall, with hands the size of oven mitts. He was born in Argentina, and his heavy accent easily sing-songed into Spanish, though Lee told him a million times he didn't speak a word. Tomás was the first man to touch the living room ceiling in their apartment with his bare hands, the first to snatch a tomato-colored ladybug off the wall and cover the insect safely in his palm. The highlights of his olive skin were surreptitiously pink—pink nails, pink tunnel of breath leading down into the catacombs of his mouth. When he looked at Lee, his nostrils flared like he smelled something bad. To pick Lee up he needed only his Spartan fingertips and the flats of his palms, and Lee began to feel he was floating on air.

The house in Newark, New Jersey, sat atop a pale gravelly slope on Palisade Road, the ugliest triple-decker on the block, its concrete foundation barnacled in two-foot-high drifts of tar and broken glass. Palisade jagged first south and then north, paralleling Route 9, racing the snail-paced commuter rail all the way from New Jersey to New York. A landfill sat in the distance like an inverted ice cream cone, gulls circling above, marking their turf. Newark was a no-man's-land of factories and trash that few survived but many passed through. In the gray polluted air that replaced oxygen, Cass sometimes said you could lose your name and no one would notice. Sometimes, looking out over the debris of glass and steel, Lee felt like the Lone Ranger in a mask, looking out but never being seen.

At night, the Budweiser Eagle that sat atop the distant brewery was lit up in red, white, and blue neon, its wings appearing and disappearing in a caged attempt at flight simulation. Rahway Avenue boasted an Italian restaurant, movie theatre, pawn shop, check-cashing window.

The only reason they lived here in this revolving door to nowhere was because of Lee's mother, Cass, who at thirty-eight had been working as a makeup artist for a lot of off-Broadway shows since before Lee was born. And there weren't that many apartment buildings in the city that took pigs unannounced—no matter how clean you said they were.

From their vantage point on Palisade Avenue, Lee and his mom had a distant view of the red and yellow squares of light that made up Times Square, Cass's home away from home. Right now, Cass was working on a rip-off of *Cabaret*, the one that originally starred Liza Minnelli and Joel Grey. She was slim and elegant and petite and wore short skirts and no makeup at all. Her lemon-yellow hair spiked up in front like duck fluff. In the morning when she woke she looked clean as the sunrise, without a worry in the world. That was theatre for you, learning how to put on a good face.

Cass was probably meant for something great, but instead got stuck with Lee. Before he was born, she had a hand in designing Cyrano's nose and the wide-eyed expressions on the actors who sang "One Singular Sensation" in *A Chorus Line*. Lee's father, Neil, a mere blip on the radar screen, was chief flavor-mixer for the Dip and Sip ice cream factory two hundred and fifty miles away in Lynn, Massachusetts. And he didn't live with them anymore, on account of Lee, and how stressful it was to live with someone who was always on the verge of a life-and-death crisis. Cass thought Lee's quirks made him colorful, which was another way of saying that she would love him no matter what.

Because Lee was a geek in dwarf's clothes, he wasn't allowed to be left home alone all day. He didn't need a babysitter and didn't wear diapers, but he was kind of weak and stopped going to school last year and had to be homeschooled and reminded to take all the medicines. There were nine different kinds of pills. His pipes were sluggish as sludge.

Tomás was not a certified nurse's aide, but he was trained in CPR. Lee wasn't sure he was trustworthy yet, not sure he'd ever become a friend, but Cass said they'd suspend disbelief these two weeks and give him a try. He had that sing-song accent that made it hard to take his words seriously. That jingle-jangle stuff that came in waves.

One thing about Tomás was different, though. Usually when people first met Lee he'd be the object of pity or buried eyes. When Tomás met him, he didn't blink or look away. Just locked eyes with him like he was reading the stony letters off an abandoned tombstone.

The only thing Lee and Cass knew about Tomás was that he claimed to have written for some kind of newspaper back in Buenos Aires, and before that played some pretty serious ball. But he didn't make it to the majors. Said his coach forced him to throw too many curve balls too young and mucked up his arm.

Lee stopped going to school last year in the seventh grade. He couldn't make it up the stairs without getting palpitations. His would-have-been-almost teachers still sent books home. Mr. Deruda in particular sent poetry and plays. When Lee was reading *Oedipus Rex* by the Greek playwright Sophocles, and the riddle came, the one with the Sphinx—who crawls, then walks on two legs, and then three—he put the book down in a flash and knew right away that the answer was an old man with a cane, on account of the fact that Lee used one sometimes.

But even more than the Greeks, all the really important information in the world that had to do with death and dying seemed to be written in Latin. All the medical terms like *morbid* and *morbidity* and *necrosis*. But American history was Lee's specialty. His one true hero was Ben Franklin. He had a framed replica of Ben's autograph and had memorized the immortal shape of his brow, both head-on and in profile. He had a picture of the first flag of the Continental Congress that Betsy Ross had sewed in 1776. And he'd read all the true stories about George Washington and Paul Revere and Sam Adams. They were to seventeenth-century America like Einstein and the Beatles were to the twentieth. But all of them, though famous, were rife with human flaws. Sam Adams was afraid to ride a horse; Ben Franklin, famous as an American, was something of an expatriate and lived almost half his life in Paris; George Washington had wooden teeth; Paul Revere was just in the right place at the right time. Lee kept his early-American-history paraphernalia on exhibit on the shelves, including a model of George Washington's wooden teeth and a copy of the Gutenberg printing press. He liked to imagine the time it took to put the letters of type in one by one. What he liked most about Ben was that he never gave up, not once, ever. What he didn't have, he managed to invent—from bifocals to the postage stamp. He could have probably done anything, even changed the direction of time.

Lee didn't exactly have a pen pal, but he did have friendships with people who didn't live with them and were hard to define. Number one, at Children's Hospital in New York City, was Dr. Bream, who first diagnosed his condition and was in charge of keeping him alive as much as possible from the point of view of science. On Thursdays, they took the train to Dr. Bream's office for a weekly check-in, where he'd measure Lee's height and weight and vital signs. He sat pale-eyed and droopy at his desk in front of a wall of color photos of red-and-white-striped sailboats parading behind him on choppy blue seas. To the left, out the window, the aluminum-colored lightning rod of the Chrysler building conspired to make him smaller than a flea. Then he tap, tap, tapped his pencil on the wooden desktop and smiled at them and blinked, but had no words of encouragement. Sometimes, when he was there, Lee couldn't help but look Dr. Bream in the eye and worry about how he was going to feel when Lee was gone. Cass, too.

But Dr. Bream gave Lee a gift no one else could have thought of. Kira Throop was Lee's soul mate, his would-be sort of girlfriend if adults ever saw fit to leave them alone for more than five minutes at a time. Dr. Bream introduced them nearly a year ago, seeing as they shared the same disease. Kira was slightly older and slightly smaller, slightly better in every way. Besides being completely bald, at three-feet-seven-inches tall she was far prettier than Lee and would tower over Thumbelina. For Kira's thirteenth birthday this past May, he made her an angel cake in the shape of an angel, without any candles. There was no use in counting when your birth certificate said one thing but your body said another. They celebrated in New York City in her parents' posh apartment. There was no such thing as privacy when your excrement was charted on a graph and your vital signs were recorded three times a day. Kira was the first person Lee talked to on the phone in the morning and the last person he talked to at night before going to sleep.

Besides having friendships and responsibilities, Lee had schoolwork to do at home, which was sent to some mostly anonymous nobody in front of an empty desk at the New Jersey Board of Education. Lee wrote the phone number on the back of his hand and tried to call several times in an hour last week just to check who it was his homework was going to, but no one answered the phone in Trenton. He imagined there must just be some mannequin in a wig. They needed to know he was still trying to learn on a regular basis or they'd throw Cass in jail.

For Lee's English requirement this year, he decided to write a biography of Ben Franklin, seeing as Ben naturally understood some of the most important things on earth: how to see with bifocals, how important lightning is, the importance of the Gutenberg printing press, and, as ambassador to France, the singular delectability of the pastry called the Napoleon.

"Time for vitals, my man," Tomás said now, robotically, like if he'd said it once he'd said it a thousand times. Lee was knee-deep in parchment paper and rumors of Tories and thinking about King James and the ego he must have had to submit to having his name on the Bible for all eternity. Tomás talked to him while looking out the window to some distant point in time. Lee sat next to him and smelled his evergreen scent, his salty sweat soaked into the pits of his T-shirt like old dried tears. Tomás unrolled the blood-pressure cuff from a soft black case tied with a string, and Lee hoisted his sleeve and sighed as Tomás pumped and listened to the hiss of histolic blood gases as they swelled and released. "One-forty over eighty," he mumbled, and wrote it down on the chart. A crooked pinky was flipped up on the outer angle of his left hand where the joint must have been broken in childhood and never reset itself right. He handed Lee a glass of water with five different colored tablets. Afternoon candy. Lee gulped them down one by one, trying to be a good sport, trying to entertain himself by wondering what form of bad behavior could drive Tomás away, wondering exactly what that would take.

"What's up, my man?" Tomás said, brown eyes woozy in the late afternoon light. "Come." He hoisted Lee sideways and carried him across the room, then set him down easy on the sofa between two ripe goose-down pillows.

If Z were here, they'd be playing Monopoly on a board cluttered with a zillion houses and hotels, and one of them would be down on his luck while the other would be cleaning up and being smug about it, lording it over whomever missed buying up Broadway and Park Place. Sometimes Lee thought he was the most clueless boy on earth, the only twelve-year-old without a sexual thought in his mind, except for the fact that he tried to see under Kira's shirt when she bent down to pick something up. So far, the closest thing he'd seen to a naked woman was Cass in a nightgown or underwear ads in the *Times*. If he were a normal boy, he'd be loitering outside the house avoiding homework, or shooting hoops, or trying to hide something from an adult, or telling out-and-out lies.

But he could barely think of those things. It's not that he was worried about dying. Sometimes he thought dying would bring him to some home away from home. Like coming back to Earth after a hazy trip to Mars.

"Gin, anyone?" Tomás said now, holding up the deck. They were sitting in the living room watching the clock, counting the minutes before Cass would return. Tomás nodded his Buddha nod and shuffled the cards in a pleated accordion way. Lee wasn't much of a strategist, was no good at games, but had become a fearless gambler on account of having nothing left to lose.

"Okay," Lee sighed, putting down his pen and closing his book. "Seeing as you're not going to take no for an answer."

Tomás shuffled, then dealt. Less than five minutes later he flipped up his hand: three jacks, four queens, a trio of tens, and Lee was done for.

"Man," Lee said. "How'd you do that?"

Tomás shrugged, reordered the cards. "Got lady luck on my side, I guess."

Lee looked up into Tomás's face, where his last breath paused so long Lee thought he had begun to take a permanent leave of absence. A thin red scar skimmed the edge of Tomás's neck where it peeked out of the collar of his dingy white shirt. The shade of red that Betsy Ross first used for the American flag.

And now Lee got the nerve to ask what it was he'd been thinking about since the first day Tomás showed up for work.

"Do you mind if I ask how you got that scar?"

Lee eyed it steadily, resisting the urge to run his finger along its zippered side. Since it looked like they may be stuck together for a while, over the past few days Lee had been trying to narrow in on any hidden secrets Tomás might have and had been doing his homework on Argentina. Bits and pieces of news articles were daily scattered through the *Evening Ledger* and *New York Times* that didn't make sense to him yet, about something called a Dirty War, which you would think was about people who were in need of better hygiene, but as far as Lee could tell was about innocent people being abducted off city streets for crimes against the government.

More than anything, Lee wanted to know if Tomás had been blindfolded and taken prisoner, if he had used a gun, or worse—had been fired upon.

"Well, that's a story for another time," Tomás said.

And if Lee hadn't needed him so much, he would probably have jumped up and down and demanded immediate answers to his questions, including: Who are you? How can you take care of me, the Elfin Head, Chicken Man?

"Time out," Lee said to Tomás, whose legs seemed to be twice the length of his torso.

❧

Tomás was stirring some instant chicken noodle Cup-a-Soup in the kitchen in an ocher mug. The smell was worse than old socks stirred with garbage, and Lee felt weak and wanted to puke.

He teeter-tottered back down the hall to his room to check on Patrick. Patrick slept even more than he did. He was slovenly by nature but had never to Lee's knowledge been sick. Sure enough he was asleep on top of the red knitted shawl with white fringes that Cass made for him, asleep like a king.

Lee closed the door to his room, where the shapes were made of angles of one kind or another. He liked shapes that had right angles. Right angles were like happy endings. They felt complete. Circles didn't have angles, but you could wrap your head around them as many times as you wished and could estimate that the diameter would be about one-third the circumference. That's what *pi* was for.

Lee's journal was on his bedside table. The one Dr. Bream at Children's asked him to keep. Dr. Bream said Lee was going to be famous one day. Said he was such an anomaly and that his treatment was on the house. He asked Lee's permission to write a book about him, which was how President Reagan's reporter had contacted him, and he took Lee's picture every week in order to watch him drying out from the inside like a prune. *Okay, why not?* Lee had said. It was hard to keep the journal up. It was only a matter of time. He knew one day soon he'd have a heart attack or die in his sleep, and his story would end in the dry white space where the ink stopped.

Sometimes he resented having to write in it, but other times it made him feel worthy. It was also part of the deal they had made, part of why his medical treatments were on the house, and why Cass didn't have to work two jobs. He was supposed to write the truth about what he felt inside. But as far as he could tell, there weren't any words created that could say why he was on this treadmill with time, or why his collarbones were disintegrating like limestone, or why his spine felt like a brittle trail of broken teeth.

In his journal he kept a list of things he wanted to do before he was gone:

Visit Washington, DC, and stand on the steps of the Capitol
Ride in a hot air balloon
Taste chocolate fondue
Trail a beetle under a dung pile
Earn a Boy Scout badge for spelunking

Lee deposited a rawhide bone in front of Patrick's nose, and he sniffed it lazily but remained asleep. He was a companion, but not a patriot.

Lee went back down the hall, where Tomás was waiting, his body stretched out like a crocodile but nowhere green.

"Poker?" Tomás asked, holding up the cards.

Lee looked skyward, checked his watch, and speculated on how many games he'd have to play before Cass was due home just past six.

They walked down the long hallway to the living room. Lee sat on a big pillow so he wouldn't scrape his sacrum bone and started gambling big like there was no tomorrow.

"Hey, little man, you always play like a high roller? Gonna risk it all?"

It had only been two weeks, and Tomás thought he knew him inside out. Well, hold on, buddy, I've got some news for you, Lee thought. It was up to him if Tomás lived to collect another paycheck.

Lee laughed and shook his head, 'cause he would never give in. Tomás could chase him to Timbuktu, and still he would outlast him. Mostly because Lee had nothing to lose.

"What do you think?" Lee said. "Think I'm gonna give in to a loser? Hit me," he said, and asked for two more cards. He smiled faintly and held his cards higher, imagining what it might be like to have a real father. How if he had been Tomás's son, Tomás would have probably squished anyone like a bug who even smiled at him crooked.

"What've you got?" Tomás asked, leaning forward from the bottle-green sofa cushion. The one gold tooth at the back of his mouth caught the light. His body gave off an unrivaled amount of heat, and Lee couldn't help thinking how in another time Tomás could have been the gladiator at the wall of a gated city.

Lee was looking down at his cards too long. He sensed Tomás was ready to fold but trying not to give it away. Lee had three kings, four queens, and suddenly picked up two more aces and was in the catbird seat.

"Satisfied?" he said, laying his cards in a fan.

Lee got up wordlessly, leaving Tomás there, his mouth open. It was already late afternoon. Outside, the wintry street was quiet, the familiar houses disappearing in a diminishing row of soft gray roofs clear to the vanishing point. Like the soft gray color that filled the concentric reverberations of an echo, like the lost sound of a voice you had to strain to hear. Made him think that time wouldn't wait, that we were always on the verge of disappearing.

If you were going to be in a race with time, you ought to be able to choose it, he thought, not have it choose you.

"Rematch?" Tomás asked.

"Not today," Lee said, collapsing next to him, intent on trying to discover where that long scar began and ended beneath Tomás's clothes. Lee had scars across his chest where he'd been invaded by heart attacks and mild strokes and wires connecting him to electrodes that depended on energy we relied on but could never actually see. And he thought how Ben Franklin really had something when he showed us electricity, and how Sir Isaac Newton was right to risk it all with his belief in the planets being juggled in space, belted by gravity. And soon Lee was exhausted from thinking of all the ideas that existed in the world and held its structure in place, because for him time was different. He didn't live within its rules.

"Guess I win by default then," Tomás said, gathering up the cards.

"No one ever wins by default," Lee said. "You only win by proving yourself the better opponent."

Furious, Lee took a sip of water. He began to choke and was surprised by how expertly Tomás caught him and pounded out the air bubble in his back. He eased back on the cushions, continuing to breathe, and tried to remember the name of that disease where people nearly killed the ones they loved and then rescued them just in the nick of time. It came to him: Münchhausen by Proxy.

Then Tomás leaned perilously close to his face, quickly out of bounds, and Lee could see the porous holes in his face scarred from acne and cross-hatched with lines at the edges of his eyes where the sub-equatorial sun had shown no mercy.

"Lee," he whispered. "*Escúchame*," he said urgently, lapsing into Spanish. "You might think I don't understand, but I do." He tapped the hallow cavity in his chest. "*Estoy aquí para ti*, I'm here for you." His eyes glazed, and Lee felt all gravelly inside. And it was like he could see tiny bits of static electricity hanging in the air, but they were really dust particles.

"Lee," Tomás said, pulling back, "I'm sorry if I offended you. I was just trying to tell you that there're things I can understand that you might not imagine, things I might be able to help with. In my country, things can get out of control. People do things, and the world goes crazy. You've got to feel a thousand years old inside sometimes with your condition. Maybe you'd like somebody to talk to. Somebody other than your mom or your doctors."

"Jeez," Lee said. "Let's not go crazy. All I did was drink water a little too fast. And I'm not exactly alone, anyway," he said defiantly, the heat of embarrassment moving up his neck. "No matter what you think," he said, standing to face Tomás. "And you don't need to feel sorry for me either," he said, his voice rising to a tremble.

"I have friends and a life and a girlfriend, for Christ's sake. Kira Anastasia Throop is my number-one best friend outside of Cass and Z, on account of she has Hutchinson-Gilford like me, though she is technically six months older and a lot better looking! And Kira and Cass and I are going on a trip to DC and Philadelphia, just the three of us, right before Thanksgiving. You're not invited. We've been planning it for months. If you actually manage to keep your job, I'll introduce you to Kira and show you our itinerary. Her parents are too old to come, much older than Cass, so it's just the three of us going on the road. Kira's practicing to be a ballerina and has seen Nureyev and the Bolshoi. She can plié and pirouette just like in the movies. And by the way, if you didn't already notice, everyone says I'm advanced for my age."

Tomás looked hurt, and Lee felt momentarily ashamed.

He was quiet for a minute, looking down at Tomás's shoes, the weight of his feet, which looked like pale red bricks tied to strings.

2

By now it was nearly six o'clock and raining, time for the changing of the guard. On Forty-Second Street at the Beverly Theatre in Times Square, Cass looked sideways at her watch and started to worry about making the six thirty-two train, while tidying up the aging actress's face with little more than a palette of primary colors and a set of sable brushes. Friday, date night, she thought—knowing she'd make a big stink about it with Lee. Takeout Chinese and watching TV was a ritual they both looked forward to.

Soon she was at the front door and turning the key in the lock. "Hey, everybody, pretty nasty out there," she said, closing the door behind her to shut it all out. She dried her hands on the damp kitchen towel twisted through the slot of the refrigerator door handle, ran her hands through her hair and turned around to scan the room to see what, if anything, had changed in the past ten hours. Her small, thin hands were calloused and strong, the tendons visible as wires. At five feet two and 103 pounds she was as sinewy as a dancer. In college she had studied theatrical lighting, costumes, makeup. Her parents had both passed before Lee's illness was diagnosed, first her mother, then her father, in the space of two years. She'd been left with a small inheritance, enough to pay off the first round of doctor's bills but not enough to answer the riddle of how to die a thousand deaths before he'd be gone.

"Date night, right?" she said. "Been looking forward to it all day."

"Whoa, little man, aren't you lucky?" Tomás's eyebrows raised while Lee threw him a glare.

"How'd everything go here?" Cass asked, giving Lee a hug. It had broken her heart to have to let go of Z, old friend to them as he was.

"Just fine," Tomás said, towering over them. "Not bad. No, sir."

Cass looked from Tomás to Lee and tried to read their expressions. Tomás's head was barely eight inches from the ceiling. He reached to the hall table for his black knitted cap and blue windbreaker with white stripes, the reflectors on his size-sixteen Nikes picking up the light.

"No, it's *ma'am*!" Lee corrected him. "She's not a *sir*!"

"Hey, Lee." Cass leaned closer and kissed his cheek, reading the smoke signals in Tomás's face. She put her bags down and stowed her key in the red enamel box on the table by the door, the box with the black-lacquer Chinese lettering that nobody knew how to read, though she enjoyed the shape of the calligraphy the way she might enjoy an abstract painting. Her purse contained backups of all the survival gear Lee required: nitroglycerin in case of heart attack, antacids, laxatives, ipecac to induce vomiting.

She stood at the window, looking out for a minute, transitioning from work mode into motherhood. The apartment, being so high up on the hill, had remained curtainless since the day they'd moved in. Streetlights came on now, and the lights from the glass storefront of the Store 24 blinked off and on across the walls in red, yellow, and green neon.

"This little guy was good company," Tomás said. "We got along pretty okay."

Cass put her arm around Lee's shoulder and squeezed lightly, feeling the winged scapula bones of his back like plane geometry, feeling his ribs poking jaggedly against the thin fabric of his cotton shirt.

"We played a lot of cards," Lee said. "Even though I told Tomás umpteen times I had important work to do. Ben Franklin, remember him?"

"Afterward," Tomás said, "this little guy took a long nap. Then we did a little salsa. Hey, little man," he called over, reaching for the doorknob. "I have one word for you: rematch. Monday. Same as usual."

"That's five words," Lee said evenly, counting them aloud on his fingers.

"No need to be rude, Lee," Cass said.

"And blackjack, baby. That's going to be our new game. Going to go for double or nothing," said Tomás. "Be ready to roll."

"As far as I know, Tomás," Cass laughed, "it's you who's going to have to watch out. When it's just the two of us playing cards, or anything else for that matter, he wins every time."

"Thanks again, Tomás," Cass said, hands on hips, feeling the exhaustion of the week. "See you Monday," she breathed, pushing her wet bangs to a higher altitude.

Then it was the two of them alone.

"Whew," she said, kneeling to Lee's level to look him in the eye. "So how did it really go? Okay? He's not too weird or anything, didn't fall asleep or start talking gibberish? Didn't do anything crazy like wash his socks in the sink or make long-distance phone calls? Didn't fall asleep like Z did toward the end?"

"So far he seems okay," Lee said begrudgingly, helping to unpack the Chinese takeout from the bag by the door and moving into the kitchen to ready the food for plates. "He's obsessed with cards, pretends he doesn't care, but I think he'd do anything to win. If you ask me, he's a little crazy. And another thing," Lee said, his eyes narrowing. "I'm sure he's hiding something big. Otherwise, what would he be doing with us? I told him about Kira and our trip to DC. I don't think he could find DC or Philadelphia on the map. I don't think he's even heard of Ben Franklin."

"Well, let's see how it goes," Cass said, passing her hand along Lee's forehead, unofficially taking his pulse. "One day at a time, right? No one says we have to keep him. His cousin Raymond didn't show up for work today, he was sick or something. That's the problem with paying under the table. Here today, gone tomorrow, but let's give him a try a little longer. At least he's shown us proof that he's certified in CPR. So far he seems to know what he's doing. Okay, kid? So far so good?"

"Sure, Cass," Lee said. "It's only been a couple of weeks.

Maybe we'll start to grow on each other, like mold or something. I don't think he's been honest. About his past, I mean. I just have a feeling. I just hope he's not a mass murderer."

Cass swallowed and turned away, felt her gut bottom out, thinking how much Lee must still miss Z. At least with Z he didn't have to say anything. With Z, for a while, he seemed to forget who he was. She had to admit, she was on her guard about Tomás too. It had been only two short weeks, and when she left the house in the morning, she still worried about what she'd come home to.

Cass unloaded the groceries and the small cardboard containers of takeout Chinese filled with greasy chow fun and shrimp with black-bean sauce flecked with dark shrubs of broccoli.

"*Brr,* it's cold in here," she said, rubbing her hands together. "Let's try to warm things up a bit," she said, rummaging through the kitchen drawer for a box of matches.

The rain continued to reinvent itself in rivulets outside the window as she stooped to light the pilot in the oven with a wooden match. The flame flared up in a gaseous blue wave, and she came out with a surprised look, her eyebrows singed.

"That'll help a little," she said. "If Tomás is a keeper, we'll teach him that trick."

Then she heard the noise of the train and watched, through the window, the familiar serpentine swag of the commuter rail jogging its way into the city, loud and rhythmic, hugging the tracks—three corroded black cars and a tarnished red caboose, stuttering into infinity, like a fire working to put itself out.

"Hey, babe, look at me," she said now, one hand on Lee's shoulder. "You know I know. You know I understand. Right? Not easy to replace somebody. No matter who it is."

Lee looked at her, saying nothing, trying to imagine what it was like for her to be around all those beautiful actors and actresses all day, people whose surfaces catch the light and can dazzle an audience from a distance. Then when she came home, no amount of makeup could change what he was.

"So, date night, right, Lee?" she turned to him, her cheeks flushed. "You up for it?"

"Guess so, sure," he said. "Why not?"

"Okay, hon, just wait a sec," she said, digging in her purse. "Just let me run down and grab a quick cigarette. It's a filthy habit and will probably kill me, but if I don't have one immediately, I think my head's going to explode."

"Sure, Cass. Go ahead. I'll fix the table."

She descended the wooden staircase, reaching to keep her balance against the too-low ceiling of the cramped back stairway, made her way to the first-floor landing within inches of the icy rain, and propped the back door open on its rusty hinge with the broken remains of a sodden brick. Crude circles of colored light bounced back and forth between the black asphalt alleyway and the convenience store across the street as she reached inside her bag for a Marlboro. A light mist sputtered across the puddles surrounding the trash as she cupped the lighter between her hands and the flames ignited into the blackness. The first inhale was good and quick and filled her nostrils till they hurt. Then she exhaled and looked down Gray Street to where it intersected with Dunn and scanned the pencil-width of light that marked the ill-stocked Store 24 across the alleyway. The choreographed movement of the dancers working themselves across the stage, the heat of the spotlights, the jag of the train, still shuffled through her brain in easy syncopation. She blew out a funnel of smoke, and her mind emptied for the first time all day as she let the geometry of the city unsettle her brain. Soft orderly building blocks spread out like forgiveness.

Then Cass inhaled and thought again about her son, and how hard it was to have a child who never had an honest shot at things, whose trusting eyes broke you every time he was sick because he was so grateful for what little you offered him in return.

She looked up at the black sky dusted with gray clouds and saw an iridescent rinse of color surrounding the bulb of the streetlight, saw the angry shape of raindrops pressing down harder, increasing the hushed timpani of their downward tilt. Her heart sank, then rose and expanded. She almost laughed. She was the unlikeliest person of all time to have become a parent. More likely for her to have become a priest. How had such a long road from nowhere taken her here, to where she wore the robe of motherhood like an ersatz Joan of Arc?

She took another drag, and then another, until there was a slight buzz to her brain and a texture to time that went grainy and gray, giving her the sense of aloneness she needed. She stood there idling, still, while the clouds moved out and the sky grew soft and opalescent in an effort to clear.

Then she looked up on an arc of distance to a place where there were no answers. But still she asked the question, because there was no place else to go: What piece of the earth did she disturb for God or gravity or the forces of good and evil to punish them like this? Why not someone else's child, why Lee? Why not have him be perfect, whole?

The raw ache in her stomach made her queasy, and she realized she hadn't eaten for most of the day. Her arms were cold where she'd pushed up the sleeves of her navy wool sweater. And though she had no talent for acting, she knew what she needed to do. The pain and love of belonging to someone is the only reason we exist, the only religion we know.

She put out her cigarette in a sea of wet pebbles, watched her shadow climb the stairs, then stepped back into it. "Hey, babe, I'm back," she called. "Where are you?"

In the kitchen Lee had set two white plates and paper napkins and identical pairs of wooden chopsticks and stood proudly waiting for her to notice he had poured her a cold beer.

"Thanks, babe," she said, nodding to him. "I'm famished."

3

By nine o'clock Cass had dozed off completely, her yellow hair plastered against the couch cushion like static electricity. Her pinky trembled a little in her sleep while the worn light on the side-table lamp flickered slightly. They sat together on the faded, red-damask sofa like two parallel lines in space, watching the James Bond movie *Goldfinger,* close but not completely touching. And for one brief, clear moment Lee took advantage of that time and leaned against her and knew exactly who he was, a deformed boy poised on the edge of time, loved for the simple shape his molecules took up in space, his blood's arrangement of particles mimicking hers. Like water, like a fountain. And he knew someday he would break her heart.

Outside, the sky was as dark as the blackest black, and each pointed white star could steal your breath if you looked long enough and tried to fathom its stellar age. And seeing was all there was for a little while. He thought to himself how he may be on a raft facing forever, but when Cass was close like this he saw no end in sight. And that's when he began to think how every minute counts, and he began to think he even understood something about love and why it was so hard to say it, to say I love you, no matter how close you feel. How it was much more than a thing with a beginning and an end, but some version of heat and light in which you're trapped in-between, and for a little while it felt good to be snug and illuminated like that. But that was temporary, and soon you would be something else. And how molecules shifted to give things shape. And how if the world were without light, there would be no dimensionality to anything, just the artist's word for it, called *chiaroscuro* in Italian, which he read about in a biography of Leonardo da Vinci last year. And which technique was also used by Raphael and Michelangelo. And so he was also grateful for shadows.

Sean Connery, who played James Bond in the first seven Bond movies, was discovered while still a small-town boxer in Wales. And it just goes to show that anything can happen. What Lee liked about James Bond was that he was a man of action. He was always able to keep his cool under pressure. He had good clothes and the most amazing gadgets.

The beautiful female pilots were getting into the crop-dusters that would spray down poison and put everyone to sleep so that Goldfinger could steal all the gold from Fort Knox. Pussy Galore wore the most incredible stretch pants, and her shellacked hair seemed to hold its winged shape despite all manner of wind turbulence. Lee nodded and knew how Cass would have liked to see that part if only she had not fallen asleep. Minutes later, when the credits rolled, and Sean Connery had defeated Goldfinger, Cass was suddenly awake.

"Hey, c'mon, kid," she said, embarrassed, sitting up, yawning. "Time for bed. Think you're going to stay up all night?" Lee allowed her to gather him easily in her arms and start down the hall.

"But I forgot to call Kira," Lee said, remembering suddenly and feeling disappointed. It was their ritual every night before bed. "It's the first time in months. She'll be worried something happened."

"She'll be just fine," Cass said. "It's late now. You can tell her in the morning that it's my fault, that I kidnapped you to watch a movie, and we both fell asleep."

Afterward when he'd put on his size-eight pajamas and brushed what was left of his teeth and removed his dentures and looked like some deranged, emaciated version of the Missing Link, Lee settled into bed, where Patrick was already waiting for him, asleep in his basket at the foot of the bed, his familiar congested snores rising and falling like radio static.

"Long day," Cass said, yawning. She smelled of apricots, soy sauce, wood glue. A little grain of rice still stuck between her bottom front teeth.

"Look, Lee," Cass said. "There's something I should have

told you right away tonight, but I just couldn't ruin our evening. And I know it's something you're not going to want to hear."

"Whatever it is, Cass, just tell me. I'm so sleepy."

"It's about our trip to DC with Kira," Cass said. "I know we've been planning for what feels like forever, and I know we're supposed to leave next week, but I'm afraid now I can't go. I'm so disappointed. They need me at the theatre, they've accelerated the rehearsal schedule so the show can open sooner, and they don't care a bit how it affects our plans. I begged the director to find a replacement, I even offered to find one myself, but this far into rehearsals they don't want to take a chance. I guess that's called being good at one's job."

"But, Cass," Lee said, fumbling for his glasses, struggling to sit up. "How could you? We've been counting on this for months. Kira even told me she was glad it was you taking us and not her parents, because you have more energy and would keep us going day and night. We already planned everything. Don't you remember? You were going to take our picture in front of the Liberty Bell."

"I'm so sorry, Lee," Cass said, feeling guilty as hell. "If there was any way I could change things, you know I would. I'm so damn pissed at those guys. I'd walk away if I could, but you know we need the money. There is another possibility," she said slowly. "I've already checked with Tomás and with Kira's parents, Joe and Louise. Tomás is willing to take the two of you instead. Apparently he has a friend there, a reporter at the *Washington Post*, whom he worked with back in Argentina. There's some possibility the three of you could stay in her apartment while she's away. But if you don't want to have Tomás take you, I completely understand. Maybe I can take you and Kira next spring," Cass said, uncertainly.

Seconds passed, though Lee had no real sense of time. He had closed his eyes, and now finally opened them and looked at Cass, wondering how quickly the conspiracy had taken shape, wondering how long they had known.

"I know it's not your fault, but I still want you," he said.

"Tomás is just…just not someone to be trusted. He barely speaks English, and he takes up too much space in the room. And his jokes aren't funny. I don't think he knows a thing about Ben Franklin. Or progeria for that matter. Knowing CPR is not the same as being a mom or a dad. And we'd be pretty far from home. But then waiting till spring might be too long too," he said. "What if one of us was too sick, or worse, died by then? But I guess I can talk to Kira tomorrow about going with Tomás rather than not going at all. But I have to tell you I don't trust Tomás. I don't believe anything he says."

"Nonsense," Cass said. "Things seem to be going okay. And if he has friends in DC all the better. Though it's true we don't know a hell of a lot about him. He seems pretty trustworthy to me. And I can keep tabs on you from here. Bream has given his okay, and I can get him to make a list of every single hospital and doctor nearby. You'd need to call every day. It would be less than a week, just till Thanksgiving. Talk it over with Kira tomorrow. I'll talk to her parents again too. We'll take it from there. Now lights out," she said, sitting beside him on the edge of his bed and stroking his skull where scores of yellow hairs once grew before falling out just before his second birthday.

Lee lay in the dark knowing he was a sight, knowing that his temples bore the soft indentations of age, that all his pressure points were visible, making him an easy target. He had broken his promise to Kira by not remembering to call. He knew Romeo and Juliet were perhaps fourteen and fifteen when they got married in secret. He hadn't told anybody he was thinking about popping the question.

"Good night, my sweet," Cass said, tucking him in. "You're my prince of princes, my king of kings."

And Lee heard how her voice was hoarse and ragged. He looked up at her, knowing he was nothing of the sort, and he closed his eyes from the pain of disappearing, knowing how he was burning himself down from the inside out, faster than she knew, like a dying star.

4

That night, Tomás Concepción put his cousin Raymond's borrowed blue Volkswagen into gear and let it careen down Speen Street, heading west toward downtown. The neon lights of the staunch Budweiser Eagle guarding the brewery across the river stuttered and realigned themselves over and over in a pointillist pattern of red, white, and blue corona, tail feathers and wings. The damn bird kept watch on him wherever he went. Within a few feet Tomás came to a forced stop on Broadway as the rush hour traffic stalled, trying to make its way toward the Lincoln Tunnel into Manhattan. The road was too narrow to pass. It was a slow process, a slow burn.

He sat behind the dogged cars, inching behind, feeling prehistoric and alone. He wondered faintly—if he lasted here in the States through winter—what falling snow might look like, or taste like on his tongue.

Finally the traffic moved, and the road widened. He took his first left on Broad Street, parked, and got out in front of an old four-story gray building filigreed with concrete. The downtown Newark YMCA was made of pale, colorless stone and would last forever. Like cockroaches, like dung. The neighborhood still felt a little like home, though he had his own place a few blocks away now on Lancaster Terrace with a separate bedroom and a secondhand fifteen-inch TV. The gym there kept him alive for the first six months while he looked for work. It was his first home after landing at Kennedy International, not knowing what his fate would be. Paradise-central was what he had hoped for, not a New York City landscape that resembled the inside of a trash can—a tangled wreck of gray and black buildings through which oxygen squeezed itself into dying foliage. And Newark, New Jersey, where his cousin Raymond lived, had made him do an about-face. For the likes of him he couldn't figure out why it was called the Garden State. No bougainvillea in sight, not even an aloe or a cactus. Instead of geckos, a spectacle of squirrels—mangy cousins to rats—that would steal your lunch right out of your hands. And pigeons that shot white pasty ammunition out their butts onto the sidewalks like kamikaze pilots. People lived in disgrace, catch as catch can, like lesser creatures than man in cardboard boxes in alleys and doorways.

Before coming to Newark there'd been a brief week in Seattle where he was introduced to other refugees granted visas under the humanitarian auspices of the American government that had taken seriously the plight of the nearly thirty thousand disappeared in Argentina. His cousin Raymond, who had arrived in the States three years earlier and found a job as a grip at the theatre where Cass worked, had helped him find a room at the Y till he had a chance to make some money of his own. When Raymond heard Cass needed a nursemaid for her ailing son, he put her in touch with Tomás, who got certified in the basics of first aid and CPR at a neighborhood health center in a matter of days. When offered the job, he took it without hesitation.

Tomás opened the trunk and withdrew his nylon Nike bag, remembering how in those earlier days the Y made him feel like a different kind of prisoner, but also helped him feel contained. One small room with a bed, table, and dresser—one window locked from the outside, and a shared bathroom at the end of the hall. At night the walls groaned with iniquity, and the rabid heartbeats of men displaced from home and family, each one's story more heroic than the next, making an attempt to justify to themselves how they had wound up alone.

He entered the building and went inside. The old run-down gym on the basement level was industrial looking and bathed in taciturn shades of gray, lathered with the stink and germ warfare of more than thirty years of sweat. It boasted a Nautilus circuit, some knee-high weight benches on steel tripods drilled into the concrete floor, and rows of octagonally tipped free weights that had seen better days. The locker room was pock-marked with identical tin lockers punched with tiny aerating holes and bull's-eyed with round silver Master locks.

Working out made him feel better, like he was marbling his human flesh into steak and made his cock lift a little, sensing life after death.

He opened his locker now, stowed his jacket on a hook. The reverberations of metal against wood on the nearby gym floor rattled his nerves even after all this time, igniting memories of disarmament and blows to the head. Three years of imprison-ment for involuntarily straddling the leftist line as a journalist against Videla's military regime. They had come for him and his wife at dawn, men in uniform shouldering guns as they tried to escape with their lives, Tomás forcing his wife Violeta to go first, racing in opposite directions across the tiled rooftop of their apartment building.

He shook his head involuntarily and tried to strangle the noise in his brain. He reached into his gym bag for sweats and T-shirt. There were all kinds of hells, he thought, as he changed into his gray sweatpants and cinched the drawstrings tighter around his narrow waist—forestalling the anger in his fists, the grievances galvanized in his bones, knowing full well that rage like his had never been known to recycle itself into anything good.

He pulled the gray T-shirt over his head, knowing how no one could have intuited the scars that creased his genitals, be-neath his clothes, the chain-link pattern imprinted along his back from hip to trapezius. He remembered all too well how pressed wood, adorned with barbed wire, could cause more pain than any other instrument. And then, the astonishment of freedom, too good to be true, making him feel guilty that his release must have somehow stolen someone else's good fortune. It was the afternoon of March 11, 1979. That was the day his luck had turned, and he had been thrown blindfolded into the back of an overheated van without warning. Then, he'd been driven for miles, over what felt like a jumbled lunar landscape, feeling a light prismatic ripple of fresh air whistle across his hands, his neck, his face—only to be dumped into a trash-filled alleyway just blocks outside the Plaza de Mayo, where it had all begun, and where the *Abuelas* still marched on Thursday afternoons. He was as bewildered as anyone as to why he had been set free. There was no opportunity to face his captors.

In Buenos Aires, in the days that followed, he came up against nothing but dead ends, and his life as he had remembered it was gone. There was no news to be had of Violeta Concepción. And their child, with whom she had been pregnant when abducted? Had they fled the country? Had she miscarried? It was already well known that Argentine president Jorge Rafael Videla, a man known for his English tailored suits and expensive tastes, had been harvesting infants from pregnant women prisoners, keeping the mothers alive only long enough to give birth. The babies were sold on the black market to high-ranking military families.

The streets had been deserted the day he had knocked at their old apartment door and a feeble, toothless man answered, claiming to know nothing of Violeta's whereabouts. She had no other family. Tomás was surprised to find some small amount of money still left in their joint bank account. He rented a room across from the apartment, sleeping in his clothes and abhorring the light, the neighborhood, in which so much had changed. He had hoped to catch a glimpse of Violeta coming or going, her hands pushing a stroller, a song on her lips, but after two months he was forced to give up. Three years away was a long time. At night the weight of unknowability, like the weight of a thousand corpses, laid its collective head upon his pillow. And for all of the other disappeared, and the ghosts of the missing who had died among him? Who would mourn for them? Who would remember they had existed?

In America there was freedom of the press, the Fifth Amendment, a Constitution of laws that made it possible to speak out. But below the equator in countries like Argentina, the secret police could get away with anything.

Every day for three years, he had been blindfolded, even

in the shower. He lost all sense of time. There was no use for soap and water, shapes invented for some human purpose he couldn't remember. In that tiny room, barely bigger than his body, what kept him sane were certain lines of poetry by Neruda, Vallejo, and Borges—that still resurrected beauty and hope in fragmented waves, the memory of their words also held in captivity, like wild birds folded into smaller and smaller spaces. He remembered Violeta's face—the angle of her cheekbones woven through his memory like hope, her breasts tilted forward, and the line of her throat, all the places his mouth had studied, uttering involuntary things that had surprised him as he had pushed in and out between her thighs—and how there are many names for the ultimate act of being; that sex, he realized, was only one of them, but that forgiveness was much harder and required more effort.

Just months after he'd been imprisoned, he was assaulted by taunting words from one of the guards saying that his wife had given birth to a baby girl in another prison, presumably just yards away from where he had been isolated. At first he didn't believe him, but then the guard said her name aloud, *Violeta,* and there was no mistaking it.

The morning they escaped, she had run ahead of him, the rose floral print of her dress lifted by the wind as she skirted the tile rooftop, revealing brown naked calves as she paused to look back at him one last time. All those days of imprisonment, lost in the dark, he had imagined her free, relocated somewhere safe. It had kept him going. He had never once let himself envision the child.

After his release, weeks passed, and all leads to Violeta's whereabouts in Buenos Aires were exhausted. He went to the clinic where she had worked, and it was confirmed by those who remained, and who could remember, that she had been missing since roughly the same time as he.

Eventually there was nothing left; he had to accept that his wife and child were likely dead, or that his child had been secretly and illegally adopted by a family impossible to track down. The idea of staying in the country that had taken so much from him was too painful to bear. He made plans to go to America where his co-worker Margaret and his distant cousin Raymond had relocated.

∽

Tomás put on his sneakers and laced them tight. It was Friday night, the activity in the gym winding down, the singles set already pooling inside bars and nightclubs. How many bench presses of the heavy barbells would it take to exhaust him before he would reward himself with scotch, a hot shower, and bed? It had been a long day, a long week. Two weeks, in fact. The kid, Lee, spooked him every morning when he answered the door looking as if he had emerged from the grave. The kid reminded him of the ghosts he had dreamed of in prison, the half-eaten people he had imagined, the soulless selves.

The theme from *Rocky* poured out of the wall speakers now, and a sleepy dark-skinned man at the front desk forked over towels as Tomás signed in and entered the locker room. A bas relief of rising and bending bodies littered the gym floor. Middle-aged men groped their way through half-hearted workouts, shadow boxing themselves back to the good graces of whomever it was to whom they mattered.

He found a spot in the corner to stretch before lifting. As a young man he could kick a soccer ball nearly the length of the field, never mind center a curve ball across the plate from the pitcher's mound. He was thankful to still be able to work up a sweat, and was still in good shape at thirty-six. No matter what he ate now, the food sloughed right off his bones and refused to add bulk. He stretched out his lower back, his lats, his thighs, and lower down along his groin, remembering how in captivity it had been considered sport to try to rupture a man's genitals.

He shouldered the hundred-pound barbell, looking in the mirror to adjust his weight. Behind him the steam room door closed with a hiss, and he could see in the mirror a tall silver-haired man walk half-naked toward the dressing area, trailed by a moist wedge of vapor that disappeared beneath his feet. A white-skirted towel hung unevenly from his waist.

"Hey, Jim," the man called to another guy as he bent to steal a drink of water from the fountain. "Almost ready for that beer?"

"Sure thing, Mike," Jim called back to the older man, easily fifteen years his senior with an twenty extra pounds on him. "Just let me make myself pretty and finish up."

Jim turned and threw a blank look at Tomás, who kneeled within a few feet of him, hands gripping a barbell resting on a rubber mat.

As Tomás squatted to pick up the barbell, he couldn't help but watch in the mirror, where the older man continued to dress. The white towel had dropped to the floor, revealing the mottled flesh of his thighs and buttocks. Piece by piece, as the man began to dress, the shapes of a familiar uniform began to assemble in shades of navy blue and steel, till the leather holster and gun emerged, cutting the uniform at his waist in half. Three inverted blue and yellow Vs anchored along the shoulder in the shape of a sergeant's patch. Last, the engraved silver badge emerged as the man turned, fastened to his chest like lesser royalty. The policeman—for that is what he was, Tomás now realized—bent to tie his regulation black shoes.

Tomás felt himself begin to shake involuntarily, his mouth suddenly dry, his heartbeat pounding in his ears. Though they had not come for him tonight, though they knew nothing of what he had been through or where he might be going, though he was in the US of A and nowhere near the heat or squalor of South American countries that had seceded to lawless livelihoods below the equator, any sign of the military made Tomás remember just how vulnerable each of us is—that no matter what side you were on, left or right, how little it took to bring men to violence.

Tomás's heart raced uncontrollably while the officer secured his belt buckle, then turned to face him from behind powerful deltoids and a thickened waist. The loud flick of a towel across the toe of the officer's shoes sent an explosive ripple through Tomás's spine. It dawned on him that he was a fool not to have noticed, after all these months, the proximity of the police station down the street, the round blue bulb of the jailhouse buttonholing the blackness. But his schedule with the kid was new, and he hadn't come to work out at night before.

He stood up, feeling weak, leaving the wreckage of twin hand weights askew on the carpet, the barbell abandoned, inhaling as he stood the odor of musk and mold and years of spent energy seeped into the floorboards. Then, trying to make his escape, he missed his timing and collided with the sergeant, who stepped back as if he'd stepped upon a rat.

"'Scuse me?" the policeman named Jim said, sidelining him. He pressed his hand on Tomás's chest where his ribs met his collarbone so there was no mistaking who had power over whom. "Where's the fire? In a hurry to get somewhere? Hurrying to meet a date, are you?"

Tomás could feel the sergeant's breath on his cheek.

"Don't think I've seen you here before, have I? What are you? Colombian? Brazilian? What's your name, *señor*?"

"Sorry," Tomás said, experience having taught him to read the proximity to violence in a man's face. "Tomás Concepción," he continued, in what he hoped was a neutral voice. "Just trying to blow off some steam, sir. Same as anyone. Didn't mean a thing by it."

But at the same time, he couldn't help looking down at the leather gun handle, snug against the sergeant's hip, that seemed to vibrate with a life of its own.

"Sorry," Tomás said again, bowing his chin slightly as he attempted to maneuver away from the policeman, reaching once again for his gym bag on the floor, his tightly arched spine made smaller as he did so in order to appear less threatening.

"Sorry," Tomás repeated. "*Lo siento,* I'm sorry," he said, wiping the damp back of his neck with his shirtsleeve. "I wasn't exactly looking where I was going. Next time, sir," he said, forcing a shit-eating smile that betrayed his better judgment, "I'll look where I'm going."

"In case you didn't know," the officer said, "I'm the unofficial watchdog over this place. You get me, boy? What are you, Mexican? That's big drug territory down south, right? No shit. Gunrunning, too. You happen to know anything about anything like that? You sure you got your papers in order?"

"Argentina," Tomás said. He could feel his pulse pumping in his fists like pocketed grenades. "I'm from Argentina, where I was a journalist, sir. A newsman."

"Well, I'll be damned. Is that so?" Jim said, with a look of exaggerated surprise, releasing Tomás from his grip. "Damned if I ever knew a real live journalist from south of the border."

"Okay, Jim, enough of that, let's go. Leave the poor guy alone," Mike said.

"Well, guess that's that," the sergeant said, surrendering. He reached for his jacket from inside the tin locker, slipping his arms into the negative spaces of the sleeves, still not willing to let things go.

"Next time, *señor*," he said, looking back with a grin, tilting his cap and dusting off his sleeves, "next time be more careful, and watch where you're going."

Within half an hour, Tomás found himself a permanent bar stool at Jose's Beef and Bun on the corner of Ninth and Main, still unnerved by the fact that he had spent his first couple of months in the States gluteus maximus to gluteus medius with Newark's finest.

The New York Knicks were playing at home on a screen too distant to see. The bartender poured him a second beer, and Tomás downed it steadily. The incident in the locker room had frazzled his nerves. It was like a bad dream, a bad omen.

Past midnight, he parked his cousin's car in front of 9 Lancaster Terrace and turned the key. The power kicked off, but the headlights were on a timer and had a mind of their own. He sat in the semi-dark and looked up at the place where the street sign should have been, but where in recent weeks neighborhood kids had made sport of turning it backwards.

He sat in the car, unable to move. The headlights stayed on, salting the air. The drop in temperature hovering steadily between thirty-six and thirty-eight degrees, playing games with the oxygen's potential to frost. Here and there something magical emerged, a lone snowflake catching the breeze, then evaporating onto the freezing windshield. His brain was frozen around a single thought: the menacing cop jeering at him inside the locker room, how men like that could put you away for life.

Across the river separating Newark from Manhattan, the familiar Budweiser smokestacks would continue to spew all night, spitting charcoal light across a pewter sky. Somewhere out there the kid and his mother with their own pathetic story were waiting for him to show up tomorrow and do it all over again.

The car headlights blinked out, leaving him in darkness. His bare knees started to shake from the cold, forcing him out of the car.

He rounded the back of the building to the basement entrance, taking the three shallow steps down to the apartment in a single leap. It was a studio apartment with a galley kitchen and worn oak floors, subleased in his cousin's name.

He set his bag down on the floor, still in darkness, and moved toward the kitchen to pull the metal chain. A troop of honey-colored cockroaches broke ranks and scattered across the counter as he increased the overhead light. The phone was a wall unit, black, the stove electric. What a man lives, a man is, he thought to himself. In America every step you took cost you something.

5

Monday morning Cass woke near six and sat arched over the kitchen counter with a cup of black coffee and the pages of *Variety*, guarding her protected private hour as the six twenty-two Metroliner sailed by outside the window. It would be a done deal, she thought; if Lee and Kira agreed to go without her, she could give Tomás the go ahead, and he would be their man.

She had argued strenuously against the decision of the cold-hearted theater director, Garth Anthony, who had no sympathy for their plans and said flat-out no, the play couldn't afford to be without her. She knew if she went against him, she could lose her job. Plan B was to discuss whether or not Lee and Kira felt safe letting Tomás take them. She and Kira's parents, Joe and Louise, had talked on the phone for more than an hour. It wouldn't exactly be the easiest thing to entrust their fragile but tough-minded children to Tomás, but Cass had already made the decision to trust him with Lee's care every day for the past two weeks. The kids had few dreams they dared dream, and they had their hearts set on going.

Kira's father, Joe, was a litigator who still fought for his corporate clients at a hectic nine-to-five, and Louise's health was compromised by emphysema. They had agreed that there was too little time left in their children's increasingly shrinking lives for disappointment. They had become each other's allies from the day they met in Dr. Bream's Park Avenue office connected to Children's. Kira and Lee had taken one look at one another's bald, frail beings and sensed they were destined to be united. Like explorers or inventors who understood something so rare and critical about the nature of the universe that no one else could begin to understand.

Cass's feet were cold on the bare wooden floor. It was nearing 6:15, and the sky was shifting from pink to gray all along the emerging calligraphy of the skyline that connected the smoke-stacks of northern New Jersey to the skyscrapers of New York.

The phone rang just as Cass placed her mug down in the sink and was preparing to take a shower, the shrill sound like an ice pick to her spine. No one sane, she thought—eyeing the clock and reaching for the receiver—called at this unearthly hour. Her parents were gone, her son was in bed, the rent was paid.

⁓

Lee heard the phone and rubbed his eyes fully awake. It was Monday. Trash day. The trucks would soon be out rumbling along the asphalt, scraping metal against stone.

Perhaps Tomás couldn't come, Lee thought when he heard the phone. He flipped on the bedside lamp and reached for his glasses in an attempt to bring the world to order. He imagined Tomás ringing the bell as usual, precisely at eight, his stony face darkening their door with his industrial lunch box and paratrooper shoes and the depressed cross-eyed delirium of an undertaker.

More and more, Lee was gaining on him. He would soon find out Tomás's darkest secrets. He had started reading news stories about the politics in Argentina sent over the UPI and AP wire feeds. There were still foreign words he had yet to decipher, having to do with a man named Videla and a group of grandmothers calling themselves *Abuelas,* whom he learned marched on Thursday afternoons in the town square, La Plaza de Mayo, at exactly three-thirty in attempt to do brave things to find missing family members. No way was Tomás going to get away with his lies. Especially if they were going to be stuck with one another and even sleep in the same room—maybe even share a bed—during their travels. It didn't really feel like an adventure anymore. Soon he would have the ammunition with which to confront Tomás squarely, and he would have to come clean. It was simply a matter of ticking off clues like eliminating letters in a game of hangman.

And what would Kira think of him? He couldn't wait to find

out. Would Tomás laugh at her, at the two of them together? Would he think they were doomed and pathetic and not worth the price of airfare? He would call her as soon as he got up. She was a light sleeper like him.

Patrick's pink-bearded muzzle emerged from the covers, his watery eyes sluiced and jaundiced. "Hey, boy," Lee said, reaching to scratch the warm heft behind his ears where the pale blue-violet texture ran coarse and veined.

The phone had stopped ringing, and Lee leaned lower in his bed to where he could see Cass's shadow shifting in the hallway beneath the crack in his door. His feet were scrawny and blue as he stepped onto the wooden floor. Her voice sounded cloudy as though sifted through a sheet of gauze.

Lee got out of bed and parted the curtain by the window. A cold-hearted sky darkened the horizon as he squinted through the venetian blinds. He fastened the drawstring on his pajamas tighter, his hipbones arched like handrails, his privates dwarfed as a snail, readying himself to face the big man. Cass had daily reminded him that what he needed was a sense of humor. Well, easy for her to say.

He moved closer to the door, opened it into the hallway, unable to make out individual words. In the freezing foyer he blinked in the direction of his mother's pale body hovering beneath the skylight, its brightness making her white cotton nightgown appear to be blown to smithereens.

Lee knew suddenly that something terrible had happened.

Cass replaced the receiver and stared past him, looking without seeing.

"What is it, Cass?" Lee said, watching her chin begin to quaver.

"Cass, what's going on? Who was that? What's happening? Is it Neil?" Lee asked quickly, thinking of his father. "Did something happen to him?"

He tried to remember his father's face from the last time he had seen him, small and avoidant and afraid. "Whatever it is, just tell me. I can take it."

She knelt and wordlessly put her arms around him.

"It's not Neil," Cass said. "It's Kira. I'm afraid it happened overnight. She's gone. I'm so sorry, sweetie."

"What?" Lee said. "Wait…"

His mouth collapsed into a tiny oval as he pressed up against the frame of the kitchen doorway, buttressing the small, bald back of his head between his palms. The plaster cracks in the ceiling seemed to ripple and spread the length of the narrow corridor, destroying everything in their wake.

"No," he said. "I don't understand. We were on the phone two nights ago going over our plans. Don't you remember? We were going to try to visit every Wendy's between the Washington Monument and the Franklin Institute. I was even reading her dumb jokes from *Poor Richard's Almanac*; she said she didn't mind. She actually said she felt sorry for Tomás even though she'd never met him. She said I should give him a chance. I want to talk to Dr. Bream," Lee insisted. "I want to talk to him right now! And Joe and Louise. I need to hear it for myself before I'll even begin to believe it."

"Sweetie." Cass tried again to comfort him. "That was Joe on the phone just now."

Patrick came into the hall and stood on splayed feet like a human soldier ready to do battle.

But not even the comic sight of Patrick at attention could change the otherworldly feeling that was beginning to infiltrate Lee's brain in wrecked curlicues of racing thoughts and imaginings. He wrapped his arms around his body and sank the length of wall beneath the window, recoiling like a spider trying to recall itself into as small a shape as possible.

Cass arched over him for protection. "Lee, my Lee, my sweetheart, I'm so sorry. I know how much you and Kira loved each other. And Louise and Joe and I—we're all still in shock. We're still a family. It's going to take a while to sink in. And Kira, I know it makes no sense that she's gone. How could it? But you and I are here together."

She closed her eyes and let it play itself back in her head, the first time the five of them met in Dr. Bream's office in the city nearly two years ago, Bream acting as a kind of matchmaker for the children when they were ten going on seventy-two. She would never forget that first meeting with Louise and Joe Throop, wealthy New Yorkers from the Upper East Side who had adopted Kira when she was a baby—even though they were older and edging toward retirement.

Cass and Lee had come into the waiting room, same as usual for the Thursday two o'clock appointment, and there were the three of them—demure as caviar on toast, huddled together on the leather sofa. Kira's pink ballerina dress a stiff mess of crinoline, her pale head bald as a cue ball, her blue eyes darting back and forth at Lee, as though seeing another version of herself for the first time. And Lee took one look at her and immediately felt she was beautiful. The five of them had gone for hot chocolate at a café on West Fifty-Seventh Street immediately afterward. What followed were weekly chaperoned social engagements ranging from high tea at the Ritz to scavenger hunts in Central Park, most often ending up with torn clothes and dirty faces in front of the bronze nursery-rhyme clock and the statue of Alice in Wonderland.

"C'mere, babe," Cass said now, squatting nearer. "Come close to me."

The six thirty-five train rumbled by across the street, accompanied by the loud screech of friction against steel, and he leaned against her momentarily, then pulled away, as the train disappeared and the window frame rattled weakly. Cass became conscious of the draftiness in the room and how they had never been able to shake it, how shock makes one feel cold and outnumbered and unnerved at once, as if their arms and legs were crawling with centipedes.

The light hum of his body next to hers kept her connected to life no matter what. It was what she lived for and thrived on in her worst moments, even now in the face of Kira's death, when she was needed most. Outside, a light circle of clouds had moved in on them, crowding the window like a sea of icebergs.

Lee exhaled hard and blew his nose into his sleeve, leaning his face against her shoulder. The word *mother* spread through her like something rouged and rough and unremarkable but impossible to break, spreading through every part of her body, from her brain to her lungs to the spigot of her heart.

As minutes passed, Lee slowly woke to the idea of the possibility, that Kira was gone in ways foretold by Dr. Bream but which he had never allowed himself to begin to imagine. They said it was her heart, but he had other ideas about what had happened. Did the west wind blow her body far out over the Hudson past the Chrysler Building? Was she at peace in the Bronx, asleep on someone's fire escape? Or stalled on a cloud atop the Empire State Building? Would her last exhale now become part of his breath? And yet air moved too quickly to see, molecules let loose from smaller atoms. He closed his eyes and saw her mouth framed in the Morse code of wanting to tell him the secrets to all these things.

"She let go very peacefully," Cass said, still holding him close. "From what Louise told me, it was easy for her. A little like, like dreaming. They had a good night with pizza and Scrabble. Kira had had some difficulty breathing, and then she'd gone to sleep happy."

Lee clung to Cass's waist, his breath coming in bursts, the tears heaving. He was ashamed he hadn't called Kira last night. He had been foolishly obsessed with learning Tomás's lies and secrets. She must have wondered what happened when she didn't hear from him. But maybe it had already been too late.

"I know, I know," Cass murmured softly. "I know we didn't think this day would ever come," she said. "The funeral will be in a couple of days." Cass wrapped her arms around herself, struggling to hold back her own grief. "Louise and Joe want you to call them if you feel up to it. It might make you both feel better. We should go and see them this afternoon and try to offer some comfort."

6

They let him go into Kira's room alone.

Cass and Lee had taken the train from Newark to Penn Station, and from there walked to Madison and boarded the uptown bus to Seventy-Second Street. Then they walked the remaining three blocks east, past somber granite brownstones detailed with wrought-iron hitching posts and the calcified poop of overbred, pedigreed dogs. A light rain started to fall, and the lower part of Cass's plaid woolen coat blew open in the wind. Lee walked slowly, delaying the worst, looking down at his shoes. He stopped to glance down an alleyway studded with silver metallic trashcans and stumbled clumsily on a loose stone. He leaned to tie his shoe, then looked up as far as he could see—to where pieces of sky were draped between buildings, which by all rights should have been trees. And he felt numb and alone, and completely without hope, wishing he and Kira could start their lives over without this disease.

The doorman at 1620 Seventy-First recognized them immediately as they made their way up the checkerboard walk. He stooped to lower a striped umbrella over their heads as they approached the maroon awning guarding the building, with its edges studded with bronze lions, claws bared. Then Lee and Cass moved through the lobby, and the elevator doors closed, catapulting them to the twenty-second floor.

Down the low-lit, narrowly carpeted hallway, they walked past the tasteful marble side table, pungent with cherry blossoms stabbed with stalks of bamboo, and arrived at Kira's doorway almost without a sound. Joe and Louise were already standing on the threshold empty-handed, as if what mattered most in the world had been stolen right out from under them.

Lee stood at attention, averting his eyes, feeling for all the world that the fact that Kira had died first, and not him, had marked him as a criminal. Every single other time he had been to the apartment it had been for some happy occasion, whether for a party or to celebrate a good check-up or to taste something good that Louise had baked for them.

"Let me take your wet things," Louise said, and he handed over his navy pea coat, feeling dry-mouthed and ashamed of the thin blue-and-white-striped seersucker sport coat floating underneath, too big and summery for such a dark occasion.

Joe had put his arm around Cass's shoulder, and together they moved into the dimly lit living room. She pressed her hand around his, the dark blue sapphire stone in his Yale class ring betraying an early solid upbringing in which he'd earned a social conscience as well as an inheritance, his father having been a circuit judge in Brooklyn, his mother a social worker reaching out to poor kids in the Bronx.

Louise, tall and big hipped, but narrow at the waist in her belted shift, had always reminded Lee of Julia Child on *The French Chef,* his favorite TV show, which he was lucky enough to be able to watch while other kids were still at school. Her usual gusty voice stilled as she bent to hug him with her large embrace, her flowery perfume making him wish all the more that he were invisible.

"We're so glad you're here, Lee," Louise said, kneeling. "You mean the world to us," she said, reaching to tilt his chin toward hers so he'd have no choice but to listen. "You always have. Do you know, Lee, how many times Kira told us how you were her best friend? And now we have to do what we can to get on without her. She was worried more about you than herself, you know. It's not going to be easy for any of us. We'll all miss her very much."

Lee stood there ashamed, looking down at the carpet. He couldn't think of any words to comfort anyone, least of all himself. He was so angry for who he was, and who he wasn't, and for who he would never become.

Cass, who was wearing her black wool crepe dress with three-quarter sleeves—usually kept hidden at the back of her closet—moved in on them and took Lee's hand.

"Such a difficult day," she said to Louise. "If there's anything we can do, either of us, we're here."

"I know," she said. "And thank you. You're the only other people in the world who can understand. I know you'd do anything. You've been our anchor all these years."

"We could never have gotten through any of this without you," Joe said, stepping in.

"Us too," said Cass.

Lee abruptly pulled away from Cass's hand and moved to the big glass picture window overlooking a skyline ripe with bronze-and-stone obelisks that seemed destined to converge, reminding him of pictures he'd seen of Stonehenge, or a handful of thunderbolts Zeus might have thrown down in a moment of rage. He pressed his palms against the glass. He could smell fresh coffee brewing in the kitchen, could see the bar cart on wheels parked beside the doorway, filled with a bucket of ice and three shot glasses, a carafe of vodka, naked as water. And another rounder bottle, its belly risen to the surface with scotch. A platter of tea sandwiches, a silver tray of pink-and-white petits fours, dimpled with frosting. The kind that Kira, who had a sweet tooth, loved.

He felt sorrier for all of them, rather than for himself, for Joe and Louise, who had lived their lives in a closet of stone and glass that only served to interrupt the flow of oxygen and preserve their time with Kira temporarily. And for Cass, who worried about him constantly. He decided to be more civilized and sociable for their sake. He turned around and found a seat on the zebra-patterned ottoman, when it occurred to him that this must be what it feels like to become a widower.

"It was really only a matter of time," Louise said weakly to Cass, from where she sat with a cup and saucer on her lap.

"Would you like to go into Kira's room and look around?" Joe asked, at Lee's side. "We'd like you to choose a thing or two of hers that would be meaningful. She would have liked that."

✦

It was thirteen and a half steps down the dark carpeted hallway to Kira's door from that corner of the living room. Joe led the way, Lee trailing behind. He turned the handle, and a quick blast of white light through the glass wall, that extended from the living room, momentarily blinded them. Lee was trembling slightly, unable to move, when Joe lay an almost weightless hand on his shoulder.

"It's okay," he said. "I understand, I really do, but our lives have to go on, even if we're the saddest we've ever been."

Slowly Lee stepped forward into Kira's room.

"What do you suppose," Joe said, scratching the back of his head and looking about the room bewildered. "What do you suppose is so enchanting about girls and ballet dancing? Anyway, I'll leave you to look around a little," Joe said, before closing the door behind him and leaving Lee alone. Lee sat on the bed and stared at Kira's white cotton bedspread tufted with embroidered red cabbage roses that reminded him of tiny detached brains. What upset him most was that everyone was talking about Kira as if she were gone, but where was she exactly? There was no sign of her body or her deadness. He lay his head on the white eyelet pillowcase as if resting his ear on the equator, listening for what he hoped might be the pulse of a submerged universe that could tell him something about what happens to the dead. But there was no such thing.

He pressed his nose into Kira's pillow, breathing in a scent of dried roses mixed with Joy parfum, and all the time the question was rising to near hysteria in his bones, wondering, what had become of her? Where was she, exactly? And if it had happened to her, what would become of him? And in how much time?

To his left, near the window, were things she had touched less than a day earlier, the diminutive oak desk with the small chair on wheels on which she used to sail across the room. On the wall opposite her bed, the posters she had explained to him, one of Nureyev, catlike, near predatory, after defecting from the Kirov and making his debut in the American *Firebird.* And opposite him, Fonteyn as Aurora in *Sleeping Beauty.*

Though she lived to be a dancer, Kira had had to accept early on—between labral hip tears and advanced osteoporosis—that her bones were far too brittle to risk even the smallest pirouette or plié. Still, she had hope. He looked into her closet and blinked widely at the rows of unworn pink satin pointe shoes, tutus spritzed thigh-high with crinoline.

It was kind of Joe and Louise to invite him to take something. Would Kira have thought he was a thief? Would she really have liked him to take something of hers? It occurred to him that it wasn't a souvenir he was after, but something that could bring her back to life. He surveyed the familiar objects on the bureau: the pocketed remains of a tiny mouse skull abandoned in the park near the sailing pond; miniature pinecones preserved in dried mud from last winter's walk in the woods; the pink paper umbrella from a Shirley Temple consumed at the Bird Cage restaurant on the fifth floor of Saks. On her bookshelf, a glossy program from the Joffrey, another from Merce Cunningham at Lincoln Center. A wide-eyed troll doll with electrified green hair, naked except for a grass hula skirt slung around her waist, and a pink ceramic piggy bank Lee had given her on her thirteenth birthday to remind her of Patrick. In all these things she came back to him and disappeared.

Then he thought he knew.

Tucked into the frame of the floor-to-ceiling oval mirror on the back of Kira's closet door was a picture Cass had taken of the two of them last summer at Coney Island. They were standing on the bleached wooden boardwalk at dusk, eating cotton candy, the huge red-and-yellow Ferris wheel at a halt behind them. He remembered the day clearly, sticky with humidity and the shrill noise of gulls ravaging through distant landfills. It was low tide, and Cass and Louise and Joe had trailed languidly behind them in shorts and T-shirts, pushing two empty jogging strollers that he and Kira had refused to ride in. It was July Fourth, and they had spent the day ricocheting back and forth between the penny arcade and the rollercoaster, dragging out the time till dark when fireworks would begin. It was nearly eight o'clock when the sun finally sank beneath a blackening sky and a ribbon of beaded white stars appeared—under which they sat huddled on the cold sand on a blanket, hips touching.

He had dared to move close enough to take Kira's hand under the blanket, his fingers interlaced with hers, his heart beating so fast that for a second he worried he might have another heart attack. But even if he did, he knew it would be worth it.

Lee sighed, remembering how that was the day he dared to predict he had a future, the day he knew he wanted to marry her. He removed the photo from the frame and slipped it inside the inner pocket of his sport coat. Cass had given him a white cotton pocket square to tuck into the outer chest pocket, and he withdrew it now and blew his nose.

Soon Joe returned, ducking his head in the doorway.

"You all right?" he asked.

"Okay, I guess," Lee said, not knowing what else to do. "I took this," he said, opening his jacket to show Joe the photograph. "Where is Kira, do you think? The truth. Her body. She must be somewhere, right? Will I ever get to see her again?"

"When someone dies, you don't always know exactly what to do," Joe said gently. "You want to keep them with you as long as possible. It's all new to us too," he said, removing his glasses to wipe them on the back of his sleeve. "I'll never forget the day we met you," he continued, sitting next to Lee on the coverlet. "Do you remember? It was so good for Kira to meet someone like her. And you're the best, you and your mom. Between you and me, Lee, I would have been proud to call you my son-in-law."

Lee beamed, but waited, wanting to hear more.

"It's her body that gave out. And now she—her body—is being attended to in order to be appropriate for the funeral," Joe said. "It'll be the day after tomorrow, and Louise and I will see that everything's done right. Then we'll see her one last time, and we'll say our final good-byes. Not our spiritual ones, of course, not our memories."

Lee buried his face in his hands.

He thought briefly of Lancelot the magician, who had come to the house for his seventh birthday and briefly disrupted the gloomy flow of their lives by making a rabbit miraculously disappear.

Who moves through walls?

Lee sat on her bed, that one last time, and cupped his face in his hands, Joe surrendering beside him, and together they cried.

7

The Charles Peter Nagel Funeral Home was located just a few blocks uptown from Kira's apartment on the corner of Eighty-Seventh and Second Avenue—in a neighborhood dense with offices and apartments and the occasional Gothic church steeple—its stiff granite steps bleached white at the top where pale winter sunlight squeezed between clouds.

Cass gripped Lee's hand tightly as they climbed the steps and approached the door.

"Wait, Cass," Lee said, his hand on her coat sleeve. "I don't think anyone else is here yet."

She checked her watch. It was nine-thirty. They could hear faint sounds of voices coming from inside, while music—thin and monastic and reedy with trills—quavered through the Adam's apple of the keyhole.

Worse still, there appeared to be no one else present who'd come to say goodbye, as if Kira's life had meant so little to so few. Lee clutched in his right hand the paper cone of red carnations bought at the underground train stall at Eighty-Sixth Street, the pale green stems sucking up moisture through a loosely wrapped damp paper towel. He tucked them inside his coat and pressed them there under the weight of his elbow, then moved away from the door to lean against one of the heavy wrought-iron posts that enclosed the landing like a Roman courtyard. Below them ordinary people passed, carrying umbrellas and briefcases, having no inkling of Lee and Cass's loss. A light came on in the Korean grocery next door, and Lee watched a clerk in a white blood-smattered smock begin to hoist a row of leathery-looking ducks—decapitated and drained of blood—in ascending order across a wire clothesline.

"Do you think it'll be just us?" Lee asked, turning to face

Cass, imagining the four of them alone facing the doomed casket. He looked back and forth down the sidewalk dismally, to see if he recognized anyone else approaching.

"Not at all," she said. "I'm sure Joe and Louise have other family, friends we've never heard of. People we haven't had a chance to meet. But we *are* early." She shrugged. "I don't mind staying outside for a few minutes."

She put her arm around him, and they moved a few steps closer to the iron railing that overlooked the alleyway. Her bare fingers were stiff with cold, and the lattice-edged diamond points of the white lace collar of her blouse forked down like fangs over her black woolen coat. She instinctively reached into her bag for a cigarette, then closed her eyes and let the wallpaper of the city abstract itself into an uneven bar graph of buildings.

A few dark-throated pigeons hobbled at their feet, making low guttural sounds. She reached into her bag a second time and withdrew a roll of peppermint lifesavers and wordlessly handed one to Lee.

What seemed like bare minutes passed before they began to hear the sounds of human feet scuffling on the brick stairs behind them and the sound of a church bell beginning to chime, signaling ten o'clock.

"Okay, that's us, we should go in and find Joe and Louise. They'll need our help to get through this today," she said. "Ready?"

"Guess so," he said, dusting off the seat of his pants, his heart doing hula-hoops.

"It's going to be okay," she said.

∽

Inside, dampness clung to the walls of the narrow foyer. The dark wooden floors were waxed slick as vellum, and a small man in a dark suit commenced dutifully toward them as soon as they crossed the threshold.

"My condolences, of course," he said somberly. "You must be here for the Throop family. I hope you'll sign our guest book before heading into the sanctuary. You too," he said, looking down at Lee, expecting to see the face of a child, but stepping back having found something else entirely. "God be with you both."

The smaller of the two chapels lay directly ahead. Four rows of metal folding chairs were arranged behind a narrow oak podium, behind which an antique ribbon of plaster angels rose in a semicircle above the open carved wooden casket. At the entrance to each aisle, boxes of white flowering tissues were arranged strategically like gardenias in bloom.

Lee had never seen a dead person. His chest heaved as they approached the open casket, trudging slowly forward at the thought of Kira lying there helpless and alone. He didn't know if he could face her. His feet came to a halt two steps before her, when he became aware of Cass still holding his hand, the blood being squeezed almost painfully out of his palm.

"I'm right here, baby," she said to him. "I won't let anything bad happen."

And then it was Kira, her face small as a doll's, her taut cheeks appled artificially with light, rouged outward toward the temples as they might have been in a wax museum. She was dressed in the crisp pink crinoline tutu and satin toe shoes, finally earned. He searched her face, knowing as he looked at her that this was not her face, but the center from which she was absent; not her eyes, but what used to be. Her hands, clenched as tightly together as a knot of failed paper-whites, rested on her narrow chest. A thin gold band, cresting her ring finger in a gleaming arc, caught the light.

And coming toward them from behind, as though skating heavily on leaden shoes, Joe and Louise.

Joe knelt to hug Lee. "You're such a help to us," he said to Lee. "You're such a mensch, it gives us strength to have you here, you know."

Lee blinked. Next to him Cass had her arms around Louise's shoulder, their cheeks touching.

And then suddenly there was Dr. Bream, maneuvering toward them through the crowd. Without his doctor's coat and stethoscope, he looked ordinary and myopic and in no position to save anyone.

"Why didn't you save her?" Lee cried, his small fists shaking, his face nearly featureless with anger. "Why didn't you do anything? What good are you if you can't save people? I never want to see you again!"

Lee moved quickly toward the door, his legs catapulted like a rocket he couldn't stop.

Bream sputtered, out of breath. "Wait, hold on, Lee . . ."

"Let him go," Cass said, touching his shoulder. "It's all been too much today, really."

Lee grabbed his coat and pushed open the heavy iron door. The wilted parcel of carnations inside his jacket fell and scattered to the floor as he made his way to the stone stoop at the farthest edge of the courtyard. The white marble beneath his bony ass was cold and hard and veined with age. He imagined, as he looked into the distance past the graying sky, the cliffs from which they were quarried, the white cliffs of Dover.

And he knew in his heart that Ben Franklin would never be a baby and deceive himself by believing in the *deus ex machina* of the gods or miracles or anything even remotely candy coated. And that Dr. Bream was not at fault after all, not really. He was as helpless as the rest of them. He had failed to save Kira's life and would fail to save Lee's. It was only a matter of time.

The disease that nature had inflicted on them, he reasoned, should have been reserved for monsters or murderers. But what happened to him and Kira was just the luck of the draw. He owed it to Kira to live the best life he could, seeing that she had gone before him. And how one comes and goes from the world has nothing to do with hard work, or luck, or even how successful you are at telling a joke or leaving a footprint. Or even how good you are at telling a lie—like the many Tomás had told them, the lies that Lee was determined to uncover.

8

Last evening, less than a mile from home, inside the low-lit inner sanctum of Dillon's Tavern, Tomás sat on a torn leather barstool, beer mug in hand, gazing out the large glass windows onto a polluted harbor of rusted out barges that would never haul cargo again. A Nets game blurred the TV screen.

It had been too easy to become a damn liar, he thought, as he downed his second beer and struggled to make peace with his conscience, knowing full well he was about to betray the two people in the world who counted on him most.

Once the kid agreed to accompany him to DC, the deal would be set. He would have succeeded at deceiving Cass, too, and could forever be counted among the lowest of the low, despite having good reason.

If there was still a chance, he had to try to find Violeta and the child.

The streets of Buenos Aires were still rife with Videla's men, and the soldiers' green Ford Falcons continued to troll for unsuspecting so-called subversives. It was a long shot that his wife and child had survived. But he had gotten new information from his old friend Margaret scarcely a week ago, Margaret who had been a colleague in Buenos Aires and who now worked for the *Washington Post* in DC, covering news of the urban war at home, including Argentina's disappeared. When he called her to explain how Violeta and the child were missing, she'd said she had no idea that Violeta had been arrested, but that she knew people who had connections when it came to the sale of black-market babies.

Within days she'd called to say she had a lead.

"You have to come and do your own detective work," she'd said. "I'm about to go on assignment in LA. People here know things but aren't always willing to talk, and some of them only for a price. Violeta and I were friends, too. I want to find her as much as you do. We've lost a lot of time, Tomás. Those were difficult years in Buenos Aires. I'm afraid I was not always your friend."

And now things were falling into place in the most unexpected ways.

He knew that Lee and Cass were headed for a bad ending, no matter how hard they tried, or what he did to stop it, and that the kid's hero-worship of Ben Franklin was just a substitute for living in the real world. They were all fooling themselves, himself included.

He drained his beer and reached into his chest pocket to scan the handwritten list Cass had provided earlier that afternoon, along with detailed instructions about Lee's care she had given him his first day on the job. The vitamins and dosages, the nitroglycerin tablets and emergency phone numbers. She had added a list of DC and Philadelphia drugstores and hospital emergency rooms.

"If you think you're going to take my son anywhere outside of Newark—whether it's Washington, DC, or Philadelphia, or the moon—you'd better be prepared to humor him and take his pulse and pretend to be at least mildly interested in American history. I know one day you might want to get a green card," Cass had said. "You might need a sponsor, or a recommendation for another job. Underneath, Lee's really beginning to like you. Not his fault his father is a cowardly deadbeat who only knows how to make ice cream."

"Cass, I know this is a huge change in plans." Tomás had tried to reassure her, knowing all the while that he was lying. "But I want you to know you can trust me. Who knows, maybe one day I'll be a father, but right now Lee is teaching me a lot of things. I'll protect him like my own child. This trip will be an adventure for both of us. I've always wanted to see Washington."

⊱

Now Tomás shrugged his shoulders and set his empty mug on

the counter. From what she had explained, none of this really mattered anyway. Lee's days were numbered, there was nothing anyone could do.

He gazed down the length of the bar to where an old drunk sat fastened to the farthest stool, shrunken down in filth and beyond salvage. When their eyes met, something inside Tomás loosened uncomfortably, and he stood up to go.

He nodded to the barkeep and lay several crushed bills on the counter.

"*Gracias,*" Tomás said, rising to his feet. He shaded his eyes against the round orange sun disappearing over the ruined harbor. It reminded him of childhood trips to the arid Pampas at the southernmost tip of Argentina with his father—who would recount long meandering tales of the fabled *gauchos,* who had once roamed there on horseback. Now he was sliding into a role of betrayal in which each step would take him farther from himself, and it made him feel like a *proscrito,* an outlaw.

He knew he would sacrifice anything to find his wife and daughter. If the rumors Margaret had heard were true, they could still be alive somewhere, living in DC. His daughter would be almost three now and quite possibly living under an alias.

9

By half-past one they were home from the funeral, standing in front of the apartment building. Cass paused at the top of the stairs before inserting her key in the lock.

"Look, Lee," she said, "I wanted to tell you earlier that I've asked Tomás to come over. Believe it or not, I have to quickly change and get back to work. Dress rehearsal is in two days. Everyone's waiting for me. I know the timing stinks. I'm sorry, sweetie. But I'll be back home in a few hours. I just want you to take it easy."

The back of Lee's throat felt hollow and empty at the thought of her leaving him alone so abruptly. The lights were already on as he trudged through the hallway, and he could smell the dark, familiar odor of Tomás's coffee coming from the kitchen. Tomás met them in the foyer, but Lee backed away, trying to avoid him.

"Lee," Tomás said. "I'm so sorry about everything...really, so sorry about your friend. *Ella debe haber significado muchisimo para ti*—I know she must have meant the world to you."

"Thanks, Tomás," Cass said, managing a small smile. "Thanks for coming. We're glad you're here."

She set her coat and bag and keys down on the small round table in the hallway and moved into the kitchen, filled a glass with water and downed two aspirins.

Lee followed behind, attempting to tug at the back of her hem like a much younger child.

"C'mon now." She bit her lower lip. "It can't be helped that Tomás is here. Two more weeks of rehearsals till opening night," she said, shaking her head miserably. "Those actors feel completely naked without a little makeup. It's a kind of selfishness that comes with the trade. I don't think those people could survive without me. Just let me quickly change."

Within minutes she came back down the hallway looking boyish and thin in a white T-shirt and dark jeans, her hair slicked back into a ponytail.

"Plus," she continued, "this will give you both a chance to talk about how it might or might not work if Tomás were to take my place and make the trip with you, Lee. Come on," she said, beckoning him to move from the hallway into the living room where Tomás was already waiting, "you have to at least sit so we can have a conversation."

Lee moved reluctantly across the wooden threshold to the faded damask sofa, eyeing Tomás skeptically. Since when did he deserve a place in their private conversation; since when did he deserve to know their worst secrets, to take his shoes off and get comfortable?

"So look," Cass said, "now that so much has changed, now that we have to start to accept the idea that Kira's gone, terrible as it is, we still need to make a decision about whether or not you want to go ahead with our plans to visit DC and Philadelphia with Tomás. Remember, Lee, I can always try to take you next spring or even in the summer if it doesn't feel right. It's up to you. Given everything that's happened, it must feel very confusing and maybe not even important anymore."

"Can't you take me anyway, Cass?" Lee interrupted. "Can't you do anything to change things back?" He removed his glasses and stood in front of them both, tottering unevenly in his socks, his small blue eyes swollen from crying. "It was just you and me in the first place," he insisted. "And now Kira's gone, and I don't know what to think, and I feel like I want to die too. It's going to be too hard to do anything without her. And the spring is too long to wait. Don't you get it? It's like I'm a time bomb inside. No matter what Bream says, or any of you. Tomás and I don't even really know each other," he said, glancing darkly in Tomás's direction. "It's just that he's a warm body for hire. Can't you do anything to still take me, Cass? Please?"

She leaned forward on the edge of the coffee table, her face propped, exhausted, between her palms.

"Right now it's just out of my control, Lee. It's just not going to happen. I wish things were different, I really do. But if I lose my job, then where would we be? Garth Anthony, our director—you remember meeting him at dress rehearsal last year? Well, he's asked for a rewrite of the final scene at the last minute," she said, throwing up her hands in disbelief. "He wants to change the ending at the very last minute! Can you believe it? You'd think the producer would have said enough already, but that's how things are looking. And I'm really sorry, Lee, I wish none of these things had happened, I wish Kira could still be here with us. I loved her like a daughter, you know that, don't you? I wish I could be a better mother. Jeez, I know that wishes don't mean a damn thing right now, do they?

"And given everything that's happened, it might be good for you to give Tomás a chance. It's just a quick week. Maybe you can think of it as a memorial to Kira, and you can do all the research you need to finish your school project. I'll insist we talk every day on the phone, and Dr. Bream's pretty confident you've got the stamina. And if you get so tired you feel like you need to crawl, I'm sure Tomás can carry you," she said, winking at Tomás. "It seems the timing's good too," she said. "Tomás tells me that his friend Margaret has an apartment near the Capitol and will conveniently be out of town, so we can save money by the two of you not having to stay in a hotel. I just need you both back here by Thanksgiving to tell me all about it. The only bad part I can see is that Patrick, poor thing," she said, looking down to where he had slunk around her ankles on the oval rug, "will have to stay home with me."

"Lee, I know this is a sad time, probably the worst feeling in your life, to lose your friend," Tomás broke in. "I've lost people, too. I understand. No rush, think about it. I'm not your mom, but I know I can be a pretty good *guía turístico,* tour guide."

"And besides, it may all be too much right now anyway,"

Cass said. "If you decide, Lee, that it's not what you want, we'll both understand. Maybe I can take you next spring."

Lee stared. His hips ached in their sockets, and he was having trouble breathing. His mind was crowded with everything that had gone wrong in the past few days. Kira was gone. That was hardest to believe. Hardest to think there was nothing in the space where she had been. He would never see her face again or share a word or have her be the last person he talked to at night before going to sleep. The person in the world most like him was gone. It was starting to sink in.

And would there be a next spring? By next spring, he could be gone.

What would Ben Franklin do?

He couldn't be sure. Would he take a chance on a foreigner like Tomás who had no idea what it meant to be a patriot? Day by day Lee was growing more and more suspicious of Tomás's past, especially since he refused to answer about those scars.

He and Kira had spent the better part of the year planning this trip, becoming more than best friends in the process—falling in love—though he doubted if anyone would take them seriously. They had collected a fat accordion file of brochures and pamphlets and bus and train schedules. First on their list was DC and the Smithsonian. Then the National Mall. After a couple of days, they'd go on to Philadelphia to the Franklin Institute and Liberty Bell. It would be the first time on a plane for them both. They'd planned to hold hands and shut their eyes on take-off. Overnight, it had all been wiped away.

Cass rose and began to put on her coat. "I've got to hurry now, or I'll miss my train. Be back tonight," she said, giving Lee a quick hug, then moving into the open doorway. "Promise me, Lee, you'll talk to Tomás this afternoon."

Reality had begun to set in. Lee's time left in the world was all about counting down, rather than counting up. He had read about Egyptian mummification and embalming and the afterlife, but none of that could save him now that he knew the truth. What happened to Kira was going to happen to him—any minute or any hour. The collapsed look on Cass's face said it all.

It was just the two of them now in the dreaded stillness. What he had wanted most was to be alone. He could hear Tomás's breathing without looking up.

What would Ben Franklin do? he asked himself again. What good was a hero if you didn't try to put yourself in his shoes?

Time after time, Ben Franklin had found a solution to what appeared to be impossible: He corrected his failing eyesight by inventing bifocals and began a campaign to introduce daylight saving time. After the tragic deaths of his son Francis and his father, Josiah, he still managed to found the first fire department and to create the Gutenberg printing press, not to mention discover electricity and become US ambassador to Paris. Lee wished he could ask Ben how he had managed to keep reinventing himself in the face of disaster.

Lee felt the other half of the couch sag beside him. It was Tomás, come to unload his weight, not uttering a word. He could hear Tomás's breathing, caustic as a vacuum cleaner.

"Kira didn't deserve to die," Lee said finally, looking up and breaking the silence. "She had so much to live for. Dancing! Our trip! It was all we talked about. And now none of it matters. It was all lies, all of it. No one—none of it—matters anymore," he said. "Nothing against you, but we barely know each other. I know for a fact you've been lying about a lot of things. You might think you've fooled Cass, but you definitely haven't fooled me. Sooner or later you're going to have to man up. I doubt we even like each other. No offense, but do you even know who Ben Franklin was? Or George Washington? I'll be honest, I don't know too much about Argentina."

"No offense taken," Tomás said. "It's the worst thing in the world to lose someone. Maybe even harder to think there's still hope. *Vivimos para amar.* We live…to love, I think. It's what makes us human. Without it, without the way you love Kira and your mom, people can become *ruin,* heartless, monsters," he said. "You want to know something about me? I've lost people too. People I loved. When I was young, and even now. When I was a child my father left my mother for another woman, and I thought I would never survive. We didn't know why or where, or who it was he still cared for. But day by day I put one foot in front of the other, and you will too."

A snowplow rattled down Palisade Road, and Lee got up to watch another angry tow truck following behind, bruising its way down the narrow thoroughfare.

"Okay," Lee said, swallowing hard. "I just lost my best friend in the world. I'm really scared. But if it's the only way, and if it will make Cass happy, I'll go with you. You can never tell Cass what I said about being scared. She works too hard and worries too much, even though she pretends to be fine. I'm older than her, my body anyway. How does that make her feel? We'll have to follow the itinerary Kira and I planned. That way, in a sense, she'll be with us, I guess. And can you please promise to learn something about American history first so that I don't have to feel like a know-it-all? I can tutor you if you want, about Ben Franklin or Betsy Ross or the Liberty Bell."

"It's starting to sound like it could work," Tomás said. "You must know that I take this job seriously, that I'll do anything and everything I can to make it a happier time. Of course, I know something about American history, I'm a journalist after all. I've written about everything from the Russian Revolution to the Taj Mahal. I wouldn't mind learning a lot more about freedom, human rights. In Argentina these things are not a given. And I'm probably going to be staying in the States a while. Maybe start over as a journalist. I know I'm not Kira or Cass or George Washington in a wig—it might surprise you that I even know that much," he said, attempting to make a joke of it. "I'll try to be a good tour guide, I'll try to make it up to you."

10

Freedom is in the air. Of thee I sing.

Two days later, the Thursday before Thanksgiving, Cass was up early and stood barefoot in the living room, double-checking the small bag of supplies she'd packed for their travels, which included Lee's daily myriad of pills, thermometer, blood pressure kit, and a CPR training manual. After a long phone conversation, Dr. Bream had approved their plans, despite citing the potential risks. Cass was banking on Tomás being responsible and trustworthy, though there was still part of her that couldn't be sure. She wondered, too, if Bream had approved Lee's going out of guilt. He hadn't been able to save Kira; what could he really promise Lee?

"Lee's due for some fun," Bream had said. "He should be okay for a week of supervised, moderate activity, his blood pressure's only slightly elevated. And if he gets in trouble, there are specialists in the area who can handle things or get in touch with me."

It was true no one could have saved Kira, and it was true, Cass thought, shuddering, that no one would be able to save Lee when his time came. Progeria had come hurtling, unstoppable, through their lives. It had made her grateful for small things, for Lee's jokes and his smile and the fact that every morning he was there in his pajamas saying something silly to Patrick or quoting the wisdom of Ben Franklin. Now she was putting him in the hands of Tomás, a virtual stranger whose cousin Raymond she knew only casually through work and whose visa and CPR accreditation were about the only real things that vouched for him. For once she wished someone she trusted—even Neil, her ex—were nearby to check in with, to get perspective. But this was Lee's wish, most likely his last chance.

Lee walked into the hallway, yawning, his backpack dangling over one shoulder, his sneakers unlaced.

"Tomás here yet?"

"No, any minute," she said, checking her watch. "Have some breakfast, then I'll drive you both to the airport. Are you pretty much packed?"

"I don't know how to say this," Lee said, sitting at the table, his bowl of Cheerios before him. "But now that it's actually happening, I didn't think how you'd feel being left alone with Patrick. I just realized I'll have my birthday without you."

"Don't worry about me, kid," Cass said. "I'll be working overtime with that pack of overaged brats. What they really need is the Fountain of Youth. You'll come to a performance with me when you're back and tell me what you think of my handiwork. But I know what you mean," she said. "It'll be the first time we've been apart since the day you were born. I'm sure you and Tomás will find something exciting to do to celebrate. He might seem a little aloof, but I think he's got a big heart."

A knock at the door, and Tomás was there. A small black suitcase on wheels at his feet brushed up against his paratrooper shoes. It looked like he had combed his hair for once.

"Morning," he said. "Beautiful day for travel. And not so far that we need passports."

"Well, that's good," said Lee. "Seeing as I don't have one."

"Next time, we'll go to Europe," Cass said. "I want to take you to see all of the Michelangelos and da Vincis in Italy. That's a trip I won't let anyone stop me from making."

"We should probably get going, Cass," Tomás said.

"Take five minutes," Cass said. "Make sure you have everything."

The plan was to fly directly to DC, where they would stay in the mysterious Margaret's apartment, explore the Capitol, then move on to Philadelphia to see the Franklin Institute. Joe and Louise had called the night before to wish Lee well and remind him that it was what Kira would have wanted, that she was with him in spirit and that they would all get together for an update when he returned.

"Okay," he agreed, "I'll try to take a lot of pictures for you."

He didn't tell anyone that he had already pinned the photo of himself with Kira to the inside flap of his jacket, the side he wore closest to his heart, taking her with him the best way he could. In the spirit of embarking on a journey, he found himself thinking not only of Ben Franklin, but of Darwin and Columbus and John Smith and Hercules. To be a real explorer, he knew, required the strength of an able body, not a dwarf. He was shrinking, tightening, losing flesh in odd places every day. It frightened him.

A light wind stirred the bare elms while they waited downstairs for Cass to pull the car around. Though it was mid-November in New Jersey, it would likely be warmer in DC, maybe even shirtsleeve weather.

They took the turnpike, arriving at the airport quickly. Cass double parked in front of the US Air terminal.

"I know I don't need to repeat everything I already told you," she said to them as they stood on the curb, exhaling bursts of cold air. "Call me every day. Have fun, but be careful. Remember, Tomás, I'm trusting you with my son's life," she said, raising her fist, only half-joking. "Make sure you take all of your medicine, Lee, and make sure you listen to Tomás. He's in charge. Any problems—call me, and I'll be there in an instant no matter what my director says."

"Don't worry, Cass," Lee said, hugging her waist. "I won't steal any national treasures. I promise to call, to take pictures, to mind Tomás and take my umpteen medicines. I've already left Patrick a bowl of dried corn and molasses and a copy of the *New York Times* to tear up under my bed to keep him busy. But can you try to read to him, even if it's just the comics? *Family Circus* and *Peanuts* are his favorites."

"We'll call you as soon as we land," Tomás said then, taking charge.

"Okay, then," Cass said, giving Lee a last hug, the boy so

light in her grasp that she could almost feel him disappearing. "I'll miss you both," she called back to them, and began to put the car in gear.

∽

All around them cabs were honking with impatience. Lee was dizzy with the noise and activity; he had never been in an airport before.

"This way," Tomás said, taking Lee's hand.

According to Lee's calculations, the 198-mile trip on the US Air shuttle from Newark International to Ronald Reagan would take only twenty-four minutes at a cruising rate of 500 miles per hour, equivalent to 805 kilometers per hour or 434 knots. Though he certainly didn't think that Ronald Reagan, our country's fortieth president and a Republican, was worthy of having an airport named after him—even if he served consecutive terms and had professionally acted with chimpanzees.

They made their way through the high-ceilinged glass-and-steel pavilion of the terminal, past the ticket counters and rows of magazines, shoeshine stands smelling of tobacco and leather, down the ramp to the gate where passengers for Flight 132 were already waiting to board.

"Are we on time?" Lee looked past Tomás, noticing how mothers with young children were already jockeying toward the front of the line. He was wearing his Yankees cap low over his eyes and could have passed for a much younger child. Now that they were there and it was starting to be real, his heart began pumping with excitement. Pre-boarding started. He gripped Tomás's hand. The stewardess offered them access first, along with parents traveling with babies and other small children. Tomás looked at Lee, who began to protest, but he pushed him along.

"Let's go," he said. "*Apúrate.*"

The cavity of the plane surprised Lee most, the low, arched ceiling reminiscent of the hollowed-out skeleton of a bird. They found their seats and buckled in, Tomás by the aisle, Lee at the window. Lee was fascinated by the foldout food tray and paper barf bag, and amused by the stewardess demonstrating the use of a gray nose-coned oxygen mask, which made her look remarkably like Patrick.

As the plane taxied down the runway, Lee's seatbelt tightened across his waist, his worries about flying were soon replaced by stories he remembered about the adventures of the Wright Brothers, and he acquired a new fascination with the inner workings of clouds.

"Are you scared, Tomás?" he asked. "Of flying, I mean?"

"No," Tomás said. "I've flown a thousand times. Besides, we're on a mission to get somewhere."

Once the plane was aloft, Lee relaxed and scanned the landing gear and seatbelt signs and placard detailing the location of inflatable life vests. He thought about how pontoons would be nice also, just in case the plane had to make a crash landing over water. He opened his jacket and stole a look at the photo hidden there of Kira and himself at Coney Island the previous year. "We made it," he whispered. "We made it." It had been less than a week since she was gone, he still couldn't believe it, and yet they were here barreling forth in a way he couldn't explain.

Twenty-one minutes later he looked out over the acres of gray rooftops and saw it—the Capitol—the chalk-white dome, the magician's hat, the pure white dove chiseled with light flourishing in the distance; all of it left him breathless with excitement and gave Lee a sense of having come home.

"Tomás," he said, elbowing him in the ribs as the white dome grew bigger and the rectangular shape of the Mall became as visible as a Monopoly board. "Tomás," he said, "look!"

Beside him, Tomás pretended to be asleep, unnerved by Lee's innocence and excitement, knowing full well his own plans for betrayal.

The blue bend of the Potomac came into view, jaggedly connecting land to water, and Georgetown to Maryland. "Sixteen hundred Pennsylvania Avenue NW, here we come," Lee said under his breath. "America the Beautiful, of thee I sing."

He closed his eyes, thinking of Francis Scott Key, and felt like a convict granted a last wish. Somehow, deep inside, he still cared about things: the Constitution; the way gold is the standard of US currency; and how getting your wish is both the beginning and the end of something. He tried but couldn't fully imagine the history that had happened here below them more than two hundred years ago, when America's founding fathers walked this soil and bathed and bled, and left their bones and fingernails behind, calcified and now part of the earth. And how Ben Franklin, with his balding head and bifocals and sweet tooth and an eye for the ladies, had turned from silversmithing to inventing and had been part of it all.

The pilot announced they were circling to land. Lee looked over to see a faint glaze of moisture bathing Tomás's forehead.

"C'mon," Lee said, jiggling his arm anxiously. "Wake up already, will you, we're about to land."

"Okay, kid." Tomás opened his eyes and yawned. "I'm awake."

෨

The grid of squares outlining the nation's capital grew bigger and bigger through the oval window until the plane touched down with a slow gritty shudder, like wheels stuttering across sand. The seatbelt sign went off amid a sea of clanking overhead compartments and moving briefcases. Lee grabbed his backpack and slung it over his shoulder, trying to climb over Tomás and occupy the aisle so they could exit ahead of everyone.

In his fervor to get going, his hat fell to the floor and he stood bald and naked in the crowded aisle, no longer fooling anyone. Businessmen and housewives, students and real children reaching for duffle bags and suitcases, stopped to stare at his elfin smallness and ancient facial features. He began to see what other people saw and wished he could disappear.

He held his breath till the engine came to a halt, and they were cemented to the terminal.

"Okay, we made it. So far so good," Tomás said, aware of

how self-conscious Lee had become. Tomás swung a big arm around Lee's shoulders and relieved him of his backpack. "I'll take this, Lee. C'mon, let's get out of here."

The backs of Lee's teeth ached as they walked through the crowded aisles of the airport, Lee feeling a little like the guy in *My Favorite Martian* trying to force his antennae down. His tongue lolled in his throat as he tried to catch his breath from all of the excitement. It was as if he could feel the last two hundred years of American history pass through him—the redcoats of the American Revolution, the cavalry of hoofbeats and marching men in blue and gray intent on civil war, and the thunder of ideas being voted into law. Then he realized it was his heart beating out of control in a giant hysterical arrhythmia—but he couldn't risk telling Tomás. Not now, not when they'd only just arrived.

"Hold on, Tomás," Lee said. "I need to stop and tie my shoelace."

He kneeled and leaned against a blue-and-white-checked Formica pole outside the men's room, counting the orderly pattern of squared-off tiles fitted into the floor and the wheeled cart of mops parked by the doorway. Slowly his heart settled down and he regained his equilibrium.

PART II

11

Outside, the air was warm as they waited at the kiosk for a cab to take them to Dupont Circle and Margaret's apartment. Signs pointed in different directions to Baltimore and Virginia. Washington, DC, being not a state, but both a city and territory in one.

"What's she like, anyway?" Lee said, looking up. "Margaret, I mean."

In November, at this latitude, somehow fall had been delayed, and the air was a balmy sixty degrees. Tomás guarded Lee's body from the bright sun while trying to hail a cab.

"Margaret is Margaret," Tomás said. "She's all business at times, but nice enough. Right now, she's in Los Angeles on assignment for the *Post*, but will hopefully return at some point while we're here."

The traffic outside the airport was busy, business as usual, less congested than they were used to in Newark, let alone in Manhattan. Lee looked up to see the white stripe of the Washington Monument tilted in the distance like a lighthouse of truth, piercing the clear blue sky. And finally he realized what it was that he felt, the thing that had been stirring inside him since they had touched down on land: *To be here was to feel young.*

∽

"C'mon," Tomás said as the next cab pulled up in front of them and he opened the door. A plexiglass partition separated them from the dark-bearded driver whose signature was posted in a foreign alphabet pastiched in swirls—Persian or Arabic, Lee thought. Tomás unfolded the square of paper in his chest pocket, refolded it, then told the driver the address, who nodded and moved quickly ahead out of the queue.

"First time in DC?" he asked, glancing at them through the rearview mirror.

"Nah," Lee said brightly, "we've lived here forever." And Tomás looked at him skeptically like he'd told a dumb joke.

They passed the Potomac laced in failed, crenellated cherry blossoms and lilacs long past bloom. Between poured-concrete curbs and manicured roads, a loosely strung fleet of black town cars with government plates maneuvered around them, sweeping easily out of the airport's cramped exoskeleton.

They drove past the interstate, paralleling the Potomac, toward signs for the Anacostia Freeway, in the direction of what Lee presumed would be the National Mall with its monuments and federal buildings. According to Lee's guidebook, Dupont Circle was a fashionable part of town with good places to eat and a real circle with a fountain, not far from Georgetown, where Lincoln was assassinated at the Ford Theatre on Good Friday, 1865. Being able to stay in Tomás's friend's apartment rent-free was what had clinched the deal, allowing them to make the trip and keeping Cass from going bankrupt overnight.

Lee had a rolled-up itinerary as big as the smallest planet, listing places he wanted to see. He removed it from his backpack's zippered pocket and began to study it. Tomás had already agreed to do whatever Lee wanted—except, of course, they had to eat and sleep. Lee could barely contain his growing excitement in the cab, feeling something like a racehorse being let out of a stall. What did he really want? he wondered A race with time? A jitterbug?

The cab veered west in the direction of the Capitol, and Lee's heart leapt as the larger-than-life alabaster dome came into view, fitted with row upon row of small curvilinear windows. But just as quickly as it had come, it seemed to disappear, and they were moving swiftly away in what felt like the opposite direction. Soon Lee feared they had taken a wrong turn.

"Tomás, I think we're going the wrong way," Lee protested, in a loud whisper. "Do you think the cabbie's trying to cheat us?"

"It's okay, *bambino*," Tomás whispered, *shh*ing him. "Have faith," he said, patting Lee's knee. "What does it matter, anyway, if we go a little out of the way? We're on vacation, remember?"

Lee's heart dropped, instantly sensing something was wrong as the landscape outside the window continued to steadily deteriorate from stately brick and marble structures to failed wood and concrete row houses. He knew for sure they'd gone too far when the sidewalk buckled into sand, and they maneuvered uneasily through a series of deeply exposed potholes. Ahead of them loomed a policeman on horseback—wearing a navy-blue uniform and enameled white helmet—directing ongoing cars at the intersection where the traffic light was out. The huge horse reared up on its hind legs, snorting loudly, as the officer pulled back on the reins to let them pass.

Two blocks later they came to a halt in front of an old abandoned Hess station, the green-and-white electric sign dead out of neon. A small fire was burning in the dirt alleyway, inside a four-foot-high metal trashcan. Next door, on a modest post-and-beam porch, a little girl in braids and a heavyset man in gray work pants and white T-shirt were talking and laughing.

"This is it," Tomás said to the driver. "Stop here." He had matched the number 44 on the abandoned building against the number written on the torn shred of paper, but it was not what he was expecting. "Okay," he said, one hand ready to release the door handle. "I'm going to get out for a minute and look around. Lee, you wait here."

"Your business, buddy," the cabbie said, "but I don't see much of anything open here. Sure you got the right address?"

"It's okay. I'll just be a minute, Lee," Tomás said, patting his shoulder. Then, to the cabbie, "Wait for me, will you?"

Lee's cheeks sank doubtfully, his lower lip beginning to tremble.

"Here," Tomás said gruffly to the driver and thrust a wrinkled twenty through the plastic window. "Keep the meter running, be back in a couple of minutes."

He took the curb and walked quickly to the front of the small boarded-up building behind the abandoned pumps and tried the door. It was locked. Tomás looked back over his shoulder to make sure the cab was still there. He reached for the square of paper from his chest pocket to double-check a third time, rereading the address, written in Margaret's flowing script. She had reason to believe this Martin Llosa could help Tomás locate his missing family.

Tomás's back was still turned away from the cab when Lee grew tired of waiting and opened the door, attempting to get out. But Tomás, hearing the noise, looked back angrily. "No, Lee, *no puedes*. Stay inside. I'll be right there."

Lee was so startled by the sharpness in Tomás's voice that he let the heavy car door swing backward on his elbow, scraping skin. He cried out, first softly and then loudly, not from pain exactly, but from what was becoming painfully clear. The man he was supposed to trust with his life had already lied to him within minutes of their having arrived.

"S'okay," the cabbie said, turning around and shrugging sympathetically through the glass partition. "Your friend's a little crazy, maybe, a little confused, eh? But not too bad. It'll be okay. Just better have the cash to pay me, is all. This may be a free country, but it ain't no free ride."

Lee removed his cap and rubbed his eyes, exposing his baldness in broad daylight. The driver eyed him curiously through the rearview mirror.

"He's got enough cash for sure," Lee said, reversing his cap and rubbing his eyes. He blew his nose into a handkerchief. "I know that for a fact. He's got enough cash to get us where we're going twice and back."

Then he got up the guts to ask, even though he already knew the answer: "This isn't Dupont Circle, is it, sir?"

"Dupont Circle? You kidding me? Rich people, senators and congressmen who go to restaurants and who get their shoes shined, they live in Dupont Circle. I think, my man, your friend's confused, that's what I think. That gas station's been closed for a year or more. Someone's playing a joke on him is all."

Lee listened, never taking his eyes off his view of Tomás through the open window.

Even the little girl and the old man on the concrete porch next door had stopped joking long enough to pay attention to Tomás's every move.

"Tomás," Lee called. "There's no one there. I need to get back and call Cass. She'll be worried. I need to use the bathroom."

"It's okay," he said, holding up the flat of his palm. "I'll just be another minute. I promise."

He tried the cheap tin doorknob again, rattling it harder to try to force it open. By now he knew it was a cruel hoax. He checked his watch. It was twenty minutes past one. If Llosa had planned to come, he would have been here by now.

From the corner of his eye, Tomás saw something move behind the back of the building. He followed, only to discover it was a stray yellow dog sidled up against a rotting fence post. Nearby a squirrel dug into a pile of dirt and stones beneath the calcified remains of a rat carcass, its skeleton undisturbed.

For the past two weeks, since Margaret had first written to him, Tomás had tried to imagine Martin Llosa's face, the man she had learned had worked with Videla in the trafficking of black-market babies in Buenos Aires and who was linked to arranged adoptions by high-ranking military officials. It was possible he could tell him something about what had happened to his wife and daughter. There was nothing to do but leave empty-handed. A small pinwheel of panic exploded in his chest, growing wider and then narrower and bathed in guilt as it shifted down into his large intestine.

He returned to the cab, this time giving the driver the right address. "I'm done here," he said, nodding. "Thanks for waiting. My mistake. Let's go."

The old Chevy cab made an abrupt turn, sending Lee tumbling sharply into Tomás's ribcage. He struggled to free himself, fighting the urge to cry out.

"What was that all about?" Lee demanded angrily. He righted himself as close as possible against the door handle, as far from Tomás as possible, sulking exaggeratedly on the torn red-leather seat. "Why did we come all this way to visit a broken-down gas station when I thought we were going to Margaret's apartment?"

Tomás exhaled, trying to steady Lee's shoulders, but Lee pulled away. "Not to worry," Tomás said. He was breathing heavy, not sure how to explain, knowing he could no longer hide the truth. "It's true," he said, "it's about time. I have some important things to tell you when we get to the apartment. We are still friends now, eh?"

12

Ten minutes passed, and the landscape righted itself, the asphalt highway seamed with concrete, and the familiar historic buildings came back into view, as they approached the Capitol. Lee could see the dome of the White House and the wide marble stairs of the Lincoln Memorial. A cross section of streets alternated between numerical and alphabetical.

"I'm going to need to call Cass as soon as we get to Margaret's," Lee said. "If there really is a Margaret. Cass is probably worried stiff. I said I would call as soon as we got here."

"No doubt she is," Tomás said, shaking his head sadly. "No doubt at all. You seem a little older today," he said. "Being away from home can sometimes make one into a man."

The cab pulled up in front of a modest brick apartment building, set behind a neat square of grass overrun with yellow marigolds, on the corner of Nineteenth and Connecticut in a populated neighborhood that reminded Lee of the better part of Brooklyn. He could hear the distant sound of rushing water, could smell the scent of cut grass, and could hear the unmistakably guttural sound of dark-throated pigeons come down from the trees, squabbling among the cobblestones. Lee knew from already having consulted the guidebook that a block away stood a large verdigris fountain made of bronze women, scantily clothed, the size of Amazons.

"Okay, this is it. Thirty-one Dupont Circle," the cabbie said. "For real, this time. At least I hope so, folks."

"Thanks," Tomás grunted, guiltily stuffing more crushed bills than he needed to through the glass partition. "I'll get the bags from the trunk."

Before Tomás could stop him, Lee raced out of the cab and slammed the door, his backpack sliding below his shoulders, his shoelaces flying. He started running clumsily up the steps of the apartment building, not caring if it was Margaret's or not, trying to escape Tomás.

"Lee, wait," Tomás shouted. "Wait," he called, trying to catch up.

The steps to the old marble building were spaced so steeply apart that Lee didn't have a chance.

"Now hold on," Tomás said, catching him by the elbow. "Hold on. I'll explain everything."

"You lied to me," Lee said, sobbing, sinking to his knees on the stone steps and removing his glasses. "You pretended to be my friend. I should have known better. I should have known you had some other reason for coming here besides being with a freak like me."

"What should you have known?" Tomás asked gently, stopping him. "That I was a jerk?"

"I should have known, because I don't have any real friends. Kira was the only one. You were only pretending. And you're being paid. Why are we here, anyway?" he asked. "If you're thinking of kidnapping me, I can tell you Cass has no money to pay any kind of ransom. Whatever it is, you're a liar and a con man, and you're probably a spy. Did you steal Cass's money? Am I ever going to see her again?"

"Now wait a minute," Tomás interrupted, lowering himself next to Lee on the stone steps, his throat dry as he searched for the right words. "We're here for you and for me. And I am a liar, but I'm not a spy. And there's no question that you'll see your mother again soon.

"Breathe now," he said. "Slowly." He placed his hand on the middle of Lee's back. "Again. A few good deep ones. Are you ready to go inside?"

"Why should I trust anything you say?" Lee said, still struggling to catch his breath.

Tomás wiped sweat from his forehead with the back of his hand and loosened Lee's backpack from where it had slipped down below his shoulders.

"I can carry you if you'd like," he said. "Here, let me help you, I'll give you the express ride."

Under protest, Lee let himself be hoisted up onto Tomás's shoulders.

Tomás opened the outer door to the building and carried Lee up the wide marble stairs braced by a wrought-iron rail to the fourth floor, moving toward the triangle of light suspended from the ceiling. He set Lee down at the top, four flights up, where a large swath of sunlight was pinned to the skylight momentarily, like a butterfly stalled on glass.

They set their things down in front of number 407, and Tomás felt for the key in his jacket pocket. He unlocked the door, unveiling the simple apartment belonging to his friend and former colleague, Margaret DaCosta, whom he hadn't seen for the better part of three years.

"Not so bad, eh," Tomás said, setting their bags down in the shadows of the hallway.

He read her life easily, surveying the contents—the smoothly sanded floorboards and the plum-colored velvet sofa; the floor-to-ceiling windows, blasted with afternoon sunlight and trimmed with voile, overlooking the busy street below, crowded with restaurants and shops. Varnished bookshelves lined the living room, crowded with paperbacks and hardcover mismatched sets and decorated with an array of terra-cotta pottery that had seen better days. Here and there, along the windowsill, he could see lapis shells, stained blue and violet and arranged like crewelwork, and tarnished *centavos* left over from her years in South America.

A stack of recent *Washington Post*s sat on a metal file cabinet, her famed typewriter on the wooden desk beside it, boxed in its black plastic crate like a time bomb waiting to explode with whatever slant her editor favored. Not all journalism was unbiased. Not in the least. The thought ran darkly through him. In Buenos Aires, they had shared an editor.

Lee still stood in the open doorway, not sure it was safe to go inside, still trying to make sense of what had happened.

"Come on, Lee," Tomás urged. "Please don't just stand there. We're going to have fun here, I know we will. I'll do whatever you want from now on."

Tomás moved to the kitchen to fill a glass with water. On the table next to the typewriter, he saw a small brass key to the mailbox and a white business-sized envelope with his name on it. He opened it immediately, reading the note within, then folded it into his pants pocket.

By this time Lee had entered the foyer and closed the door behind him, his body weighted down from traveling, curious now about the person who lived here and starting to feel the distant rumblings of hunger.

"I'm sorry for not telling you about the detour, Lee," Tomás said, clearing his throat and handing him a glass of water and the familiar lunchtime installments of heparin and aspirin. "I just didn't know how, that's all. I didn't know if you'd understand."

Lee accepted the glass of water, then saw the phone on the kitchen counter next to a dried-out African violet that someone had forgotten to water. Tomás held back Lee's hand, preventing him from dialing.

"Before you call Cass and tell her what a liar I am and how you want to go home, just give me a chance to explain. Five minutes. As you've already guessed, there are things I haven't wanted to tell you."

"Cass will be worried if we don't call," Lee said. "Thanks to you we're already late because of that stupid detour. I need to tell her big time that you're a traitor and a liar. Unless you plan to kidnap me, or bury me alive. Unless you're a mass murderer."

"Now hold on, Lee, please," Tomás said with a nervous laugh. He stood and thrust his hands into his back pockets. He took a step closer but then changed his mind and sat back down on the loveseat near the window, where a molten patch of sunlight momentarily blinded him. "Just give me a few minutes to explain," he said. "And then, after you've heard me out, if you want to ask Cass to come get you or to have me arrested, I'll live with that."

Lee looked at him, wondering what possible explanation would make sense or matter. He had just lost his best friend—the woman he loved. He had come all this way to see the White House and the Declaration of Independence. And before they even had a chance to get going, Tomás had already spoiled it.

"Well, I guess I could wait a few minutes before calling Cass," Lee said, unbuckling his wristwatch and setting it on the windowsill. "It's ten minutes to two. You have ten minutes to talk. I'm only doing this because I know that if Cass were here, she would give you a fair chance and at least listen, I know she would," he said, sitting down on the kitchen chair opposite Tomás. "Okay. So tell me what the big secret is, and why you took me to Timbuktu on a wild goose chase."

For a few seconds Tomás had no voice, and then it started to become clear to him. "You see, it's like this," he began, glancing down at the jagged, broken scars that crossed his palms, lines arranged in a kind of story, the kind that could almost be read from a book.

"I know you know a lot about American history," Tomás began again, "but there's a part of my country's history that you might not know too much about."

"You mean about the kidnappings," Lee interrupted, remembering what he had read in the newspapers, "the secret army?"

"That's right, though I don't know how you know about these things," Tomás said, eyeing him skeptically. "Almost three years ago, in the fall of 1977, my life fell apart, Lee. I was married and living in Buenos Aires, the capital city of Argentina. You know that's my home, right? We lived close to La Plaza de Mayo, the city center. I was a journalist for *Las Postas,* the local newspaper where Margaret and I were colleagues. Violeta, my wife, was a physician's assistant, a kind of nurse. We had been married for two years."

Lee listened, nodding, his fingers gripping the arm of the chair.

"But our government was out of control. The economy in chaos, destroyed by poor leadership and corrupt labor unions.

Videla had become a dictator overnight and was calling for what he called the Process of National Reorganization. Nearly everyone was accused of being subversive—students, members of labor unions, lower-level workers, and people like myself and my wife. People were disappearing off the streets every day, picked up in unmarked green Ford Falcons, the unofficial car of the military *junta.*"

"I read about that in the newspaper," Lee said, "but I didn't know if any of it was true."

"It was true enough," Tomás said. "Though we went about our daily jobs, every day was becoming more dangerous, people were being picked up off the streets and taken to detention centers or worse. We later learned about the unmarked graves, crushed human remains turning up in trash piles and private gardens, children burned alive, people thrown from planes or drowned in La Plata."

Lee listened, wide-eyed. "How could they have let that happen?" he asked. "How could anyone?"

"It happened because the military let it happen," Tomás said. "Like most things that happen as a result of greed and corruption. No one was safe. As more news of the disappeared, *los desaparecidos,* became known, we became more afraid. Every night we turned off all the lights in the apartment and pretended no one was home. One night I felt so much despair that I told my wife I wanted to start a family. She looked at me like I was crazy and said no, the times were too frightening. But eventually, several weeks later, she gave in, and two months after that she was pregnant. It was about that time, too, that my editor assigned me to write a story about a youth circus in the barrio.

"A group of teenagers, all of them orphans whose parents had been abducted by the military, were living in an abandoned shoe factory near the waterfront, where they had set up a makeshift trapeze and other circus paraphernalia. They were led by an old bum who called himself Ruiz though that probably wasn't his real name. It was a little like the story of *Oliver Twist.* You've read that, right? They stole for him, they begged on the streets."

"Yes," Lee said, "go on."

"The morning I went to interview them my fate was sealed. Hours after I finished my session with them, they were rounded up and never seen again. My article appeared in *La Posta* on Thursday, not about their stealing, but about their heroism.

"Early the next morning the soldiers came for me. Somewhere in the building a dog had started barking. We lived on the top floor, and I could hear heavy footsteps on the stairs. I woke Violeta and told her to hurry and dress. The look of terror in her eyes told me she heard them, too, hammering the wooden staircase with their heavy boots. The front door was splintering behind us as I opened the window to the roof and told her to run.

"I climbed out after her and started to run across the rooftops, but the guards chased me. I leapt across a smaller rooftop, then down a set of stairs. But more men were already there at the bottom waiting. They called me *payaso*, clown, for my article about the youth circus. They struck the back of my skull with the butt of a rifle and I lost consciousness.

"Hours later, I woke in a tiny cell with a terrible headache and dried blood on my clothes. I knew there must be others like me nearby, but I couldn't see anyone. I was kept in the dark for days, weeks, months. The soldiers stood outside the bars of the cell in their green uniforms and military boots, touting machine guns and yelling death threats. All of Argentina's military forces had formed into one—the army, the navy, everything."

"So that's how—" Lee began.

"Yes, now I'll tell you how I got these scars," Tomás said. "We were blindfolded twenty-four hours a day, experimented on, tortured. Electrical prods and wooden clubs. I forgot what it was to be a man, Lee. But more than anything, I feared for Violeta and the baby, and my thoughts constantly turned to whether or not they had made it to safety, if they were alive.

"One day, what seemed months after I had been arrested, two guards were laughing outside my cell. One said, 'Congratulations, you've just become a father, you have a little girl.' I had been alone in the dark so long I didn't know if they were talking to me or to the walls. One of them came close, sweating through the bars, taunting me with the news. 'Congratulations,' he said. 'Your woman is a whore, your baby deserving of a better family. Too bad you'll never live to see either of them.'

"I was so weak I wasn't sure I had understood. I had no way of knowing if he was telling the truth. But then, nearly a year later, I was released from prison as miraculously as I had disappeared, probably because of the efforts of Amnesty International and other human rights groups working to free journalists. So much had changed. Violeta was gone. I searched for her...but there were only the *Abuelas*, the grandmothers and mothers who gathered on Thursdays in La Plaza de Mayo to protest the abduction of their missing children and grandchildren."

"I read about them," Lee said. "They look like nuns or something. They don't have guns but they're not afraid."

"*Sí*," Tomás said. "Violeta disappeared the same time as me and nobody had heard of her since. I had no other family left except a distant cousin, Raymond, who had relocated to the States. Somewhere in New Jersey, I knew, close to New York.

"My colleague Margaret, from *Las Postas*, had taken a job in America at the *Washington Post*. We began to correspond, and she promised to do whatever she could to help me find out what had happened to my wife and child.

"So I came to New Jersey to stay with my cousin, and he introduced me to your mother. Then, two weeks ago, I received another letter from Margaret. She had information from a colleague working on a story about the illegal adoption of babies in Argentina. She knew people connected to black-market baby brokers who had networked in Buenos Aires at the time Violeta and the baby would have been abducted. And she knew people who had access to the Abuelas's carefully kept records of the missing and dead. Besides the human rights offices, there were underground networks of people who knew people. You understand? But it was a delicate situation, and these informants needed to meet me, to trust me. Margaret urged me to come to DC myself.

"And so when Kira died, and you were so sad, and your mother couldn't make the trip, it just seemed like the perfect opportunity to come here. Even though Margaret needed to go to LA to cover another story, she was happy to try to provide me with leads. She'll be back in a few days.

"She's the one who pointed me in the direction of Martin Llosa—the man I was supposed to meet today at that gas station. She said he had trafficked in the illegal adoption of babies in Buenos Aires around the same time Violeta disappeared. It was a gamble, but one worth taking. But as you know, today proved to be a dead end. Now you know as much as I do. I'm sorry this has been such a long story. I'm sorry I tried to deceive you, but I didn't know how to explain or if you would understand."

"Are you still in love with her?" Lee asked. "With your wife I mean?"

"*Sí*, of course," Tomás answered, without hesitation. "I had nearly lost hope of finding her. And my daughter, if she's alive, I would do anything to find them. Now do you understand why I didn't tell you the truth? But I'm also here for you, Lee. I'm determined to take care of you, believe it or not."

"Then your secret's safe with me," Lee said. "Well, I guess I'm sorry I got so angry with you. It's not your fault, really. Well, it is and it isn't…you could have at least told me the truth a little sooner."

Tomás pushed back his chair and cradled the back of his head in his hands. Now that he had told Lee everything, he was responsible more than ever for the consequences of what would happen.

"And the fact that you have progeria isn't your fault either," Tomás said to Lee, his fist striking the table. "Fate, you know, what the gods have dealt us. What's not fair is never fair. If I could help you get rid of this disease, I would do it. And I would set that father of yours straight, too, and have him take better care of you and your mom. Though your mom says things are a lot better without him. But then maybe I shouldn't have told you that."

"My dad's a first-class jerk," Lee said coolly, leaning forward. "I almost don't remember him anymore. And if I did, I don't think I'd want to see him."

"Dads have a way of doing that sometimes," said Tomás. "My own was quite a *cabrón*, a bastard," he said, glancing out the window at the moving traffic. "I would have liked to have been a good father, Lee. I don't know what happened to my wife or the whereabouts of my daughter. For all I know, my child might be asleep on the ocean floor, with seaweed growing out of her ears. Or she might be rich and eating candy and pouting over some small disappointment, the child of a murderer. If she were adopted by a military officer, then my wife must surely be dead. These are the questions that haunt me still. But," he said, with a deep breath and a shaky smile, "whatever we find out, I'll try to accept it and move on. I won't say you need to keep this a secret from Cass. That's up to you. But I could use your help while we're here. Let's do everything you want to do, let's climb the Washington Monument, for god's sake, or jump into the reflecting pool in front of the Lincoln Memorial, or ride the goddamn elephants at the National Zoo. Let's make sure this is the time of your life! What do you say, kiddo?"

"I'm not sure yet what I think," Lee said. "But I do think we should eat now. I mean, to keep our energy up," he said brightly, "so that we can get to work on this mystery tomorrow. We need to start thinking like detectives. Not exactly like Sherlock Holmes and Watson, but I mean we've got to put our brains together to find your missing family. There's a ton of things I'd like to see here while we're at it. I don't know why we can't do both. Right now, though, I'd better call Cass," he said, reaching for the phone. "I'm sure she's already worried enough. I won't say a word, Tomás, about anything you told me, not Llosa or anything, because her imagination's even worse than mine, and she'd get on the next plane and come and shoot you, then drag me home. Then I'd never get to help you or see the Lincoln Memorial or the Declaration of Independence. And why the hell did Ben Franklin move on to Philadelphia and take that Liberty Bell with him?"

Tomás leaned closer, his arm around Lee's shoulder. "For a little guy, you're kind of a giant, you know. I mean it," he said. "For someone with so many serious health problems and things you should be worried about, you're a king."

Then he picked Lee up and put him on his shoulders, careful not to let the top of his soft bald head graze the ceiling, and carried him the length of the apartment from one end to the other and back again.

"When we get home, I want you to carry Patrick like that too. Promise?"

"I promise. You're on, kid," Tomás said as he carefully set Lee on his feet. "Make the call to your mom while I go across the street and get us something to eat."

"Hey, Cass, it's me," Lee said when she answered. "Yeah, me, your son," he said even louder, as if distance apart was reason to shout. "I've already seen the Washington Monument from a distance. And the air's a little cleaner here because it is, after all, the nation's capitol. And President Reagan must have passed a law that says nobody farts or smokes cigarettes outdoors. It's that clean, I'm telling you."

On the other end of the phone Cass was laughing. "Well, that's great," she said, her voice husky with cigarette smoke.

"So seriously, how are things? Tomás still hanging in? How's the apartment? And what do you think of DC? Have you seen any senators yet?"

"Everything's great," Lee answered enthusiastically. Tomás let himself back into the apartment with Margaret's key, carrying cardboard boxes of hamburgers and French fries. "Tomás is a lot nicer than you'd think," Lee said, winking at Tomás, who was setting the table and pretending not to listen. "Well, so far, anyway. He doesn't mind carrying me, either, which is a damn good thing."

"No swearing, Lee," Cass interrupted, "even if you are on your own for a little while. Even if you guys think you're men.

Understand me, kid? How was the airplane? I really hoped I'd be the one to fly with you your first time," she said.

"I didn't see any angels or anything," Lee said. "But we flew through clouds and close to the sun, and I now officially believe in gravity."

"Well, that's quite a lot for one day," she said. "But seriously, Lee, I miss you. And Patrick misses you. Even though he's trained to use the litter box, he's already pooped on the floor out of spite and is curled up on your bed looking sad-eyed and lonely."

"Can you give him his blanket and rub his belly? Can he sleep in your room tonight? I mean if he really looks lonely?"

"Sure, hon, you got it. Listen. I don't want you exhausting yourself. And I don't want you giving Tomás a hard time, either. Dr. Bream said to have fun, but not too much fun. And remember to take your medicine, promise? Tomás has the list and knows what to do."

"Sure, Cass," Lee said, cooperating. "All nine of them. Twice a day. You know I will. And Tomás knows it, too. This guy is serious. He doesn't kid around."

"Okay then, sweetie," Cass said, relinquishing him. "Now let me say a quick hello to Tomás. Love you, baby."

"Love you, too," Lee said, holding the receiver up for Tomás, who began to roll his eyes melodramatically.

"Quite a son you've got," Tomás said. "Seriously, Cass, everything's fine. We're both excited to be here. The apartment's fine, too, within walking distance of everything. It was a good decision to come. Lee's really excited. We're a pretty good team."

"I'm so glad to hear it," she said. "If not for our damn opening, I'd be there in a heartbeat. Tell me you don't think I'm a terrible mother for bailing on him at the last minute. Especially when his best friend just died. Tell me I'm not an absolute asshole, for letting Lee think that making money is more important than keeping a promise."

"You have to do what you have to do, Cass. No guilt, please. The two of us are fine."

"I believe you," she said. "But listen, promise me you won't run him around. Remember he's a sick kid, even if he acts like he's fine. Lee's health is only going to get worse, not better, just the way it was with Kira. It's his heart and his lungs working overtime. You need to be the one to tell him to slow down. If anything should happen to him without my being there, I'd never forgive myself."

"I'll get him back to you safely," Tomás said. "I'll guard him like my son, like my own child. Try not to worry about anything, *por favor*, please."

"I want to trust you," she said. "But I'll worry every minute till you're back home safe."

"Okay then, Cass," Tomás said. "We'll check in every day, twice if you want. Try to get some rest now, and good luck with the show. *Buenas noches,* good night."

He hung up the phone just as Lee was waltzing down the hallway toward Margaret's bedroom. He was examining a small portable alarm clock, turning it upside down and sideways, forcing the rims of the two tin bells on top to collide and make a thin vibrating sound.

"I want to be up early and get a head start, don't you? Do you think six is early enough?" Lee said. "Kind of spooky to be in someone else's apartment using someone else's things. By the looks of it, Margaret doesn't spend a whole lot of time here. There's almost nothing in her closet except a few old clothes and some running shoes. She's your friend, though," he said, yawning. "You must know something about her, even if you haven't seen her in a while. She's not in the witness protection program or anything, is she?"

"When we worked together, I thought I knew her pretty well," Tomás mused. "Now that I think of it, I'm not so sure. People will surprise you when you least expect it."

"You can say that again," Lee agreed, thinking how different the world looked to him in the space of a few hours, now that he knew Tomás's story.

They ate off white paper plates at the little round table

overlooking the street. Tomás opened a beer, sipping it slowly as the early evening light coated the living room furniture in shades of pale gray and violet. Across the street, near the noisy public fountain, an arrangement of townhouses were painted cinnamon and parchment. Lee craned his neck out the open window to get a better look at nearby federal buildings supported by stately Doric, Ionic, and Corinthian columns. Behind the wrought-iron balconies and marble terraces, he imagined, politics were played. It was too easy, he thought, to forget how just blocks away American laws were being voted into existence by congressmen and senators.

For once Lee had stopped talking long enough to eat his food. Neither he nor Tomás seemed to mind sitting in silence. Near nine, Lee yawned and wiped the crumbs from his face and stood to clear the table. "Bedtime," he acknowledged. "I'm surprised you're not on top of that, señor. Cass would have a fit if she knew you let me stay up this late. And I have to remember to brush my fake teeth. They're not wooden like George Washington's, but they're bad enough. There's no radio, I checked. I guess I'm going to have to sing myself to sleep."

"Maybe not," Tomás said. "Let's check out your room. I'll be sleeping comfortably on the couch. It looks pretty nice, actually."

Together they moved down the hallway toward Margaret's bedroom, the small, square room furnished simply with Shaker furniture, a queen bed, a straight-back chair, and a white oval rug banded in blue. On the wall above the bed hung a lone black-and-white photograph of a dozen or so elderly woman gathered in a circle, dressed in kerchiefs and shawls, clutching posters with the faces of children.

Tomás's heart raced, recognizing the location immediately. "La Plaza de Mayo, the town center in Buenos Aires," he told Lee. "Near where I lived and worked. Those are the *Abuelas*, the grandmothers, who march for their disappeared, their children and grandchildren. On Thursdays they gather, no matter what. This woman here," he said, pointing to one in the center, "is

Margaret's grandmother. They never found Margaret's younger brother Rafael, who was accused of being subversive and was assumed to be among the disappeared, though of course he was only a student at the time."

"How many?" Lee asked solemnly, understanding in pieces now how Tomás's story was real. "How many people disappeared?"

"It's impossible to say," Tomás shrugged. "Some say thirty thousand, but there is no official count, no way to know. And then there are the ones who are left, like me. We are alive, but we will never be the same," he said.

"But tonight, we're both free," he said to Lee with a faint smile. "Tonight, you can slip into your dreams and become anyone you want. I insist on it," he said, deftly turning down the covers. "I understand now why it's important not to waste any more time, not for either of us. And as for me, it's not so much the future, but really lost time that I remember. And forgetting and remembering are tangled up in one. Come get in bed, it's late."

After Lee brushed his teeth and changed into his pajamas, Tomás unfolded the covers to white cotton sheets, and Lee slid inside. "Let's see what we can do about making some music, because music is good medicine for us all," he said. "I don't have my guitar. And maybe that's for the better, because maybe you'd think I sound like a loon, or a wounded chicken, or a dying *toro, a* bull. But my mother used to sing to me, and I'll give it a try with you. Did you ever hear a lullaby sung in Spanish? This one's about *los caballeros,* the cowboys, lost in the Pampas, the long-lost grassy place in the southernmost part of Argentina where sunlight stretches out for days and where mirages and myths are born."

13

Long after Lee had gone to bed, and the street noises had subsided, Tomás lay in the dark on the couch in Margaret's living room, watching the night sky yield to a flat black wash, luxuriant with stars, and still sleep wouldn't come. As much as he was looking to the future, there was so much of the past he was unwilling to forget. He tried to imagine his wife's face, the way it felt to hold her, to kiss her, to say good night. He had taken it all for granted.

He picked up the phone and dialed the number Margaret had given him for the hotel where she was staying in California, but there was no answer. He lay with his arms folded across his chest. The past few years of uncertainty had rendered his nerves paper-thin. Now there was a chance. He was getting closer, despite today's failed meeting with Llosa.

The youth circus story had been a mistake, of course. At times he had suspected his editor, Eduardo Alfonso, of having been bribed by the military to set him up, but he also knew it might only have been a matter of days before he would have been arrested for something else.

Tomás kept reliving that afternoon, wishing there was some way he could go back, do things differently. He'd parked his car some distance from the *barrio* and walked the long road past the ancient shipyard scarred by retired oil tankers and tugs and rusted-out fishermen's shacks. Though he should have known better, he was unafraid and had been humming "The Long and Winding Road," a favorite Beatles song. The air stank of rotten fish, the June sun already too hot at ten a.m. He was sweating through the sleeves of his white button-down shirt. But the part of him that believed in free will kept him joyful, humming, despite himself.

He stopped across the street from the old shoe factory where the circus had taken up residence. The windows were boarded up, but a primary-colored Jackson Pollock-style paint job had been added to the façade above the doorway.

The youth circus—*Patas Arriba,* or Upside Down in English—was headed by an aging trapeze artist named Ruiz. He was rumored to be nothing more than a confidence man who likened himself to a priest. Tall and bearded and difficult to read, he was suspected of manipulating the orphaned children of the disappeared, having them perform for money, most of which he pocketed. Tomás knocked, and Ruiz answered, moving aside the wooden slat that guarded the door.

"*Hola! Entra.*" He came out of the shadows walking on his hands. He met Tomás feet-first, with his feet almost in Tomás's face. Then Ruiz righted himself with a half-flip and extended his hand.

"*Estoy tan contenta de verte,* so glad you could come," he said. "We are at your service. The tortured, the homeless, the wallflowers, the bold. The poor, even the rich," he said with a sardonic smile.

Behind him Tomás could see several teenagers lounging in the shadows, children newly molded into adults, but with faces, he thought, that were less sure. The warehouse was tentlike and cavernous. A thin wire tightrope bisected its length. A few feet away, a pale blond girl in tights had wrapped her body over the tightrope, stretching the length of her torso, arm extended toward her toes. A young boy with the beginnings of a beard wordlessly watched Tomás's every move, most likely distrustful of his presence in their sanctuary.

One by one, the children came forward and began to tell him stories of how their parents and brothers and sisters had been taken from home in the middle of the night. Heartbreaking stories of screaming family members shot in front of them, of babies stolen from cribs, and older siblings hiding to survive.

As soon as Tomás stepped inside the converted factory, he knew the story he was after was not the story for which his editor had sent him. He immediately sensed something deeper welling in the darkness, needing to be told.

What creates a native people? he wondered. What gave us our human origins? Long before the escapades of Perón and his wife and the failed attempts of the labor party and the military *junta,* Argentina was populated by aborigines and other nomadic tribes. What lived in their hearts? What made a family?

In the Camín Cosquín Museum, in downtown Buenos Aires, was an exhibit he'd often visited at lunchtime—a glass case containing the complete skeletal remains of an aborigine. *Reconstrucción de un enterratorio aborigen* was the description on the brass plate. The skull lay on its side, the limb bones assembled in kneeling position, the accordion-pleated length of vertebrae spaced evenly apart like piano keys. Perhaps that was why he had been so moved by Patas Arriba. Like the skeletal aborigine at Camín Cosquín, they were nomadic in spirit; they shared no real ties with anyone. That could have also described his own youth, Tomás reflected, before he'd straightened out and gone to college, before he'd gotten a job at the newspaper, met Violeta and got married.

That day, when he'd said good-bye to Patas Arriba, after listening to the gruesome stories of Karla and Miguel and others, all of them children of the disappeared who bore witness to atrocities, he promised Ruiz, "I'll do what I can to tell your story, the right story. Maybe help reconnect these kids to their families. Get you some help, maybe begin to fix the world."

Afterward, he stood outside the building in the failing light and realized more time had passed there than he was able to account for. He walked forward into the dusk, forgoing his car in the parking lot, continuing under the bridge, not sure where his footsteps were taking him. The average human brain weighs three pounds and has twelve pairs of cranial nerves, he mused as he walked. Which part of that was reserved for evil? Which part for faith?

It was growing darker. Tomás felt so weighted down by the stories of the children that he took a series of wrong turns and walked past much that was unfamiliar. He stopped at a convenience store for a pack of cigarettes, though it had been years since he had smoked. He lit one and choked back the pain in his throat. He hailed a cab, finally yielding to the fact that he was lost. He longed for a drink of vodka and the homing device of his wife's unconditional love.

Now, alone in Margaret's living room, with Lee's tiny body asleep down the hall, Tomás craved whatever truth he could find. He searched the sky for signs of humanity—not as an astronomer might, but as a hunter who anticipates a hunt. Somewhere this same sky contained the coordinates for all of them, all of the disappeared—his wife and child among them. Though he couldn't see them, he was able to sense their presence. Though he couldn't see their faces, he could hear their names.

14

Lee woke the next morning at dawn and sat up in bed, instantly groping for Patrick under the covers, only to realize he wasn't at home. His head felt light for a moment in the darkness as he remembered that he was in DC with Tomás, whose mystery was now beginning to unravel, and whose story had started, oddly, to make sense. It pained Lee to know that Tomás had lost Violeta, in what might have been some horrible way. And his daughter? He hoped with all his might she was still alive. In a sense he and Tomás were brothers, both having lost the women they loved.

If life was for the living, despite the troubles of sickness and war, then equally important was a sense of humor. And for that reason, Lee had long ago understood why he had been so taken with the works of Ben Franklin. Not only was he a founding father of America, not only had he been involved in the signing of the Declaration of Independence and the drafting of the Constitution and the aphoristic humor of *Poor Richard's Almanac,* but Franklin—the tenth son of seventeen children whose father made soap and candles for a living—had written what was probably the world's only elegy to a squirrel.

Lee took out his notebook, to where he had pasted the words:

EPITAPH

Alas! poor Mungo!
Happy wert thou, hadst thou known
Thy own felicity.
Remote from the fierce bald eagle,
Tyrant of thy native woods,
Thou hadst naught to fear from his piercing talons,
Nor from the murdering gun,

Of the thoughtless sportsman.
Safe in thy wired castle,
Grimalkin never could annoy thee.
Daily wert thou fed with the choicest viands,
By the fair hand of an indulgent mistress;
But, discontented,
Thou wouldst have more freedom.
Too soon, alas! didst thou obtain it;
And wandering,
Thou art fallen by the fangs of wanton, cruel
Ranger!
Learn hence,
Ye who blindly seek more liberty,
Whether subjects, sons, squirrels, or daughters,
That apparent restraint may be real protection,
Yielding peace and plenty
With security.

Then he sighed, remembering his promise to keep a journal for Dr. Bream, though it could hardly compete with the words of Franklin. He took out his notebook and began:

Dear Dr. Bream,

One if by land and two if by sea... Do you remember the words of Paul Revere warning that the British were coming? Tomás and I are here in Washington, though Paul Revere is nowhere to be seen. It would have been far better if Kira were with us. Every day I miss her. I know you probably did your best.
More later. Etc.

Lee

Then he hid the journal in his backpack and withdrew the photo of Kira, plus another of Cass holding Patrick in a baby blanket—and took a good, long look, committing them to memory.

He got up and walked down the hall, detouring into the tiny bathroom, where his kidneys took over, then out into the kitchen, where Tomás was already sitting at the table reading the *Washington Post* and *El Mundo*. He was sipping coffee. Lee could smell the odor of tobacco on his breath. It was clear he hadn't shaved.

"Morning, my man," Tomás said, pushing back his chair. He had dark circles beneath his eyes, which Lee now understood to be more the norm than the exception. "Been waiting hours for you to wake up," Tomás said. He poured a glass of orange juice for Lee, along with a bowl of Cheerios and milk. The morning's regimen of medicines was already laid out on the countertop, his complete arsenal of multicolored blood thinners and vitamins and other poisons. "Our little rainbow," Tomás said. "To keep you happy."

"Says you," Lee complained. "I've been taking all of these for so long, I don't know how I'd actually feel without them."

"Do me a favor," Tomás said. "This is not the time to experiment. Keep to the routine or your mom will kill me." He made a mock gesture as if to slit his own throat.

Lee rolled his eyes and sat down at the table, glancing out the window. Ordinary people, dressed for business and shopping, were moving in fits and starts toward buses and subways. Tour buses filled with foreign visitors rattled past. Lee could sense the onset of the day's humidity.

While Lee ate his breakfast and downed the daily regimen of pills, Tomás was quietly plotting their next move that might bring him closer to Martin Llosa. He was unwilling to entirely let go of that connection, though Margaret was still three thousand miles away, not answering his calls.

Margaret had always managed to be one step ahead of danger. Miraculously, she had been absent from the newspaper offices on the day he had been arrested.

By the time he arrived in the States, she had already been working at the *Post* for more than a year, having left Buenos Aires while he was still in prison. Her first job was to report on the human rights abuses in Argentina and in other Latin American countries. Two years later, when Tomás was released and had nowhere else to turn, he contacted her, and she wired him money for his ticket to the States, purposefully—it seemed—not encouraging him to come to DC. He had a brief time in Seattle, and then decided to go to New York, where his second cousin Raymond had already immigrated on a student visa and had promised to help him find work.

Then, after less than a month with Cass and Lee, while he was still getting his bearings, Margaret had called to tell him she had met an Argentine refugee, Isabel Arona, who had started coming to meetings at the cultural center downtown where Margaret volunteered as a translator. Isabel had been a maid for a military family in Buenos Aires and told Margaret about a nurse she knew at the hospital connected to Campo de Mayo prison. The nurse had told Isabel about a woman prisoner who sounded a lot like Violeta. This woman had been brought to the hospital to give birth and was very scared. Unfortunately, Isabel suddenly stopped coming to the cultural center, and Margaret had been unable to question her further or confirm her story. But she had offered a couple more clues.

"There is a chance," Margaret had said to Tomás over the phone, "that Violeta's child could be here in Washington. Isabel told me that the captain and his wife had recently adopted a baby, but then they were arrested by Videla's men one night for some kind of betrayal. Their daughter was visiting from the States at the time. After the captain and his wife were arrested, no one bothered to find out what happened to the child. It's possible, even likely, that the captain's daughter brought the baby back here as her own. Isabel also claimed that the captain's daughter sent a letter, postmarked from DC, to the house months after the parents were killed. Isabel gave it to the *Abuelas* for safekeeping. The captain's daughter's first name was Sofia, but Isabel thought she had a different last name, which she couldn't remember."

"And the mother?" Tomás asked, breathless. "What did the nurse say became of her after giving birth to the child?"

There was silence on the other end, followed by Margaret's

matter-of-fact answer: "I know of none who survived, Tomás. I have heard stories that many were shackled and thrown into the sea. But you're a journalist, after all, and you know how to ask the right questions. This job can't be done long-distance. The last name of the family in Buenos Aires was Sanchez, Sofia's last name before she changed it. It's just a shred of something. If you want to know more, you'll have to come to DC to piece things together yourself. You can stay in my apartment while I'm in LA. And remember, if the baby is adopted, you'll have no proof that she's yours."

Tomás hung up the phone and tried to make sense of what Margaret had told him. It was the smallest of clues, yet it had given him hope. And when the opportunity came up to put himself exactly where he needed to be, it seemed like an act of divine intervention. He called Margaret and told her he was coming, and she, in turn, set up the meeting with Llosa. "Llosa," she'd told him, "besides being a thief, was the liaison between Campo de Mayo prison and several adoptive families in Buenos Aires. He can't be trusted, but perhaps for enough money, he might provide some useful information."

Tomás returned to the present and looked across the table to where Lee was happily eating his breakfast. Bright morning sunlight was streaming through the kitchen window like butter, forming a thin lacy pattern through gauze curtains across his cheek. Tomás got up and began opening kitchen cabinets at random in search of a local phone book. It might be that simple to find Llosa on his own.

"So, you and me, we're detectives, eh?" Tomás said.

"Call me Sherlock," Lee said.

Tomás knelt, starting to search the dining room shelves, but all he found was an old transcribing machine with a foot pedal and some tangled wires. Glancing toward the kid, he felt guilty to see the fatigue on Lee's face, his watery blue eyes pale.

"What are you looking for?" Lee asked, intrigued.

"Phone book," Tomás said, with a sigh. "DC, Virginia. Anything close. I can't seem to find one. We'll look once we get on the road. Where to first today? Your wish is my command."

"Well, it seems to me we now have two purposes," Lee said. "Indulging me with my tourist experience and helping you find your family. I guess your family is really more important. So we can figure out both, because everyone knows I never give up."

"I don't want to believe we won't find them," Tomás said quietly. In the back of his mind, he didn't know how much Lee was capable of understanding, though he had, Tomás knew, lived through his own version of torment and disappointment. He was certain that losing Kira had been the worst moment in Lee's short life.

"Where would you be if you were lost?" Tomás asked him, reconsidering.

"Well," Lee said, "you're only lost if you belong to someone who can't find you. "It's possible they're looking for you, too. Trust me. If I have anything to say about it, we'll find them."

∞

They crossed Nineteenth to Constitution and headed toward the National Mall. It was already seventy-seven degrees—the sky delft blue and cloudless with molecules packed as tightly as the pristine air before snow. In the distance, the Washington Monument pierced the air like an inverted lightning rod.

Lee was visibly excited, struggling to contain his delight at the fact that he was actually in DC. He fairly danced on ahead, his backpack dangling.

They walked briskly down ordinary shaded streets, past office buildings and coffee shops and souvenir stands manned by Asian immigrants selling American Eagle key chains and George Washington T-shirts and wads of fake hundred-dollar bills bearing Ben Franklin's lopsided ironic face. The colorful flags of many nations were set up on a distant hill, moving gently in the breeze.

If Lee were alone, he might have been afraid to show his freakish face in public for all the world to see, his birdlike body being pecked and prodded by the breeze. But Tomás was his bodyguard, a Tory turned spy.

Now that he had learned Tomás's secret, he felt certain this trip was the mission he had been waiting for all his life. Wherever they went, there would be clues, and a search for the poor baby who had come into the world not knowing who she was. Violeta, Tomás's wife, seemed everywhere and nowhere at once, like something too thin to touch. His heart ached for Kira in the same way. It was a lonely thought, he realized all at once, to not know where lost love went.

⁓

The Mall itself was predictable in its geometry—framed at one end by the Washington Monument and the Capitol, with its convex white dome and row upon row of curved square windows; and framed at the other, toward the east, by the Lincoln Memorial, whose steep marble steps led to a gargantuan seated statue of Lincoln himself, a statue so big that you could land a Cessna on one knee and seat a battalion of school children on the other. In between the two, loomed the shallow rectangular reflecting pool, designed by Henry Bacon in 1922, in which one could lose one's thoughts, or find them, depending. How many copper pennies could be raked from the bottom in a day? Lee wondered, as he and Tomás stood before it, staring down at their own reflections.

"Should we throw some in?" Tomás asked, "And make a wish?"

But Lee was busy digging in his backpack for his camera. "Sure," he said.

"Say cheese."

"Spaghetti," Tomás said.

It was after ten. Toward the east a troop of Boy Scouts, dressed in military green with pinched hats and bolo ties with badges, began a slow, knee-socked march over the crested hill in the direction of the bronze World War II Memorial. Lee and Tomás followed behind them at a distance, then down a narrower path, where in a thinly disguised cadre of low-lying trees lay the Vietnam Veterans Memorial—a seemingly endless bandage of black reflective marble inscribed with the names of all who had given their lives to the war. They stood for a moment before it in silence.

Lee looked up to see Tomás in tears.

They walked north toward the Smithsonian Air and Space Museum, moving out of the way of two hovering patrolmen on horseback, wearing ultramarine jackets and pants, their fellows patrolling the dry, distant hilltop, where between monuments the grass had gone to seed.

"So many names of the dead," said Tomás as they continued on, walking past two boys playing pretend army games on the concrete paths, blasting twig rifles in one another's faces, shouldering makeshift flags. "And here we are with sunshine on our faces and money in our pockets and something good to eat. I can almost feel all those lost soldiers standing next to us. Like a crowd."

Lee tried to think of something comforting to say. "Have you ever heard of the Tomb of the Unknown Soldier?" he asked. "It takes into account every soldier, every hero, and it's nearby somewhere in Arlington National Cemetery."

"But it's only your American heroes," Tomás said. "Americans don't have a sense of the larger world."

"Maybe we can trade," Lee said. "Maybe you can teach me something about Argentina's history when we're finished here. Or better yet, you can take me there one day."

It was beginning to make sense to Lee why American history mattered so much to him, and why he'd wanted desperately to come to DC. Even as his life was disappearing, history persisted with the fact that they all—he and his countrymen, and those visiting its shores—existed as a country, as a people. The accomplishments of the founding fathers demonstrated that human ingenuity had a purpose, and that we could use it to fight big battles, to outlive the worst. George Washington knew it when he signed the Treaty of Paris, even if he was wearing a ridiculous powdered wig. Jefferson knew it in his early drafting of the Constitution, and John Adams and Abraham Lincoln, each contributed something along the way. Without them, there'd be no America to speak of. And Benjamin Franklin, even though he had defected to Philadelphia, where he pawned the Liberty Bell and printing press and the unknown future of chocolate, knew that the air in America, despite war and independence, was ripe for creating something that would stick.

"This way," Lee said, stuffing the frayed street map into his pocket, having already memorized everything they needed to know. The barometer fell, forcing the clouds above Connecticut Avenue to swell. He hoisted his bag across his shoulders and adjusted his baseball hat to shield his eyes from the sun.

Tourists had descended from all over the country. A brass horn blew, gathering a crowd, and a large group of people assembled before the Washington Monument, its gaunt white pinnacle a 555-foot obelisk disappearing into the sky. Lightning rods, like golden fangs, clawed the top. "Did you know, Tomás, that the law states that no other building in DC can be built as high as the Washington Monument?" Lee exclaimed, eyes shining.

When a six-man Marine Corps color guard, outfitted in navy blue uniforms with brass buttons, stood to attention and began to play "The Star Spangled Banner," Lee took off his hat and stood to attention too.

As Lee listened to the music, his heart almost bursting with pride and excitement, he could not help but reflect that the purpose of their trip had shifted overnight. He wished he had the clever tools of James Bond at his disposal to better help Tomás find his missing family. Wasn't it human beings' ability to make tools that had allowed us to evolve? Wasn't it our opposable thumbs that helped us grip objects? If only Lee could invent a cool new device for finding missing persons, for turning shadows inside out, for broadcasting unknown facts and phone numbers. As it was, they were low on clues.

The music stopped, and the Marines disassembled, their gloves a bright and gleaming white.

"Okay to go on now?" Tomás asked. "Had enough?"

"Sure," Lee said, a little disappointed in Tomás's lack of interest.

"Let's find the Smithsonian," Tomás said. "At least that will get us out of this heat."

They moved south, away from the fields and furrows of the larger Mall, and crossed into a neighborhood of heavily trafficked streets where the sidewalks were higher and poured with concrete. The air was heavy with bus fumes. Soon they passed a modern sculpture garden and signs for the Smithsonian Museums.

15

One Thousand Jefferson Avenue SW brought them to the Castle, also known as the Smithsonian Information Center. Lee remembered reading about a guy named James Smithson, a rich English scientist and illegitimate son of the Duke of Northumberland, who had willed his fortune to the museum even though he had never even visited the United States.

"The Smithsonian is actually a bunch of museums," Lee explained to Tomás, who already knew, but humored him. "All of them," Lee said. "Air and Space, National Gallery, Anacostia, Hirshhorn, National Museum of American History. They've got exhibits planned till the next millennium! Look," Lee said as they entered the Castle building, a huge glass-and-steel structure with its ceiling exposed. "They've even put all the visitor information in braille!"

Tomás ducked his head as they entered the turnstile. The elaborate ceiling was pasted with galaxies and mock geodesic forms. They checked their bags and approached the information desk for maps and ideas.

The woman who greeted them wore a name tag that said *Doris*. She was short and thin and neatly dressed with gray-white hair and pale blue eyes. Assessing her small stature, small hands, and round wire-rim glasses, Lee wondered if she might have been a descendant of Henry Adams. Unfolding the museum map in front of them, she spread it across the visitors' desk so Lee could get a better look. Tomás leaned on the countertop, growing increasingly impatient. He checked his watch as if he needed to be somewhere.

"Can you tell me what it is you're interested in?" Doris asked, not sure what to make of Lee.

Lee was moon-eyed, plush with the thirst for knowledge.

"Almost anything," he said. "What's in this building with the X on it? Skeletons, muskets, coonskin caps?"

"Let's take a closer look," Doris said, trying not to smile too big at Lee's enthusiasm. "If it's American history you're interested in, then I would recommend you go down the street to the Museum of American History. They've even got Dorothy's ruby slippers from *The Wizard of Oz* and Abraham Lincoln's top hat."

She circled the building in yellow highlighter.

Lee spied something on the map that sparked his interest. He turned it upside down to get a better look. It was an exhibit on osteology, the hall of bones. For what was a brain, he wondered, minus its skeleton? He had read stories about a certain Dr. Walter Freeman and his use of a lobotomy mobile—and a portable apparatus that applied an ice pick to the brain—in his experimental treatment of the mentally ill.

The noon bell chimed, and Tomás interrupted.

"Lee," he said, looking like a man about to bolt. "Wait right here for me, will you? Forgive me, Doris," Tomás said, seizing her hand. "Can you keep an eye on him for a few minutes? There's something I have to take care of. So sorry. I'll be back as quickly as possible."

Before Lee or Doris could say anything, Tomás was hurriedly crossing the great tiled hall, cutting across diamonds.

16

Earlier that morning, while Lee was in the shower, Tomás had finally managed to locate the DC phone book tucked into a drawer in Margaret's desk in the hallway. He had traced the long list of names with his finger, finally arriving at the double *Ls*. There were two Martin Llosas and one Martina. The neighborhoods were unfamiliar to Tomás, one in the Anacostia District and another in Georgetown. He had dialed the first while Lee was singing his *do re mi*s alternately with *bravo* and *bravissimo*, but there was no answer. Then he dialed the second number and let it ring seven times before a male voice answered.

"Is this the number for Martin Llosa?" Tomás asked, trying to make his South American accent disappear. He held his breath waiting for the man's response.

"Maybe," he finally answered. "Maybe not. Who wants to know?"

"I'm a friend of Margaret's. Margaret DaCosta, the Margaret who can be trusted. The Margaret who is right now on the other side of the country."

There was silence on the other end and a soft shuffling sound like someone combing through pages of water.

"Margaret said you might be able to help me. I'm looking for some friends who have relocated to the States from Buenos Aires. They may be tourists. Or they may be citizens."

Tomás's breath stalled in his lungs. He had to be careful how he worded things or risk driving Llosa away.

"What's your name?" Llosa asked.

Thomas thought again. "Carlos, a tourist here, looking for old friends from home."

"And that home is?" Llosa demanded.

"Buenos Aires, like you," Tomás answered. "My friend is

very young, not more than a few years old. She may have been adopted here in the States. She may be with or without her mother."

At that Llosa hung up the phone.

Tomás stood silently, heart in his throat, listening to Lee singing in the shower down the hall, not knowing how to get Llosa to talk. His body had gone cold, and he began to feel the old tremor in his right hand from where he had been struck repeatedly with a splintered two-by-four. He waited, feeling his pulse quicken, then picked up the phone and dialed again. After three rings, Llosa answered.

"I don't know who you are or what you want, but nothing is free, you know," Llosa informed him.

"I need some information and I'm willing to pay," Tomás said, knowing that he had little more money than what Cass had given him. "I don't plan on telling anyone anything. The laws are different here, and you and I are strangers without faces."

"Does the name Violeta Concepción mean anything to you?" Tomás asked in a rush. "Did you know her in Buenos Aires? Do you know what happened to her baby? I have news for her about her husband."

"Her husband?" Llosa said.

"Yes, he's dead," Tomás said, not willing to give himself away. "But he left some accounts for her, some money for the baby. She didn't know."

"And some of that money might be used to reward me for my trouble if I were to help you?"

"That's right," Tomás said quickly, seeing how things were falling into place. "If it is of use to you, that money would be at your disposal."

"When can you meet?" Llosa asked. "I'm returning to Buenos Aires in the morning."

Tomás and Lee had planned to spend the morning exploring, and Tomás couldn't ruin the plans for the kid again. Not after what had happened yesterday.

"Meet me at the lobby of the Castle of the Smithsonian, twelve o'clock," Tomás said. "Do you know it?"

"What, you have no loyalty to your own country? I'll be there across from the information booth at one of the kiosks. I'm easy to find, easy to spot, I am very short, almost like a baby, so be careful not to step on me."

And with that he hung up the phone.

Lee was still in the shower when Tomás stole guiltily into his backpack, knowing the boy had his own small stash of money hidden there. If he could combine that with what he already had, he'd be able to pay off Llosa. Tomás withdrew two hundred dollars in wrinkled tens and twenties, hoping the kid wouldn't notice it was missing until he'd have a chance to explain.

It was twelve o'clock on the Roman dial of the huge clock in the hallway. Tomás crossed the vast lobby, fired up with hope, but his spirit sagging. So much so, he thought, that if he had been Noah in the story of the Ark, he would have had no names for the animals. All of his efforts were now channeled into staving off the creeping feeling of ruin that surrounded him. He didn't know what would be more devastating, finding out the worst, or having Llosa not show.

He looked back quickly across the great hall to see Doris and Lee sitting comfortably on a wooden bench with a pile of pamphlets. It seemed for the moment Lee was in good hands.

Tomás approached the kiosks, knowing that if Cass knew what he was up to she would fire him in a flash, maybe bring him up on charges. The thick wad of bills was pressed against his chest pocket. He had no idea what made an appropriate bribe. The riddle Llosa told him about his size seemed somewhat akin to the riddle of the Sphinx. What kind of man looked like a baby? he wondered.

Then he knew.

Martin Llosa was a gruff, jowly sack of crap badly in need of a shave. He skulked against the kiosk like an animal in pain. Tomás recognized him immediately and without introduction. He was not quite as small as a baby, but round and disheveled. He kept his hands in his pockets and his sunglasses on.

"*Margaret,*" Tomás said, approaching him and using the designated code word. "I'd like to reward you for your trouble, but first, what can you tell me?" He pressed his hand involuntarily to his left chest pocket, where the wrinkled bills straddled his heart. "What can you tell me about the woman Violeta Concepción from Campo de Mayo prison? And her child? Margaret said you can be trusted, that you're a man of your word."

Tomás knew that a baby broker was nothing more than a thief of the lowest kind. For all his height and weight, Tomás's breath was flitting like a hummingbird inside, so desperate for information that he had to fight the urge to choke the man.

"I might be able to help you," Llosa replied, his voice high and nasal. "But then again I might not. It depends on what you have to offer. My business is in the legal adoption of babies. It is a lot of work to sort through the paperwork. It is a lot of trouble to keep track of. And it's very expensive." He sighed, shaking his head sorrowfully. "There have been many women named Violeta, there have been many babies."

Tomás looked across to where Lee was still held rapt under the spell of Doris's history lesson. He felt himself growing more furious by the second. The bastard was toying with him.

He seized Llosa's elbow. "Look, *señor,*" he said, "I intend to make this worth your while, but first, tell me what I need to know. Her name was Violeta, and she was in Campo de Mayo prison, and she was a good person and she didn't belong there. She didn't deserve to die or to have her child taken from her. She had the bad luck to be married to the wrong person. My friend, who died in another prison, would have wanted me to find out. The baby would have been born in March, she would have been sold to someone in the military, the operation handled secretly and delicately, by someone innocent and helpful, someone trustworthy, like you."

He set Llosa's arm free and reached into his left chest pocket, his gold wedding band catching the light, and he knew, in that moment, that Llosa understood the truth. Inside the billfold he had placed a photo of Violeta taken shortly after they were married, long black hair swept behind her ears. "This is the woman I'm looking for," Tomás said. "Take a look and tell me either you know her or you don't. *Dime la verdad.* And whatever you do, don't fuck with me."

Llosa cleared his throat and smiled. "Well, seeing as you're after the truth," he said, "for your friend, that is, I can see I have no choice." He shook his head sadly. "You know a woman is not the same as a man. Mothers in Videla's camps aren't worth anything once they've given birth. Women are like animals, really, bringing babies into the world, and then they're no good to anyone. May she rest in peace. Yes, I knew her. I don't think she made it out of the hospital, at least not alive. But then it's not my job to know."

Tomás felt the shock of what he'd already guessed, gravity disappearing beneath his weight. "And the baby?" Tomás asked hoarsely. "What became of her?"

"Well, lucky for you I do know what happened next," Llosa bragged. "I arranged for the adoption myself. Perfect from head to toe, the baby. A girl. Took her to the home of a captain in the military, a high-ranking family close to Videla. But for that information I want to first see the money."

Tomás removed the bills from his pocket and counted them out in front of him, still not ready to hand them over. "Go on," he said through gritted teeth.

"The wife's name was Camila and the captain, Pedro," Llosa said. "I never knew their last names. And there is no use trying to reclaim the baby. They have probably relocated and assumed aliases. I'm sorry for your loss. Of your friend of course. That's all I can tell you." With that, he seized the money from Tomás's hand and strode rapidly away. Tomás, unresisting, motionless with shock, watched Llosa disappear through the crowd. He stood dry-mouthed for a few long seconds, letting himself imagine what he couldn't have before, what Violeta must have endured in prison—the rape and torture and humiliation, mingled with an anticipation of their baby and the need to hold on. He had a vision of Violeta, alone and blindfolded as he had been, intimate with the language of shadows. She must have hoped for a miracle, that he'd find her. She might have assumed he was dead. The old grief came alive again like ice in his veins, propelling him into the outer arcs of a brain that could mutate past pain when necessary. His impulse, almost overpowering, was to run.

And then he remembered the baby.

Wherever she was, he would find her.

⬧

Now the money was gone, and Tomás was filled with guilt. He looked across the nameless heads of tourists and students and museum officials milling about the museum with notebooks and headsets till he finally saw Lee and Doris still standing together alone, patiently watching his every move.

"Thanks, Doris," Tomás said, upon returning to them. "Just a bit of a stomach bug. Better now. I'll take over from here. Lee, can you tell me everything you've learned so far?"

"What happened, Tomás?" Lee asked in an urgent whisper a few minutes later when they were seated on a concrete bench pressed against the lobby wall, his lap piled with maps and brochures. "Who was that creep? Did he know anything about Violeta and the baby?"

"Later," Tomás said. "I'll tell you everything in just a bit. I just need to settle down a little."

They ducked into a planetarium show that was just starting, and sat in darkness watching the phosphorescence of stars and planets circling on the huge screen, not speaking, until afterwards when they came back out into the light and approached the museum cafeteria.

"Please, Tomás. Can you tell me everything now?" Lee begged.

The ceiling in the overly bright cafeteria was strung with double-winged paper airplanes, inspired by the aerodynamics of dragonflies, paying tribute to the Wright Brothers and the history of flight. Over cold pizza and lemonade, Tomás shared with Lee the report of his meeting with Llosa, as if doling out bread crumbs to an ancient ant.

Lee's eyes were ringed and bulging as he took in the details. "Is that everything?" he asked finally, brushing crumbs from the corners of his mouth. "Everything? Are you sure? What did you leave out? And how much did you pay him?"

"That's something else I need to confess," Tomás said, shifting uncomfortably in his chair. "I borrowed a little money from you this morning when you were in the shower. Two hundred dollars. I gave the bum two hundred dollars, and I still don't know if I can believe him."

"You did what?" Lee asked. "You took my money? That was my allowance for a year. Do you know how hard Cass works and how long it took us to save? I thought you said you weren't going to lie to me anymore, Tomás. But I guess maybe I can think of it as a loan for a good purpose. Though Llosa stole it in the end, didn't he? He looked like a coward even from far away. A big fat slug. I wanted to run up there and punch him in the face. I'll be looking for you to pay me back when we get home. Cass can deduct it from your pay."

"I'm nothing but a poor bastard sometimes," Tomás said, shaking his head. "Cass can definitely deduct it from my pay, and I hope you'll both forgive me. Money won't matter much by the time we're done with all of this. I haven't been much of a caretaker, have I? It's more you taking care of me."

Lee didn't know what to make of Violeta likely being dead. He wanted her to be alive somehow but kept this to himself. Instead, he began to focus on the idea of the baby, suspended somewhere like a pod caught in a tree, precariously in need of being rescued. "Next time you need to let me be in on the meeting," Lee said. "From the beginning. Promise?" He released the straw from his lips and wiped his mouth on his sleeve, looking over the tops of his wire-rimmed glasses. "I know a lot more about these things than you think."

"I know, you're right," Tomás said slowly. "I should have told you. But I didn't know what to expect. Men like that are dangerous. He could have had a gun for all I knew. And I couldn't risk you getting hurt. So now we're left empty-handed."

"What would Ben Franklin have done?" Lee asked intently. "Well, first of all he would have needed his bifocals. And I don't think his experiments with lightning and electricity would have been much use. But he would have thought of something!"

"*Sí*," Tomás said, catching on, "it would be valuable to have use of his inquiring mind. And perhaps also, that of a pirate. It's a good question. What would Ben Franklin do?"

Lee leaned forward in his seat, growing more and more animated, despite his suspicion that Tomás was being sarcastic and didn't believe there was anything Ben Franklin had said or done that could be useful in this situation. After all, Franklin was an inventor, a diplomat, who had at one point been ambassador to France. But wasn't an ambassador a lot like a spy? Wasn't it part of his job to attend party after party, ferreting out information while eating as well as possible?

"Franklin would have had a plan," Lee said. "He didn't take no for an answer. He improvised."

"You're right, my friend," Tomás agreed, standing to stretch his arms above his shoulders, feeling a familiar chain-link pattern of pain scatter the length of his upper vertebrae. It was approaching seven o'clock. He had checked his watch dutifully, remembering his promise to Cass to uphold Lee's bedtime.

"We'd better get you home. Let's go, *ándale*. If it's dark enough, maybe we can test our new knowledge of the cosmos."

"Franklin would have faith that his plan would succeed," Lee said. "He believed he made his own luck."

⁓

The planetarium show they'd watched earlier had revealed the many secrets of the Milky Way, enlivened by the heat of lasers. They were headed back to the apartment, when Tomás stopped beneath a street lamp to light a cigarette, even though it was against Cass's rules.

"I'll try not to breathe," Lee said. "The smoke, I mean."

He stood several steps away, shivering in his windbreaker,

and pulled the zipper up to his Adam's apple, mimicking a spy, perhaps one from Eastern Europe traveling incognito.

"That will be my last," Tomás said. "Cross my heart. Cass would have my head on a platter, and I know it's bad for you. I just run out of excuses sometimes."

They walked side by side, the sky having become dark enough to sustain the early debut of a few distant powdery stars. To the north, the prince of light emerged, then Venus rushing to outshine it, kneeling at its feet.

"Look." Lee pointed up as Venus pirouetted into view. Orion would come later, then the great Ram, followed by the seven sisters of the Pleiades.

Lee could feel his heart flutter against his ribs. Things inside were speeding up again. He didn't think he believed in God, but he believed in gravity, that gravity had a plan for each living thing, a kind of intelligence lying in wait. He was grateful that Cass had seldom babied him and had told him the truth about most things, even about sex.

He had read once that Ben Franklin had had the good fortune of being born twice. There had been a change in the European calendar, extending his age by eleven days in 1752—when calendars switched from Julian to Gregorian—in a struggle to stay aligned with the earth's orbit.

Was it possible, somehow, some way, that his own life could be extended? His life mattered more than ever now, not just to Cass and to himself, but to Tomás and his family. He needed to live as long as possible in order to help them.

Past the White House the streets were named for the fifty states, arranged alphabetically. Alabama, Alaska, Arizona, Arkansas. They turned south. The shops along Connecticut Avenue were still open, the cafes lamp-lit. Tomorrow they had plans to visit nearby Georgetown. They would visit the Ford Theatre where Abraham Lincoln was assassinated.

Lee shivered, his hands stuffed inside his jacket pockets. Night was coming on. Having no fat on his bones, he was hard to insulate. He even had to wear a wet suit when wading in a heated swimming pool. Guitar music played, faintly sweeping across a distant hill where college students camped out, protesting some kind of injustice. The Constitution ensured their human freedoms. He was old enough to know about famous decisions of the Supreme Court, such as Brown v. the Board of Education and Roe v. Wade.

The underground rail system that operated beneath the Capitol was reserved for VIPs and senators. Surely President Reagan had umpteen escape route options by air, land, and sea. The Pentagon straddled an unnamed airfield like a death star, like a giant spider.

⌐ふ

They turned onto Nineteenth Street without speaking, and several blocks passed in a seemingly endless straightaway, each entertaining thoughts of loss and longing. Lee was thinking about Kira, and the pain of her absence, trying to conjure her face in an arrangement of stars. Then he began to imagine Tomás's baby as a tiny new caped planet coming into view that could change the universe; or perhaps a meteor at the tail end of Pluto, but even tinier, having previously been mistaken for a moon.

In the quiet, Tomás's long legs aligned themselves with the shadows of the tallest trees.

"C'mon, little bear," he said.

Little Bear. It was the name of another constellation comprising Ursa Minor and Major, the Little and Big Dippers. Lee's face lit up like a firecracker, illuminating chipped broken teeth and curdled breath, hardly able to believe his winning good luck.

"C'mon," Tomás said, "here we go, get you home good as new." He hoisted Lee up onto the scaffolding of his shoulders. Little Bear and Big Bear, staggering into the night.

17

Do I really know anything about anything? Cass shook her head incredulously, lighting up a cigarette on the trash-strewn platform of Penn Station. She was on her way home from work, it was Friday and raining. She looked down into the darker recesses where the tracks met a deeper indistinguishable blackness. Since the call from Lee and Tomás the night before, she had spent the whole day worrying. It was reckless of her to let them go off without her. Now she opened and closed the nearly spent lighter and stowed it neatly in her purse.

Thanksgiving loomed in the distance like a natural disaster. That was the day they'd be home from their travels. Tomás would have exhausted Lee. But she couldn't have risked letting Lee die before he'd gotten to live some part of his dreams.

Early November winds had already begun to blow across the darkness that led from Forty-First Street to the station. A blaring, pointillist cacophony of small, round, primary-colored traffic lights torched the broken sidewalks of Broadway like a Mondrian painting, and Cass swore there was enough stored neon in the overhead marquees and billboards to keep a hospital emergency-room generator powered for hours.

She had gotten off work at six after carefully sorting and putting away her brushes and pots of color. Every day the idea of beauty reasserted itself in new ways. She had spent a dizzying day getting the cast ready for dress rehearsal. Life in the theatre brought with it the intersection of many lies. Her job was not always to make the characters seem youthful. But she was always to make them beautifully sad, or beautifully romantic, or beautifully envious, or beautifully at the end of their rope. To be beautiful in hope, or despair, was to be believable to an audience, no matter how ugly one truly was.

She had walked the few blocks to the station, her cheeks flushed. Then, inside, there was the world at sea, people mushrooming in and out of benches and kiosks. Money changed hands constantly like lightning, like a magnet.

Her platform was announced for the 7:02, and she took the stairs down, powered by the sheer momentum of the crowd. She pulled her coat tighter around her torso, absently digging the toe of her black boot into a crack in the cement floor. Her jeans felt good and tight. Secretly she knew her mind had always been too selfishly alive to have room for a baby. Her marriage to Neil Adams had been a brief and dishonest punishment for everything unresolved in her life. She was never sure if she'd ever loved him, or if she'd simply needed somewhere to be. They'd gotten married because she was pregnant. When Lee was born, he'd surprised them both by being the one thing they loved most in the world, and their lives seemed to work for the first time. But Lee's illness put it all in reverse.

By the age of one, Lee's growth had dramatically slowed. Before his second birthday, he was still bald as an egg, and progeria had been diagnosed by Dr. Alexander Bream at New York Hospital. Cass had been terrified, and her concept of time was forever changed. By the time Lee was five or six, he was well on his way to arteriosclerosis and had developed a beaked nose. My little old man, she'd crooned to him at night, tenderly improvising. Children shunned him, and their parents looked away. By the time Lee was ten, he'd outlived some of his progeria-ridden friends and had broken both hips, along with her heart. His life expectancy, at best, was fifteen. No amount of trips to Dr. Bream's office changed the facts. There was no cure, and not enough time devoted to research. All Bream could do was rub his own ancient thumbs together and say beatifically: *Bis pueri senes,* Latin for "old men are twice children." Whatever that meant....

At times, she felt, guiltily, that she'd given birth to Frankenstein's monster. Lee's life was raging past them, faster than a speeding bullet, more powerful than a locomotive. In the brief interval since he'd been born, Cass had gone from being vivacious and purposeful with hopes of becoming a legitimate artist to feeling like she was clumsily trying to piece together a cyborg out of mismatched broken parts. She was a broken artist, a sham.

But then, weren't there sometimes miracles?

She had heard from an anthropologist friend of her father's that in Nigeria and other poor rural African countries albinos were killed, their body parts sold to local witch doctors who believed they had magical powers. What might they have done to Lee? Confused his premature age with premature wisdom? Made him a king?

She had agreed to have Lee go off with Tomás before she had agreed to empty nearly half her savings account. Now she stood waiting on the dank platform chastising herself. She should have checked Tomás's references beyond his cousin's vouching for him. After all, he was paid under the table. But Saint Dr. Bream had sanctioned the trip, saying it was a good idea as long as they were careful, and there was no point consulting Lee's father, the king of ice cream, the prince of nothing.

The train appeared first as a distant black dot and then like a silver fist savaging its way into view. She boarded the train bound for Newark and found a seat next to an old woman who slept noisily on a sheet of crushed newspaper.

The ride took barely twenty minutes. She secured the top button of her tweed coat and walked the few blocks east from the station, then let herself in and picked up the mail, ascending the stairs through the dark hallway two at a time. Lee and Tomás had been gone two days now. Their absence made the rooms look strange and unforgiving. She hung up her coat, turned on a light, and saw Patrick running to greet her.

"Ugh, not now," she said. In the past couple of days, without the distraction of Lee and Tomás underfoot, she'd begun to notice how over the years the bleached pine floors had become worn with age, splintered in places, the window curtains gone from white to gray. The refrigerator was empty, except for beer, olives, and cottage cheese—her staples. The very first night, after Lee and Tomás had departed, Cass immediately reverted to her nasty after-work habit of smoking cigarette after cigarette on the poured-concrete porch overlooking the alley.

Cass turned on a second lamp and took off her shoes, then opened a Corona and sat on the couch. Patrick sat squinting up at her over his pink crepe muzzle, trying to insinuate his way into her lap, seemingly trying to cheer her up. Cass looked at him now and saw him for what he was: 130 pounds of ham sandwiches, a pork roast or a belly. In a fleeting thought, Cass weighed his inconvenience versus his virtue. But, no, she couldn't do that to Lee.

Worried again by thoughts of Lee without her, Cass tried to calm herself. Vermilion, the red-orange name of a color, drifted through her mind for the sound of it. The word like the newly born petal of a beach rose, soft and floating with edges tinted the darker, sueded colors of a Cape Cod sunset. And then flamingo, a vibrant pink, breaking into neon. She'd wanted to be a painter once, a yearning that had flowed through her like a river since she was a little girl.

Cass had grown up in Providence, an only child, and had gone to the well-heeled Mary C. Wheeler School, then on to Pembroke, sister college to Brown, where her father August Rhodes was a professor of Elizabethan poetry. He was an expert on the British poet Edmund Spencer and had devoted his scholarly life to unearthing the elusive secrets of *The Faerie Queene*. Cass's mother, Sara Broome, was a decade younger and bohemian in nature, a painter who taught part-time at RISD, the Rhode Island School of Design. They'd lived in a nautical-looking wooden house on Benefit Street—a street that bridged the middle distance between the two colleges—with round, porthole-shaped eyes for windows.

Being an only child with parents like that hadn't been easy. Cass was dreamy and secretive. She saw the world in overly vivid oblique patches of color. Her parents fought regularly over her welfare in a way they called healthy but, from Cass's perspective, made them seem out of their minds. She felt more an object to them than a child.

Then, when Cass turned seventeen, her mother was diagnosed with lung cancer. It took less than six months for her to die. It was too late for chemotherapy, the cancer had infiltrated her lungs and liver. Unbeknownst to anyone, she hadn't had a check-up in over fifteen years.

The shock of time ending without warning had devastated Sara. When her mother told Cass about the cancer, she was still in denial: "I'm not dying," her mother said. "I'm just fading to black-and-white. I'm not going anywhere."

Cass's father had wordlessly set up an easel in the bedroom where her mother lay dying. The thin camel-hair and sepia brushes, arranged simply on the wooden tray of the ancient easel, looked like long, dark musical notes coming apart at the seams. August Rhodes was a man whose life was crumbling. He did what he did best to respond to the tragedy. He read to Sara at night from Shakespeare's love sonnets, "Let us not to the marriage of true minds admit impediments, love is not love which alters when it alteration finds."

Cass listened outside the door and wept. This was love, even though Cass hadn't realized it at the time.

Five days before her mother lost consciousness, while she was still capable of drinking sips of water through a straw, Sara whispered to Cass: "Paint me a feeling, any feeling. You've always been so secretive. I have no idea what you feel."

Cass saw her mother's eyes on the verge of death, time overtaking her, and reached for a brush. She had no idea what to paint, but within minutes she slowly began to paint, in cobalt blue, the outline of a small square box, and inside that another box, and inside that some five-pointed stars. She imagined a catalog of angels like the ones painted by da Vinci and Michelangelo and Raphael, paintings she had copied in charcoal during her Saturday art classes at the museum. She loved Raphael's drawings the most. They were the ones she could most fit her own feelings into, the ones that were most her, flesh leaning against bone. And when she had copied them over and over—the boy, the angel, with long, loose cascading curls and softly crosshatched cheeks that neared the impossibility of owning a pulse—she felt something taking shape that was more powerful than anything else. Because her subjects were always "becoming," they would never be done, never completed, never quite alive. Each line gave way to another, and after that to the possibility of what might come next. Her mind reset itself every time.

Twenty minutes later, she set the brush down and turned to show her mother. In her mind she knew that the repetitive straight lines of the boxes represented a desire to keep going. She thought of the closeness of the two words *angels* and *angles,* the difference being the order of the *e* and the *l.* What did we really know of death anyway? It contained the words *heat,* and *hat,* and *head.*

Her mother was asleep. It took her three more days to die, slowly and slower still, her head tilted involuntarily back on the pillow as if she'd slept and suffered there for a thousand years, her eyes wide open, staring into infinity.

It was getting late. Cass walked back down the hall to Lee's abandoned bedroom, Patrick tiptoeing at her feet. Light from street lamps leaked weakly through the window shades, barely outlining the Civil War relics Lee had collected from both Confederate and Union armies, showcasing a fake sword, an antique flag, and a quill pen. The push-pinned counterfeit one-hundred-dollar bill engraved with Ben Franklin's face centered on his bulletin board. Was it really only a week ago that Kira had still been here with them, talking and laughing? Cass sat on Lee's bed and thought of Joe and Louise, whose grief she understood as her own. She picked up the phone to call Lee and Tomás in DC. It rang and rang with no answer.

18

On Thursdays the *Abuelas*, the grandmothers of Plaza de Mayo, marched in a circle carrying handmade signs bearing photos of their missing children and grandchildren. At exactly three-thirty p.m., when the Buenos Aires church bell clanged, and the shadow cast from the granite obelisk of Pyrámide de Mayo—marking Argentina's freedom from Spain in 1810—shifted to the right, they assembled, wearing identical white kerchiefs and cotton shifts. These mothers and grandmothers and aunts, coifed in the white headdress of doves, began their protest march.

It was an act of defiance, meant to provoke the attention of General Jorge Videla, whose military brigade stood at close range, armed and watching from the safety of their circling green Ford Falcons. It had begun in 1976. Buenos Aires had drunk its own blood, it had swallowed ordinary people up, and a name emerged, *los desaparecidos,* the disappeared, a name that would shame the country for years.

The *Abuelas* would make their way clockwise around the Pyrámide de Mayo, ten or fifteen or twenty, sometimes more. And not just old women; the *Madres,* mothers of all ages, marched too, along with the young. With the defeat of Evita Perón, the city had fallen, and would fall again under its own petty spiritual bankruptcy. Like warm-weather Antarctic penguins, like spies, like men, the *Abuelas*—having outlived their children—had already suffered a fate worse than death.

In nearly every home, a question mark at the table remained for the missing: a daughter stolen during the early morning hours while studying for a college exam; a father taken from his lab in the middle of the day while dissecting the wings of fruit flies; a newspaper reporter; a nine-year-old piano student practicing Beethoven's *Für Elise* in a humid living room next to his snoring grandmother.

Rooms were preserved. High school trophies sat abandoned on bureaus, and unworn wedding clothes of the betrothed still hung mutely in the closet. Running shoes were abandoned, their laces forever tangled. While some things remained the same, during the worst of the regime, it seemed that nature itself had become disrupted. Creatures normally shy had abandoned their habitats and ventured into the open. Aplomado falcons swooped down from the hills, creasing the sky. April bird populations shifted—warblers, and Creek, and hummingbirds nesting too soon in ocotillo cacti. In a country that had killed more than thirty thousand of its own people in the blink of an eye, it was ironic that the region had seen a resurgence of wildlife, with more than 320 species of birds having been counted.

In those troubled and turbulent times, the tango, it is said, was born in Buenos Aires. Some believed that other, far stranger things were born from the history of oppression and the heat and sensuality of Argentina's moderate climate, something that caused rapidly occurring mutations that attracted evolutionists like Darwin and his followers. Perhaps, some thought, it was the spirit of the two-hundred-thousand-year-old fossilized remains of the armadillo's ancestor, the Glyptodon, whose skeleton was discovered miles deep beneath the city plaza, a creature much like an armored tank, that had somehow lent its characteristics to the struggle of the *Abuelas.*

To those who understood, but were afraid to act, the *Abuelas* were the real revolutionaries. They searched not only for their own missing family members but also for the missing children of others, keeping careful records in the hope of one day reuniting families torn asunder. Babies born in prison were being adopted illegally by high-ranking military officials, their true identities vanquished. DNA testing would come years later. But for now, the women meticulously tracked crumbs of information, as in a fairy tale, following uncertain leads and conducting interviews, trying to match eye color and cleft chins. To express the fierceness of their love out in the open was more powerful, and more inspiring, than to fall prey to the drowsy ether of despair. Without weapons, Videla's men were cowards.

If, over the course of years, the *Abuelas* and *Madres* might have possessed the souls of trees and their accompanying wisdom, they would have grown tall enough and wide enough with outstretched arms to reach above the clouds and try to obtain forbidden knowledge. As it was, on almost every Thursday afternoon in La Plaza de Mayo, rain or shine, the sky temporarily lifted when the women marched, old and young, their white billowing kerchiefs starched and determined. While high up on the clay terraces of the circle of buildings that enclosed the square the blue-black iridescent crowns of exotic birds flew in on the wings of tolerance, the knowledge of flight giving them the advantage of another place to go, their range of sounds speaking the language of the dead.

19

Lee and Tomás were finishing breakfast, getting ready for the day. The kid had gotten a good night's sleep but was coughing raucously. That can't be good, Tomás thought. He would need to check Lee's temperature and pump him with lozenges.

They had planned to go to Georgetown, followed by a visit to FBI headquarters, both within walking distance. Founded before Washington and fronting the Potomac, Georgetown had been home to the Nacotchtank Indians before it was trampled upon by politics, tobacco, and slaves. It was the site of Ford's Theatre, where Abraham Lincoln was assassinated, and home to several foreign embassies.

Tomás leaned out the window in order to gauge the weather outside, accidentally upsetting his mug of coffee. His nerves had been on edge since the meeting with Llosa, and he had begun to obsess about whatever it was Margaret wasn't telling him. If she had known about Llosa, what else did she know? And how did her research on youth gangs fit in, if at all? What was she hiding? Margaret had never been fully honest with him, even when they were colleagues tracking down the same news story. She was careful never to reveal her sources. She would skillfully point him in one direction and then go in the opposite, leaving him hanging out to dry.

Lee sat by the window on a high stool overlooking the street, his journal in his lap, his bare feet dangling. His baldness caught Tomás off guard, Lee's skull's resembling a lightbulb on its side. And he thought of how fragile the world was, and how the blue and white of Lee's skull was like the blue and white of ocean waves. Suddenly, he wanted to tell a joke.

"I learned something yesterday, Lee," Tomás said, mopping up his coffee. "About human nature." Lee looked up from his notebook. "Here goes," Tomás said. "Never wrestle with a pig. You just get dirty, but the pig likes it." At Lee's perplexed expression, he explained. "Llosa is the pig."

"Got it," Lee said, "though I don't exactly see why you have to pick on pigs. If Patrick were here. I wouldn't want him to feel he was being made fun of."

Shrugging, Tomás returned his attention to the yellow legal pad on his lap, where he had begun to draw a timeline of everything that had happened—from when he and Violeta were abducted to the likely timing of the birth of their baby. He was trying to predict their future, based on how well he could approximate their past. "*Dios mío*," he mumbled, frustrated at how pieces of memory seemed to have disappeared, how his brain felt locked when pressed.

Lee poured himself more Cheerios and slowly chewed. His teeth were feeling more and more tightly crammed inside his mouth, and it was getting harder to work his jaw. For the past several days he had been staring at the calendar on his digital Timex. He would be thirteen in two days on the eighteenth of November, the same birthday as Louis Daguerre, who had invented the daguerreotype. He had never been away from Cass on his birthday before. Time was steadily counting down, getting past thirteen was pushing it, fourteen would be a miracle. A cake seemed out of the question. A cupcake maybe. He wasn't planning to tell Tomás about his birthday. The idea of becoming even older was too difficult.

"It's a nice joke," he said, glancing up at Tomás, while trying to pry the cereal from between his teeth with a fork. "At least one of us has a sense of humor."

Getting to Georgetown from Dupont Circle would be relatively easy. They could either take the metrobus or walk the distance of less than two miles. Cabs were out of the question with their finances shrinking.

Despite the fact that Tomás knew it was his job to be a good sport and cart Lee around, and despite what he felt was a growing mutual affection, Tomás was on the verge of exploding at the idea of wasting more precious time sightseeing. He had the urge to stand out in the middle of the street, next to the overflowing fountain in Dupont Circle, and beg the incognito CIA agents and senators to help him find answers. Every dark-haired, dark-eyed woman looked to him like some version of Violeta; every toddler in every stroller from the Washington Monument to the nearby metrobus platform was perhaps his daughter.

And all the while they were being squeezed by time. Tomás worried about how they would make their money last the remaining days in Washington. He worried that Cass would pull the plug before he had time to discover anything useful. He worried that Lee would do something dangerous or stupid, like chasing a suspect into the open doors of the Capitol, and that they'd both be arrested. Worse than that, he worried that when it came time to leave, his family might still be utterly lost to him.

Cass had told Tomás about Lee's birthday before they left and made Tomás promise to take Lee out for a celebration. "And for god's sake," she said, "splurge a little, get him ice cream."

So now he was supposed to practice being a teenager's father?

⌇

Rain-coated fall leaves, splayed with finely veined exoskeletons, were deconstructing at their feet. It was drizzling across Washington, across every monument, across every dollop of secreted dog turd, every abandoned newspaper and soggy Chock Full O'Nuts coffee cup. A slick pearlescent rainbow stained the slate walk that led from Margaret's door out onto the thoroughfare of West Nineteenth Street in an upside-down V.

Tomás looked up at the overcast sky and sighed. *Mierda,* he thought to himself, shit, Mother of God. He reluctantly hoisted the huge black umbrella he'd borrowed from Margaret's closet, holding it over the two of them. Lee looked so excited at the prospect of the day's adventure that Tomás felt ashamed at his impatience. He put an arm around Lee's shoulder and felt through the thin casing of flesh to the bone.

"*Vámanos,*" he said.

They set out walking, Lee's shoelaces double-knotted, his inhaler hanging from his belt loop on a string. Tomás had slathered Lee's neck and chest with viscous smears of Vicks VapoRub, which stank of eucalyptus and something waxy like crayons. The air was still raw at nine a.m., and Lee's cheeks held a mild flush—which Tomás was hoping against hope was not the beginning of something deadly like yellow fever or malaria or typhus, not really sure what the American immune system could tolerate. Nonetheless, Lee's spirits were high.

"This is going to be the best day!" Lee said, excited. "I've already figured it out on the map. This way."

"I'll follow you then, Lee," Tomás said.

They made their way easily down P Street NW toward the Rock Creek Park Trails, then right at O, and left on Twenty-Seventh, past coffee shops and newsstands and restaurants with smokestacks that smelled of steamed coffee and inflated hot dog buns.

Lee, having quickly caught sight of something in a nearby shop window, raced ahead and stood staring into the glass window of Squire's Ten Cent Antique Shop. "Whoa," he said, impressed.

Under a yellow cone of light were two white plaster-facing busts, one of Wolfgang Amadeus Mozart and the other of Benjamin Franklin. The window was dripping with tantalizing antiquities, ropes of pearls, and brass candlesticks. But a sign hanging from a rusty chain said the shop was closed until further notice, locking in place a forgotten world of antique coins and old crystal watches and Victorian doorknobs.

"C'mon," Tomás urged, having caught up to where Lee appeared hypnotized. He nudged Lee's elbow. "We'll come back later if you'd like. Take a look inside and see what kind of crackpot runs the place."

Lee's eyes lingered on the enchantment of broken, irreplaceable things, letting go, finally, of his own reflection. He was used to the pawnshops along Broadway in New York, and those in Soho, filled with the cast-off, seemingly animal remains of gamblers and addicts, including snake skins and watches. But these objects were different—and were likely authentic.

"Okay," he said reluctantly, knowing Tomás was right. But he still clung to some dumb secret thought, some crazy idea that he could find something that could save Tomás's family. Some talisman or key or handwritten letter, tucked into the trick drawer of an old wooden box, that would give them a needed miracle.

Soon the sidewalks changed from boring asphalt to the excitement of cobblestones. Lee quickly learned to tap dance over the stone topography with minimal turbulence, his backpack dancing across his shoulders, as if straddling sheets of bubble wrap.

The first stop on Lee's list was Ford's Theatre, then the Old Stone House and Oak Hill Cemetery, then they'd move on to the FBI Building, where J. Edgar Hoover was rumored to have roamed the halls in women's skirts.

Tomás traipsed along, trying to be a good sport, but inside his thoughts grew darker and darker, more impatient to get on with his search. Every wasted step they took as tourists was a step away from finding Violeta and his daughter. They had four days left, and he had already used most of the discretionary cash Cass had given them.

Once, modestly known as the river of geese, the Potomac washed northward, its current carrying soft-shell crabs and protozoa smaller than the eye could see, coursing into parts of Maryland and Virginia, before emptying into the Chesapeake Bay.

They didn't come upon Georgetown, insomuch as Georgetown came upon them—its commercial streets, M and Wisconsin, intersecting at the hub of foreign embassies, postwar relics, abandoned slave tunnels, and the campus of Georgetown University. Many a night, George Washington was reported to have attempted federal land deals over tankards of beer in nearby Suter's Tavern.

Narrow sidewalks were bracketed by Colonial hitching posts and wrought-iron gas lamps. Georgetown appeared to Lee to be a stage for life in miniature, like Munchkinland in the *Wizard of Oz*. He had read, but not fully believed, that the average height of a man and a woman in 1751 was five feet six and five feet one-half inch respectively. Lee smiled to himself, realizing that at his current height of three feet eight he'd nearly fit right in.

They stood opposite the Francis Scott Key Bridge, rain misting intermittently, the sky struggling to clear. Lee looked at Tomás, who was lost in thought, and wished that Margaret would call or send a message or just do something to help them discover another lead.

Lee folded his street map into his back pocket and adjusted his glasses. "Don't worry, Tomás, this won't take long. I want to find your family almost as much as you do. But as long as we're here, we might as well see some things, right?" Lee smiled up at him brokenly. "Remember, I could have come here with Ronald MacDonald and the Make-A-Wish Foundation, I should have been here with Kira, and I could have come here with Cass if I had made a big enough stink about it. But I let myself get stuck with you. I'm trying to make the best of it. Don't forget, I'm your number-one detective, and I always get my man."

"Whatever you say, Lee," Tomás replied, shrugging indifferently.

They crossed the road against the wind. Post-slavery, these same streets, lined with handmade bricks and row houses, had been home to slaves, whose dark spirits manned the Underground Railroad. The oldest African American church—Mt. Zion United Methodist—was just blocks away, built in a flash like an Amish barn raising.

At the intersection of F and Tenth, they came to a gradual stop in front of Ford's Theatre, with its late-Victorian brick-and-stone facade, impaled with a central row of shale recessed windows.

"This is it." Lee exhaled, bowing his head in respect. "Even though it's a museum, I read they still perform plays."

Tomás nodded. He lowered the windblown, inside-out umbrella and waited till Lee was ready to go inside.

It was hard for Lee to believe that Abe Lincoln, our six-teenth president, who was six feet four and a mythical beast of a man, had been shot while watching something as bland as *Our American Cousin.* They climbed the carpeted stairs, past a smattering of tourists examining antique-framed programs and other memorabilia, and stopped in front of the roped-off box where the tragedy had occurred. Lee removed his hat, recalling what he knew of the events of that night. Ulysses S. Grant was supposed to be sitting in Lincoln's place, but at the last minute he'd canceled. General Robert E. Lee had already surrendered. The Civil War was essentially over. Halfway through Act III, Scene 2, Johns Wilkes Booth, an actor at the theatre, delivered the single shot from a derringer that lodged behind Lincoln's left ear. According to the brass plaque, Lincoln didn't die right away but was carried across the street to the Petersen House, where he lasted the night but was pronounced dead the next morning.

Around them, the eleven a.m. tour was assembling. School groups and retirees all leaned in to hear.

Tomás had had more than he could take. He was fed up, his blood boiling. He couldn't stomach hearing one more word about American history or tourists or the fact that Lincoln had been assassinated and had his face stamped on a penny or a five-dollar bill. He didn't give a rat's ass about any of it. Not the Emancipation Proclamation, nor the American flag, nor the Constitution. He knew better than any of them that in a time of war, no matter where you lived, it would only be a matter of hours until human rights collapsed and dictators took over. Americans were fools.

Inside him something else was breaking. The little bit of hope divulged from Llosa was eating away at him like a slow poison. If Llosa believed Violeta to be dead, then it must be true, and yet Llosa was known to be a liar. The kid's problems were Tomás's problems while they were here. He wasn't about to go back on his word and desert him, but this trivial stuff was eating up time. Something neither of them had to spare.

Beside him, a young Hispanic woman leaned against the dark stairway, a small baby in her arms. Tomás watched them, and something shifted in the pit of his stomach. When you love someone, he thought, you belong in ways you can't describe. The hard part was the longing. It was longing that made people do criminal things.

Lee could see Tomás's face shifting irritably, his tolerance for Abraham Lincoln exhausted. Being a tourist didn't suit him at all. But Lee's work wasn't done. He would never have a chance to return. He consulted his guidebook, noting many corollaries connecting Abraham Lincoln to John F. Kennedy, the thirty-fifth president, also assassinated. Lee wrote a list of the striking similarities between them and posted it in his notebook.

Comparison of Events

Lincoln	Kennedy
Lincoln was elected to Congress in 1846	Kennedy was elected to Congress in 1946
He was elected president in 1860	He was elected president in 1960
His wife lost a child while living in the White House	His wife lost a child while living in the White House
He was directly concerned with Civil Rights	He was directly concerned with Civil Rights
Lincoln had a secretary named Kennedy who told him not to go to the theater *1	Kennedy had a secretary named Lincoln who told him not to go to Dallas *2
Lincoln was shot in the back of the head in the presence of his wife	Kennedy was shot in the back of the head in the presence of his wife
Lincoln shot in the Ford Theatre	Kennedy shot in a Lincoln, made by Ford
He was shot on a Friday	He was shot on a Friday
The assassin, John Wilkes Booth, was known by three names, composed of fifteen letters	The assassin, Lee Harvey Oswald, was known by three names, composed of fifteen letters
Booth shot Lincoln in a theater and fled to a warehouse *3	Oswald shot Kennedy from a warehouse and fled to a theater
Booth was killed before being brought to trial	Oswald was killed before being brought to trial
There were theories that Booth was part of a greater conspiracy	There were theories that Oswald was part of a greater conspiracy
Lincoln's successor was Andrew Johnson, born in 1808	

When Lee was done, he was excited to share his findings.

But Tomás waved him away with his hand. "I guess I'm not exactly an historian…but let me ask you something," he said. "What's so important to you about all this history stuff anyway? What does it matter? Is history going to be good to you? Is it going to save your life? Or bring Kira back? I don't think so. And who was Lincoln anyway, besides a con man with a beard?"

Lee's eyes grew wide, his pupils dark. He wasn't expecting Tomás to turn against him in this way. His small fists clenched and his heart beat wildly in his chest.

"Well, number one," Lee began, his voice skipping an octave, "you may not know this, but in 1865 the average life expectancy for a man was forty-eight. Lincoln lived to be fifty-six! Number two, the history of this country is like a puzzle. And Lincoln's a major piece, like a shape as big as California or Texas. If he were a chess piece, he'd be a king. He abolished slavery, he enabled freedom. Without men like him, like Benjamin Franklin—men who actually *do* something in life, not like my father or you who waste time feeling sorry for yourselves—there'd be nothing to believe in."

"Now hold on, Lee," Tomás said, wishing he could take back his thoughtless words. "You know I have a lot on my mind right now. We're on a tightrope, a leash. Before long, this game of ours will be over. I'm desperate not to go back without my wife and daughter. I need to know what happened to them. Can't you understand that?"

But the damage was done, leaving Lee feeling mocked and worthless.

"You know I know," Lee said. "And I've promised to help. Anyway, you'll be glad to hear I've seen enough. You win. I know you must be bored to death. C'mon. We can get out of here."

Lee took the lead, ricocheting down the two flights of stairs, stopping to take one last look by the exit at a table of leaflets and maps depicting Lincoln as president in hat and beard. He grabbed one of each as souvenirs, stuffing them into his raincoat pocket. He lifted his chin and pressed forward, beneath the dark teetering sky and onto the soggy cobblestones. Tomás followed behind, feeling guilty, as they made their way against the wind down M Street, which would eventually lead them to Pennsylvania Avenue NW and deposit them in front of the FBI Building. It was still a long walk, and Tomás, feeling ashamed at his outburst, sheepishly let himself trail a few paces behind.

Two destinations still remained on Lee's must-see list before exiting Georgetown: the Old Stone House and Oakhill Cemetery. He checked his notebook and decided to stick with the plan, no matter what Tomás might think.

Newly restored, Old Stone House was the oldest private home in Washington. Lee came to a standstill before its granite walls, eyeing the foundations skeptically. How do things last, he wondered, how do they survive? Houses like this, built by hand? Lee felt so angry at Tomás that he refused to look at him, even as he sensed Tomás now beside him

Lightning flashed, piercing the sky with a jagged yellow Z, followed by a rumbling explosion of thunder. Clouds shifted darkly like animals on the run.

Lee cleared his throat, taking stock of the historic cemetery gone crystalline in the rain, its mausoleums and crypts toned silver and charcoal. Among those buried here were George Washington's great-nephew and several expired senators. The deteriorating late-fall gardens were pungent with amber and violet mums and zinnias, shy and unpetaling, becoming shadows of themselves. He gripped the cold metal gate and peered through its large cartoonish keyhole.

Then the faltering sky opened, and an angry rain followed, drenching them to the bone. Lee wiped back tears and pressed ahead. Though he was angry at Tomás for his bad behavior, another part of him understood his frustration. They still needed to find Violeta and the baby.

20

If Harry Houdini had been a famous criminal instead of a famous escape artist, he would surely have made the FBI's Ten Most Wanted List. Lee had read stories of his famous jailbreak in 1906 just a few short blocks from where they walked. Houdini had not only freed himself from handcuffs and a straightjacket, but he'd freed eight other prisoners on murderers' row. Then, if that weren't miraculous enough, he rearranged them, locking them all in the wrong cells—all in less than twenty-seven minutes. The FBI's infamous public enemies, Lee reflected as he trudged through the puddles, had included Capone and Dillinger, the Rosenbergs, the abductor of the Lindbergh baby. Crime sprees that shook the public to the bone.

The rain slowed as they approached Pennsylvania Avenue and Tenth. Tomás continued to hold the black umbrella over Lee's head. He walked silently by his side till they slowed finally, and the FBI Building came into focus. The building struck Lee as a collection of oddly intersecting waffles, with row upon row of small sand-colored square windows fitted neatly into right-angled slabs of concrete. He sighed and thought of what little he'd learned about math, how all the shapes on which we base our mathematical calculations relied on the theorem of an ancient Greek named Euclid. Lee would never make it to study tenth-grade geometry; but his intuition told him that if there was a square in sight, nearby there'd be a circle, and somewhere close to that a triangle. The human eye needed to entertain all possible angles, trading pieces of lines interchangeably like colors.

Centuries from now, Lee had a feeling, there'd be new shapes, new dimensions.

Lee climbed the FBI's concrete steps, trying to take them two at a time—thinking of all the TV shows he'd ever watched that featured secret agents, from Bond to the Untouchables to Efrem Zimbalist Jr. as inspector Lewis Erskine in *The FBI*. In his mind, he imagined a secret door behind which were hidden silencers and polygraph machines and poison pens and even a convertible—only to stop in his tracks, feeling short-circuited by the huge CLOSED FOR RENOVATION sign plastered to the front door.

"This can't be possible," he said. "There must be a problem with national security, Tomás." Lee's chest heaved with misery, and his eyes darkened. They had come all this way in the rain for nothing. "Now what?"

Tomás was beside him, drenched and sweating, his body smelling strongly of roasted pumpkin seeds, his long dark hair plastered to his forehead. He took one look at Lee's miserable expression and pushed ahead to see for himself.

"The guidebook said it would be open," Lee lamented. "It says so right here on page thirty-four. Just because J. Edgar Hoover is dead doesn't give them the right to lie."

"Sorry, kid," Tomás said "I know how much you were looking forward to this. Those are the breaks. It's a bum deal. Listen, kid, we've got to clear the air. I'm really sorry about what I said back there—about not caring about Abraham Lincoln and Ben Franklin. I didn't mean it. The truth is I need America. I need you, and I need Cass. And even Patrick. I've never been so afraid in my life. I didn't think there was even a chance that Violeta and my daughter could be alive. And now that I know it's possible, I can't stop thinking about them. We're only here for a few more days, and it feels like finding them is going to be impossible. It's like the whole world has amnesia, and I'm the only one who remembers."

Lee retreated to a wooden bench out of the rain. Tomás joined him. Lee understood about the killings and abductions and the work of the *Abuelas*. He understood, more than Tomás thought, about how things—or people—who have disappeared can never be brought back. Violeta and Kira.

Across from them, on another bench, a man sat

pretending—made of bronze. A bronze newspaper lay open in his lap, his legs crossed, his gaze directed downward, as though he were reading.

"That's government for you," Tomás insisted, touching Lee's shoulder lightly. "They never need to have an excuse for anything. They just do what they please."

"Maybe there's some kind of national emergency," Lee continued. "Maybe they're entertaining a foreign president or discussing enemy secrets. If only we could x-ray the building and find the secret dungeons."

Fistfuls of windblown red and ocher leaves caroused around their feet, stirred by the wind. Tomás looked on, feeling level with the bronze, abandoned man whose life went on without feeling. How do you right a wrong done to a kid? How could they learn anything about finding a missing person when even the FBI had closed its doors to them?

It seemed they had come to another dead end.

"What are we going to do now?" Lee asked. "Do you know tomorrow's my birthday?" It had been on his mind all day, and he was missing Cass. His small dry mouth felt stitched with sadness as he remembered the birthday parties every year at home, with hats and cake and trick candles.

These days a birthday felt more like a death sentence than a celebration. His father sent the obligatory cards every year with the same primary-colored cartoonish pictures of elephant shapes or bright balloons or zoo animals meant for a younger child. Who was more ashamed of whom?

So many miles away from home, who could make him believe he mattered? Cass would call tomorrow to wish him a happy birthday with her false good humor and say that she and Patrick couldn't wait to see him again. But the thought of that made him even sadder. Who would take care of Cass when he was gone?

Lee's head ached. His chest hurt, and he was short of breath. All of the walking had tired him out. But if he died in DC, at least it would have been his choice. They had come this far, there was no going back.

"Okay there, Lee?" Tomás asked, patting his knee. "We should have paced ourselves better, it was probably too much today, all this walking in the rain. Who ever heard of the FBI closing its doors? Did they think we were KGB?"

But Lee wasn't listening. He watched a pair of sparrows twittering on a branch and began to think about a story he'd heard on the news about rich people who sat down in exclusive secret restaurants in France to illegally eat whole small *ortolan* birds as delicacies, first placing a napkin over their heads to hide their delight and shame, then downing the bird—bones and all. It seemed inhumanly barbaric, the crushed marrow jammed in a human throat, the violent compression of tiny captive wings, the ornamental beak emptied of song.

He looked across the gravel path to the locked-down building, knowing it was staffed by the country's best espionage teams, secreted in the geometry of squares within squares. Somewhere inside, he thought, there must be a league of expert code breakers at work, filling countless reams of watermarked paper with things too dangerous for the public to know.

Despite mechanical weapons, nuclear missiles, and radar, Lee suspected that beneath it all, it was mother nature who was ultimately in charge, with her earthquakes and tsunamis. When all else failed, it was nature who most often destroyed and restored. During World War II, hadn't American spies and generals devised code spoken in Navajo? Hadn't passenger pigeons been trained to deliver messages into enemy territory, defying radar?

And for this reason, Lee firmly believed that the answers to Tomás's missing family were within plain sight, among the everyday familiar objects they took for granted. They not only needed to know *what* to look for, but *how*. And they needed something concrete to happen quickly, something better than a Ouija board.

The rain stopped, and Tomás stood and tried to brush the dampness from his clothes. "I'm sorry your dad is a jerk," he said. "He's losing out, you know—on being with you," he said, rubbing his palms together. "You're so smart, Lee, and so funny, and you can do things a lot of people can't."

"Like what?" Lee asked, becoming interested.

"Oh, I don't know," Tomás said. "Like taking on mountains. Like being more than most people, more than a Mummy or an Invisible Man."

Lee listened like an adult with adult thoughts and plans. Keeping to himself his thoughts of how history was full of disguises, and how the ingenuity of the Trojan horse made a remarkably good hiding place.

"I'm sorry you've had such a hard time, Tomás," Lee said. "I'm determined to help you find your wife and baby, so help me. I swear on the soul of Ben Franklin."

"Thanks, Lee. I know I've been a colossal disappointment," Tomás said. "I know Cass would have had me shot by a firing squad by now. I promise I won't let you down again. I promise to carry you upside down anywhere. Just say the word. I'll get you a shopping cart, even a stroller . . . I'll even steal the Declaration of Independence."

With that, Lee started laughing, prepared to forgive Tomás at last. "I guess you're okay," Lee said, biting his lip as he began to shiver. "But I think we're going to need some warmer clothing. Maybe Washington Redskin jerseys, maybe a helmet and mouth guard," he said. "We gotta get hats and gloves and cheeseburgers or something."

"What do you say we walk back toward the apartment and stop at that antique shop you were so crazy about and see if it's open?" Tomás said.

"Deal," Lee said, slipping his arms into his jacket and zipping it tight. "We might find something that will bring us luck."

"Deal," Tomás said.

A starling awoke in the bushes, black and screeching, alarmed at the proximity of human contact.

"Tomás," Lee said, turning to him, unable to get the thought out of his mind, "do you happen to know anything about the ritualistic illegal dining habits of the French?"

21

Lee was so tired from the day's disappointments that Tomás carried him into the bedroom and let him sleep with his clothes on. But the following morning, Tomás woke him with the sun in order to get an early start. Lee emerged from the bedroom, rubbing his eyes, his shirt askew.

"Happy birthday, kid," Tomás greeted him. "You're thirteen, you made it."

Breakfast was already on the table: Cheerios and OJ, and the regimen of pills. Two matching maroon-and-yellow Washington Redskins jerseys with matching knitted hats lay on the kitchen table. A small package wrapped in foil sat on Lee's chair.

"What's this?" Lee asked.

"Happy birthday, Lee. Just open it."

Lee tore open the paper while Tomás watched. Inside was a small black-and-white plastic panda on a keychain. "Is this what I think it is?" he asked.

Ling-Ling and Hsing-Hsing were the two giant pandas who had become the overnight darlings of the National Zoo. Given to the United States in 1972 by China after Nixon's visit to confront Communism, the couple had become overnight celebrities, with twenty thousand people coming to catch a glimpse of them their first day on the job. In return, Nixon sent to China a dowdy pair of musk oxen.

Hardly a fair exchange, thought Lee, gazing at the wide-eyed expression on the seven-year-old pandas, who sat comfortably at home in a terrain of rough gray rock and eucalyptus, delicately chewing stalks of bamboo.

Tomás and Lee had taken the Red Line to the Woodley Park–Zoo/Adams Morgan stop and walked the remaining distance. Wearing their matching Redskins jerseys, they followed the crude stone wall to their right, past aisles of traffic. Lee thought he could smell the lions from blocks away. The only other zoo he had been to was in Central Park, where ancient polar bears smelling of naphthalene swam in a chipped stone bath, and lachrymose alpacas grazed in a narrow field, their pointed yellow teeth resembling candy corn.

They passed through the curved iron gateway and into a mock jungle, where they obtained a map and beelined for the pandas, whose feeding time they had learned was ten a.m. Several asphalt pathways fanned out in different directions, dividing the zoo into separate houses for vertebrates and invertebrates, marsupials, birds, reptiles, and creatures too small to name. A long line of tourists were already queued up, a quarter of a mile long, against a thin rocky ridge within view of the panda habitat. Children—two, three, and four years old—sat high atop their parents' shoulders, craning to get a glimpse. Lee glanced at Tomás, who hoisted him to eye level.

Then a hush was followed by a burst of applause. Like a Chinese brush painting come to life, Ling-Ling and Hsing-Hsing ambled forward over the crests of giant boulders in search of lunch, their shaded eye sockets resembling Hollywood sunglasses. Ling-Ling, in front, was the larger of the two, reaching with his black oven-mitt-shaped fist for a stalk of bamboo, skillfully stripping the leaves with his teeth, then stopping to stare at the crowd for a photo op. He sat beatifically on the edge of a log, jammed, perhaps, with termites and centipedes and the dung of ants. Hsing-Hsing yawned, took one look at the crowd, and went back inside. It was a good performance. The children cheered.

Lee was ecstatic. "Thanks, Tomás! Thanks so much for bringing me. It's a great birthday gift. Cass would approve."

The crowd dispersed, and Tomás set Lee down on a granite boulder across from the visitor's center to study the map. The sky was blue and clear, buoyantly tattooed with high cumulus clouds. Behind them in a furrowed field a row of sunflowers had fallen to seed.

"This way, c'mon," Lee said, grabbing Tomás's arm.

They followed a narrow dirt path littered with fallen yellow leaves toward the African elephants—their huge gray hides like small distant hills.

"This is an important birthday," Tomás said. They stopped to buy Italian ice and some roasted peanuts in a brown paper sack from a vendor's cart and sat themselves at a wooden picnic table.

"Cass would give anything to be here," Tomás said. "I'm sure she'll call tonight, and she'll probably have some celebration cooked up for when we're home. You're thirteen now," he continued. "That means you're a man in some cultures."

"I guess you're right," Lee said, as he scraped the melting ice with the back of his spoon. "Like Jewish boys and girls who have bar and bat mitzvahs, like Maasai warriors. Like aboriginal walkabouts. This might sound silly for a kid like me," he said, "but I keep trying to make my life mean something. Else why am I here? To torture Cass and take care of Patrick? To make fun of you? What have I done that history could care less about? What does any of it matter? Kira was my best friend, but I never got the chance to tell her I wanted to marry her. Because I'm sick I'm not supposed to make plans? Thirteen is an unlucky number. I'll feel better when I even out at fourteen," he said, avoiding Tomás's eyes. "If I make it."

"You'll make it, all right," Tomás said evenly. "*Te lo aseguro.* If I say so, you will."

"My best birthday," Lee said suddenly, gripping Tomás's hand across the bird-poop-stained picnic table. "Much better than any I can think of," he said, "except maybe when I was seven and Cass hired Lancelot the magician. Of course, it would be perfect if Cass and Patrick were here."

❧

On Lee's seventh birthday Cass had hired Lancelot the magician to entertain them. Barely five feet tall and dressed in a cape and top hat, he arrived at the apartment precisely at four p.m. on a Sunday afternoon in November, courtesy of Manhattan's yellow pages, carrying with him up the three flights of stairs a dignified white dove named Snow who slept peacefully in a wire cage.

Lancelot's purple velvet cape was embroidered with gold stars. Cass had set the cake on a wheeled cart, in a room decorated with tinfoil-clad cardboard swords and the names of King Arthur and the Knights of the Round Table written in glitter. Blue balloons hugged the walls. A circle of eight white-wax candles sat atop the cake, seven for Lee's age and one for good luck.

"Are you going to cut anyone in half?" Lee had asked, scrutinizing Lancelot's bag of props, looking for a metal saw.

Lancelot had laughed, showing a gold tooth. "That's for me to know and you to find out," he said, opening the cage to set Snow free. The bird landed on his index finger.

"How do you make a rabbit come out of your hat?" Lee had asked, examining the outer brim and inner silk lining for secret compartments. "The only other hat I've seen like this belonged to Frosty the Snowman."

"That's for me to know and you to find out," Lancelot had said, tapping Lee lightly on the shoulder with his plastic wand. "Or maybe for you to know and me to never find out." He set about busying himself.

Cass stood in the background, leaning against a wooden post, as the magician carried forth, calling sunlight out of shadows, working colored scarves into rope, inviting Lee to tug them apart. "*Presto, change-o,*" he said, and two pieces of rope separated, then fused back together with a tap of his wand.

Lee watched as Lancelot put Snow back into his cage, covered it briefly with a silk scarf, then tapped it three times: "*Wikki wikki wakki,* don't smoke tobaccy." He lifted the scarf and the bird was gone.

Lee was wide-eyed, dazzled. He had never seen anything like it. He scoured the room but couldn't find the bird. He stood on a step stool and combed the ceiling, then looked under the sink in the bathroom with a flashlight.

"How did you do that?" Lee asked, mystified, returning to the tiny living room where the light was fading.

Later, after Lancelot had collected his fifty dollars and a generous five-dollar tip, and had eaten a slice of cake and packed another to take with him at their insistence, Cass and Lee watched him disappear as easily as he had arrived, carrying the empty wire cage down the back steps, the magic hat packed in a plastic bag. They watched out the window as he unlocked the back of the white VW van parked in the alleyway, absent of markings or identifying bumper stickers. When he opened the door and lifted the hatch, they were amazed to see the bird already inside, unharmed, in another cage.

To this day, Lee still didn't know how Lancelot had done it.

Life's like a shadow, a magic trick, Lee thought, his mind returning to the present with Tomás. What if we don't find them? he panicked. How could we possibly go home empty-handed? But, no, he wouldn't let himself believe that Violeta and the child were gone.

"I'm sure Cass will make it up to you," Tomás said, bringing Lee back from his memory of Lancelot, feeling somewhat overwhelmed by Lee's show of affection. He instinctively reached inside his chest pocket for a nonexistent pack of cigarettes, remembering that smoking was not an option.

At the table next to them, a family of four was setting out food for an elaborate picnic. Tomás watched, noting how he had forgotten it was the right of families to move about easily.

"Hands down. My best," Lee repeated, pulling on Tomás's hand and trying to get his full attention. "Because of you," he said, still expectant, still wanting, waiting for him to say something.

"When we get home we'll call Cass," Tomás said. "I bet she'll have some great surprise for you, something you can't begin to guess. It was a good day for me, too, Lee. Let's be grateful for small things."

"Do you think we can sleep here? Upside down with the sloths?" Lee asked, gazing past a shallow pool of basking pink flamingos, wet up to their ankles in pond scum. "Gravity inversions are supposed to be good for my health on account of they could interrupt the flow of age. At least that's what Dr. Bream said, but Cass and I knew it was a joke."

"I hear sloths are very quiet," Tomás said as they arrived in front of the creatures in cages, suspended upside down from trees, pretending to sleep. They were larger than raccoons, but with the same coloring.

"Not lazy, but slow, water on the brain or something," Lee ventured, straining to get a better look.

"I feel sorry for their tortured souls—a lifetime in captivity," Tomás said. He waited, letting Lee take his time, feeling proud of having handled the birthday celebration adequately. He was happy to have redeemed himself in Lee's eyes. Violeta had often said he was too proud, and that he needed to come down from his high horse and make things right with people. He knew that same strategy had served to make him a better journalist.

They watched the sloths for several minutes, waiting for one of them to make a move. "I never thought of the zoo when I thought of visiting Washington," Lee admitted, struggling to crack open a peanut shell. "But then I guess there's room for national everything. George Washington had it all under control."

"Here, let me help with that," Tomás said.

"I haven't felt anything anywhere near happy in a really long time," Lee said. "I still don't understand it, what happened to Kira, I mean. I know she's supposed to be buried in the ground. We saw the coffin. But I still don't believe it. I still see her everywhere. I keep thinking we're going to run into her by the lions or the elephants. She would have liked the pandas. Do you ever feel that way about Violeta? Do you think that's crazy?"

Tomás shook his head. "You know as much about these things as I do. I don't think it hurts to believe."

"You're not so bad, Tomás," Lee said. "Not really. But maybe I am crazy?"

"No, never," Tomás said, soberly. "*Es mui triste,* it's so sad she's not with us. But we'll keep her here...somehow together with us. I'm afraid, for better or worse, you're stuck with me for the time being."

They walked in the direction of the dying sun, whose orange husk was just beginning to unribbon from its inner molten yellow sphere. It was past five-thirty, and the zoo would close at dusk.

"One more animal?" Tomás said, checking his watch.

"Okay," Lee said, torn between signs pointing to the big cats, bird house, and butterflies.

"You pick," Tomás said. "Our last stop."

◈

Because gorillas and humans are so closely related and can transmit diseases back and forth with ease, the Great Ape House was enclosed in glass. Lee had never seen a live gorilla before. He stood humbly facing his closest ancestor. Its humanness startled him, its slow dark eyes that moved side to side. Its gray leather palms were heartbreakingly detailed with a careful network of heart- and health- and life-lines, its consciousness palpable.

"If you gave a gorilla a lie detector test," he asked Tomás, "would its grunts register truth and lies?"

"Not likely," said Tomás, admiring Lee's sense of humanity, wishing he had more power in the world.

"I'm ready to go now," Lee said, after a few more minutes of watching in silence.

They exited the zoo gate and crossed to Connecticut Avenue, waiting for the metrobus to take them back home. Evening had come on. Lee's teeth began to chatter involuntarily through the Redskins Jersey, and he felt dwarfed and gloomy leaving all of the animals behind. The branches of the tallest trees threw shadows across the darkening street, while the rush-hour traffic moved on as usual.

"I would have liked to have set them all free," Lee said when they found their seats on the bus alongside students and businesspeople heading home from work. "Though I guess there are some good reasons that they're here. Ling-Ling and Hsing-Hsing could never find their way back to China by themselves, that's for sure. They wouldn't get far without a passport. And the gorillas would at least need to learn sign language. Don't you think so, Tomás?"

Back at the apartment, Tomás kept his promise to Cass and delivered on the cake and ice cream. He turned out the lights in the kitchen and living room and lit each of the thirteen candles on the cake, plus a fourteenth for luck. "Happy birthday, kiddo," Tomás said, cheering him.

"Happy birthday to me," Lee repeated, his face aglow. The cake was chocolate with vanilla frosting, a drawing of the Capitol done in silver icing on top. He leaned down to blow out the candles, their light illuminating the hollows of his skull, making him look like a carved-out jack-o'-lantern.

He closed his eyes and made a fervent wish, then made quick work of blowing out all the candles.

"Good man," Tomás applauded, reaching for the knife.

After cutting generous slices for each of them, Lee settled next to Tomás on the couch, his white socks grazing the coffee table. The sky had turned a deep Prussian blue. They turned on the TV to some sort of variety show where the acts were loud and nonsensical and unnaturally colorful. Within minutes Lee felt himself drifting toward sleep. Tomás didn't move a muscle, but let him lean there against him free and unhurried, allowing the weight of Lee's body to dissolve into his shoulder.

Now the Brothers Karamazov, an acrobatic act, were performing on Margaret's ancient TV, going through hoops and other tricks on ropes and unicycles. The TV had poor reception, and the wavering outlines of people made it appear as if it were snowing in Las Vegas.

The phone rang; it was Cass, calling to wish Lee a happy birthday.

Tomás woke Lee and handed him the phone, and Lee quickly

remembered her face the day they left and realized how much he missed her.

"Three days and counting," she said. "That's how long you've been gone. That's how much I miss you. How's my birthday boy? This weekend I'm going to get my shotgun down and go out into the woods and start hunting our Thanksgiving turkey. Patrick's going to sniff him out, point his tail, and then I'm going to shoot him between the eyes."

"You're kidding, right, Cass?" he said. "I can't imagine you shooting anything."

"Of course, I am," she said. "I miss you. The show opened to good reviews, but what good is it? I sure wish I could be with you and Tomás instead. You know that, right?"

He thought of past opening nights, the way she always let him watch the play from backstage, then introduced him to the cast and crew at the end of the night.

"Sure," Lee said. "Though I think we're getting pretty good at managing."

"Hey, kiddo," she said, "was it a good birthday?"

"It was terrific, Cass," Lee said, trying to keep the homesickness out of his voice. He didn't think she would mind that he was starting to like Tomás after all. "We went to the National Zoo, and there was national everything, more animals than I'd ever heard of. I wanted to take one of the gorilla's home, but Tomás wouldn't let me."

"You know you could come home earlier," she said, "tomorrow even, if you're getting tired. How are you feeling? Has Tomás been checking your vitals? Do you feel like he's paying attention?"

Lee contemplated the offer. It would be so easy to return home, climb in bed and take naps when he needed them. Snuggle with Patrick, the big lug. Their mission to find Tomás's wife and child had changed everything though. Tomás was in the next room, probably worrying that Lee would betray him. He could hear his footsteps pacing back and forth outside the door.

"It's just a couple of more days," Lee said, his voice cracking.

"So far, so good. Tomás isn't perfect, but he's not as bad as I thought. And we haven't made it to Philly yet, either. That's a big part of why we came. Wouldn't want to disappoint old Ben Franklin."

Cass paused, cleared her throat. "I'm so sorry Kira couldn't be with you, Lee. Joe and Louise have been calling every day. They send their love. I have to admit it's hard to be away from you so long. Patrick's missing you too. I don't know what I'm going to do with him. Meantime, big hugs, sweetie. Happy birthday. Can you put Tomás on?"

Lee handed over the phone, feeling guilty for lying to Cass. It wasn't exactly lying so much as withholding the truth. He was relieved when, after a few minutes of questions and answers, Tomás hung up.

"Tomás," he said, "I don't feel right not telling Cass what's going on. I've never really lied to her, not really, not since I was little and Patrick pooped all over the floor and I cleaned it up myself. I know she'd be really upset if she knew. Do you think we should tell her anyway? About Violeta and the baby?"

"I can't tell you what to do, Lee," Tomás said. "But consider this: if you do tell her, we leave without finding the truth about my daughter. Am I selfish? Yes, but I've waited a long time for this moment and nearly lost everything in the process. We have return tickets in a few days. Maybe Margaret will still find some way to help us. Either way, I leave here as a father with a child or as a childless father," he said.

Lee knew in his gut that helping Tomás was probably the most important thing he'd do before he died. He didn't know how long his body would last. He had seen pictures of volcanoes erupting without warning. "I guess I can wait a few more days," he said. "When we get home, though, promise me you'll tell her right away. I have to admit that with lying to Cass, this whole thing doesn't feel as much fun anymore."

"We'll have plenty of time to figure out how to tell your mother," Tomás said. "I'll take the blame for everything. It's me she'll be mad at."

Lee got undressed and climbed into bed, thinking of the gorillas and sloths, for whom it appeared time had magically slowed, if not stopped altogether. Tomorrow would be devoted to Tomás and figuring out where to look next. He wished with all his might and in all of his bones that he could slow things down for both of them so they'd have more time to solve the mystery. But like the predilections of a good race car driver, his curse was speed.

PART III

22

The red eye from LA was late.

Margaret DaCosta had been sitting on the LAX runway since twenty minutes past midnight. It had been a long trip, and she was anxious to get home to the nation's capitol and put her troubles to rest. Once the plane took off, she stretched her legs across the two vacant seats beside her. The lights were dimmed, the plane half empty. The temperature in the plane began dropping steadily as they crossed the Rockies and neared Michigan.

Margaret shivered and slipped her arms into her lime-colored down jacket, arranging her waist-length black hair loosely around her shoulders. At thirty-seven years old, her right temple was already streaked with a bolt of premature gray like Cruella de Vil from *The One Hundred and One Dalmations*. Like Susan Sontag, like her own mother. Lightning seemed to strike all of the women in her family with tragedy in one way or another. As a Latin American woman covering politics and youth violence and as an investigative reporter for the *Washington Post,* she had a reputation for being a hard-ass and had scared off many of the American men with whom she worked. For others, she inspired erotic fantasies that would never come true.

Time after time she had put herself in uncertain, dangerous positions, never knowing who or what she'd face when she knocked on a stranger's door. The art of asking questions was delicate and intuitive. Push anyone too hard and they'd shut down. Her work with former political prisoners had taught her when to shut her mouth, when to press, and when not to cross the line of human dignity.

When the flight attendant asked if she'd like a beverage, Margaret ordered a scotch. Night flying made her batty, she had too much on her mind.

In Buenos Aires during the Videla regime and the atrocity of the Disappeared, she had been one of the lucky ones to play the political game and walk away seemingly unscathed, playing it safe by writing about propaganda-ish so-called women's stories: garden parties, engagements, petty complaints of the upper class—never complaining or exposing anyone within inches of the military.

She was the only surviving child of Jewish immigrant parents who had managed to escape the ghetto in Poland and emigrate to Argentina after losing everything, with hopes of living out their lives in relative quiet. She and her brother Rafael—nine years younger—spent their childhood tiptoeing around their parents' lives, living under the radar of the past.

Now Margaret sipped her scotch and felt the swell of heat and licorice and burnt apples streak her tongue. She wondered what was awaiting her at home. Tomás and his charge, whom she knew very little about, were already camped out in her apartment. She was simply returning a favor. Or was she?

She had not seen Tomás since their work together in Buenos Aires. She'd never told him how she felt responsible for his disappearance and also for that of his wife, Violeta. But now she thought she had a solid lead that could actually help him locate his missing family. She had put him in touch with Llosa, whom she had learned about through the underground contacts at the paper. But one could not reveal one's sources. And if Llosa was a dead end, she would find another way to help Tomás.

When they were reporters together on *La Posta* in Buenos Aires, Tomás was assigned stories he knew might be considered subversive. The youth circus story had been offered to her first, but she'd refused, telling her editor she was far too busy and encouraging him to offer it to Tomás instead. It was sure to be something that would pique his interest.

When he was abducted afterward, Margaret had felt guilty for months. She had gone to his apartment to visit Violeta and was shocked to discover that she, too, had been taken.

Three years later, when Tomás washed up in New York,

asking for help, Margaret thanked God, but cursed herself. She could see without looking into his eyes that he had experienced the worst imaginable. She knew from her interviews with other political prisoners who had survived and made it to the States that every single one of them had left something behind.

Her job at the *Post* had been a dream come true and had kept her connected to Human Rights Watch and Amnesty International. After her brother Rafael and his girlfriend were tragically killed at home, Margaret's life changed drastically. Part of her work was to uphold the Universal Declaration of Human Rights, to try to free prisoners of conscience around the world. Conscience implied that in every man and woman there existed a basic degree of morality. But torture, applied via electrical prods, waterboarding, sleep deprivation, and rape seemed to have removed that gene from the human conscience—revealing the true nature of men to be no different from monsters.

She had gone to LA to cover a story on female youth gangs and had returned with a story on a murder that had happened over a pair of sneakers. She had seen the shoes in the photo of the corpse, blue like the Pacific. At eighty-five dollars a pop, they hardly seemed worth it. As if one's feet could moon-jump out of the ghetto and out of poverty. She would need to type her notes and go over the details of the story with her editor. Murder over a pair of sneakers was tragic but hardly front-page news.

It was nearly five a.m., and light had begun seeping through the plane's half-shuttered windows. The few passengers on board began to stir and grope for misplaced shoes and abandoned newspapers. Her attention shifted back to Tomás and his situation. She still had contacts among the *Abuelas* and the *Madres.* They were sure to know something.

❧

The Boeing 727 angled east, and the hazy panorama of the Capitol came into view. The plane released its landing gear and skidded to a standstill. Margaret retrieved her bags from the overhead bin and began making her way briskly through the sparsely populated gates of National. Outside, the blue-gray November dawn began to separate dark from light, prying open the day like a freshly shucked oyster.

She hailed a cab, her heart beating faster as they spun onto 395 and dove-tailed south with the morning traffic before exiting onto E Street, crawling toward the Circle. Two alabaster landmarks were visible in the distance: the dome of the Capitol and the obelisk of the Washington Monument. How many years had she come home to these man-made symbols of freedom the way some people reclaim the desert or the ocean?

She was well aware of whisperings around town, in the inner political circles, of circumspect glances and circulating rumors, that she was counter-intelligence. No one knew about her double life in Buenos Aires and the stories she'd secretly written under an alias for the underground papers. Years later, she realized her actions might have led to the murder of her brother Rafael. A notion she felt she could never come to grips with.

For now, she was expected to be in LA for another week and had no intention of telling her editor she was back. The better to try to sort things out with Tomás and check on what was going on in the apartment.

The cab pulled up in front of her building, and she paid the driver and climbed out. She looked up to see the sun imprisoned inside a bank of dark clouds, the trees nearly naked. In LA it was still hot, the temperature well into the eighties. Thanksgiving was almost upon them. She felt at home in the kitchen and longed to cook something with butter and liquor and oranges.

Knowing that Tomás was likely still asleep, she walked to the French café on the corner, its plate-glass window already lit from within. She inhaled deeply, breathing in the smells of baking bread and the aroma of freshly brewed coffee. She had avoided answering Tomás's phone calls while she was away, wanting to be sure she could really help him before she divulged any further information.

She bought a copy of the *Post* and checked the headlines in order to inspect the work of her colleagues. An ex-minister had escaped a bomb in Paris; Congress was meeting to decide yet again on tax reform. The former president Carter had already overridden Kissinger's support of Argentina's cleansing of the government. Now what was Reagan to do? Americans were egocentric and would do well to acquire world maps rather than additional vacation homes. The price of gas or cigarettes didn't seem to deter them from vices.

Her story on *Los Diablos* would take months to sort out and would likely make the Sunday magazine. Gangs were clubs held together by fear. She folded the newspaper in half and checked her watch. It was nearly eight, late enough for someone to be considered a visitor and not an intruder.

23

She stood in the vestibule and rang the buzzer twice, then went back outside and stood on the sidewalk. Tomás was already up and drinking coffee in the kitchen, sitting near the window that faced the street.

He heard the bell and opened the shade. Margaret waved up to him from the sidewalk. It was the first time in three years they'd been in the same time zone.

He opened the window and said, "Margaret, is that you? *¿Qué demonios estás haciendo aquí?* What the hell are you doing here? We thought you'd be gone for another few days. Wait, I'm coming down."

At the bottom of the stairs, he was breathless, opening the door for her.

"One of my main witnesses was killed," Margaret said. "Over nothing, over a pair of sneakers. Long story. I'm sure you can imagine."

He pushed back the dark strands of hair that hung over his forehead. "*Terribles*...I know you'll tell me more about it. But enough, come upstairs. I hope you can at least wait a few days before kicking us out. We've gotten rather comfortable here."

Margaret laughed and began to climb the stairs. He was ahead of her, taking them two at a time, then stopped. "Here, let me take your bag," he said, seizing it. "*Dios mío,* good god, you *are* a light traveler. What's in here, air?"

"Some notes for my story, my tape recorder, a few dainties," she said.

She stepped into the apartment, placed her coat over the back of the kitchen chair, and set her bag on the counter. Everything looked the same but different. The smell of coffee was pungent and dark. The curtains, usually left closed, were wide open. "Now let me say a real hello to you," she said, and reached to embrace Tomás, leaning into his chest with rare surrender. He hugged her also, kissed both cheeks, then stepped back.

"The red eye, eh?" he teased. "Can't the *Post* afford better than that? Remember all those nights working late in Buenos Aires, with Violeta calling every ten minutes, wondering what I was up to, when I'd be home? And I'd come home smelling of whiskey. You know, I think she was a little jealous of you. Those were good times. We did good work before Videla, Margaret. The rest, well, the rest has been like being lost at sea. And your man Llosa was a thief! I still don't know if he was lying about Violeta and the baby. I didn't believe a word he said. Though he did manage to steal my money."

Margaret gazed at him with a great enduring sympathy, as if truth alone was never enough in any story. Her downfall, she knew, was the desire to fix things that weren't fixable. She took his hand and told him the truth. "*Mierda,* I'm sorry," Margaret said. "About Llosa. He was a yes-and-no man all along, meaning we never knew if we could trust him or if his information was any good. There are other trustworthy people here, some other contacts I can try. We have to keep going until we can't go any farther."

"*Gracias,* thank you, Margaret," Tomás said. "I don't know if I can tolerate another false lead. If I only had some idea of what happened to them, I could live with that. I could make some kind of peace. It's not knowing that's driving me crazy. And we'll only be here a short time, really. Just till the day before Thanksgiving. Then I've got to return Lee to his mother," he said, nodding toward the closed bedroom door, "in New Jersey. You're not going to throw us out right away, are you?"

"Well," Margaret said, "that depends on you, and Lee, is it? And how well you can spoil me in order to pay me back."

"Just so you know," Tomás said, glancing at the closed bedroom door. "I'm here to see to the kid's dreams too."

"The kid?" Margaret asked, curious. "Tell me about him."

"Well." Tomás thought for a moment. "My friend is a little

hard to explain. He's not quite a baby, and he's not quite a man. His name is Lee, as I mentioned. He's sort of an historian. A detective historian. You'll see."

"What is this, the riddle of the Sphinx?" She reached inside her bag for a cigarette. Within minutes they heard movement coming from behind her bedroom door. Lee was awake.

He opened the door, the bed sheet twisted around his body like a toga. "Hey, Tomás," he said rubbing his eyes, "it's cold in here."

Lee was blinded for a moment by the column of white light streaming through the gauze living room curtains. He yawned loudly.

Margaret's mouth opened, then closed, but she said nothing. To see a dwarf adorned like that was a privilege. His egg-shaped skull set her teeth on edge. "I get it now," she murmured, repeating Tomás's words: "child, old man."

She vaguely remembered knowing something about this syndrome or disease, remembering some of what she had read but never seen. "*Hola mi hombrecito.* Hello, Lee. I think you must be one in a million, aren't you?"

Lee blinked back at her, embarrassed. "Well, actually, one in eight million," he said. "It's called Hutchinson-Gilford. Or progeria. I age too fast," he explained, "but I don't get big." He slipped on his glasses to get a better look at her. His feet were cold, and his pajamas snagged above the sharp barbs of his bony ankles. "Margaret? I mean who else could it be?"

Nothing really shocked Margaret. She was tough as nails and breathed in information like a naturalist. Her eyes grew wide as she took in the Brancusi-like winged deconstructing creature in front of her, neither man nor bird nor beast nor epiphany.

"This is *the* Margaret, our host, my old friend. Our *landlord*, for the moment," Tomás said. "Good thing she came home sooner than we thought. We need her help badly. You'd better be nice to her if you expect to stay."

"Oh," Lee said, stepping back. "The Margaret who owns this place, the expert on youth gangs? Jeez, we didn't expect you for another few days. We've kind of taken over here. Sorry… oh, I guess you'd like your sheet back," he said, letting it drop to the floor.

"Oh well," Margaret laughed, "never too soon for a party, right? Looks like you two had one without me last night," she said, gesturing toward the kitchen, where the remains of Lee's birthday cake still sat on the counter.

"I turned thirteen yesterday," Lee said proudly. "There's some cake left. I can cut you a slice that has frosting from the dome of the Capitol."

"Well, that's damn nice of you," Margaret said.

She didn't exactly know what to make of him. It was trouble enough to try to think about helping Tomás, but now a boy who was not even a boy, but an old man? Who was a riddle but not a joke? Was she supposed to treat him like a toddler and hold him on her knee? No, he would want to be treated equally, with respect.

"I see," Margaret said, moving into the living room, "that you've made yourselves at home. Don't mind me if I take a load off. Those red-eye flights get a little tougher as you get older."

She took off her shoes and stretched her legs out onto the beige woven ottoman. Lee could see how her recent time spent in the LA sun had scored a faint sock line. Early-morning sunlight scorched the coffee table near the window, where his umpteen bottles of pills were arranged in two intersecting circles resembling the Olympics logo. His upside-down sneakers stuck out from under the upholstered sofa, a guidebook to the city was folded open and sticking out from under the carpet. Tomás had draped the wet towel from his morning shower over the back of an antique chair in the hallway.

"Didn't take you guys long to turn this place into a men's club," Margaret observed, matter of factly. "What's it been, three days? I hear you've been sightseeing in between detective work. You guys making any progress? Me, I get out of breath just climbing the steps to the Lincoln Memorial. His head's too big, it gives me nightmares."

"I suppose I should tell you," Lee said. "I suppose if anyone could understand, it would be you. You *are* a journalist, you should, theoretically, be interested in everything."

"Go for it, kid," she said, lighting a cigarette. "Tell me."

"Well, here goes," said Lee. "I wasn't exactly born like this, though in a sense I guess I was, but my parents didn't know right away, not until I was two when all my hair fell out and I started going backward instead of forward. It has to do with genes and stuff, and right now there's no cure. I guess you could say I'm fast at everything, well not exactly at catching or throwing a baseball or grabbing an arrow out of the air like Robin Hood. My doctor said I could die in my sleep any day, or die wide awake from a heart attack. But anyone could die crossing the street when you think about it, or choke on a potato chip for that matter.

"I'm an American history buff, a big Ben Franklin fan, and my best friend, Kira, who had the same disease—just died. Just like that, and I didn't get a chance to say good-bye. She was supposed to come with us on this trip—with me and my mom, Cass. And now I'm so sad, and I really miss her. We wanted to see the Capitol and the Smithsonian together. Kira had only been thirteen for two months. In the end my mom couldn't take me 'cause she had to work. Her job is to make people look good on stage. I was so disappointed, but then she asked Tomás. And Ben Franklin is my hero," he added. "You know about his printing press, right, and his bifocals and *Poor Richard's Almanac*? He was really good at telling jokes. Tomás has been a good sport and all," Lee said, glancing over at him, "but I bet you know how to cook a little better. Do you, Margaret? I sure hope so, because I'm tired of hamburgers and pizza. Are you going to let us stay here? Because we're practicing at being detectives, and Tomás has a big fat secret he needs help with. He's searching for people, and I'm trying to help him. But then I guess you know that. That Llosa guy was a creep. I think he had a gun in his pocket. Is there anything we can help you with, Margaret? Then maybe we can all help each other. And one more thing, I have a pet Vietnamese potbellied pig named Patrick. We couldn't bring him on account of he's too big and doesn't like to be on a leash."

Lee paused, out of breath.

"Are you done?" Margaret asked, getting up to put out her cigarette in the sink. "You about done, or is there more?"

"Well, there is one thing, "Lee said. "We were really disappointed when the FBI building was closed. You don't have any kind of secret key, do you, Margaret? You don't know any spies?"

At this, Margaret breathed deep and laughed out loud. She leaned closer to Lee on the ottoman.

"Well, number one," she said. "You guys don't need to leave. And number two, I think you are quite charming. And number three, I have a few more ideas for Tomás. But I expect you both to help me, and I expect we'll have a good time."

Lee stared up at her broad tan face, the cheekbones high and angled, giving him the distinct impression she was descended from lions. He decided he liked her. He was sure she could lecture him on a thousand different subjects.

"Deal?" Margaret asked. "Let's get to work already. I understand you have a very important date with a Thanksgiving turkey!"

"Deal," Lee said.

24

Sometimes, in order to solve a mystery, the best strategy is to work backward from something you already understand.

Lee sat at Margaret's side as she withdrew a small black-and-white spiral notebook from her bag. It was double-rubber-banded together, its narrow-lined pages torn, folded, and paper clipped, secreting a lifetime of essential information and private contacts along with retired passport photos, foreign embassy phone numbers, and a tattered last letter from her father telling her how much he loved her before he died.

"Are you a code breaker?" Lee asked. "Are you good with numbers? Is there anything I can do?"

"*Shh,*" Margaret said, searching through her notebook. She sat at the round table in the living room overlooking the street, with Lee glued to her elbow monitoring her every move, his steady, sure focus like an Eagle Scout. She spread the pages across the table, trying to map an idea. Tomás sat in the stuffed chair by the window, his deep-set, melancholy brown eyes admonishing the universe at large. He had resumed his old curmudgeonly self, relieved to let Margaret take over the care of Lee for a little while. He bit into the cuticle on the index finger of his right hand till it bled. His separateness assaulted him. In his mind he traced the spare, effortless shape that hawks made in flight, silhouetted and soaring, holding onto nothing, riding currents of air.

"Do you know anyone in the FBI who can help Tomás find his missing family?" Lee asked Margaret outright, desperately trying to think of ways to help before they ran out of time, desperate to be part of it.

"Not exactly," she said, "but there are other alternatives to that J. Edgar Hoover crowd."

Margaret turned the pages slowly, going down lists, muttering aloud. Every time she knew she was about to confront something difficult in her life, she'd tried to picture herself sitting on an imaginary, numbered line, precisely at zero—as though a pendulum on a swing—in order to weigh the odds. She looked up at Tomás and sighed, sensing he was suffering beyond repair.

"Sometimes," she said finally, reaching to close the window, "the best cure for what ails you is a road trip."

It was still early in the day. She closed the notebook, replaced the rubber bands, and stuffed it in her purse. Then grabbed her coat from the back of the door. C'mon, guys," she said. "Grab your gear. Let's go. I have another friend we need to talk to," she said, dangling her noisy keys shoulder-high.

"Right now?" Lee asked, excited. "This minute? I knew you'd think of something! C'mon, Tomás, don't just sit there. Let's go!"

❧

The car had fins like a fish but was the dark reddish-brown color of a salamander. Its worn vinyl seats blanched to a pale tripe, its rear length far too long, the Virginia plate hanging by a screw. Almost forgotten and hardly used, the car was stored in the garage behind the apartment building, along with sealed crates of Margaret's forgotten belongings, including a retired typewriter and broken Dictaphone machine. She unlocked the garage door, unveiling the car like a svelte naked lady. Its exhaust pipe was rusted over, but the engine started up immediately when she turned the key.

"What are you waiting for? Get in, *caballeros*," Margaret insisted, her cheeks flushed.

"Do you think I'm a magician and can make it drive by itself?"

Lee paused, his hand on the door handle, struggling against his better judgment. He looked first at Tomás and then at Margaret before deciding it was safe to get in. He clambered over the hump in the middle of the backseat and found the seatbelt trussed down with metal clips, folded so neatly it must never have been used. When Cass drove, he never used it. But now he quickly secured it across his hips, then clutched his ears, readying for blast-off. Tomás slid easily into the passenger seat beside Margaret, nodding as if something familiar was about to happen, and stowed his sunglasses in the glove box that closed with a loud click.

"Should we blindfold ourselves?" Tomás asked. "Or are you going to tell us where we're going?"

Margaret had the best poker face, the best at bluffing and bringing down the house. She looked at him and rolled her eyes. She was at the wheel, the window cracked an inch, her hair flying behind her ears like some minor superhero, heading for the highway. Large round white sunglasses framed her eyes like an ant. They were traveling incognito, staying loose and anonymous. Tomás next to her, Lee in the rear, holding on to his ears as if poised to break the sound barrier. It was a standard shift.

The gray funnel of the highway warmed to them as the big Buick throttled over it, the suburbs of Virginia angling distant and small as the compass speculated first west and then east. Margaret tuned the radio to station WRYR out of Sherwood, Maryland. Van Morrison's "Tupelo Honey" was airing, a playful tune. Tomás glanced back at Lee and rolled his eyes. Lee snorted out loud, noticing how in the company of Margaret, Tomás seemed to have regressed to some adolescent place, struggling with himself to let her be in charge. They passed road signs directing traffic to Baltimore, Maryland, and places farther north in the direction of Philadelphia, as Margaret drove northeast, following directions for Gettysburg. It was an hour-and-a-half drive to Adams County, Pennsylvania, just north of the Maryland line. They exited onto I-270 North to US 15 and followed the signs.

"Where are we going?" Lee asked.

"You'll know when I know," she said.

They settled back into an easy cruising speed and Margaret and Tomás lost no time picking up where they had apparently left off, speaking Spanish with increasing fluency.

"Hey!" Lee yelled from the backseat. "Cut it out, why don't you? Just pretend I'm not here. You know I can't understand a word you're saying. But, no, don't pay any attention to me."

"Just give us a few minutes," Tomás called out. "It's been a long time. There's a lot to catch up on."

Lee smiled to himself, thinking how in reality he was relieved to get a break from Tomás, who took everything so seriously. As much as Tomás had been taking care of Lee, Lee found himself taking care of Tomás. Now he was happy to look out the window, letting the scenery thread through his eyelids like a movie. He was feeling a bit like royalty to be chauffeured around. He drummed his thighs lightly to the beat of the music and thought that the only thing missing that might make this moment perfect was some chocolate candy.

They passed a gray painted-over school bus, parked high on a threadbare hill above the county highway. Convicts in orange jumpsuits—seemingly choreographed like a corps de ballet, and overseen by a handful of prison guards—were bending in synchrony at the waist, working with what looked like the devil's pitchforks to collect scraps of litter and broken bottles.

"*Presidiarios*. Convicts," Margaret said, shaking her head. "From the local minimum-security prison, I bet. One small mistake and you're doomed in this country. You'd think they'd be busy enough making license plates, but I guess they could use a little fresh air like anyone else."

Lee stared intently out the window, noticing how the individual bodies formed a collective orange streak as their car swept past—wondering exactly what crimes they had committed.

They crossed the Pennsylvania line and exited the interstate, following the traffic toward Exit 47A and signs for Gettysburg. The Battle of Gettysburg in July of 1863 had produced the largest number of bloody casualties in the Civil War, Lee remembered. Any good history buff worth his salt had spent time reenacting it over and over with toy soldiers and grass mats and vials of fake blood.

"Are we going to Gettysburg?" Lee asked, piping up excitedly.

"Do you have any leads, Margaret?" he added quickly. "Are we going to do a citizen's arrest?"

"Well, yes on one and two, but no on three," Margaret said. She could barely see his small shrunken head in the rearview mirror. She thought of cannibalism and excrement and blood. She tried to picture the disease inside him, hungrily eating his cells like a game of Pac-Man.

The white line of the highway pitched and folded in on itself as they crossed hills and valleys taking them deeper into farmland and roads with fewer cars. The painted lines changed from solid to dashed, then narrowed to a single lane. Cows grazed on thinning fields framed by leafless trees and abandoned shacks.

Soon the famed embroidered battleground of Gettysburg came into view, the rolling fields and valleys enameled in shades of umber and ferrous oxide. Lee remembered how he had once made gunpowder by mixing iron filings with sulfur from a two-bit chemistry set Cass had given him for his tenth birthday, the results of which made the house smell like rotten eggs for days.

"Gettysburg was where Lincoln stood on Cemetery Ridge and delivered his *Four score and seven years ago* speech," Lee announced, craning to get a better look out the front window. "It's where Robert E. Lee was defeated, and the Confederates began to get a major headache."

"Well, aren't you a know-it-all," Margaret said.

Three quarters of a mile later the country road forked sharply, leaving them no choice but to pull into a huge parking lot that faced the forty miles of grounds that made up the historic battlefield.

They got out of the car, Lee sliding easily out from under his seatbelt, Margaret and Tomás drifting ahead, still speaking in Spanish, their bodies nearly touching, sharing a single slanted shadow.

Across the highway, in the middle of an empty field weighted down by a sinking horizon, a small rectangular sign advertising miniature horses caught Lee's attention. He stood still, letting the two of them walk on ahead. The idea of a miniature horse, like a miniature adult, made Lee wonder if they had parts of their genetic code in common. Were they old, but small, like him? What was their excuse? he wondered.

They crossed the frozen ground, approached the Visitors Center, and stepped inside to see a large-scale Civil War diorama that dominated the room, detailing the battle, with legions of tiny plastic Union and Confederate soldiers positioned with miniature guns and cannons. A tour guide was narrating the details of the final and bloodiest battle to a group of tourists who had made the trip from Ohio. Outside, somewhere in the adjacent fields, hundreds of reenactors were engaged in mock combat, turning the clock back to the first three days of July, 1863.

It was bad acting, Lee knew, sizing up the men in uniform easily, but exciting nonetheless.

In the corner of the big room a fireplace crackled. Margaret scanned the faces of the volunteers quickly. "Maybe she's outside. I know she's here somewhere. C'mon," she said and took Lee's arm.

"What makes you so sure—" Tomás began, but Margaret ignored him.

"There's someone I want you both to meet. An old friend, I promise."

Margaret led the way, pulling each of them by the hand around the side of the building, till they arrived at a rough-hewn, two-storied wooden barn, its inner frame insulated with hay bales and raw lumber. A bearded blacksmith, shirtsleeves rolled above his elbows, was bent over an anvil and hammering out a metal horseshoe. Bare electrons smarted out loud, uttering sparks of red and blue electricity.

All around, actors dressed in the blue and gray of the Union and Confederate armies were reenacting the simple activities of the time. Chickens scratched the sawdust floor for nibs of food, while pigeons squawked above, holding stubbornly to un-shaved rafters. The smell of wood resin was strong throughout, the odor of hay mixed with dung.

In the spirit of wartime, women were rolling white gauze bandages across a butcher-block table, attending to the hand-ful of actors portraying the wounded men who lay flat out on stretchers or bales of hay. A tall, slight woman, dressed in layers of skirts made of wool and cotton, silently stirred a large cooking pot over a fire, while another sat at a treadle machine spinning sheep's wool into yarn.

Lee noticed a frail woman under a gauze bonnet—her back turned to them—making butter in a churn, her calfskin shoes strapped tightly to her ankles like thimbles.

Margaret zeroed in on her, having finally found who she was looking for.

"Alicia, Alicia Patmos! *Mi amiga, mi querida amiga!*"

The woman turned quickly, letting the wooden paddle sink into the churn. "*Dios mío*, Margaret, *cómo estas amiga?* It's been too long, eh? I am too old," she said, wiping her hands on her skirt. She stepped back to absorb her friend's glowing face. "But you're still beautiful, still strong. And you've come to see me. How is work? Still working for the movement?"

"*Sí, sí,*" Margaret nodded. "I'm fine and busy, and I've brought my friends."

Tomás stepped forward to take Alicia's hand. She reminded him of those small wooden Russian nesting dolls, their delicate features painted on with as few strokes as possible, as if to suppress any expression of true feeling.

"Alicia, this is Tomás," Margaret explained, urging him clos-er. "A friend from Buenos Aires. *Un amigo muy bueno,* a very good friend. We were coworkers once."

The three spoke quickly in Spanish, Alicia nodding. Tomás saying little, a simple *sí* or *no.*

"Alicia is a good friend." Margaret spoke now in English so that Lee could understand. "Her son Rodrigo was one of the first to be made an example of by Videla's army. He was burned alive in La Plaza de Mayo. His crime was being too outspoken, though he was only a poor university student. Alicia can tell you many things, but she will not tell you about that. She has many active contacts among the *Abuelas* and the *Madres*—many still looking for their missing families. She may be able to help us look for Violeta and the baby. But you can see why we needed to come. Talking on the phone wouldn't have been enough."

Alicia tipped slightly forward on her toes, leaning toward Tomás, her pale brown eyes clouded with cataracts, her cheeks cross-hatched with age. "I'm so sorry," she said to Tomás, "for your *dolor*, untold grief, for what life has made of you." She took his hand and pressed it between hers. "There are still ways to know things," she said. "Murder is as traceable as birth. You have to think in reverse. There are witnesses, birth certificates, real or fake. If your baby was taken from Buenos Aires to the States, someone will know. People talk. Sometimes too much. We are not phantoms yet in life. I'll let you know in a day or two what I can find out. I'll need to know the name of the family— the father and mother, and their daughter, who you suspect may have intercepted the child. And you," Alicia continued, looking down at Lee. "*Quién eres tú?* Who are you?"

"I'm Lee," he said. "Their stowaway."

"Ah," she said, "you and me both. Stowaways. I'd better get back to work. Here I have no shame but to make butter. There is still some sweetness in life, *sí?*"

"*Gracias*," Tomás said, putting his hand on her shoulder. "*Gracias* for whatever it is you think you can do. We're grateful, all of us. My wife would have thanked you also."

"I'll be in touch," Alicia said. "Give me a day or two."

As they walked away, Lee pumped Margaret for answers. "Who is she?" he asked. "How do you know her, and what makes you think she can help us?"

"You ask a thousand questions," Margaret said. "Alicia was almost like a mother to me once, she worked for my family. She doesn't exactly have superpowers, but she's powerful nonetheless."

25

As they walked back to the parking lot, Margaret's thoughts couldn't help but turn to the past, to remember the death of her younger brother Rafael and how Alicia had saved her life afterward. Word had traveled quickly about the murder of Rafael and his girlfriend, Anna. Another story of untold grief that had the effect of tearing off one's skin in broad daylight. It was 1978, and the police were in bed with the murderers. The police lied and said that they had stopped the couple to answer a few simple questions and that Rafael and Anna had refused to cooperate. The tables quickly turned as they tried to flee. Afterward, Margaret tried to locate the crime scene, to find a witness, but to no avail.

For years afterward, Margaret often wondered if it had been a case of mistaken identity. What was subversive about their lives could have filled a thimble. Rafael's death had turned her thoughts inward. The human skeleton has 206 bones, with 22 of them belonging to the skull. What temperature did a flame require to melt human tissue and bone? Later it was determined that more than 65 percent of their bodies had been burned.

It wasn't long before Alicia came to her home just outside Buenos Aires, representing the *Abuelas* and the *Madres*. A week passed, then two, and on Thursday morning Alicia knocked at Margaret's door, arriving like a dusty pearl, having walked more than two miles from the city to find her. Alicia, whom she hadn't seen in perhaps two years, but who had worked for her family when she was a child, and who demonstrated without fail every Thursday at three-thirty in La Plaza de Mayo in the name of the disappeared.

Margaret had grieved her parents after they'd died of old age, but Rafael's death had dismantled her language of being entirely. There had been no body to bury, no face to identify.

Alicia had come alone—her oval face gaunt with age, her

cheeks cross-hatched with asterisk-shaped stars at the edges of her eyes, having lived through too many indignities to name. "I've come to help you," she had said, sitting across from Margaret at the small kitchen table. "Listen to me," Alicia said, taking Margaret's hands so that their wrists touched. "Even though I didn't know your brother as a young man, I knew him as a boy, and I'm sure he made you proud. I'm sure he could have toppled the earth," she said, her voice gaining urgency. "Each of us has lost someone we loved to this massacre, this indecency. May Videla rot in hell, with his army and his mistresses and all his fine suits. If I could get him alone in a room, I'd waste no time murdering him myself. He's stolen the identities of our children and our grandchildren. And his conscience is clear.

"Some may think we're poor old women capable of nothing," she said, waving her hand in the direction of the window, to where an imaginary army waited outside. "Some might think we're poor washerwomen without courage or brains," she continued, drumming the table with her fist, her voice beginning to quake. "And they might be right or wrong, it doesn't matter. What matters is this: We're as strong as any of these men, and what's more, we're smarter. We haven't given up by a long shot. It's simply not allowed. We'd like you to come march with us, help document things. Be our ally."

Six months after Rafael's and Anna's murder, on June 7, 1978, little over a year after Videla had taken power, Argentina was pitted against the Netherlands in the final game of the World Cup. Mario Kempes scored a goal to gain the lead, followed by a final goal by Daniel Bertoni, giving Argentina a 3-1 victory. Buenos Aires erupted into riots. The celebration went on in the streets for days and nights, in a frenzy of excitement so disproportionately passionate it verged on civil violence.

Margaret had been so distraught at the thought of a civic uprising on behalf of a sporting event, rather than on behalf of those killed by a murderous regime, that she knew she couldn't stay there any longer, and she made the decision to leave Argentina. She was thirty-four years old. Deciding to go to America meant not only losing her brother but her country.

Alicia, who had by now moved on to join Amnesty International and Human Rights Watch in America, had been encouraging her to come for months. She was the closest thing to family Margaret had left.

Over the course of the next few days, Margaret had sold her meager worldly possessions—a sofa inherited from her parents' house, her mother's sewing machine, and a small black-and-white television. In Rafael's room she found a lone tattered copy of Darwin's *On the Origin of Species* gathering dust on the shelf, his name scrawled tentatively in the frontispiece. She wrapped it in tissue and tucked it into her suitcase. Divested of all useful things except memory, she looked lastly at her mother's wedding ring, thin and silver and tarnished where it had failed to deliver on the promise of forever, and she placed it simply on the kitchen table, where it caught the light and shivered slightly, like a small circular moonrise on a hill.

She had sat on the Boeing 747, waiting for takeoff. The sun was sinking on a lost city in which she had no more reason to stay. Left behind were the hybrids and anomalies that begged for exception in the Natural world: the steamer duck, the plover, the platypus, the rhea (cousin to the ostrich), and the sad song of the penguins who mated for life, not knowing what near-human tragedies awaited them.

It was believed that birds were the closest living relatives to dinosaurs. Did that explain their leftover soaring overtures secreted in the wind, their presence everywhere trying to break down roofs and enter houses? To look inside their beaked cavernous mouths was to look into the caved anonymity of an uncertain future for humankind.

Somewhere in the distance, she knew without a doubt—aided by the glow of light over the hills— the bones of the dead and disappeared sent out a flare to wish her well, to let her know they believed she would continue their work abroad. And she finally understood—perhaps for what was truly the first time—that, as deeply as she had ever dared to love and grieve for anyone, Rafael was gone.

26

It was still early afternoon. Lee hoped that now that they had taken care of business and were walking across the parking lot, the rest of the afternoon might be devoted to whims and impulses. Across the road the thin blue sky stretched as wide as a serving platter where it neared the horizon, and Lee remembered what he'd read about Ben Franklin's obsession with hot air balloons. It would take a sky like that to launch a man-sized pod full of helium, to test the wind. It felt as if his heart stood outside his body, feeling the overwhelming immensity of the earth. He had a desire to be selfish, to ask to visit the miniature horses across the road and enter the four-legged wilderness that belonged to the Latin genus of *Equus*.

Margaret and Tomás were ahead of him, arm in arm.

"Margaret," Lee called out before they reached the car. "Is it okay if we make another stop while we're here?"

Across the highway, set back from the road, the Land of Little Horses Farm Park was staffed by urban cowboys and aimless drifters. Admission was five dollars a head, to benefit the Adams County SPCA. Money well spent, thought Lee, as they went inside, knowing he wasn't the one paying out of pocket. He had already tried and failed last Christmas to persuade Cass to pay twenty dollars a month to adopt an orphaned African elephant named Little MiMi whose mother had been slaughtered for her ivory tusks. He had watched a TV documentary and dialed the toll-free number. But Cass would have nothing of it. Margaret and Tomás were easier marks. He was their orphan, their charge. He could probably score three hot chocolates and a Mars bar in one hour with them if he tried.

No bigger than a Great Dane, the American miniature horse stands thirty-four inches tall read the placard on the barn wall. Besides a stable of miniature horses, the farm boasted six dwarf llamas, a pinstripe zebra, and two gray flannel donkeys. Lee stood leaning over the rails of the largest stall, inspecting a variety of tiny Icelandic descendants of wild ponies, their combed white-blond manes the same color as the hair of Scandinavian supermodels. He read how to groom a horse's hoof with a pick and saw their maleness protruding naturally. In another stall were creatures that defied the imagination: the hinny and the zorse—hinny being the offspring of a male horse and female donkey; zorse being part zebra, part horse.

Margaret and Tomás sat on top of the weathered split-rail corral fence, legs dangling, looking for all the world like an old married couple, while Lee inspected the premises. "Take your time," Margaret said. "We're not in a hurry to get anywhere."

Lee looked up at her, his eyes sparkling. She made a good temporary mother, the way Wendy did in *Peter Pan*. Even Tomás nodded agreeably. He was holding a Styrofoam cup of coffee and a bag of kettle corn and looked more relaxed than he had in days.

The average life span of a horse measures between twenty-five and thirty-five years, Lee read from the bottom of the placard. *It has the largest eyes of all land animals, and its hoofs are softer than they look, the equine version of a human fingernail.*

What Lee discovered next he loved best of all. A small brown wide-eyed pony named Cocoa was nuzzling along the side of the fence, a sprig of hay glued to its nostril. Lee fell in love instantly. They were nearly the same height, Lee reached out to pet her. Cocoa's large, clear, brown eyes peeled back from decadently lush lashes, her warm breath a moist oven lit from within, her tail a marvel of overgrown protein. Lee wondered how he could feel so much for her so quickly. Hutchinson-Gilford had turned him into a kind of pet also. People either felt sorry for miniatures or loved them. Did Cocoa have any clue they had something in common?

Lee caressed Cocoa's forelock appreciatively. It curled a little in front, the same as Superman's. Then he sat down on the straw-covered ground at Cocoa's feet and reached inside his backpack for pencil and paper. He hadn't written a word for Dr. Bream in his notebook in two days.

He took out his Number 2 pencil and began to sketch Cocoa on a piece of blank paper, knowing intuitively that in some instances it is what is shown, not what is said, that tells the best story. This is what Cocoa looked like:

He finished the drawing and placed it neatly between two clean sheets of white paper in his backpack.

A children's rodeo game was being announced over a loudspeaker. Lee looked around, searching the grounds to determine where the gravelly voice was coming from. Soon a short, disheveled carny, his cowboy boots trimmed with glue and sequins, his eyes glazed raw, came limping around the left side of the barn.

"Howdy," he said to the three of them, scanning for victims. "The three o'clock children's race is about to start. Rain or shine, we do it every day, even on the weekend. Always a prize. To win you gotta run down these here twenty-five yards and tie a ribbon round that goat's tail. First one to get it done wins a slice of apple pie."

Lee scrambled to his feet, turning first to Margaret, then to Tomás.

"Sure, why not?" said Tomás, knowing that Cass would not approve, but wanting Lee to have some fun.

"But not so fast that you're at the Olympics, Lee," Margaret yelled between cupped hands. "And try not to split your pants. If you win, we'll buy you a pair of cowboy boots."

That was all Lee needed to hear. From what he could see, the only other potential contestant was in diapers, slumbering in a stroller at his parent's knees.

The nameless carny eyed Lee skeptically. "Looks like it's

just you. No contest, but still a contest, eh, kid," he said, his forehead bathed in sweat, his sideburns gnarly as sheep's wool.

"Fair's fair," Lee replied happily.

"What's your name, kid? Them there your parents?" Lee noticed his breath smelled of salted peanuts and bourbon.

"Sure," Lee said. "My name is Ben Franklin Muhammad Ali. I bet I can run faster than that baby!"

"Well, seeing how the baby's just a baby, he's automatically disqualified," the carny said with a wink. "It's gonna be just you, kid. Hope you like pie."

Lee squinted up at the expanse of blue sky, suddenly cleared of clouds, thinking maybe his luck had changed. He pressed the tip of his sneaker on the red-taped starting line and scrutinized the goat, who grazed mutely at the other end.

"Ready, on your mark, get set, go!" the carny shouted. He fired the starter pistol and a tiny flag dropped down. Lee scrambled toward the confused, beleaguered goat tethered to a rope at the opposite end of the field. He took the biggest breath he could and advanced steadily, clambering over the matted straw ground laced with dust and dung and the sloughed-off wings of dragonflies, his hips wobbly as a warped hula-hoop, his legs cycling in sideways pirouettes, the ribbon clamped in his teeth. He reached the goat in thirty-two seconds, then worked to tie a bow around the creature's tail.

"There," he said, trying to catch his breath. "I did it! I won!"

"The winner and new champion," the carny was announcing to no one in particular. He had sashayed lazily to join Lee, and now raised up Lee's small, skinny arm like a champion boxer before Margaret and Tomás.

"Whoopee, ride 'em, cowboy!" shouted Margaret.

"Way to go! Nice job," called Tomás.

They were beaming and proud of their perfect "son." Not only was there pie for Lee, but pie for Margaret and Tomás also. They sat on oak stools at the small afterthought of a café tucked into the tiny raw-planked barn and enjoyed the pie with vanilla ice cream.

"I didn't know you could run that fast," Margaret said, her mouth full, patting Lee on the shoulder.

"Me neither," said Lee, wolfing down the pie.

"Just goes to show you don't know what you're capable of until you try."

They looked through the dingy glass window at the dehydrated pasture. It was feeding time for the ponies also. They watched the gloved carny pouring dry oats into rubber feed pails, then hosing water sloppily into troughs.

They finished eating, then strolled around the back of the barn, entering the woozily lit twilight zone of the Hobby Horse Gift Shop. It was staffed by a lone blond-wigged matron in pigtails, red-checkered shirt, and jeans—who watched their every move from her stool behind the counter. The floors were brushed sawdust; raw pine walls were weighted down by wrought-iron hooks shelving worn-looking riding gear, leather bridles and saddles, and assorted tack.

"We're looking for riding boots for our son," Tomás announced, lifting the lids from a couple of tired-looking shoeboxes lined up along the wall. "The best you've got."

The pair of children's size-eleven Corona boots that they bought for Lee were "genuine and made to last," stitched from golden-brown calf's hide, with white embroidery around the ankles and up the sides, the toe pointed in an exaggerated V.

Margaret paid the saleswoman eighteen dollars cash, and Lee put them on immediately and refused to take them off, swaggering a little as they ambled toward the car.

"Thanks, guys. That's about all the action I can handle for one day," he said, yawning. As they walked back through the dusky parking lot, the soles of his shoes clicked loudly against the matted yellow dust. He stuffed his hands in his pockets and leaned back on his heels, staring up at the slurred sky, where red and orange stripes had begun to glow like an Arizona sunset.

"Wish you could have raced me," Lee said, calling over his shoulder to Tomás. "Though I still think I would have won!"

27

Margaret glanced back at Lee, keeping one hand on the wheel, while the black highway barreled out before them, smooth and steady as jam over toast. Lee had fallen asleep nearly as soon as they had hit the road, leaving behind the historic battlefields and flat furrowed farmlands of Gettysburg. She shivered in her leather jacket. The temperature had dropped. The sky was beginning to be marked by new flakes of freshly falling snow. As the road began to whiten, there was no telling how much accumulation there'd be.

As she drove, she wrestled with her conscience. Her recent trip to LA had been brutal. The short life of the sixteen-year-old *Diablos* member Miguelina Ortiz, dead over a pair of sneakers, tortured her. Since when had human lives become human garbage?

Seeing Tomás again reminded her of all of the things she had both lost and gained since her days as a reporter in Buenos Aires. She had changed faces a dozen times since coming to DC, having been earmarked, while still in Seattle, as one who could successfully maintain a double life.

If she was a spy, she avoided the word. *Intelligence* was a more palatable term. To say she was good at keeping secrets, that she knew how to use state-of-the-art navigational tools—and when needed, state-of-the-art weapons, having found places on her body to secret microscopic things that one might not have thought possible—was hard enough to believe. But this mission with her friends was an interlude from her real life, entirely off the record.

Road signs emerging up ahead signaled a choice of directions. Lee was waking up in the backseat, rubbing his eyes. Margaret was already working against the thread of an idea that would soon require a decision. To the left marked their return to

DC, and to the right a detour into historic Philadelphia, home of Ben Franklin. She slowed the Buick to a halt at the stop sign and let the motor idle quietly. Lee roused and stretched. "Where are we, Tomás?" he asked, straining to see out the window.

Margaret gripped Tomás's hand tightly. "What do you say we go on to Philadelphia and spend the night, Tomás?" she suggested. "Weren't you planning to go to the Franklin Institute? Tomorrow we can see the Liberty Bell and Betsy Ross's house. We could be there in two-and-a-half hours or less—a little over a hundred miles."

"Let's do it!" Lee called out excitedly from the backseat. "C'mon, Tomás, say yes! It'll be a lot easier and a lot more fun to go with Margaret than by ourselves. We're so close." The carotid vein in Tomás's neck pulsed. He was taking too long to answer.

A large red tractor-trailer appeared out of nowhere, honking loudly behind them, its cab forced to veer sharply to the left. "*Sí* or *no*, Tomás!" Margaret repeated. "Now and not tomorrow," she said. "*¿Qué te parece esta idea?*"

A tow truck rattled dangerously toward them, the driver making obscene gestures. Margaret thrust her middle finger in his direction, still waiting for Tomás to answer.

"Tomás, is it because you're afraid we'll lose time looking for Violeta and the baby?" Lee asked. "Alicia said it would take a day or two before she had anything to tell us. You can spend time catching up with Margaret without me. I'll leave you two alone to talk. I'm old enough to take care of myself."

"You've got way too much bravado for someone who only weighs thirty-eight pounds, Lee," Tomás said. "Don't forget I'm responsible for your safety."

Scattered snowflakes continued to fall, salting the air.

"I can't wait here all day, Tomás!" Margaret persisted. "You're his guardian here. It's got to be your call."

"Okay," Tomás said. "*Sería bueno para él.* It would suit him. *Es el destino.* It's a good idea. I have all of Lee's medications with me. I'll call Cass when we get there, let her know we've gone out of state. Let's hope no police car pulls us over along the way, or it might be considered kidnapping."

Margaret snorted loudly. "Since when did you worry about those kinds of things? Since when do you care about the police, or anyone?" Privately, Margaret knew that with her security clearance it would never happen. She glanced back at Lee, tethered to the confines of his small arthritic shell, his cratered face a lunar landing, his tiny ribs a ukulele of bones. The raw power that came from him was all but prehistoric.

"Okay, we have a plan!"

Margaret scanned the rearview mirror, waiting for an opening, then gunned the gas pedal and shifted into gear, darting between a Chevy and a Land Rover. Signs ahead signaled the interstate was approaching.

She switched on the wipers, obliterating the snow. She had driven these roads a hundred times through all seasons and every kind of weather, having spent days at a time on assignment in Philly covering visits from foreign dignitaries, always staying at the plush Four Seasons, upholding the appropriate image that the paper wanted. Some nights she was required to wear gowns and gold jewelry and to entertain foreign diplomats and senators in the grand ballroom with both her political savvy and her impressive cleavage, two competing distractions.

Now she quickly leaned into the wheel and spun the Buick into gear, letting its headlights bruise the open road in the direction of the City of Brotherly Love. The sky was slush-gray and whitening, the icy ragged remains of the day underlit with a torn pale violet indifference. Snow continued to fall softly, like an arrangement of quarter notes scatted illogically to music.

"Just sit back and enjoy the ride," Margaret said to Tomás and Lee evenly. The road was an island she enjoyed navigating. Within minutes she settled down, breathing in sync with the wheels' steady rotation. Lee pretended to sleep, but struggled to stay awake in order to eavesdrop on their conversation.

Margaret finally took the opportunity to say the things she had kept secret from Tomás for too long. "A long way from home, eh Tomás?" Margaret began.

"A thousand years. And then some," he said. "When did the earth become like a cubist painting, a landscape by Picasso?" He wondered what her life had been like before he had arrived, if she had taken a lover, if she had cared about anyone.

"You always thought like a poet," Margaret said. "To your detriment, I suppose. You could never *not* follow a story. It would be too much for you."

"The youth circus was worth it," Tomás said. "Almost. Subversive as it was. I think I can tell you, I think you'll understand, that there's a kind of—for lack of a better word—*poverty* in my soul. My instinct is always to try to find the underbelly of something and expose it. The last time was at the cost of Violeta and the baby, I'm afraid. I'm a stupid man. *Stupido…*"

"Not *stupido*, a little blind, *ciego*, maybe," Margaret said, touching his knee gently.

Tomás studied the dashboard, wanting to get at the truth. "Who is Alicia Patmos?" he asked, leaning forward. "Who is she, really? Tell me now, and please—out of respect for both of us—leave out the *mentira*, the bullshit. Who is she?" Tomás repeated when she didn't answer. "Is that an alias, the way I suspect your whole life here in DC is an alias? You may be able to fool others, but you're not fooling me. Your apartment is virtually uninhabited, you haven't aged in years, you're the same but different. Don't forget I shared an office with you. I could smell your perfume. I could hear you breathe."

"I am no one, really, an interloper perhaps," she said. "In Buenos Aires it was my job to protect my parents. They were like sheep put out to pasture. Here I don't belong to anyone. I have no loyalty, no conscience. And as for Alicia, you're right. In her own way, she's very dangerous. She's fought bravely, courageously, and given up many things. She will have access to information we can use."

Margaret quickly glanced through the rearview mirror to see that Lee had fallen asleep. "And now I have to confess something," she said to Tomás, finally coming clean. "Do you know that I was at the paper the day Eduardo, our editor, gave you up? It was a setup. They needed a scapegoat, an example from the press that Videla's men weren't taking any shit. They had infiltrated the newspaper and were using us for propaganda. They used you, the way they tried to use me. I had arranged to be out of the office...I didn't know it was going to be you, Tomás. I should have warned you, but it all happened so fast. I never dreamed they'd actually take you, a warning, yes, but the rest seemed unheard of with your status, your byline."

He looked at her, his mouth open. "I knew it had to be someone at the paper, I never imagined it was you," he said. "Did you have any idea what would happen to my family? How our lives are broken forever? How stupid I am now to ask you, of all people, for help. I'm an idiot. How can I trust you...even now? Is this another setup? Is there something more you can take from me?"

"Tomás, you have to believe me. I didn't know names. Only that it could happen at any time. And for that I'm forever sorry. But it was the times too. The city was becoming a jungle. We were all at risk."

For a brief moment he wanted to strike her hard against the leather seat, her teeth set in her jaw. He wanted her to feel a fraction of the pain he had endured. "Why are you getting involved now?" he asked. "After all this time? Is it because you feel guilty? Do you really think you can make it up to me?"

"Not at all," she said. "Too much has already happened. But you still deserve to know what happened to Violeta and the baby. Maybe it's the reporter in me. Maybe it's because I care. And there's Lee. He's invested every single part of himself in your cause. We owe it to him to make something good happen."

"He's only playing detective," Tomás said. "There's nothing he can do to help us."

"Don't you get it?" Margaret said. "He has so little time, he's living for this. In a way he's responsible for bringing us together again. I don't think you should underestimate his value and the gift he's given you, the opportunity."

"What do you suspect Alicia can tell us?" Tomás asked. "Does she really think she can bring back what's gone? Can she find Violeta and our child—can she find out if they're alive?"

Margaret cleared her throat, then swallowed. "She's in touch with people in Buenos Aires who've kept careful records of missing black-market babies given up for adoption. There were countless placements, mostly with the military. It's a horrible betrayal to both the birth mothers and their children to be sold to the enemy. *Dios mío,* God save us. Luckily people kept records, the way Hitler kept records of his insane experiments on old helpless Jews, the mad scientist, the Frankenstein. There ought to be a newly created weapon just for them, for people like Videla and Stalin and Pinochet, that would incinerate the part of their brains that remembers what it is to love—robbing them of all pleasant memories."

"So it's possible that Alicia will be able to tell us something?"

"*Sí,* I'm almost certain of it. Or she wouldn't have offered to help. She's done it many times for people in your situation. Each case for her is like her own child. She won't let us down. Think of it. Think if you were her, and your child had been Rodrigo. Would you let anyone give you no for an answer?"

"In Buenos Aires we worked next door to one another, we collaborated on stories. You were a guest at my wedding," Tomás said. "Look at us now, Margaret. What's become of us?"

"I was no good to you before, Tomás," she said. "But things are different now, I'm probably the only one who can help you. If you'll let me. Do you think Lee dreams?" Margaret asked, glancing back to where he slept on. "Do you think the pictures behind his eyes are the same as ours, or different? Older somehow?"

"They're the same," Tomás said. "I don't imagine there will be a positive outcome for any of this. But I have to know in order to stay sane. In order to go on. Then I'll at least know what choices I have. You're right, if it hadn't been for Lee, I would never have come to see you now. I owe him something."

"The truth will either set you free or kill you while trying," Margaret said. "If there is such a thing as truth." Her eyes were dark and roaming, the road a metaphor for all things that eventually come to an end. But for now they were encapsulated in the safety of motion, like a moving picture.

"I've never been to Philadelphia," Tomás said, glancing at the time. "Most kids Lee's age are out playing ball and starting to go girl-crazy, not thinking about dead inventors like Ben Franklin. Every day I'm scared he's not going to wake up, and I'll have to call Cass and break the news. He's a time bomb—literally. Now that I know him, I'm convinced he's better than me, every molecule. I mean that. He's like a soldier of the earth. I feel a little like his bodyguard."

"You sound like a man who believes in something after all," said Margaret.

"Maybe," Tomás said. "Maybe I'm getting good at living for someone else. Maybe Lee will defy the odds and live till he's one hundred and be written up in *The Guinness Book of World Records*. You never know. Did you ever read the American comics about Superman? Most of the time I don't care about myself," he continued. "I always believed that we should be grateful for gravity, that gravity alone keeps us from being asteroids."

"The persistence of the physical world makes us prisoners of our brains," Margaret added. "The old human condition. To me, it's simple. Our minds are caves, and if we're lucky we know how to amuse ourselves for a little while inside them, with memory, with fashion, with hope."

She stopped talking and let the silence take over. They headed north, over the flat single-lane highway, then deeper into the trills and valleys of western Pennsylvania, indented with black-dotted ski tracks and the dashed lines of telephone poles, strung out over the listless hills and snow-capped mountains. They passed rows of tiny extinct mining towns marked by vacant houses and abandoned factories, towns with names like York and Hersey, famous for barbells, peppermint patties, and milk chocolate.

Margaret was relieved to have finally told Tomás the truth. She dimmed the dashboard, staying on course, while lanes of cars bearing New Jersey, New York, and Connecticut plates swarmed north alongside them. The thought of Lee's tender, temporary consciousness adrift in the known world made her already grieve for his absence. She found herself wondering what Lee's mother, Cass, might be like. A woman whose every waking hour must have been filled with uncertainty in a world that had betrayed her. It was a long shot that Violeta and the child were alive. And if they found the child and she were adopted, what then? How could Tomás prove she was his?

The speed limit increased to fifty-five, and Margaret dimmed the dashboard further, blackening it to stealth, leaving only the speedometer visible.

They continued east, the asphalt road pulled taut as tarpaulin, growing nearer and nearer the City of Brotherly Love. The snow had vanished abruptly, the sky painted eerily black. One by one, white pointed stars, punched clean as tintype asterisks, traced the arc of the road in a higher octave.

Now she looked in Tomás's direction, where he appeared to doze fitfully.

"So far so good," he said. "You don't mind driving?"

He leaned closer, swept a strand of hair from her eyes.

"*Gracias,*" she said. He was a man after all. She found his attempts at kindness to be moving and suddenly intimate, though not in the least sexual. She had rarely thought of him as a man, apart from her job and the competition. But now as he eased the hair from her face, his tenderness made her long for everyone she had ever loved and desired who had since faded into oblivion. She hadn't kissed anyone in a very long time.

They were getting closer. Signs for the Ben Franklin Bridge appeared at the southern fringes of New Jersey, then signs to the Schuylkill Expressway—a highway rimmed with arched stone bridges and timber light posts, its sole job to tame the Delaware.

Street lamps and billboards increased with every mile and stood out in jewel tones, picking up traffic like the blast-currents of jazz. It was nine-thirty; they were golden.

"See, I told you it wasn't far," Margaret began. "A stone's throw to the bridge. It's late, I know. We can check in at the hotel without a problem. A little rich for your blood, maybe, but on my expense account it won't matter. We can spend the night like royalty, and in the morning eat pancakes and tour the Liberty Bell and the Franklin Institute, then return our stowaway. No one will have noticed. Isn't that why you're here with him anyway, isn't that why you've come? And if I hear a tinkling of bells, Tomás, I won't assume it's you getting your angel's wings either."

"I have a lot of things to be ashamed of," he said. "With all the lies I've told, it doesn't exactly feel like a party. His mother would have my head if she knew what we were up to."

"Did you ever wonder what it's really like to have a child?" Margaret mused, biting her lip. The road urged her on. She was tired and not thinking. "The responsibility is forever. Few things are really forever. Breath, the sun, the moon. Death, depending on what you believe in."

"I don't think it really matters," Tomás said. "I think what matters is when you realize that you alone can make a difference in someone else's life. And then you have to decide if you're able to act. At home, in Buenos Aires, if you knew someone who disappeared, it made you feel on fire with a need to do something. Then if you became one of the disappeared yourself, like I did, or like Violeta, you learned for the first time what you were made of. A very frightening prospect."

Margaret stared down the freezing highway swarming with urban traffic trying to squeeze itself into the approaching single-lane. She set her teeth and ruthlessly began to calculate her way through it, heading for Route 15 as though gunning for the enemy.

It was almost ten as they coursed onto the Schuylkill inbound, circling the roller coaster of converging roads leading into the city, following the scope of the river through West Philly, past the big art museum on Twenty-Sixth where it intersected with the Ben Franklin Highway, past the University of Pennsylvania medical research centers, their basements cuckolding live animals for the spoils of genetic research. They sped past Symphony Hall and the four-star restaurants serving up edible gold, past the slums and row houses, knee deep in squalor and rodents, that could rival the poverty almost anywhere else in America. The city had come a long way from hoisting a key atop a building in a lightning storm to claiming the discovery of electricity.

28

One Logan Square marked the big parking circle of Philly's Four Seasons Hotel. They pulled up in front, the old Buick proudly taking up two spaces, the valet on the move in an instant to greet them.

"Pretty fancy," Tomás exhaled. He got out of the car before the valet could reach them and stood with his hands in his pockets, leaning back on his heels. Above, the sky resembled a bowl of black ice. A yellow half-moon slid in and out of the freezing temperatures.

"Are you sure this is where we belong?" Tomás asked. "Not a Howard Johnson's?"

"Not a problem," Margaret said coolly, unzipping her outer self to reveal a new sleeker version inside. She unfolded her wallet to find two dollars for the valet and her American Express card. Three huge verdigris statues modeled after Native American river gods swam sideways around Swann Fountain, spewing water at one another.

"The *Post* has given me a fat expense account," Margaret explained. "I'll worry about my editor later. You only live once, but in your case, maybe twice, depending how you look at it."

The valet held the door as she crossed the asphalt driveway to the hotel entrance. Tomás scooped Lee out of the backseat, cradling him in his arms. Lee opened his eyes for a second, then closed them just as quickly.

Inside, the hotel foyer was well-lit and glistening. "Good evening, Señora DaCosta," the receptionist said, smiling, as Margaret approached a dark-skinned woman whose nameplate read *Clara*. "I see tonight you've brought your family."

"*Sí*," Margaret nodded. "Yes." Her lips were newly lacquered with red lipstick, her smile flashing. "Is Suite 507 available? I apologize for the late hour, an impulse, a quick holiday."

"Of course," Clara said. "I'll check for you."

Tomás had followed Margaret inside, Lee still in his arms. He winced at the hotel's sumptuous carpeted foyer, its high molded-plaster ceiling fitted with brass and crystal chandeliers. In the middle of the room a gigantic arrangement of blazing orange-and-lavender birds of paradise nearly set the entryway on fire.

The exaggerated affluence made him crazy, but he sat with his back braced against a bronze urn, guarding Lee while Margaret finished checking them in.

"Ah yes, no problem, Señora DaCosta. It's available. Just give me a minute."

"*Gracias*," said Margaret, flashing a smile.

"Do you need a bellman?" Clara offered, returning Margaret's credit card and handing her a set of keys.

"*No, gracias,*" she said. "We're here on the fly. I think we're good."

"Will you be needing anything else then? A crib?" Clara said, gesturing to where Tomás held Lee in his arms. "A bottle of warm milk or cookies?"

"No, no, thank you very much," Margaret said. "I think we can manage."

A few people were lounging comfortably in the plush lobby bar, watching the 76ers pound the parquet floor against the Celtics at an away game in Boston. Margaret, Tomás, and Lee took the mirrored elevator to the fifth floor and followed the carpeted hallway to where it dead-ended.

"I've stayed in this room before," Margaret whispered, unlocking it. "It's very comfortable."

"Apparently," Tomás said, rolling his eyes.

❧

Margaret pushed the door open, allowing Tomás to go ahead of her and place Lee's slumbering body comfortably on the king-size bed. He set Lee down gently in the middle of the four-poster, on a quilt splashed with yellow sun flowers.

"Don't turn on the lights," Margaret said, *sshh*ing him.

She went to the window overlooking the balcony and pulled the heavy curtain open. Their room faced the fountain, several stories up, but they could still hear the sound of rushing water below.

"Who lives like this?" Tomás asked, opening the door to the bathroom, where the brass knobs of the faucets were sculpted swans, and the Jacuzzi tub was bigger than the width of two linebackers. He opened the hall closet and found Egyptian cotton terry-cloth robes as thick as sheep's wool. "It must cost a fortune."

"Never mind," Margaret insisted. "They owe me. In the capitalist land of American credit, they owe me big time. And a lot more than this."

Tomás moved to the bed, where Lee still slept, his body taking up hardly any space.

"Still out like a light," Tomás said to Margaret, watching Lee's chest rise and fall softly.

"Do you think we should do something?" Margaret asked, moving closer to inspect Lee's breathing. "Is this *normal,* is there a way to check him?"

"*Sí,* I think it's time. *Nunca lo he visto dormir tanto.* I've never seen him sleep this long. But then, he had a busier day than usual."

Tomás removed Lee's cowboy boots and set them on the floor at the foot of the bed. He placed the Yankees cap on the night table next to a bottle of Evian and two squares of Godiva chocolate. He lifted Lee's wrist and felt his pulse. It was slow and steady, with small, aerated gaps interrupting the usual flow.

"A minor arrhythmia is normal for Lee, but I still worry," said Tomás, lowering his head to Lee's chest to listen. "Let's hope he's just wiped out from today's excitement. But we'd better keep a close eye on him in case anything changes. I have a list of doctors within a ten-mile radius of Philadelphia. Cass saw to that. I'm going to call her and check in. Let her know where we are. She made damn sure I knew what to do in case of an emergency. I have Lee's beta-blockers in my pocket. We should probably wake him soon and give him something to eat."

"Thank goodness," Margaret said. "I'm so worried about him from minute to minute. Like his mother, I guess. I don't know how she does it." She slipped off her shoes and sank her feet into the plush carpet, moonlight glancing off her shoulders. "I'll sleep next to him," she volunteered. "I'm sure that couch will be as comfortable as any bed you've ever had. Let's put some pillows on the floor on the other side of Lee in case he rolls off the bed in his sleep. He could break a hip or something."

"Maybe I should sleep on the other side of him," said Tomás. "There's room enough for all three of us, if you feel all right about that. That way he won't have a chance to fall."

"It's okay with me. *Esta bien conmigo.*"

Tomás picked up the phone, but Margaret stopped him. "A drink first? It's still early." She unlocked the small minibar with a tiny key and withdrew two small bottles of bourbon. "*Salud,*" she said, offering a toast. "To invention, to Ben Franklin. Without whom at night every city in the world would be in blackness."

❧

In the end they made a Lee sandwich. The two of them sleeping on either side of him. A *sandwich,* that's what Margaret's parents used to call it when she or Rafael lay in between them at night as young children.

Tomás lay in the bed fully clothed, staring up at the crystal chandelier. He would have liked to have been able to share a hotel stay like this with Violeta. She would have laughed and said it was too much money.

"He's our little prince for the night. Kind of cute like that, isn't he?" Margaret said, whispering into the shadows across the bony crest of Lee's body. "I don't think I've slept through the night in years," she said. And then she did something so involuntarily intimate she couldn't stop herself. She kissed Lee's forehead, but to her horror it was cold. "Tomás," she said, alarmed, getting to her feet. "I think there's something wrong with him. He's so cold. He's freezing!" She lifted Lee's arm, but it dropped limply to the mattress. "Tomás," she said, "I don't know what's going on, I don't know if he's all right. Check him again, please! *Date prisa!* We may need to call a doctor. *Prisa,* Tomás, what is happening?"

"Let's try to sit him up," Tomás said, taking charge, checking Lee's pulse with his thumb and forefinger. He propped Lee's head up against the pillow and tried to wake him, shaking him until Lee's eyes blinked open.

"Where am I?" Lee asked, confused.

"Breathe, Lee," Tomás commanded. "Breathe." Lee was breathing hard, but with a sluggish rhythm. "Get him a glass of water, Margaret. Quickly. Let's give him one of these beta-blockers, it'll help regulate his heart no matter what's happening. *Ándale,* Margaret, *ándale.* He's going to be okay," Tomás said, his voice steady as she went to get the water. Tomás unscrewed the small plastic vial of pink pills stored in his chest pocket, and set one on Lee's tongue as they both waited. "Better now?" he asked.

Lee's chest heaved, but Tomás was relieved to see him sitting up, his cheeks gaining color.

"Not the first time, right, Lee? Cass told me to expect that this could happen, it's just stiffness of the aorta, the largest artery in the body," Tomás said. "It can raise your blood pressure. How much did racing that goat exhaust you? Was it worth it? I think you'll be okay now," he said.

No diapers, Cass had explained when she had first interviewed Tomás in the tiny apartment. *Just drool, coughing, sluggish bowels. All par for the course in old age. His hands are soon going to be useless. Advanced arthritis. Chances are good that one day soon he'll have a heart attack or a blood clot to the brain, leading to a stroke. Everything that happens to an old person will happen to him eventually, only faster.*

Tomás recalled the conversation now, and for a moment began to think that coming to DC and Philadelphia had been a mistake. Away from his mother and his doctor, Lee was at far greater risk. For god's sake, his best friend had just died in the middle of the night. Anything could happen. He should never have let Margaret convince him to let Lee race that goat or sashay around in cowboy boots. The kid was too fragile for that kind of horseplay. The kid was not a real boy, not really. The kid was more like...Pinocchio.

"Where am I?" Lee asked again, squinting without his glasses, trying to sit up.

Tomás squeezed an overstuffed pillow behind Lee's head and shoulders, and together he and Margaret propped him up. Lee was disoriented, confused, not sure where he was or what day it was.

"Lee," Tomás said, "you fell asleep in the car right after we left the horse farm. We were so close to Philadelphia that we decided to keep going. We're in a hotel. A fancy one. We're only a couple of miles from the Liberty Bell."

Lee smiled, his chipped broken teeth squished into a lower jaw that had never fully synced with his age. His chest heaved and then relaxed. His breathing was starting to look normal. "Maybe I did do a little too much running around today," he said weakly. "Maybe it was the pie. My bones kind of ache, and I feel kind of cold on the inside. More water, please. I've never been in a hotel before," he said, swallowing, then glancing around the room toward the open window. "I thought I was dead and I'd woken up in someone else's bedroom. Except the ceiling's so high, and it's so dark. Where's Cass?" he said, looking around a little desperately. "Where's Patrick?"

"Hey, Lee," Margaret said, leaning over him, "*mi querido.*" She held his small bony foot, translucent with blood vessels and tiny capitulating bones. "We're here just for the night. You can have anything you want to eat in the morning. We have room service. And there's a minibar with candy and a combination safe in the closet. Maybe you can crack the code, eh?"

Lee looked around and saw that it was true. The room went on for miles, bigger than their whole apartment at home.

Then a worried look crossed his face.

"Who exactly is paying for this?" he asked. He already knew that Tomás was guilty of spending almost all their money too soon. "Tomás? You know we can't afford it."

Tomás looked at him sheepishly, his chin pointed towards Margaret. "Not me, kiddo. The lady's in charge."

"My newspaper has a deal with the hotel," Margaret said, not wanting him to worry. "A penny here, a dollar there. What're they going to do, shoot me? And you," she said to Lee, "you should go back to bed immediately and let your medicine do its work. Let me get you some more water. You can pee in there," she motioned to the bathroom.

The enormous bed was too high for Lee to get in and out of on his own. Tomás found two thick telephone books and a Gideon bible in the desk drawer and piled them in a stack at the side of the bed so that Lee could climb up and down to relieve himself. There were no pajamas to speak of. Tomás took the white terry-cloth robe monogrammed in gold with the letters F and S from the closet and wrapped it around Lee like a security blanket, using the belt to rope him in at the waist.

They made Lee a sandwich, and within fifteen minutes, he was safely back asleep and snoring. The dim shapes of the furniture were crested with moonlight. Tomás looked at his watch and decided it wasn't too late to call Cass, knowing she'd still be awake.

She answered after two rings.

"What's going on, Tomás? Is everything all right?" Cass sat up in bed, preparing for the worst, feeling the heft of Patrick at her feet.

"It's nothing, Cass," Tomás said quickly. "Everything's fine. I just thought you should know we're in Philadelphia ahead of schedule. We were visiting Gettysburg this afternoon and realized how close we were. Lee's really excited that we'll see the Franklin Institute and Liberty Bell tomorrow. We're just staying the night."

"Who's we?"

"Oh," Tomás said. "I guess I didn't tell you. My friend Margaret has returned from California."

"What's really going on, Tomás?" Cass asked, cutting to the chase. "Why are you calling this late? Something's wrong, I know it."

"Lee's fine," he said. "We had a small scare tonight, just an arrhythmia after an active day, but I gave him his pills and he calmed down right away. He's sleeping now."

"You're not a very good liar," Cass said. "I wish to god I could be there now. How do I know you're telling the truth?"

"Listen to me, Cass. Lee's having a great time. He's completely safe. I'm actually jealous of you, being his mother. He's the real thing, you know; he's smart and funny and great to be with. And he loves you, he misses you."

"I know you're not telling me everything," Cass said, imagining Lee's worn-out DNA hanging by a thread. She had already been in bed for an hour, but sleep wouldn't come. She wanted to tell Lee how much she missed him, how he had been the one thing she'd done right in life. Now Patrick snored at her feet, his thin, veined ears folded daintily in half, his tail curled round as a bull's-eye. She was embarrassed to admit she found him to be intelligent, companionable. His overall pinkness a sweet consolation.

"I only hope you have the sense to know when to ask for help," Cass said. "He's my baby, you remember that. And even though it's only going to be a few more days, if I have to, I'll come get him myself."

"We're having a good time," Tomás said. "Your son is very brave and keeps us laughing."

"You tell Lee I love him," Cass said. "Make sure you call tomorrow first thing. I'm counting on you both coming home safe, with a lot of stories to tell."

"Will do," Tomás said, feeling humbled at how mothers know instinctively when they've been told a lie.

∽

The three of them slept enveloped in the protection of one

another's arms, a small boat of losses thrown together on a stormy sea.

Tomás woke first and walked out to the balcony to see the day. The sky appeared ancient and pink, a red sphere being filtered through a swan dive of gauzy clouds, the sun summoning itself. In a few minutes he came back inside to see Margaret coming out of the shower, her hair in an ivory turban, fully dressed. Lee was awake and tinkering with the combination safe in the closet, the long robe trailing being him like the train of a wedding gown.

"Hotels are pretty fun," Lee said, happy, his tiny ears tilted upward like an elf.

He had already set up the ironing board and had sampled two chocolate bars from the minibar, along with a handful of sugared almonds. The coffee maker was on, brewing loudly.

"Now, what's for breakfast?" he asked, staring down at the room-service menu.

"Well, I guess I don't have to tell you to make yourself at home," Margaret said. "Here, kid, let's all have a look at that."

Twenty minutes later room service arrived with a knock at the door, the bolero-jacketed waiter wheeling the overstuffed cart into the suite with a flourish. He set the table near the window where they could hear the gurgling fountain, then removed the stainless-silver lids of the chafing dishes one at a time. He tied the large white cloth napkin into an elaborate bib below Lee's chin. Then, from beneath one of the silver crowns, slid a splendid yellow omelet sprinkled with scallions and a drizzle of hollandaise, and next to that, a stack of chocolate-chip pancakes, both for Lee. Margaret and Tomás watched Lee enjoying the ceremony of it all. They had ordered strong cups of Italian espresso and croissants with squares of butter and strawberry jam.

"This beats IHOP, hands down," Lee said, syrup dripping down his chin.

Within an hour they were dressed and downstairs in the

lobby, cleaned up and ready to go, having received directions to the Franklin Institute and the Liberty Bell from the concierge.

"One more thing," Tomás said with a bit of a flourish before Lee could attempt the revolving-door. "For your safety and your comfort! No license required!"

Tomás reached down and withdrew a preschooler's umbrella stroller from behind the concierge desk, its small round wheels ratcheted to the frame with steel ball bearings.

Lee took one look at it and didn't know what to think. His lower lip trembled. He already knew that he was, day by day, losing something he couldn't keep, and that the world saw him differently. He looked pleadingly first at Tomás and then at Margaret—each trying to keep their expression neutral. What good would it do to fight them?

"Okay," Lee said, with a noisy exhale. "But I'll only use it if you take turns pushing me. And I'll only use it while we're in Philadelphia."

29

Silence Dogood, Polly Baker, Richard Saunders. These names were among Ben Franklin's known aliases. Inventor of swim fins, bifocals, electricity, the glass armonica, the long arm, the lightning rod, the odometer. Philadelphia had taken root in his footsteps and made him their hero.

Margaret, Tomás, and Lee had arrived at the Franklin Institute, Philadelphia's alternative to the Smithsonian, which was devoted to everything Franklin and Franklin-inspired. As they walked into the great, classically appointed hall, they found themselves facing the giant seated statue of the man who had fought for freedom and changed history.

"I can't believe it!" Lee said. "It's him, it's really him! Why couldn't Cass be here, why not Kira?"

He felt sad and awed at the same time. He climbed out of the stroller to get a closer look at the twenty-foot-high marble statue of Ben, seated with his great coat, knee breeches, and buckled loafers. Elsewhere, on Franklin's tombstone, were the words Lee knew he had written before he died:

The Body of
B. Franklin
Printer;
Like the Cover of an old Book,
Its Contents torn out,
And stript of its Lettering and Gilding,
Lies here, Food for Worms.
But the Work shall not be wholly lost:
For it will, as he believ'd, appear once more,
In a new & more perfect Edition,
Corrected and Amended
By the Author.

He was born on January 6, 1706.
Died 17

Those words suited him, thought Lee. He knew it would be the responsible thing to do the same, to one day soon write down how he'd like to be remembered. His head swirled with all the plans he and Kira had made, how in some ways he felt lost without her, especially on this trip, which should have been a celebration for the two of them.

He knew she would have wanted him to go. He began to climb the stairs to the second floor, holding the rail, Tomás and Margaret trailing behind, to see an exhibit that couldn't have been more perfect, that claimed to contain the workings of the human heart.

Sized for a 220-foot-tall human and made of four tons of plaster and papier-mâché, the giant heart was painted candy-apple red and lined with paisleyed corpuscles. It boasted a blood fountain and surgical theatre, with four chambers linked to memory and forced resuscitation.

Lee stood inside the model of the walk-through exhibit, facing the four identical chambers, and thought that this was how Bruce Lee must have felt in the famous scene in *Enter the Dragon* in which he confronts himself reflected in a dozen mirrors, not knowing which one is him.

"Cool," Lee said to no one in particular.

❧

Lightning, it turns out, is nothing more than static electricity on a massive scale. They walked farther down the hall, parking the stroller outside the entrance to a large, high-ceilinged room devoted to the history of electricity, filled with endless rows of prehistoric-looking lightning rods and row upon row of shelved, rudimentary lightbulbs—each one the small pocketed progression of an idea. It struck Lee that the series of clustered transparent lightbulbs were like small domed fragile heads—strung with various types of wire filament—in place of brains. If Franklin had learned how to harness lightning, Edison had learned how to channel it into copper filament. By the end of the nineteenth century, Edison had revolutionized the notion of bedtime reading, of hearth fires, of candles.

Lee inspected a table fitted with a series of interactive bulbs, their metal bases riveted into an oak block, each one fitted with a small black switch. He stood before a replica of Edison's incandescent electric lamp, carbon triple arc filament, circa 1879, which was said to burn for 1,065 hours. Lee flipped the switch, his eyes growing big as a sliver of yellow heat narrowly wormed its way through.

Then, not meaning to be disrespectful to Franklin or to Edison, he found himself starting to feel overwhelmingly...*sick*. His stomach lurched, and he wanted to keel. In the opposite corner of the dusty room he could see Tomás and Margaret chatting animatedly, catty-corner to a museum guard who was busy grooming his cuticles.

If they knew he was sick, they would make him leave. Not just from the Institute, but maybe send him home for good. They would think the stroller was a good idea.

Lee crept away, making for the exit where he hoped he'd find a bathroom. He had spikes in his chest, an effervescent volcano about to blow. Somewhere deep inside, the morning's chocolate-chip pancakes were slowly undergoing a chemical change, giving way to a blinding surge of gas that would soon erupt into a shattering fart or worse. His body see-sawed from head to toe, but he didn't shit his pants. His eyes blinked, and his groin burned. Then a loud rivulet of farts broke loose, and he clung to the wall for safety.

"Franklined-out?" Tomás asked sympathetically, appearing at Lee's side. "Had enough?" Tomás kneeled down to get a better look and checked Lee's pulse. Lee straightened, anchoring his arms against the doorframe. "The dust in here is probably as old Edison," Tomás said. "I bet we could still find his fingerprints somewhere if we looked hard enough. I think you're suffering from too much breakfast. Let's head out and get some fresh air."

"Okay," Lee agreed, his stomach still grumbling. "But it's Margaret's turn to push."

"I'll steer," she said, taking over for Tomás. "*Vámonos.* I'll handle the driving from here."

✍

The Liberty Bell was several blocks away and more than they could muster on foot. Tomás hailed a cab that took them to the corner of Market and Sixth. During the short ride, Margaret silently chastised herself over and over, trying to wish away the pancakes. The omelet alone would have been enough, she realized. Not knowing how to say no, she was not fit to be a mother by any standard.

The Liberty Bell lay coyly inside the glass pavilion of Independence Hall, a symbol of American freedom recast by the partners of Bell and Stow, installed in the State House steeple in 1753. The bell weighed in at 2,080 pounds, the majority of it copper, with lesser amounts of tin, lead, zinc, arsenic, silver, and gold. The famous crack was a meaty half-inch wide, its length twenty-four-and-a-half inches. The bell's musical note was a zinging E-flat.

The bell had been rung in dire circumstances and during patriotic celebrations.

Lee's fascination with the crack was equivalent to his fascination with the lean in the Leaning Tower of Pisa. The button on the wall promised to play a recording of what it sounded like.

"Go ahead, try it," Tomás said.

Lee pressed the button and clutched his ears. Not only was it loud, but it sounded awful. He stepped back and stared at the bell as though he were looking at an early dinosaur, wondering how many times it had been rung during its existence. There was no way to tell.

"Okay, this was pretty great, but I guess I've seen enough of Philadelphia for now," Lee said, tucking his hands into his pockets. They still had an important job to do. "I'm ready to go back to the apartment. I wonder what news Alicia will have."

30

If Lee had been someone other than a kid afflicted with Hutchinson-Gilford, he might have considered etymology as a career. He was in love with the coincidences of words, their dramatic inversions, spellings, and mishaps. A verbal polygamist, married to far too many nouns, he was viscerally bothered at the near miss in meaning contained in the order of letters in certain words, among them the reverse order of the *n* and *a* in *Satan* and *Santa,* and the ambiguity of one *s* that distinguished *desert* from *dessert.*

Latin roots bloomed through the history of Romance languages like flowers opening in slow motion across the centuries. No wonder Lee loved the writings of Ben Franklin. What a privilege it would have been to have met him, to have to think on one's toes. As was the case with Franklin, Lee was captivated by historic firsts—the first baby gorilla born in captivity, the first safety pin.

They had made it back to Dupont Circle easily. No sooner had they made it back than Lee decided to work on his own epitaph, in the tradition of Ben Franklin, not wanting to leave his last words to chance.

It was early afternoon, he sat on the couch in the living room with his brittle legs beneath him in a loose parallelogram. Tomás had taken a shower and then gone into the bedroom to collect his thoughts before telephoning Cass. Margaret had gone to the store for groceries.

In days, Lee and Tomás would return home to New Jersey. He thought of inviting Margaret to come with them. She and Cass would no doubt get along. The sense of loss he felt for Tomás was bigger than his own problems. He knew they were running out of time and that good detective work was sorely lacking. He had his doubts about Alicia Patmos, whose gnomed stature appeared too fragile to do anything useful, but then, who knew better than Lee that good things come in small packages.

Lee opened his notebook and saw his drawing of Cocoa and remembered her fondly: the peace in her dwarf eyes and her instinct to run. Dr. Bream was a good egg after all, encouraging him to write things down. He hoped he'd have more things to show for himself when they got home besides picture post-cards and plastic pandas.

They had brought the stroller back to Margaret's apartment. It sat in the foyer, a reminder of Lee's failing health. Three phantom words, *congestive heart failure,* loomed in the back of his mind like the grim reaper. It's what had happened to Kira. It could happen to him at any time.

Which left him with the remaining question: What was the best way to die? Taken by surprise or walking toward it? If he could choose, what would he want his last thought to be, his last image, or touch, or taste? Was the last thing one saw really imprinted on one's eyes? If that were true, many more murder mysteries would have been solved.

Lee's epitaph should be clever, like Franklin's. Comical. Leading with his name, the tombstone would be engraved with the years of his birth and death, followed by a list of pseudonyms, to include Sherlock Holmes and James Bond, and beneath that a diagram of a hangman and a list of clues, or the blank-fill-in-able lines of a Mad Lib. Something interactive that would somehow keep him alive.

He started to write his epitaph:

> Here lies Lee,
> too old to drink,
> too young to die.
> Too cold to swim,
> too hot to fry.
> A mother's son,
> a son of a gun,
> a historian!

He looked over the words skeptically, trying to force the off-rhyming *n* of *historian* with *son* and *gun,* unhappy that it sounded forced.

It was an okay beginning, he thought. He heard the key in the lock. Margaret had returned, carrying two brown paper shopping bags. Green-ferned carrot tops peeked thinly out over the top of one of the bags, next to feathery bunches of parsley and cilantro.

"*Hola,* Lee." She lapsed into Spanish, unloading the bags on the kitchen counter.

"*Hola,*" Lee said quickly, heat creeping up the back of his neck and shoulders. Margaret had a warm musical utterance that couldn't be copied. The angles of her eyes made his squared edges curve.

He quickly slipped the notebook into the dungeon of his backpack, embarrassed at his own morbidity, his final words suspended on a tightrope.

"Where's Tomás?" Margaret asked.

"Back in your bedroom, getting ready to call Cass. She asked for an update. I promised Tomás I wouldn't say anything about Violeta and the baby, but I feel bad lying."

"It's not an easy thing to lie to one's parents," Margaret said, "though I have to admit I found it necessary from time to time. Your mother is a mother, part of her will understand. No doubt she'll also be angry."

She took a pair of shears from the kitchen drawer and started trimming back the stalk from the first of a dozen yellow roses, fitting each into a glass vase in the kitchen. Her back to Lee, she was busy thinking how if she couldn't exactly baby-proof the house for him, she could at least manage to remove thorns so that he didn't prick himself.

"Cass likes yellow roses too," Lee said, pulling himself up on a wooden stool. He wished he could somehow connect Margaret and his mother. "Yellow roses with blue irises," he added. "That's her favorite combination."

"Pretty," Margaret said, still working to excise the sharp thorns from the stem. "There," she said, finally placing the vase on the table. "¿Bonitas, no?"

A triangle of sun skirted the windowsill and landed brightly on her forearms.

"Four more days," Lee said quietly. "Four more days till we go home. Back to Cass and Patrick." He searched Margaret's face for a reaction. "You could come with us," he said, trying to make it sound exotic, trying to make it a question she would want to say yes to. "If you wanted to. Newark's really close to New York City. We could hop on the train, I could show you around," he said, almost swaggering. "I could show you my room, and you could meet Cass and Patrick."

Lee tried to picture the Thanksgiving table set for feasting, the same every year. In the center of the table the bird, browned in butter and sage, its stocking feet trussed up with string, culminating in white, fringed paper booties. Next to that the moat of gravy adrift in its narrow scull—a mysterious blood juice made of flour and gizzards and neck drippings infused with red wine and marrow. It was Cass's father's recipe, which she dove into making with diabolical enthusiasm.

And the centerpiece—always the same—was an arrangement of yellow roses and blue irises. Cass said the combination reminded her of the framed print of Van Gogh's *Irises* that hung near the dining room table in her parents' house.

Lee looked at Margaret's roses, still tightly closed with no hint of blossoming.

"I'll think about it," Margaret said. "*Mi querido,*" she said, impulsively giving Lee's hand a careful squeeze. "I'm so grateful for the invitation," she said, leaning against the window. The season was changing again. Bicycle wheels moved in and out of the bare-boned trees in the park below, where the shallow bowl of the fountain was beginning to glaze over in a slick layer of ice for sparrows to skate on. "But I may be needed here. There's Natalya to think of. You know, the teenage girl I mentor, or at least try to mentor." She made her eyes go cross-eyed, as if to impress upon Lee the difficulties involved. "I've been neglecting her. She's very young, always in trouble, gets in with the wrong crowd. Not like you!" she said. "And now she's got a damn boyfriend! It's about time I give her some attention. And Thanksgiving," she said, "is a time for families, no? Your mother must really miss you. And that pig of yours, if he really exists. I'm not sure I believe you." She reached to find some of Lee's nonexistent belly fat to pinch. "Who keeps a pig to poop in an apartment? Only a crazy person," she said. "In Argentina we don't have Thanksgiving, exactly. Halfway around the world our seasons are mixed up, our summer begins in December. I used to travel with my parents on vacation to Bahía Blanca, where there're the most beautiful beaches in the world, covered in waves of white salt. And where there're too many legends to sort out, of *caballeros* and *malones*, aborigines on horseback who invaded the city when it was still a fortress."

Lee's chin dropped, sensing she was trying to let him down easy. He guessed Margaret wasn't really that worried about Natalya at all, but it was something else she was thinking. Was she waiting to get rid of him? Was it fear? Fear about being part of something? And equally, fear of being left alone? Those were things Lee already understood, long before Tomás had come.

31

If love were a face, it would be moon-shaped and honest and tenderly yielding.

It was Saturday. Last night's conversation with Tomás had kept Cass up worrying. She got out of bed and pulled open the shade, the tops of the buildings appeared eaten alive by frost. She sensed in her gut that something was different, that the shape her son took up in the universe was shrinking.

She dressed, combed her hair with her fingers, then ate a breakfast of coffee and buttered toast. By eight-fifteen she was out the door in blue jeans, a pea coat, and a yellow scarf, walking quickly to the station, climbing the stairs in twos.

She took the commuter train to Penn Station, then changed for Eighth Avenue and the E that would travel uptown, past Harlem to 190th Street/Fort Tryon Park and the Cloisters, where the land jutted out over the Hudson. Saturdays were usually reserved for Lee—his whims and disasters—which called for ice cream sundaes and treasure hunts for which they hardly ever left the apartment. But today Cass had a promise of her own to keep. Arthur Wilson, with whom she'd been friends since college, had asked her to look in on his apartment while he was away visiting his aging parents outside of Memphis. The job involved taking in the mail, which he implied—looking over the tops of his glasses—there'd be plenty of, and watering a few meandering acidophilus plants.

Cass had thought it would help keep her mind off Lee's being away, and had immediately agreed to check on his apartment. She had never been to his new place, and didn't realize it would involve a sluggish forty-five-minute train ride along the rusted-out hollows of New York City's antiquated subway system. The crowded train shadow-boxed its way coarsely above and below ground, screeching intermittently.

At 110th the human traffic thinned. Two thirds of the people got off, and Cass could finally see the walls plastered with balloon-shaped graffiti and the floor scattered with filth.

She had known Arthur since they were freshmen in college in Rhode Island—Arthur at Brown and she at Pembroke. Distinctly southern, Arthur's aging parents still lived in a suburb outside Memphis in a white colonial, brick-and-clapboard former plantation, which still retained the dirt-floor cellared remnants of slave quarters.

Arthur had arrived at school with a pair of wine glasses and the jacket-and-bow-tie half of a tuxedo—the pants never found. He was the oldest friend she had in New York and had managed to make a career as an artist. He taught life-drawing classes at the Art Students League on West Fifty-Seventh Street across from Carnegie Hall. Cass once visited him in his studio for lunch when he'd first moved to town, sitting with her legs tucked neatly beneath her on a gray metal stool under the opalescent light in the life-drawing studio, while he offered her a newsprint pad and a stick of vine charcoal and invited her to draw the nude model along with the class. The female model sat motionless on a wooden block for the better part of an hour, while Arthur lectured to the class about how the secret to drawing the human body is based upon the repetitive pattern of an egg.

The train jolted to a stop at 190th Street, and the metal doors breezed open. All the years of working in New York, Cass had never come this far uptown. She'd never seen the neighborhood that bordered the medieval Cloisters where campaigns were once launched and battles were fought on horseback. Somewhere up here, she had read, was the highest elevation in New York City, where infinity hung on, narrowly sweeping the edges of clouds.

Cass exited the train into the cold. The tin, chiseled-out sounds of a working-class neighborhood rang out from street corners and curbs, and the big wheels of a beverage delivery truck roared past her.

She crossed the street and walked through a damp, stone tunnel, its coarse concrete canopy like the upper curve of a covered wagon. Signs at the opposite end pointed left to the Cloisters and right, toward Arthur's apartment. She followed Arthur's directions, walking briskly past a small public park whitened by recent snow and splintered with icicles, broken bottles, and graying scraps of newspaper.

Arthur's run-down building was a tall, fort-like structure of cornflower-colored stone, outlined in faux bricks. She unlocked the door to the foyer, which smelled faintly of laundry detergent and baby formula. Three flights up, she dismantled two locks and unharnessed the deadbolt.

Besides teaching life drawing at the League, Arthur had another part-time life as a custom pornographer who drew sexual art to order. Cass didn't judge him, he had a right to make a living on his own terms and it wasn't illegal. He filled orders for art the way a milkman filled orders for milk or eggs. Clients were explicit, but he didn't take it too seriously beyond the scope of good draftsmanship.

Cass pulled the chain in the center of the ceiling and the lights came on, the room an unexpected diorama of hot-house plants and acrid oxygen. African violets and nasturtiums, gardenias, anthurium in pots. Plants she didn't recognized by name but which hailed tiny purple blossoms. Arthur's talents were openly displayed on the walls—a supine threesome laid bare against a fire escape next to a small potted geranium; and another featured two men engaged in fellatio before a hummingbird drilling a bonsai. Cass looked closer and noticed that somewhere in each of the drawings or paintings Arthur had left his signature in the shape of a green plant secreted somewhere in the scene. It was what Hitchcock had done, inserting himself somewhere in each of his films.

A worn, brown-leather chair on wheels and an ottoman were the only other furniture in the room, besides the wooden easel and a table laid out with drawing supplies, brushes, a rapidograph pen, an extra pair of spectacles, and a package of Tums.

Cass sat in Arthur's chair and put her feet up on the ottoman, still wearing her coat. Never staying, but always leaving. She often slept in her clothes and didn't seem to notice.

In the corners of her mind, it was clear that part of the reason she had come here was to lose herself, to remember what it was like to be set free.

She sat in the chair and breathed, remembering the one night she had slept with Arthur, years ago, when Lee was almost two, shortly after Neil had left and all hell had broken loose. Arthur had taken her to dinner in Little Italy, and, over too much red wine, had listened to Cass's story about the magical boy who had popped out of her body without a single birthmark, who'd heralded a perfect Apgar score, who had smiled and grown bicuspids on cue, but at two was facing arteriosclerosis.

Later, in Arthur's apartment, not this one but another downtown near the flower district, he had kissed Cass tenderly, like a friend and bodyguard. His long blond ponytail come loose around his shoulders, his body pallorous, ripe, softer than ether. Cass made love to him with care, as though it were herself she was trying to steal back. Her arms spread wide to take him, her back curved forward, the cobra of her spine loosely unzipping toward her pubic bone, the reality running in circular motion in a rotunda of words that simply would not stop: *her baby was sick, he would never get well, he would die a ruin.*

She didn't have the words to say any of it. She made love to Arthur as if she were capable of turning the world inside out, as if science could not recuse itself and would never be forgiven.

She watered the plants and stacked the mail, each letter according to its chronological postmark. She looked up now and judged Arthur differently. The figures in the drawings appeared to exist on another frequency, as if a picnic on the subject of love, a diatribe of nourishing one's self. She thought to herself how lucky Arthur was. How he was brave and had moved past sex like some kind of secret gardener.

32

Lee was lying on the couch in the apartment, reading a news article about the invention of the hula-hoop when the telephone rang. It seemed to him that it was the motion of the hips and waist that made it happen. He tried rotating his hips to get a feel for it. In 1963, twenty-five million hula-hoops were sold in the first four months they were on the market. Lee looked around the room and wondered what he could invent if he tried. If he stacked a thousand black ants one on top of another and pressed them together into a solid line, could he make a durable shoelace? Could he make bubble gum that could bounce? Bubble gum continued to astound him.

The telephone rang, and Margaret answered it. Tomás came into the living room looking somewhat rejuvenated after a short nap. He ran his hand through his hair and sat on the couch, stretching his arms behind his head. The aroma of *carnitas* and black beans wafted from the kitchen.

"Who could that be?" he said.

According to what Alicia told Margaret over the phone that afternoon, nearly four years ago, three babies had been born during the month of March to women held in the converted prison of the Navy Mechanics School. The school had been connected to the newborn ward in a hospital in downtown Buenos Aires. The dates fit the approximate timeframe for when Violeta would have given birth.

Two of the babies were boys, so they could be ruled out entirely. But reliable testimony about a baby girl had come from a maid who worked in the home of a military family. The maid knew a nurse at the hospital where prisoners were taken to give birth. The nurse said she had cared for someone whose description closely matched Violeta. She described the birth and lack of anesthesia, accompanied by ungodly cries, and how afterward a military officer with a gun stood over her as she was forced to clean up her own bloody afterbirth.

The nurse also knew that the hospital kept secret birth records. She was able to find a record from March 29th about a baby girl adopted by Captain Pedro Sanchez and his wife, Camila, who already had an adult child living abroad. The captain, who worked in the concentration camp connected to the hospital, had been dealing in black-market babies for months on the sly.

But unbeknownst to Sanchez, Videla had gotten wind of the captain's embezzlement practices and had issued his death warrant. On the April night that Sanchez brought the baby home, the sky was clear. His wife, Camila, had held the infant up to the light, and had seen the sparse black curls scroll across her forehead in a sea of tiny waves, her small peony-shaped mouth fashioning love out of the air.

By morning they had settled on the name Maria Teresa. There were few details that Captain Sanchez could offer about the baby's birth parents. Camila had fought the urge to ask more questions, reading in her husband's eyes that he had something to hide.

33

Two months had passed by the time Sofia came to Argentina to visit her parents and meet the baby that June. At twenty-seven, Sofia was newly married and enjoying her life in Washington, DC, where she had settled after getting a master's degree from Georgetown. She was working as a translator of botanical books for the Library of Congress. Her husband, Daniel, was a well-respected carpenter and craftsman, and he had spent the last couple of years traveling around the country, restoring carousel horses to their authentic manes and tails. Things between Sofia and her parents had never gone smoothly, and she wished Daniel had been able to accompany her to South America.

On the third night of her visit, after Sofia and her parents had finished dinner and Isabel, the maid, began to clear the dishes, Sofia's mother, Camila, put water on to boil for tea and her father sat back from the table to smoke a cigar.

"So good to have you home," her mother had said, "even if it's only for a little while. The baby reminds me of you, Sofia— so active, so busy even this small."

"Let me take her for a walk," Sofia said. "The night air will help her fall asleep. "It'll give you two a break."

Outdoors on the concrete walk, *luciérnagas,* fireflies, ricocheted off the sidewalks and flittered high up in between the leaves of the *tipa* trees, their tail lights sparking fits of electricity. Sofia followed the fallen purple blossoms of the jacaranda down the street, their perfume sweet as honeysuckle, their twisted shadows cast around her like crewelwork. A bat flew up into a tree and sat staring down at them, huddled on the tip of a branch.

The last several days had been dry, the parched yellow lawns begged for rain. Maria Teresa slept like a queen in her carriage.

Sofia looked at her and wondered what trouble she would bring. She thought of her father's large, menacing hands and remembered how his attempts to discipline her as a child often verged on bouts of cruelty.

They had circled the block twice, the air netted with mist and the smell of rain, dark clouds moving in overhead. Sofia turned the carriage around, heading back. As she approached the familiar neighborhood of stores and houses, she saw several human shapes moving in the shadows near her parents' house. Four men emerged from a green Ford Falcon and pushed against their door.

There was no way to warn them.

Inside, her mother might have been checking her watch and pouring water for tea, her father loosening his collar and drinking his scotch.

Soon, an ungodly cry welted the air. Sofia stood still next to the alley, where trash burned in a metal can, and the smell of smoke filled her nostrils. She felt sure her father was guilty of some terrible crime. She had known it all her life. Her childhood friend Elena had disappeared last July. Elena was a teacher at the elementary school downtown but had lately become a lapsed Catholic and was rumored to have had an abortion. After Elena disappeared, Sofia had asked her father if he'd heard any news. He paused and smiled coldly, his mustache giving way to his weak upper lip, and said, *The world gets what the world gives.*

Now Sofia looked down at the baby's pale crown, her pulse visible at the tender spot on her skull, and knew that trying to help her parents would do no good. She backed the stroller into the alley and waited. Before deciding to visit, she had planned to take her vacation somewhere warm, perhaps on an island in the Caribbean, in which case Daniel would have come with her and rubbed suntan lotion inside the space between her shoulder blades where she couldn't reach. But her mother had begged her to come and see the baby, and her husband had encouraged her to go ahead, it would be a quick visit, and they would soon be together again. Now the baby's perfect mouth glistened even in the dark. Sofia's pulse quickened, pushing her back on her heels. The wind picked up. She wanted to cry but refused to give in to tears. She knew she would never see her parents again.

It began to rain. A strong wind pelted the ground, shutters beginning to bang in place. The wind blew harder, and Sofia stood perfectly still as a shower of gold and purple flowers swarmed down from the trees and covered the tips of her shoes, threatening to bury her standing up.

She peeked out of the alley, still shielding the stroller, and saw the shadows of two figures being hauled out of her parents' house—first her father, who had difficulty walking, then her mother sagging behind.

Sofia waited another ten minutes until she was sure they were gone. The rain had stopped as quickly as it had started. Gray puddles pooled at her feet. She secreted the carriage behind a drain pipe in the alleyway and tucked the baby inside her coat, barely giving her room to breathe. Maria Teresa began to whimper and cry. Sofia kissed the top of her head, then went around the back of the house to the servants' entrance. Inside, on the back stairs, she paused long enough to see the empty living room, the coffee table overturned, and the lit tip of her father's cigar still glowing red in a glass ashtray. Her mother's purse sat demurely on the sofa. Isabel, the maid, was nowhere to be seen.

Sofia began to shake, but had no time to waste. There was blood on her father's chair.

At the top of the stairs, on her mother's bureau, was a jewelry box, and inside, hidden beneath a gold necklace for safekeeping, was the baby's birth certificate that her mother had shown her earlier that afternoon, a passport, and some other papers she didn't have time to read, all tidily bundled with a green rubber band. Maria Theresa's scrawled name on the birth certificate looked fainter now, disappearing, as if written in invisible ink.

"Maria Teresa Sanchez," Sofia whispered to the infant as she stood in the shadows. She buttoned her into a sweater and leggings and found the diaper bag, feeling the child's fragile weight like a carton of eggs she was now obliged to deliver to some other safe haven. "Maria Teresa Sanchez, or whoever you are," Sofia repeated, her breath fighting jolts of adrenaline. Downstairs, she took one last look at the home that had held her childhood. She felt sorry then for her mother, who must surely have known something of the heinous nature of her father's crimes but had long ago made the choice to keep his secret.

Sofia left the worst thought for last. She knew that in order for her parents to have inherited this baby, someone had to have died in a terrible way. She stared into the darkness, wondering whose pantomime of eyes, whose bewildered expression she was really looking into. Maria Teresa stared back at her, not speaking or giving anything away.

34

Margaret put down the phone and returned to Tomás and Lee.

"*¿Qué está pasando?* What is happening?" Tomás demanded.

"That was Alicia," Margaret said. "*Con noticias,* with news. *Iré,* I'll go," she said, not wanting to expose Tomás to false hope. She reached for her coat from the kitchen chair. "Just a short walk to meet her at the National Gallery. Tomás, you stay with Lee, I'll be back in no time and tell you everything."

Tomás stared back in disbelief. "How could you even think of going without me?" he demanded. "This is my life, my family." As if on cue, Lee released a series of raucous coughs so violent they sounded like they might separate his ribs from his sternum.

Margaret was quick to read the injured look in Tomás's eyes, but her maternal instincts took over. "Tomás," she said, "*por favor.* Stay with him. Nothing important will go on without you."

It was clear since their return from Philadelphia that Lee had taken a turn for the worse. Something in his face had begun to sallow and set, though he insisted he was fine.

"I see it too," Tomás had told Margaret privately. "Cass warned me he was getting weaker. It's this damn disease. It has its own momentum like a motorcycle or a rollercoaster. There's nothing anyone can do. Once we're home he'll see his doctor right away." Tomás didn't want to believe it was happening. Even in prison the human body responded to pain and injury, but afterward tried to heal itself. Lee's body couldn't signal a response to live. His short life was slipping through their fingers.

"I promise to report everything." Margaret attempted a forced smile of reassurance. "Don't forget that's what I'm good at. That's my job."

"Are you sure, Margaret?" Lee complained. "Why can't we go with you?"

"Because," she said, "it will be easier if it's just one of us."

"Whatever Alicia tells you, no matter how good or bad, you have to tell us everything," Lee said. "I would never forgive you if you didn't."

"That goes for me too," said Tomás. "I guess I'll have to trust you, won't I? Though we know that in the past that wasn't always for the good."

"But we also know things are different now," she said.

Margaret fastened her coat on the way down the stairs, then hugged her woolen scarf tightly around her throat, walking brusquely toward Constitution Avenue and the National Mall. She cut across at Third and Ninth, beneath a darkening sky that had absorbed all extraneous color into gray, as if to signal snow. In Buenos Aires it would be approaching summer, the mercury just beginning to rise. Ten minutes more, and she took the steps to enter the West Building of the National Gallery, which housed European sculptures and paintings from the thirteenth through the nineteenth centuries.

Inside the exhibit hall of the main lobby, *The Art of Romare Bearden* was bannered over the walls—paintings filled with colored light outlined by black lines, reminding her of stained-glass windows.

She nodded to the guard at the turnstile and opened her bag for him to inspect the contents. *"Gracias,"* she said.

On the second floor landing she confronted Vermeer's *Girl with the Red Hat*, the girl's raised eyes and doubtful look mirroring Margaret's own uncertainties.

What were the chances that Alicia would tell her that Violeta was still alive, that her daughter could be found? For Tomás, simply knowing would never be enough. Margaret knew of many cases in which the lone survivors of atrocities like his had eventually taken their own lives.

It was Sunday, and the museum was crowded with tourists for whom only the most famous paintings mattered.

In the soft light of gallery six, Margaret finally found her sitting before Leonardo da Vinci's portrait of *Ginevra de' Benci*. It was the only da Vinci painting in the US. Fifteen inches square, painted in 1474, it was most likely the wedding portrait of a sixteen-year-old girl who was described as a poet married to a merchant. She bore a strong resemblance to the *Mona Lisa*. Originally the painting had included her hands. A line of her poetry was inscribed below the portrait: "I ask your forgiveness, I am a mountain tiger."

Alicia sat on the bench facing the portrait, the curved shape of her back slurred in quiet concentration.

Margaret joined her wordlessly, letting their shoulders touch.

Alicia took Margaret's hands in hers. "I have news," she said.

"Creo que te ayudará a encontrar lo que buscas. I think it will help you find what you're looking for. *Esperemos que sí.* Let's hope so."

"Sí," Margaret said, her body tensed for what was to come. She held her breath, knowing Tomás's fate lay in the balance.

"Okay," she said, bracing herself. *"Dime,* tell me. Tell me everything you know."

⌘

Alicia had kept her word and had found out everything she could about Violeta and the baby from her still strong connections among the *Abuelas*.

"It turns out," Alicia said evenly, "that much has been learned in the three years since things happened. And that is good news for us, eh?"

Margaret nodded. *"Sí,* yes. Go on."

"According to my sources," Alicia continued, "unbeknownst to Videla, Captain Sanchez had been running a prosperous side business of his own in the illegal sale of babies. When he brought home the newborn to his wife, Camila, she was not so stupid as to think it was delivered by a *cigüeña*, a stork, and had distrusted him immediately. So much so, that without telling her husband, she bribed their maid to do some detective work to find out who the baby's biological mother was. The maid's name was Isabel Arona, and she had been sympathetic to the *Abuelas* all along. After some work, Isabel was able to make contact with one of the nurses in the civilian hospital where the babies belonging to prisoners were born. The women who gave birth there were often listed as *NN*s (not named), but sometimes mistakes were made and a real first or last name was given. In this case, luck had it so that the record included the mother's name—Violeta Concepción—but the baby's father was listed as unknown."

Margaret almost cried out loud when she heard this. At last it was confirmed!

"According to Isabel," Alicia went on, "Camila knew the truth within days of receiving the baby."

"Go on," Margaret said.

"She was afraid to confront her husband, and she was afraid to know what had happened to Violeta," Alicia continued. "She was afraid someone would come for her and take the baby away. Earlier that morning, before she and her husband were arrested, Camila shared this information about the baby with her older daughter Sofia, including Violeta's full name. Isabel, the maid, was folding laundry in the next room and heard everything. She said there was no mistaking it, that Sofia *knew*. Unfortunately," Alicia said now, lowering her voice to a whisper, "Camila was killed for her husband's actions. This information was written into the *Abuelas'* records after Camila and the captain disappeared. Isabel barely escaped through the back door that evening when the soldiers arrived. She was afraid for her life."

Margaret nodded; things were adding up. She fought the urge to be hopeful.

"From what I've learned regarding your friend's family," Alicia continued, "the daughter's name was Sofia Sanchez. She lived and worked here in DC as some kind of translator at the Library of Congress. She was at home visiting her parents when Videla's men came, and she must have felt she had no choice but to take the baby back to America. But then, after leaving Argentina, her conscience must have gotten the better of her. She needed to be sure. A week or two afterwards, she sent a letter to the house. The phone had already been disconnected. The letter arrived and was intercepted by Isabel, who had come back to collect her things. Isabel was the one who gave the letter to the *Abuelas*, who were kind enough to place it in their archives and have forwarded it to me. I have it here."

It seemed impossible. Margaret's pulse raced as Alicia reached into her purse and withdrew an ordinary envelope with a canceled stamp dated May, 1979. The museum guard leaning against the doorframe at the entrance to the gallery shifted his weight, moving nearer. For a brief second Margaret was afraid she was under suspicion. Years of being surrounded by the military regime had shattered her sense of personal safety. In another context this meeting might have cost her her life or had her thrown into prison. But then she remembered that this was America. Here you could burn the national flag and call it art.

Alicia handed Margaret the envelope. She turned it over carefully, understanding the sum total of the weight it carried.

"According to the letter," Alicia explained, "Sofia came back home to DC with the baby and planned to go on sabbatical with her husband Daniel, probably to hide Maria Teresa, just in case. Sofia must have written the letter because she needed to know for sure if her parents were dead, and maybe to find out if anyone was looking for the baby. She was smart and wrote in a kind of code, not mentioning the baby directly. Take a look, you'll see what I mean."

Margaret carefully withdrew the letter from the envelope, reading what looked like words written in a hurried hand:

Querida Mamá,

I hope you and Papa are well. I have received your precious gift. We are all safe and well. Daniel and I are about to go on sabbatical. I'm not sure for how long. We are thinking of starting a family. He follows the horses and I go along for the ride.
Go with God.

Love Sofia

Margaret reread the letter three times. It was like a nursery rhyme that offered insufficient clues. What was Sofia afraid of? Surely, she and the baby were safe here in America. But no one could know for sure the extent of Videla's revenge. And with the money her father stole still unaccounted for, there was no telling how far he would reach. Her last name on the return address was Sanchez. Good news. She had kept her last name!

"You are a magician, Alicia," Margaret exclaimed, grateful. "How can Tomás and I ever thank you? Now at least we have something to go on. In so many ways this information has exceeded our hopes."

A young mother, carrying her sleeping baby in a backpack, accidentally bumped into Margaret, jostling her slightly, while trying to get a closer look at the painting of Ginevra.

Margaret smiled up at her, then returned to Alicia.

"Just a few more minutes and I'll be done," Alicia said. "We know that the captain and his wife were killed in one of the prison camps days after being kidnapped. Their remains were thrown into the open road outside the city. Later, forensics used dental records and old injuries to identify them. Broken bones. Videla was not easy on them," she said, looking into the distance. "Especially the captain, who abused his power and was responsible for placing more than a dozen other infants with civilian families for a price amounting to more than one hundred thousand American dollars. The money was never recovered. And there's something else." Alicia stopped, sitting up straighter, a smile beginning to play across her lips. "*¿Crees en el destino?* Do you believe in fate?"

"What do you mean?" Margaret asked, not sure what she was getting at.

"*Examine más detenidamente,* take a closer look," Alicia said, placing the envelope in her hands. "Here," she said, pointing to the return address.

Margaret inspected the scribbled handwriting in the upper left-hand corner, then let out a gasp, accidentally dropping the envelope to the floor.

"*Dios mío,*" she said, stunned. "I can't believe it. They were two blocks from my house? A stone's throw. And now they are surely gone!"

Margaret's heart sank like a stone. It wasn't enough to have been so close and to fail. She glanced across the gallery for some sign of hope and saw Raphael's portrait of the Alba Madonna, the Madonna of Humility, stealing a glimpse of heaven from within an aureole of clouds, her infant son racing across a landscape made of sand. "We're a year too late," Margaret said, gloomily. "Two years, maybe," she said, laying the envelope on the bench between them.

"*Es un presagio.* It's an omen," Alicia said. "A good omen. That you are traveling in the same direction, that you both want what's right. Keep this," she said handing Margaret the letter. "You might need it to prove Tomás is the father. They could still be nearby, *mi querido.* Maybe closer than before. Surely there will be marriage announcements and perhaps news articles. Someone who has lived so openly in a city of public records like this is sure to have left a trail. Someone with a child. And now I'm afraid that I have to get back to Gettysburg and the work of making butter. A fine job for someone as old and toothless as me. A friend has been kind enough to wait for me and will drive me back."

She took Margaret's hands in hers, kissed both her cheeks. "*Escúcheme,* listen. If anyone can track them down, I know it's you. Please tell Tomás he has my love. *Besos a los dos,* kisses to you both, and to Lee also."

"*Gracias,*" Margaret said, not wanting to let go of Alicia's thin, frail hands. "Not just for now, but for all the time you were a friend to my parents at home, and to me when I first came here. And for Violeta, may her soul rest in peace somewhere, finally. And for the child, who will hopefully one day know how important she is, so important that her father has been looking for her all this time."

Margaret watched as Alicia traveled down the stairs and continued on her way. She was beyond grateful. What she felt seemed to come from some other, deeper place. They had come so close, but had missed their chance.

She sat on the edge of the wooden bench, still facing the portrait of Ginevra. They had come to the end of a long dark road and were now left to weigh their inheritance. One can never give without receiving, or receiving, give. In the fading light, she hoped to pay her final respects to the young woman in the painting, whom time had forgotten. Through the fists and clothing and shadows of the viewing crowd, she could barely discern the difference between taking and borrowing. Somewhere in the world of art lay the answer to the question of good and evil, in which the quality of shadows had to do with the quality of light. And throughout all of it was a kind of courage. With a leap of faith, Margaret said aloud: "I ask your forgiveness, I am a mountain tiger."

35

Margaret exited the museum, taken aback by the drop in temperature. It was past three, the sky gone gray. To her great surprise, Lee was waiting for her on the stone steps, hunched over like a tiny gargoyle. He started to run in her direction.

"What are you doing here, Lee?" Margaret exclaimed, immediately upset that he was alone and shivering. "Where's Tomás?"

"Please don't be mad Margaret. Tomás fell asleep almost as soon as you left," Lee said. "He stays up most nights like a vampire, in case you didn't know. I couldn't stand to have to wait to hear everything. I left him a note that I was going to find you. I knew where you were going and I followed you, but you didn't see me. Did Alicia give you any good clues?"

"Better than clues," Margaret said, pulling Lee close to where his jaw met her hemline. "I should have known that a detective like you would insist on working overtime. But aren't you freezing and exhausted from all that walking? Didn't you think Tomás would be scared to death when he woke up and you weren't there? Your poor mother, what would she think?"

"I was afraid you'd leave me out of things," Lee said, feeling guilty, knowing Margaret was right. "Tomás puts up a good front, but I don't think he's as tough as he thinks he is. We really would have been stuck without you. I think it's time we took over, Margaret, don't you?"

"We're going to have to call Tomás immediately to let him know you're safe with me," Margaret said, regrouping quickly. The afternoon light was fading. She pulled her wool cap over her ears and locked arms with Lee. "This is our lucky day. Not only did Alicia provide critical information, but she gave us this," Margaret said, opening her purse to show Lee the letter from Sofia Sanchez and she started to explain, at which point he gasped openly.

"We are *so* lucky," Lee said. "I told you little people can accomplish a lot. I knew Alicia would come through with something."

"And do you see now, my darling," Margaret said, bending to zip Lee's coat up to his chin, "that we were so close but didn't know it? It seems more of a coincidence than we could begin to imagine."

"What do you mean?" he said, wide-eyed.

"C'mon," she said. "I'll explain as we go, but first let's call Tomás and let him know you're okay and that we'll be back soon."

36

Two hundred twenty-three Sixteenth Street was a nineteenth-century brownstone with ivy growing up its front. Margaret and Lee had taken the route home from the museum that would bring them past Sofia and Daniel's old address. Tomás had been angry when Margaret called from the pay phone on the street to reassure him. He was angry and embarrassed, but had no choice but to understand. "Lee is fine," she said. "Though I don't know how you could have let him escape like that. I'll tell you everything when we get there," she said. "There's reason to think there's good news."

It was late afternoon, a few dark clouds inched across the horizon in a cavalcade of lost light. They stood in front of the building, glancing up at the stone façade. A carved pediment at the top guarded a dove-colored plaster angel, as if to signify that children would be safe here no matter what.

"We're two years too late," Margaret said wistfully. "But maybe we can still find something."

They walked toward the modest entryway, holding hands, knowing that Sofia and Daniel and the baby had once lived here. Through the glass entryway, they could see brass mailboxes and a flight of stairs. Six units in all. At the top, a chimney forced a chiaroscuro of smoke into the clouds.

The vestibule door was open, emitting the smell of limes accompanied by Lysol.

"C'mon, Margaret," Lee said. "Don't just stand there."

There was no evidence of a child—no toys, or stroller, or signs of any kind. Just the usual ghosts of adult possessions—an umbrella stand, a table for oversized mail. Lee crouched beneath the stairwell to sift apart two mildewed magazines—*Runner's World* and *Common Cause*. A copy of the *Post* lay on the tiled floor among the cobwebs.

The names on the mailboxes belonged to Sorensen, Verner, Ignacci, McCall—all single names, except for one: McDougall/Hernandez.

"Doesn't seem like they live here anymore, Margaret," Lee said, disappointed. "We missed them, but by how long?"

Margaret wanted to believe more than anything that McDougall/Hernandez might be aliases, the couple fearful of Videla's attempts at retaliation.

"I'm going to try the buzzer," she said. "Just to be sure. At least it sounds like a Spanish name, if they changed their names to hide…"

She rang the bell and waited. Then rang it again, along with all of the others. They waited and waited, and no one came. What did they expect? It was four o'clock in the afternoon on a Sunday. People were napping over spent newspapers or meandering their way home from shopping and the movies.

"Margaret," Lee said, "wait, I need to rest a minute." He sat on the granite steps outside the apartment building and took a few deep breaths after so much disappointment. "I know we don't know each other very well, not really," he said, looking up at her from beneath the brim of his Redskins hat. "But I know what you did. About betraying Tomás, I mean. You both thought I was asleep when we were driving to Philadelphia, but I heard everything. About how you let him get arrested instead of you. Cass taught me that you need to be right with the world before you can be right with yourself," he said, swallowing hard, thinking about how lonely Cass must be in cold New Jersey with only Patrick for company. They had never been separated this long.

"I'm not surprised," Margaret said. "You seem always one step ahead of us, always knowing more than we expected. I'm ashamed of what I did, though at the time I didn't have all the facts. It's impossible to know what one will do in that kind of situation before it happens. And do I regret it? Of course, I do. So now we're doing our best to help him. And when we're done, I'll still have to live with myself and my actions. Meanwhile, I can see where you get your brains," she said, putting her arm around his shoulder. "Let's go. I have another idea. We have another mission ahead of us before we meet up with Tomás."

"Okay," he said, "but where are we going?"

"You'll know soon enough," she said, squeezing his hand a little tighter.

Tomás had waited almost two years to learn the fate of his family, she thought to herself, and he could wait a little longer. Enough time, she thought, for them to make a detour to her office at the *Post*, minutes away, and give the microfiche machine a whirl. She hoped her editor, Glen Keating, the kind of busybody who left no stone unturned and who insisted on dotting every *i* and crossing every *t*, would be at home for once with his family and not sniffing compulsively over someone else's byline. By now he had read her draft of the story about *Los Diablos* that had been couriered over and would be looking to challenge her facts and determine whether it was good enough to make the lead article of the magazine, or to be buried in the back pages.

Alicia was right. There would likely be evidence of Sofia's and Daniel's lives in the form of a wedding announcement or a school committee blurb. Something that had to do with Sofia's work at the Library of Congress. The local papers were all over things like that.

They approached the familiar Times Roman logo of the *Washington Post* stretched across the width of the building. Underlit now in the fading afternoon hours, it wore the dim reflected floodlights of a hospital emergency room.

They moved through the revolving glass doors. Margaret flashed her security badge to the guard, and Lee's unsteady heart beat faster. "Lee's with me tonight, Jim," she told the guard.

Lee held up his hands. "You can search my coat if you need to," he said.

"That won't be necessary," Jim said. "You can go on up."

"Do you realize," Lee said to Margaret in the elevator, "that this is where the story about the Pentagon Papers broke, and where we learned Nixon was a thief?"

"Of course, Lee," Margaret said. "Woodward and Bernstein are my colleagues."

Lee looked down at his windbreaker and sneakers and wished he had worn something more grown-up looking in case he met them—a suit and tie, and maybe a briefcase instead of a backpack.

﹇

Margaret had been away for two weeks. As they stepped out of the elevator, she took a cursory glance at the gruff orchestration of desks and pages of news pouring in from the wire services. A skeleton crew of copyeditors with rolled shirt sleeves were laboring over galleys, proofreading the final copy for tomorrow's paper in a stench of cigarette smoke and stale coffee.

Lee inhaled and started coughing.

"You okay?" Margaret asked, pounding his back. "We can go back home, you know, I can come back myself tomorrow."

"No!" he shouted, hating the way his sickness always held him back. He was on the trail of what was probably the discovery of his lifetime.

"Here's a glass of water," Margaret said, filling a paper cup from the nearby fountain. Lee drank, sputtering a little, as the water worked its way through his creaky esophagus.

"What's our plan?" he managed to say, fighting the spasm in his chest.

"Hold on a minute," Margaret said. "Hey, Ted." She flashed a smile at the editor she knew to be the weekend quarterback overseeing the rest.

"Margaret! Welcome back. How was the West Coast?"

"I'm not here," she said, feigning a whisper. "Remember, you haven't seen me, and by the way this is my nephew Lee. Someday he's going to be a famous detective. Over here, Lee," Margaret called to him. She dumped the contents of her bag out on her desk and switched on the lamp, then unlocked her drawer for a packet of aspirin. A fading black-and-white photo of her parents at home on their thirtieth anniversary was pinned to the cork board on the wall, along with ticket stubs from a championship Phillies game, and a takeout Chinese menu from a nearby restaurant. The sleek taupe IBM Selectric typewriter still waited for her like a trusty animal. She turned it on, just to hear it purr, then quickly silenced it. On Friday she would be back to work. Tomás and Lee would be gone. She realized slowly that it would be Thanksgiving by then, and she 'd have nowhere to go.

"First things first," she said. "We call Tomás and update him that we'll be a little late. Tell him you're okay. I'll dial, you talk."

Lee was embarrassed, but when she handed him the phone, he was apologetic. "Tomás, I'm sorry, but you were sleeping and snoring really loud. I just wanted to help. We'll be back in a couple of hours. Maybe with good news."

"Nice job," Margaret said. "There's always a good way to say you're sorry."

"Okay, Lee, this is where you come in." Margaret led him down the corridor into what looked like a huge storage room. "Do you see those machines over there?" she said. "Those are microfiche machines, kind of our treasure chests. Somewhere in there is proof that Sofia and Daniel came to this country and put down roots. We just need to find out where they went after they left that apartment building."

Decades of back issues of the *Post*, encrypted in the yellow glow of microfiche, were kept in a separate alcove in the rear of the loft, dating as far back as 1877. Reading monitors were set up on carrels, the small lobotomized machines threaded with film, magnifying glass, lightbulb. Margaret had last used one of these when researching a college paper on Eumenides—the Greek god of vengeance—but it had been a while.

"Here you go," she said, positioning Lee on a metal chair with wheels in front of the plastic microfiche machine next to hers.

"But what are we looking for, exactly?" Lee asked, bewildered, adjusting his glasses. "Daniel and Sofia could be anywhere."

"I'm going to turn it on for you, and you're going to scan like this," she said, showing him how to turn the crank and watch the news slide past in flattened-out pages. "We're searching for weddings, engagements, marriage announcements. Anything that says *Sofia Sanchez* in connection with Daniel somebody or other, any combination of their names together. We'll start by going back two years. Can anyone really survive in this town without getting their name in the paper?"

Margaret sat in front of the machine and began to search. Back issues were organized by year, month, and day, and were accompanied by an alphabetical index. She took a piece of paper and pencil and tried to sketch out a timeline, thinking through the history of Sofia's visit to Buenos Aires, trying to picture Sofia's face in her mind.

Out of the corner of her eye, Margaret watched Lee, his face close to the glass as he scrolled. She could only begin to imagine the kind of wild unspoken thoughts going through the kid's head: how impossible their mission was, how they were likely to fail. He was fired up with concentration and had not strayed an inch. Margaret returned to the timeline, securing her long hair with an elastic band.

The machine continued to hum quietly. The paper was a living, breathing thing. She could smell stale cups of coffee deadening in trash cans and something worse, the skeletal remains of a rodent, long marooned and decomposing on a glue trap, slowly revealing its tiny occipital skeleton. Being an investigative reporter was like being a detective without a gun.

Margaret turned the crank and continued to read. The words jumped fluidly to the surface like a startled school of silverfish. According to the timeline, Sofia had last visited her parents in June of 1977, so she must have been married at least a year before that. Margaret tried to imagine Sofia's face, in turn patient, anxious, afraid. Safe to assume, Margaret reasoned to herself, with an inner, slightly sardonic smile, that having lived in America for some years, Sofia may have wanted to be a June bride.

Wedding announcements were reserved for the *Post*'s Sunday lifestyle pages. Two solid pages of these were published on

June 3, 1977, several of them accompanied by photos of the engaged and newly married. Susan and Sam Moore, Charles and Dorinda Pickering, Federica and Andrew Von Hippel. All in all, they had something to smile about, being generally healthy, young, and accomplished.

Beside her, Lee silently read on, from time to time adjusting his glasses to better lean forward, his legs crossed beneath him on an eager slant. He flashed through pages of debutantes from Bethesda, newly graduated MDs funneled into residencies, looking to make their homes in Dupont Circle or Georgetown.

Trite love stories that looked good on paper but would end in disappointment. Margaret looked at the big overhead clock with skepticism, the monotonous, black second-hand stalking the hour-hand dispassionately. It was nearing five-thirty and already dark. Tomás would be looking for them with a thousand questions. They needed to hurry.

"Any luck?" She leaned over and kissed Lee on the forehead.

"Nothing yet," Lee said, not lifting his eyes from the rolling pages. "*Shh,*" he said. "Don't interrupt me, I'm almost up to June 1978."

"Okay," she said. "A little longer, but we're going to have to quit pretty soon and go home and tell Tomás everything. We can always come back tomorrow."

Lee took off his glasses and blinked, put them on again and refocused. The notices were spread out randomly like jagged puzzle pieces needing to be inspected one by one. It was stuffy inside the newsroom. Those who remained were starting to pack up and go home. Margaret could hear the distant digitized music of the UPI and AP news feeds rippling like waterfalls. The financial markets switched off for the weekend. Somewhere in the distance a vacuum cleaner skimmed the carpet in a buzz. Her mouth was dry. She asked herself reluctantly—and for reasons she didn't understand—why it was important to love.

৵

Ten minutes more, and nothing. Lee's eyes were beginning to

blur, but he continued to scroll forward. Nothing else in his life had mattered like this before. If Kira were here, she would feel the same way.

He yawned and stood, then sat back down. He was starting to sweat. Stray news articles caught his eye, the words becoming blurry and inflamed: On June 10 the Senate committee announced its Permanent Select Committee on Intelligence; the Concorde made its first commercial flight from Paris to DC. He cranked faster, closing in on another slew of wedding announcements, when the name *Buenos Aires* caught his eye as a small unfamiliar block of type at the bottom of the right-hand column on the last page. As luck had it, there was a small black-and-white photo of a couple, the woman in white, the man smiling sheepishly as if he had been caught by the camera doing something illegal. *Sofia Sanchez and Daniel Orozco, newlyweds.*

"Margaret!" Lee shrieked. "I think I found something."

The brief article said they had met the year before and were married by a justice of the peace in the county court house.

> Ms. Sanchez, daughter of Pedro and Camila Sanchez of Buenos Aires, completed her master's degree at Georgetown, and is a translator—and sometime illustrator—of botanical books with a particular interest in orchids, employed by the Library of Congress. Mr. Orozco, who also graduated Georgetown, works as a master craftsman and carpenter, with an interest in restoring fine antiques, in particular the restoration of carousel horses. The couple will make their home in Washington.

So that part of the story was confirmed!

"Now what?" Lee asked Margaret. "I can't believe we found them! Tomás is going to be so happy!"

"Good work," Margaret said. "A-plus. I wouldn't expect anything less of you. Sit tight, Lee, while we dig a little deeper. We could, of course, check with the Library of Congress or ask for alumni records from Georgetown, but that would take time. Let's keep digging while we're here."

Now that they knew that Sofia and Daniel had moved, they

needed to find out what happened next. When Sofia brought Maria Teresa back from Buenos Aires without warning, did Daniel accept her as their own? Were they afraid someone would try to steal her back? Did Sofia believe she'd be asked to pay for her father's crimes? More than one hundred thousand dollars in blood money was still unaccounted for.

Now that they knew Daniel's last name, Margaret's training as an investigative journalist took over.

"Come sit with me," she said to Lee, and he climbed into her lap, as they searched for Daniel's name, Margaret sorting through the microfiche like a rabid tiger, perhaps channeling Ginevra in her wake. She wondered how common it was for someone to be a restorer of carousel horses. Restoration work like that was expensive and time consuming. It took patience, she imagined, and with its appeal to children might make good human-interest news.

The question then became one of horses.

"If Daniel were a restorer of carousels, he might live near a seaside community with a boardwalk and arcade," she said to Lee, trying to piece it all together.

She worked for answers, trying to think. Nearby Cape May, New Jersey, boasted a beautiful stretch of sand without a developed boardwalk. But Rehoboth Beach in Delaware and Ocean City, Maryland, were two towns within a three-hundred-mile radius that possessed full-scale honkytonks and arcades, making them better candidates.

A merry-go-round with carousel horses was the property of children and could steal their hearts with its promise of forever. Wasn't that its appeal? The thrill of *always* and *never* and the continuity of *forever* that a circle suggests?

She checked the microfiche index under *C* for carousel horses, *B* for boardwalks in the states of Virginia, Maryland, and Pennsylvania within a three-hundred-mile radius, finally coming up with a small article in the *Post* from last year's summer tourist season in Ocean City, Maryland.

Eureka! There it was, almost too small to notice, buried in the fine print in the Things to Do with Children section. *Restorations to Yield New Life to Trimper's, Beloved Merry-Go-Round, Ocean City, Maryland.* A small photo accompanied the article of a group of carousel horses opposite the boardwalk and a stretch of jetty. Beside them was a youngish, dark-haired man wearing a torn white T-shirt, with a small sterling-silver sea horse on a black leather cord around his neck. And the caption: *Daniel Orozco enjoys painstaking restoration work…project to extend another year.*

"That's got to be them, Lee!" she said, pushing back her chair. "Tell me what you think, tell me you believe it!"

Lee leaned in to see the photo. "Who else could it be?" he asked excitedly, his insides gone crazy, letting himself finally realize he was exhausted.

The article was brief and from the summer before, but it was a solid lead. She searched under *T* now for Trimper's and found another article, more recent, dated October 20th, just the month before, with more details and photos. She quickly skimmed it to discover that Trimper's was a large vintage amusement park with a hand-painted carousel, closed to the public for the winter months while undergoing renovations. Not just horses, but giraffes and lions and elephants.

"We did it, we're golden, Margaret! I can't believe we found them! Now we can tell Tomás the good news."

"You mean *you* found them," she said, beaming. "None of this could have happened without you. You were the one who found the announcement that got us on our way."

She sent the articles to print and shut down the microfiche, feeling excited by the prospects, but at the same time worried about what they'd find. If they found the baby but she belonged to someone else, what could Tomás do? And Violeta? She shivered at the thought; she knew better. But at least they could go back now and give Tomás the good news.

37

In less than half an hour, Lee and Margaret were back in the apartment hanging up their coats, excited to share their findings about Sofia and Daniel with Tomás—who had not fully recovered from Lee's leaving the apartment on his own.

"You really scared me, Lee," Tomás said, shaking him lightly by his thin shoulders, careful not to hurt him. "What were you thinking?"

"I'm sorry, Tomás. I'm really sorry. But I just couldn't lie around and wait any longer. I needed to know things right away. You fell asleep, I tried to wake you. I knew Margaret was going to the museum. And it was all worth it. We brought good news!"

Margaret let Lee explain their findings—both from Alicia and the *Post*—the details of which she realized sounded almost like a fairy tale. She opened her bag to show Tomás the news clippings, like stale crumbs of bread that could provide a trail, both the wedding announcement and the story about Trimper's Amusements.

"Here," she said. "Take a look. Tell me it's not my imagination."

Tomás seized the clippings, bringing them under a more powerful lamp in the living room, where he held them side by side, comparing both Sofia's and Daniel's profiles, looking at Daniel's first, wondering what it was that had drawn him to her. Wondering if he had what it takes to be the right kind of father to the daughter who was possibly his. A man who worked with his hands commanded respect. But did Daniel care about the child, especially if she wasn't his flesh and blood? He looked younger than thirty, perhaps younger than Tomás. It was hard to tell. It was harder to look at the wedding picture of Sofia, whose soft features and inquiring eyes showed no knowledge of murder.

He handed the clippings back to Margaret, who passed them on to Lee, who was fairly salivating waiting to reread them.

"What do you think, Tomás?" Margaret asked. "It sounds like Daniel's still there, working. If we're going to go, it'll have to be tomorrow. I'm due back at work in a couple of days, and you and Lee will be on your way too. It's your choice, Tomás. Do you want us to go with you? Or do you prefer to go alone? Either way is fine, *mi cadre*. I don't mind the drive."

He looked at her wild-eyed, unable to believe she would ask the question. *"Todos nosotros!"* he said. "It's been the three of us all along. I couldn't imagine going without both of you."

"We're like the three Musketeers," Lee interrupted. "All for one and one for all. I'm going to have to write this down for Dr. Bream. He's never going to believe we made it this far without the FBI."

"I'll take that as a *carpe diem*, a yes," Margaret said, trying to keep her voice light, her worry at bay. Her maternal instinct was telling her that another car trip like this was not the right choice for a sick kid like Lee. His health was at risk every day, and still he carried on like a brave soldier. She closed her eyes and tried to picture his mother's face, knowing how betrayed she would feel if she knew what they were up to. From the shadows of the kitchen the smells of burning rice and beans took over, and she realized Tomás had forgotten to stir the supper pot on the stove while they were gone.

"What's the difference between *carpe diem* and *quid pro quo?*" Lee asked, showing off his scant knowledge of Latin.

Tomás looked at him.

"It's the difference between life and death," he said quietly.

PART IV

38

The sky was pleated and gray as Margaret drove the Buick east that morning in the direction of Annapolis, leaving the formal white architecture of the Capitol behind, with its domes and spires and arpeggios of curved windows.

They followed the Capital Beltway toward US 50, which would take them past Baltimore and across the Bay Bridge, eventually depositing them into Ocean City, Maryland. Tomás held the map on his lap, charged with the job of navigating the 150-mile distance, but he was too anxious to be of use and soon handed it over to Lee in back. Margaret maneuvered the Buick easily, coursing through the city traffic as it panned toward the highway—having abandoned her high heels for blue jeans and sneakers and a maroon sweatshirt.

Lee was bundled securely in the backseat under an avalanche of woolen blankets, doused with medicines, his throat aspirated with Vicks. On the seat beside him, two bottles of Hires root beer jostled freely, next to a jumbo box of Saltines. Silently he was praying to the god of lost families—whomever that might be—that they would not only find Daniel, but Sofia and the child. That Violeta might still be alive. That somehow Tomás would walk away happy.

He opened his notebook and began an overdue entry to Dr. Bream.

"You okay back there, Lee?" Margaret called out after a little while, as telephone poles whizzed by in imitation of trees.

"Who me?" Lee answered, not taking the time to look up. "Nothing better than a road trip where I can count cars in the breakdown lane and fields full of cows."

He was trying to make her laugh, but he was also trying to make up for lost time by attempting to write another entry to

Bream. He hadn't written anything since the trip to Gettysburg. He held the notebook in his lap, trying to recall everything that had happened during the days they were away from home, everything from Capitol Hill to Gettysburg to Philadelphia— from the taxi ride that took them to the outskirts of town the day they arrived, to Tomás's rendezvous with Martin Llosa, to Alicia and all the rest. But what he couldn't begin to describe was how he felt about his new friends, particularly Margaret, whom they would have to say good-bye to in only two days. Cass would be glad to see them and they'd have to confess everything. He knew she'd be mad at Tomás and disappointed with him. He wondered how Patrick would behave on Thanksgiving with the turkey on the chopping block. Last year he had climbed up onto the table, taken one sniff of the rigor-mortic bird, and disappeared under the couch for the day.

Toward Easton, Margaret shifted gears and leaned into the straightaway, following the curve of the highway as it glanced sideways past broken guardrails and dented hubcaps. The nearby Chesapeake appeared sunken and blue.

Next to Margaret, Tomás was going crazy, unable to sit still or believe they might meet his family after all this time. His nerve endings were on fire. The idea of being disappointed, of this being a wild goose chase, of the child not being his, and of Violeta gone filled him. Every part of him was fighting itself. Margaret looked over and touched his shoulder but didn't say a word.

✥

Nearly two hours later, 130 miles dissolved into the east, and the land began to drop, unraveling toward the sea.

"Not far now," Margaret said. "A stone's throw."

The road grew narrower, the traffic single-file, as they passed small wooden houses decorated with sand dollars and shells. The soil along the roadside increasingly mixed with sand, the scrub trees dwarfed. They passed the tiny town of Salisbury, which sat like a chiseled emerald brooch on a peninsula of land, push-pinned with fishing shacks and boats at anchor, and was just as quickly gone. Then a green-and-white flash of a municipal sign announced Ocean City ahead.

Lee sat up and closed his notebook. He blew his nose into a rag, cracker crumbs tar-papered to his teeth, and grinned with satisfaction. "Are we almost there?" he asked, feeling a jiggle in his pants. "I hate to tell you, but I need to pee."

"Almost," Margaret called back to him, feeling unnaturally calm and relaxed. "I wouldn't mind getting out of the car myself," she said, "to stretch my legs and get a sandwich."

They finally crossed the bridge linking land to sea, which gave a full view of a series of tiny canals and waterways, the narrow, striped coves steeped in marlin and oysters, in plain view of the larger Wight Inlet. A series of tiny islands, some of their waters home to a single fish, were lost between houses fitted with individual docks and skiffs at anchor. Then the Atlantic itself stretched as wide and gray as the eye could see, wallpapered to the wind in a single glimpse. No horizon to speak of in the distant fog.

Margaret pulled into the beach parking lot, lined with empty spaces in the off-season, and killed the engine. A public bathhouse and toilet yards away, behind abandoned picnic tables and a boarded-up life guard's shack closed till June. It was too cold for swimming, but the sun was shining. A blue-and-white coast guard flag buckled above them in the wind.

"Look," Lee said, spying a brown pelican basking idly on a wave, seemingly for the pleasure of its own company. "What is it?" he said.

"Don't tell me you've never seen the ocean," Margaret said. "Or fishermen?" She pointed to three men with reels and rubber waders spaced along the jetty. "C'mon." Margaret opened Lee's car door and took him by the elbow. "I'll take you to pee, then we'll find something to eat."

They could feel the sun on their backs, could smell the salt air, and hear waves crashing on the shore like a smattering of distant voices.

"What about Tomás?" Lee said, pulling on her arm.

"I Just need a few minutes to stretch my legs," Tomás said, yawning, but not yet opening his door. "I'll catch up in a few minutes."

The ocean was a gift Lee was excited to give Tomás. Benjamin Franklin had crossed the Atlantic eight times in his lifetime, his first voyage at eighteen, his last at seventy-nine.

"Well, don't wait too long, Tomás. Aren't you excited?"

"Don't worry about him," Margaret interrupted. "He's slow as a dinosaur. We might have to light a fire under his butt if he doesn't start moving soon. All this anticipation is too much for one day. If I were him, I'd probably be just as nervous. I'll take you to the bathroom, and when we get back we'll drag him up. It's already lunchtime."

Despite it being November, it was nearly sixty degrees. They took off their shoes and began to cross the cold sand in their bare feet.

"Just think, they're here somewhere," Lee said, looking back across his shoulder in the direction of the boardwalk.

They had been so busy working to help Tomás, she hadn't been able to concentrate on Lee. Margaret stopped to really look at him, at his pale eyes and fading face, realizing how things were quickly fitting into place. It was because of Lee they had come this far. She hugged him to her waist. "You're the reason Tomás has this chance," she said. "He might never admit it, he might not even know how to thank you, he's so terrible with words," she said. "But you've been an amazing friend to him. We could never have gotten this far without you."

"They don't even know we've come," Lee continued. "Just think, they're here somewhere. Somewhere close. And the baby …I wonder who she looks like, Violeta or Tomás? Do you think she has hair?"

"Well, she's got to be at least three by now," Margaret said. "So it's likely she has hair, though I can't say how much. I hope we find them as much as you do, and if we don't, well, we'll have to accept that, too, and go home and know we had the guts to try. At least Tomás will know that much."

❦

Ocean City, Maryland, was a good place to disappear.

As soon as they were gone, Tomás got out of the car and leaned against the door for balance. He needed to have this time alone in order to face the possibility of disappointment. Across from the parking lot, toward the ocean, the sun shone in horizontal lines across the breaking waves, momentarily blinding him. He shielded his eyes and looked across the street in the opposite direction along the boardwalk, knowing that's where they'd find the carousel.

The boardwalk itself appeared Pleistocene gray and frayed in places, its worn planks resembling the baleen of whales. Its amusements shadowboxed with the better part of one hundred years, Trimper's being built in 1902.

Most of the shops were lashed down for a storm, the open-air cotton-candy and fried-dough concessions, the games sealed tight with clown faces and bits of gum and saltwater taffy. At the far end, distilled to gray, he could see the huge sign that said Trimper's in red-painted letters surrounded by neon, and below that the carousel, where a horse's painted wooden mane peeked through a window.

"Like a bad dream," Tomás said aloud. And he remembered briefly the members of Patas Arriba, the youth circus, and what it had cost him to find himself here.

By the time Margaret and Lee returned, Tomás was standing outside the car breathing in the salt air.

"Tomás," Lee exclaimed, breaking free of her. "We made it! We're here. Aren't you glad?"

"*Sí*, I had a good rest and now I'm ready for anything," he said, lifting Lee up onto his shoulders.

"I see a Ferris wheel," Lee cried out. "And the carousel too," he said, cupping his hand around his eyes, "where Daniel probably works."

"Okay, first we'll eat," Margaret said. She handed Tomás a po' boy sandwich of fried oysters wrapped in newspaper, some fries drenched in vinegar and catsup, and a bottle of Coca-Cola, and they sat on one of the picnic benches and ate immediately.

"Nothing like the sea air to make you hungry," Margaret said.

"I've never had oysters before," Lee said, prying at his sandwich curiously. "I'm not even sure what one looks like in its shell."

"Messy and gooey," Tomás described, as he finished his off and washed it down with cola. "Okay, let's go," he said.

They crossed back to the car and unpacked Lee's stroller from the trunk, under protest. "You know I don't need this," Lee said, angrily, sliding in. "You know this is for babies."

"Maybe so," Tomás replied, trying to make light of it, "but a man of your stature deserves special attention." He couldn't help noticing the gaunt grooves in Lee's temporal lobes, which dimpled his skull and made him look more vulnerable.

"Whoever the original Trimper was, he must be pretty rich by now," Lee said, looking up as he glided across the concrete sidewalk and up a shallow ramp to the other side of the road. "He must have had all the money and candy he could want. He must have really spoiled his children."

The boardwalk appeared nearly deserted—the summer population extinct. It extended for nearly half a mile, in some places the concessions were built up two stories tall. They could hear the thin, pressed sounds of merry-go-round music up ahead. They began to make their way slowly toward it. It was rough going with the stroller. Still more stalls along the promenade were boarded up and battened down for the winter. Over the years, tidal waves had occasionally overcome the retaining wall. But in November, in Maryland, it was anybody's game, and it was still possible to get a seventy-degree day and a slice of summer.

Tomás could see that the majority of the rides along the midway were based on the old-fashioned work of simple machinery—pulleys and levers and gears—and had seen better days. The ceramic Mixing Bowl ride appeared faded and chipped, the painted carriages of the Scrambler ordinary at a standstill, the Fun House a beleaguered tunnel without doors. They stopped to peer inside one of the covered wooden buildings to see the penny-ante arcade vending machines out of order. Frozen in time was the Atlantic movie theatre, its marquee plastered with the faces of Julie Andrews and Christopher Plummer, where *The Sound of Music* had been replayed for more than a decade.

"Do you think Daniel is working today, Margaret?" Lee asked.

So far, the boardwalk had proven to be somewhat of a disappointment, which was not what he'd imagined at all.

"Good chance," Margaret said, patting Lee's small head, where he sat protected from the elements in windbreaker and sunglasses. "We'll know soon enough."

39

They had reached the end of the boardwalk, where the land fell abruptly to the sea. A tall gray and white lighthouse, the color of a seagull at rest, stood valiantly across the bay on a lone peninsula, witness to those both lost and found.

Yards ahead, a faint up-and-down music was becoming louder, emanating from the rustic wooden building that housed the carousel. In towering letters, the name Trimper's Amusements swayed above them in a building three quarters of a century old, housing the nostalgic centerpiece of summer—its original forty-five animals, three chariots, and one rocking chair, once powered by steam.

But upon entering, it was not at all what Tomás had expected. Inside the temporary pine structure, the entire carousel had been disassembled and was lying in pieces. Absent of all color and stripped down to gears, the central cylinder broken down like the eye of a storm—the gasket and dispensing wheel dismantled and spread out on drop cloths along a sawdust floor.

The detached torsos of wooden horses were propped up on tables. Without manes or tails, their naked trunks in various states of disrepair, they were relieved of their glass eyes and gilt edges. Not just horses—but the inside-out souls of zebras, and giraffes, and elephants—the second skins of their saddles and bridlery draped over rustic sawhorses like retired suits of armor.

On the opposite wall, filtered sunlight coming off the bay shone through a dusty glass window, like light through a vast keyhole. But a real horse, Lee knew, has 205 bones, 10 in each ear alone. And who knows how many muscles.

They followed the pungent smells of cut wood and leather into a larger workroom where a makeshift lamp hung by a chain from the central support beam of the ceiling, beneath which a lone craftsman was working. He had his back to them, but they could hear the repetitive blows of a rubber mallet striking wood.

They moved toward the sound, Tomás in front, leading the way. For once Lee didn't speak up or complain or cite any anecdotes from Ben Franklin. Margaret squeezed his hand tightly, sensing that his heart was racing faster than he could maintain, and felt subconsciously for the small bulge in her hip pocket where at the last minute she had stashed Sofia's letter to her parents, proof that Maria Teresa wasn't theirs.

Tomás's heart beat like a drum as he involuntarily reached for his worst moment. After they had applied electricity to his testicles and to his gums, and had delivered him unconscious to the cement floor of his cell, slowly, day by day, he came to understand that his life was over. Months passed, then a year, then more. And then just as abruptly, the beatings stopped, and they had allowed him enough nourishment to recover his muscles. But by that point the meaning of his life had vanished, his body a leftover suit of skin like a valise or a sofa.

He trembled now, unable to stop his brain from maneuvering. It would take all of his courage to meet his past face-to-face. The screen door behind them banged shut, and he looked backward involuntarily toward the sea to where the wind blew across the ocean, delivering low tide. The exposed flats mottled like human footprints, leaving behind what it couldn't carry—shells and seaweed and tumbled rocks.

The odor of glue reached him first, the smell prying at his nostrils, then the rectangle of the workroom that had been transformed into an artist's studio. A butcher-block table balanced evenly on sawhorses, upon which several glass jars of acrylic paint shimmered, translucent in jewel tones, a wall of handheld carving tools resembling surgeon's scalpels, and sheets of gold foil for embossing. On another wall, there was a tableau of illustrated horses, labeled in Latin and dating back to carousel horses of eleventh-century Europe. Of the three categories of horses—the stander, the jumper, and the prancer—only the jumper was suspended on a pole.

Bringing the carousel back to its original beauty required the sensibility of an artist, not a carpenter.

Tomás could see Daniel leaning over his work, his head bowed, evenly applying pressure with which to shape the animal's fetlock, as if feeling his way blind.

As Daniel worked, it struck him as amusing that within the trade of carousel restoration, the body of an unfinished horse was known as a *coffin*. If it had been a real horse, he would have been able to feel its moist breath on the back of his neck, snorting as he reached to pat its flank or stroke the coarse wiry strands of its tail. But as it was, he was used to the ways of inanimate objects. In their own way, they talked to him.

As he worked, pale, thin slivers of pine curled down roughly to the floor, forming a tidy pile like something a spider might deign to live in for the better part of a day. The raw smell of wood, mixed with sap, was nearly intoxicating, shaved clean as a human bone and the color of marrow.

Daniel put the tool down, satisfied, and reached for a square of sandpaper to begin to smooth away the roughness. His biceps were lean, his forearms browned-over from what remained of summer. Working alone, he was often given to his imagination and could get lost in his thoughts for the better part of a day.

He leaned the horse's body on its side and set down the chisel on a sheet of leather, its edges curled thin as paper, careful to wipe the blade clean.

He stood up, removing his safety glasses, and dusted off his hands on his thighs as he turned around—his hip banging into the edge of the wooden table that held the bandsaw—then saw the three strangers standing before him.

"I'm afraid we're closed for the season," he said dryly. "Off-limits to visitors. Please, you'll have to move along now."

"We're visiting from DC and were hoping to get a glimpse of the carousel," Tomás said.

Lee stood up in his stroller to get a better look. He couldn't help but gasp out loud when he noticed the silver seahorse catch the light from the leather thong around Daniel's neck. *Bingo,* he thought to himself. *Bull's-eye.*

"We won't re-open until May," Daniel said, his body calming from his initial fright. "Restoring the horses to their original magnificence is a big job. Should be up and running come spring, if you can come back."

Tomás moved forward, feeling vaguely like a criminal, wool hat pulled down low over his ears, his jaw shadowed roughly with two days' stubble. The exhaustion of despair filled the bags below his eyes. It was not his talent to make a good first impression. Not to a crow or a rat—let alone anything human.

"Do you mind if we take a look, maybe watch you for a few minutes?" he said, his attempt at hiding his South American accent beginning to falter.

"Lee, especially, will be disappointed," Margaret said, interrupting Tomás. She could see something shift in Daniel when Tomás spoke. "We're from Buenos Aires, a long way. Not Lee," she said gesturing towards him. "He's more like our borrowed son."

Perhaps Sofia had been right, thought Daniel. Perhaps they were not safe anywhere. A feeling of panic began to circle his intestines. There was something familiar in Tomás's face, a light in his eyes and cleft in his chin that matched those of his daughter. In the next room, under a navy quilt covered with neon-yellow moons and stars, their child was sleeping on a makeshift cot. Sofia, only a small distance away, had gone to get coffee for the two of them.

A stripe of blue sea filtered through the open window behind where Tomás was standing, so serene it made Daniel not want to have to face the possibility that these Argentinian co-patriots were here for his child. They had made a life here. They had disappeared for all practical purposes, living beneath the radar.

Daniel hoped Sofia would linger and make small talk with the clerk long enough so he could get rid of them before she returned. For a mad moment, he entertained the notion of killing them, hurling their bodies into the sea, before they could ever discover the truth and find Maria Teresa.

He thought of the Trojan horse, how it was best to befriend your enemy. To stand your ground next to them in broad daylight. He decided not to panic, but to work to befriend the child.

"Hey there," Daniel said, leaning down. "What's your name?"

Lee answered quickly, trying to control his pitch, which was high and thin and vibrating with excitement. "I should tell you right away that I'm older than I look, you don't need to treat me like a baby. It's called Hutchinson-Gilford," he said, lowering his voice to an exaggerated whisper. "Long story."

"Oh, I see," Daniel said, stepping back a little.

"Nice to meet you all, but I don't work well with an audience, unfortunately," Daniel said, turning to get back to work somewhat abruptly. "I've got some cleaning up to do before I can quit for the day. You'll excuse me, won't you? Come back in the spring, I'll give you a tour myself."

"We're just here for the day," Margaret broke in quickly, trailing a few steps behind him, trying to keep the conversation going. "If you don't mind, before we go, suggesting some ideas for what to do with children, something to do with Lee this afternoon before we go home."

"Not too many visitors from Argentina come all the way to Ocean City," Daniel said then, deciding to confront them. "Why here, and not Atlantic City? Or Asbury Park? Just curious."

"We read about Trimper's in the newspaper," Margaret said. "It's famous. Lee's thirteen and has never been on a carousel. He's going home to his family in New Jersey in a day or so. We thought he should give it a try."

"My parents didn't take me to such things in Buenos Aires either, when I was a child," Tomás said. "Buenos Aires these days is not exactly just the home of the tango." He picked up a metal carving tool that had fallen to the floor and set it on Daniel's work table.

"I hear there're many sad stories there. My wife," Daniel said hesitantly, looking into the distance, "lived there for a while, and there were many unhappy times, families deceived, lives ruined." Daniel bowed his head. "We are largely impotent, right? Governments like the Argentinian one controlled everything. But I'm speaking to those who already understand this, correct?"

"*Sí.*" Tomás spoke quickly, lapsing into Spanish. "There were many *desaparecidos*. Many disappeared. Many of us, including myself," he dragged out the words for emphasis, "lost members of our families."

"I'm sorry to hear that," Daniel said, squaring his weight evenly. "One's family is like a lock and key on the universe. You have to protect it at all costs."

The air in the workroom was warm and stuffy. Daniel watched as Tomás walked to the open window overlooking the bay, removed his wool hat, and stuffed it into his jacket pocket, revealing to all his profile as he glanced sideways across the room in the direction of the broken horses—the slant view of his face taking on a deeper shade of sadness. Then he turned to look at them. His eyes were familiar, more alike than different, like hers in late afternoon light as they often strolled across the jetty, hand in hand, to watch the fishermen reeling in their catch. The cleft in his cheek was masked by five o'clock shadow, but still the same parted nimbus. But above all, the unmistakable tenor of feeling come alive in his eyes, which had not existed anywhere else in the world apart from his daughter's face until this very moment, and which now filled the room with its ungodly explanation. And with that, the answer to the question that had eluded Daniel and Sofia both, as Maria Teresa had learned to walk and talk and face the world: a mirror image of the same melancholy look so unmistakably odd in the face of a child.

Daniel stood, feeling the natural world turn to sand at his feet. The hair stood up along his arms. He searched for air in its purest form—and wished to hell this day had never come.

Lee's mind was turning like crazy. No amount of detective work from the FBI or Superman could have gotten them to Daniel and Sofia and the baby. He suddenly missed Cass uncontrollably. He thought of Hansel and Gretel leaving a trail of breadcrumbs, wanting to be found. Why did the world need fairy tales, he wondered, if they only made you feel lonely?

"Things to do with children," Daniel repeated. As long as Tomás had never seen Maria Teresa, he could never be sure. He had to get them out of here as quickly as possible.

"Hmm." He squatted down to think, leaning against the wooden doorframe, feeling the cavity in his chest where the blow had been delivered, his breath pumping like crazy. Tomás was easily three inches taller and forty pounds heavier. He could lose it quickly, and go into a rage against them. He leaned against the raw pine boards, cupped his hands around his mouth, concentrating on how to keep Maria Teresa hidden until he could get them out of there.

Tomás stood, hands behind his back, assessing Daniel brusquely as he appeared to search for ideas, and he couldn't help but conclude that he looked like a boy who had stubbornly refused to become a man and was still guarding early innocence.

"There's a ton of things to do here even in the off-season," Daniel volunteered at last, coming to stand. "A boat trip, a visit to the playground, a stop at the maritime museum, and, at the very least, *ice cream,*" he said, licking his lips to get Lee's attention. "If you go around the corner by the harbor you'll see Christina's," he said, motioning to the right. "Best there is. I'd go for the mint chip myself. I don't think they stay open too late in the afternoon. I'd hurry, if I were you."

40

But at that moment Sofia was unlocking the car door and returning from her trip to the market. She came in quietly, sawdust muffling the scrape of her shoes. But Diego, their large yellow Lab, came running in ahead with his loud uncontrollable bark.

They all turned to look at Sofia.

"*Diego, ven acá,* come here!" she chided, trying to pull him from the sawdust and tumult of horses. Then, as she saw they had guests, she apologized. "I'm so sorry," she said, somewhat bewildered by the group of them. "*Diego, ven acá,*" she said again. But the dog ignored her and dutifully padded toward the back room where Maria Teresa slept peacefully.

"Daniel, you didn't tell me you were expecting company," Sofia said, shaking her finger and smoothing her damp hair. She was the face in the wedding announcement photograph. Tomás knew it at once. Four years older now, but there was no mistaking it. A thousand times in Tomás's imagination their meetings amounted to nothing more than a lifeless pantomime in which no one breathed and the world fell apart brick by brick. But here in the flesh, Sofia's face was radiant, unsuspecting, washed over by mist skimmed off the surface of the ocean. Tomás's mind played tricks on him. He immediately saw her abstracted to the shape of his missing wife, as if Violeta had been momentarily resurrected and had walked into the room with the same benign pleasantries—the long legs and dark hair—the woman for whom he had pawned his past, present, and future, all gone.

"This is my wife, Sofia." Daniel stepped forward to relieve her of the cardboard tray of espressos and kiss her cheek. They could see that her body was in bloom with another child, a charcoal-gray sweater buttoned high over her pale-pink dress, painted with a mixture of white lotus and Chinese pagodas.

Her long dark hair hung loose around her shoulders, her skin slightly olive, her cheeks flushed. Around her neck, a simple gold chain betrayed her faith, in the shape of a tiny hammered cross.

"Hello," Sofia said, at ease, with no inkling of danger. "I'm sorry if we're interrupting anything. Did you come to see the carousel?" she continued, turning toward the guests. "Unfortunately, it's closed down for now, but we still sometimes have visitors. My husband is a master craftsman, but he is very slow. He is a perfectionist, and he is doing such a great job, the only problem is that it's going to take forever," she said, joking. "We eat, sleep, and dream these horses. My daughter," she confided, "loves them, though she is too little to ride them alone." Then, turning to Daniel: "*¿Está bien?* Is she still napping?"

At that moment Daniel gave her a dark look, as if to urgently silence her, but it was too late, the final question in their minds now answered, out in the open. Sofia faltered, her mouth parted in mid-sentence, picking up his cue and suddenly afraid of what she might have done.

Daniel moved to stand beside her and put his arm around her shoulder.

"These people are visiting from Buenos Aires," he said. "Maybe you know people in common. I wonder, but of course it's such a large city." His voice trailed off, trying to tell Sofia to be careful. "But it is always possible."

At the mention of Buenos Aires, Sofia's chin dropped, her heart began to pound. She involuntarily put her hand on her belly and shifted her eyes to Daniel only, whose face shared her fear.

Then she regarded the strangers, who looked neither dangerous nor innocent, but guilty with hidden knowledge. One could never be sure. Her parents had sat comfortably in their own living room for years, unsuspecting, just minutes before Videla's men had stormed through the door.

For those first few months after she had returned to the States, they had lived in constant fear of retaliation. Until Daniel was offered the job in Ocean City, and she got the brilliant idea to ironically make themselves disappear. Sofia took a leave of absence from her job and decided she would try to write a book about Oncidium orchids, also known as dancing ladies, and illustrate it herself, plant a garden. She had always loved the sky along the shore that was painted blue and white—two colors that she knew, like the backdrop to Mount Olympus, cleansed the world.

Maria Teresa was sleeping in the next room, her small head of dark curls given over to a world within a world. Sofia could smuggle her out the back door if necessary, excusing herself politely to walk Diego.

But it was all meant to unravel differently.

In the back room, Maria Teresa, her scalp damp from turning restlessly in her sleep, overheard voices and sat up and felt alone. She stood up in her socks on the sawdust floor, which seemed to her like dry flakes of fallen snow. She tiptoed in her stocking feet to eavesdrop on the other room, excited by the company of Diego at her side. She ran to them now, her thumb caught in her mouth, still clinging with her other hand to the muslin horse with Xs for eyes that Sofia had sewn for her and stuffed with raw cotton.

Coming into the workroom, Maria Teresa found them all assembled. She reached immediately for her mother's arms, her body smelling of sweat and milk and life in its fullest form.

"*Tú mi amor*, my sweetheart," Sofia cried, hugging her with all her might. "*Mi pequeña!* My little one. *¿Fue Diego quien te despertó?* Was it Diego who woke you?"

His daughter's arms encircled Sofia with such certainty, Tomás was convinced Sofia was the only mother the girl had ever known. He couldn't resist the temptation to come closer, to see Maria Teresa in the light. Bringing with him as he did the natural phenomenon of a perfect storm.

It was when he saw the child's face that Sofia saw *his* also. Perhaps for the first time—the exchange was complete. Standing side by side, their two shapes overlapping, though disproportionate in size. Sofia was startled by the eruption of her own tears. She had known her daughter's face better than anyone's: the shade of her eyes, the color as it strayed and delivered on every possible emotion.

Sofia was having the overwhelming sensation that for the first time their lives were real. How many nights had she lain awake trying to picture them, the ones who had given Maria Teresa life? And at what price? How many times had she imagined the dreadful birthing room, a woman like herself hollowed out and grieving, bereft of the most important being to her on Earth. And the father, if he were anything like Daniel, would have gone crazy from longing. She understood instantly that their good fortune had come at the cost of Violeta's and Tomás's loss. She looked at Tomás and put her hand to her mouth.

Maria Teresa and Lee had joined forces on the floor to explore Diego's belly. The big beast lay flat on his back, flattened as a rug, begging to be loved and petted, his pink tongue hanging lopsided out of the side of his mouth. Lee took off his hat, becoming bald. Maria Teresa touched Lee's naked skull, her fat pink hand exploring him gently. Then, looking up wide-eyed, she asked the obvious question: "Baby?"

"No," Lee answered, pointing at Sofia's pregnant belly. "I think the only baby around here is in there."

And now it was Tomás's turn. He kneeled down to join them. Within inches of Maria Teresa's small, soft cheek, he could see that her gray eyes, tinged with brown, were unavoidably his, Her small mouth ribbed in a duplicate latticed pattern. Her chin tilted in both knowing and uncertainty.

Daniel stooped down protectively and whisked her high in the air, held her, and kissed her. "My sweetheart, darling girl," he said fiercely, looking directly into her eyes. "My Maria Teresa."

Tomás watched as his daughter was turned upside down, then swung around and deposited in the leather saddle of one of the near-finished ponies, the blunt tip of its tail missing as though bitten off by a wild animal.

"She has your eyes," Lee cried out. "She has your chin. Don't you see it, Margaret?"

Daniel turned up the portable boom box, making the carousel music louder, the scratched recording of "Tinker Polka" coming off the Wurlitzer.

"You know, don't you?" Tomás said to Daniel. "You know why we've come. She's my daughter; we've been searching for her for months. I've come to take her back with me. I have proof." He took out the letter that Alicia had rescued. "It's all here. You and your wife have stolen her. I don't know how, but isn't it clear? After she was born, my wife, Violeta, was tortured by Videla's men, and thrown into the sea like garbage. How can you stand there calmly—you and your wife—knowing what we've been through, and still try to hide the truth about my child?"

Daniel looked at him like a drowning man. All was at risk, worse than he could have imagined.

"All she knows is us," Daniel broke in, beginning to stammer. "We're her world, and she's ours. And if Sofia hadn't rescued her, something worse might have happened. If I could turn the clock backward so none of it would have happened to you and to your wife," he said, opening his palms, "I would have done everything in my power. Surely you can see we're a family now. We're prepared to fight for her, we both are," he said, nodding to include Sofia, who had come forward.

"We've been together every day since I brought her home," Sofia began. "I know you haven't had a chance to be her father, to love her the way it should have been, and that isn't fair. But every single inch of her is alive and well because we've cared for her as our own."

"Mama." Maria Teresa ran to her now, slipping on a small pile of sawdust on the floor. Sofia reached for her, hugged her.

"And now she's about to be a big sister," Sofia added. "You can't take her. It's too late. She's ours. A judge would side with us and not you. I pray you'll find another way to have a family someday."

"Actually, I'm not so sure Tomás would lose in a court battle," Margaret stepped in. "Anyone can see she's his daughter, we'll get a blood test to prove it. Tomás has rights too."

To have come all this way in search of her had meant everything. Day after day, she was all he had thought about. Now he had confirmed her existence in the world. He knew she was safe. Perhaps, he thought, that should have been enough.

And yet it all came crashing down. It would be no use. He could imagine endless meetings with lawyers asking for money he didn't have. Strangers trying to make her understand that he was her real father would confuse her, crush her. He could try to grab her now by force and make a run for it with Lee, try to keep on going without looking back. But what would that accomplish?

Tomás knew Daniel and Sofia were right. His head began to throb in the dim light of the workroom.

"The truth is, this is what will happen," said Daniel. "Court dates, endless bills, and a child who was once happy becoming depressed and confused and still wanting the only parents she had ever known. If I were in your position," said Daniel, "I would be knocking down doors trying to find the people responsible. But I can tell you already, it won't get you anywhere. The war has ended in Argentina, and the real criminals have gone underground. And very soon we'll be welcoming another child," he said, glancing in the direction of Sofia and Margaret.

"We know how much you've suffered, Tomás. Your wife also," said Daniel. "We've been wrestling with those thoughts since the beginning, knowing that our good fortune was at the cost of someone else's terrible loss. And we've had to struggle in our own way to keep the ghosts of that time out of our lives. Videla had Sofia's parents killed when he found out Sofia's father was embezzling money from illegal adoptions. As luck would have it, Sofia and Maria Teresa were out walking only a block from the house when the soldiers came for her parents. If not for that bit of luck, we would never have Maria Teresa. As far as I'm concerned, she'll never know what happened."

"Daddy," Maria Teresa called out, as the music neared an end, and both Daniel and Tomás turned in her direction.

❧

Tomás looked around the sawdust-covered room. The wild-eyed carousel horses cast their frenzied stares into the shadows, mute except for the promise of being put back together.

It was how Daniel held her that made him sure. That, and how he could see they were a family.

She was loved.

Not just by one, but by both of them, and soon to be loved, too, by the baby. Tomás's certainty grew from all his lost days, in which despair had arrested him and picked him clean to the bone.

He closed his eyes and replayed the image he had created in his mind over and over: *A thousand dreams away, his family lived, whole, together underwater in a place where it was safe to breathe, arms wide and flooded with affection. The three of them undivided, sharing the same common connection. If the world had happened differently, not once, but twice.*

"You're a lucky family," Tomás said then, looking first at Daniel and then Sofia. "Anyone can see that. You're very lucky. Though I can hardly think of leaving her here alone with you, either. And yet I don't know what choice I have."

"We had no way of knowing that anyone in her family was still alive," Sofia said. "We did our best to take care of her. You can still be part of her life if you give us a chance. We can find a way."

Tomás closed his eyes and felt a tremendous wash of devastation swell over him, having lost what he had come for.

Lee smiled weakly up at Tomás, not having been able to hear any of their conversation but sensing something was terribly wrong. They had found Maria Teresa, they had solved the mystery, and yet from what it looked like, she wasn't coming with them. He didn't understand what the problem was.

"Isn't she coming with us, Tomás?" Lee asked, feeling helpless to make it happen. "You need to fight for her," he said. "Please, Tomás, don't do what my father did, don't leave her behind. She'll hate you for it later."

"Daniel and Sofia love Maria Teresa the way Cass loves you,"

Tomás said. "At least we know where she is. I need to consult an attorney and find out what my legal rights are."

∽

On the ride home, Margaret drove. The full moon followed them, the sky laden with longing and the distant reach of stars.

"Why didn't Maria Teresa come with us, Tomás?" Lee asked again from the backseat, his face buried in tears. "She's your daughter, isn't she? How could you do this, how could you leave her behind?"

"Sometimes," Tomás said, "you have to do the wrong thing for the right reasons. Sometimes you can't bring back what's gone. No matter how much you want it or miss it or think it's the way it should be."

41

It was November 22nd, and Thanksgiving morning. Lee woke out of a watery dream in which he was piloting a plane into enemy territory. His feet were cold, and he sat up instantly. It was twenty years to the day since president John F. Kennedy had been assassinated in Dallas, Texas—shot from a sixth-story perch in the Texas School Book Depository by a common man named Lee Harvey Oswald. In Arlington National Cemetery the flag of the nation's capital was hung at half-mast—the boundless lit flame facing off against eternity. Kennedy's death had brought America to its knees.

He looked out the window past the fire escape from Margaret's bedroom and was surprised to see a light dusting of snow covering the sidewalk. Two hundred miles northeast in the Garden State he knew Cass was awake and powering up the oven, putting together the makings of a humble feast, waiting for them in jeans and sneakers. He and Tomás would say goodbye to Margaret and be on their way.

He sorted the few remaining possessions into his backpack, preparing to head home—his keys and compass, and the journal for Dr. Bream with his sketches of Cocoa. He stood in the kitchen, glazed over and reeling, counting the artifacts of their recent days. The small plastic snow globe of the Capitol sat quietly on the mantel, and in his hip pocket, was the panda keychain from the National Zoo, both of which had served to bring them together.

Deep in his heart he missed Kira, knowing things would never be the same. Did he need to stand on the equator, looking sideways for his shadow, in order to know what direction loss would assume?

Lee had found someone new to love, despite the fact that Maria Teresa had not come with them. He was angry at Tomás for leaving her behind. The wheels of his mind were turning with her. Maria Teresa—aloft and alive—had ignited a field of fireworks in his brain. He wondered feebly if one day he might come back and visit her with Tomás and make a better impression on Sofia and Daniel, meet the new baby, bring her a stuffed giraffe, that alone would be worth the trip.

But for now, he thought, tightening the ripcord on his backpack and cinching the clasp, Cass was eagerly awaiting them with plans of her own—despite everything new he had become a part of. He was anxious to tell her all about it. Except for the lies, those would be up to Tomás to explain.

✍

Margaret had insisted on driving them to the airport for the seven-thirty a.m. flight to Newark.

"Are you kidding?" she'd said. "It's part of my job."

The old Buick stood idling against the sidewalk, Margaret behind the wheel, warming the engine against a sudden snow squall. They had stepped out of the apartment building and been surprised by it, the ground swirled with white, the frigid air. Black lines of telephone wires were studded with iridescent crows, alighting in trills. A snowplow rumbled down Connecticut Avenue, uprooting debris like corn ripped from fields. It wasn't even six o' clock, the city already ringed with exhaust, smells of coffee and French toast rising off the stoves of all-night diners.

Lee tried to take it all in. He stood outside on the frozen walk waiting for Tomás, who had run back upstairs, having forgotten his keys.

In minutes, Tomás opened the third-floor window and waved down to them, showing his keys. The scent of the snow had a particular swell, the way you could feel the moist air of the ocean peel off a jetty. The soft white powder sifted cleanly over the contours of street lamps and railings and the oblique shapes of trash cans strewn haphazardly in alleyways. Tomás had needed to bear witness to his own resolve, knowing he had chosen to leave Maria Teresa behind, knowing they had settled what they had come for, finally.

Tomás stood alone in the empty apartment, searching for words that could convince him of his existence. To be alive in the human world—he measured quickly—meant buying into its deals, sleeping in beds, eating food from bowls. He was the husk of a man in a body in which he all too often felt scaled back to his skeleton. He realized now as the slow motion of Lee's small, dwarfed body came gradually into focus, just what it was that connected them. No matter that it was fate that had granted them permission. They had come to the same place, though by different means. If ever there was a natural son who belonged to a natural father, Tomás concluded with sudden intimacy, it was the two of them.

"C'mon, Tomás," Lee called up, cupping his hands into the shape of a megaphone. He pointed to his wristwatch exaggeratedly. "Time waits for no one," he called up playfully. It was as close to any aphorism Ben Franklin might have said, though Lee knew full well the credit belonged to an unknown ancient Greek. "Hurry, Tomás," Lee called again, his voice cracking, as he began to realize they could actually miss their flight. "Cass is making apple pie! Do you know what that means?" he asked urgently. "Margaret's getting mad. Hurry up, she'll leave us behind."

Lee had borrowed Margaret's chunky red-and-white-striped hat and knitted scarf from the hallway closet, having outfitted himself unintentionally like an elf. He had wisely put on the cowboy boots at the last minute to cope with the sudden change in the weather. His footprints now punctuated like tiny bite marks in the snow, leaving behind a mystery for sparrows to wade in.

"Got everything." Tomás was downstairs now, relieving Lee of his backpack.

"Only took you two years," Margaret said when Tomás slid into the passenger seat beside her.

Inside, the car was wildly overheated, like a jungle cat panting.

Lee removed his hat and gloves and pressed his palms together. Margaret's face appeared oddly naked of expression, her hands bound in nefarious black leather gloves, bright-orange ceramic chili peppers dangling from her ears.

Tomás half-smiled at her apologetically.

"Sorry," he said. "Thanks for waiting. My keys must have fallen out of my pocket behind the couch when I was asleep."

Glancing back at Lee, Margaret teased, "You boys are like old ladies. The traffic will be crazy, don't forget it's a holiday, the busiest travel day of the year. The airport will be jammed. They'll have to put you in the cargo area. *Ándale* then? Finally?"

Then she steered the car away from the sidewalk, shifting in the direction of the airport with a vengeance.

42

The night before, Tomás had planned a celebration for the three of them. A guided walking tour of the monuments at night along the National Mall—the White House, the Capitol, and the Washington Monument. He had seen it in a brochure, a description that said Washington at night resembled Paris. He thought it would make a good farewell.

They had eaten dinner at home, baked chicken and rice that Margaret had prepared. Lee was excited at the prospect of going out their last night, to be sophisticated and daring and to be treated like an adult. But the truth was, he had been feeling steadily worse since Philadelphia, his intestines running interference between his stomach and his lungs. With each small bite of food, he felt worse. He pushed back his chair, leaving most of his dinner uneaten.

"I think I'd better lie down for a few minutes," he'd said, trying to hide his discomfort.

"Go ahead," Tomás had said, reading between the lines. "We won't be leaving till dark anyway."

But after Margaret and Tomás had cleared the dishes and wiped the table and come back into the living room some ten minutes later, Lee had fallen asleep on the couch with his shoes on.

It was nearly nine before Tomás carried him in the stretcher of his arms to the empty bedroom for the last time, removing his shoes and checking to see that his pulse was steady, his lungs clear. Leaving the two of them to their own devices.

The living room was dark, except for reflected light from the street lamps outlining the furniture, and the faint sounds of a television. Margaret was waiting for him on a worn leather chair, her feet up on the ottoman, having poured two glasses of vodka over ice.

"Imagine what real parents go through," Margaret breathed. She set her drink on the table and waved Tomás to the chair opposite her.

"*Gracias*," Tomás murmured, taking a sip and setting the glass down, noticing how the fading light cast deep shadows behind Margaret's eyes, aging her prematurely. The small dot of moisture clinging to the outline of her mouth, making her appear uncharacteristically still and vulnerable. The end had brought them so far from where they had started from, to this final moment alone, leaving them to reflect on how fate had seen fit to give them a second chance. When they were colleagues in Buenos Aires he knew almost nothing about her personal life, only how their egos knocked up against one another constantly, like feuding children, vying for the right to cover the meatier stories and gain the reputation of being tougher than the rest of the pack. Back then he saw Margaret as a woman attempting to do a man's job. But no more.

The war had come to them disguised as civil disobedience for which they were unprepared. To be *desaparecido*, disappeared, was almost worse than to never have existed, Tomás thought. Because it hurt so much to remember what was lost.

Margaret sat there feeling the guilt of one who had betrayed a friend against her better judgment—over things that appeared selfish but for which she'd had no choice. If the war between Videla and the common man had taught them anything, she thought, it was how to endure, but not to forgive.

Margaret lifted her glass and clinked it against his, her eyes melting under the weight of the alcohol, her thoughts drifting apart, fighting to keep her admiration for Tomás from being mistaken for anything else.

"*Está bien*," she said quietly. "Your daughter is safe, and there is some hope you can be with her again?"

"*Sí, está bien*," he said. "And also, *eso no me satisface*, not so well," he said, feeling the effects of the vodka spreading like a slow flame along the length of his spine. "I came here to find my family, to find my wife and daughter, and now I am leaving empty-handed. Though to know that Maria Teresa is safe will let me sleep at night, will let me think carefully about what to do next. I can only hope Sofia and Daniel will keep their word."

"Tomás," she said, shifting forward, "I know there'll be opportunities to visit Maria Teresa as time goes on. They're good people, Daniel and Sofia. There'll still be time for Maria Teresa to come to know you if that's what you decide. They're good people, her parents. I'm sure of it."

"*Sí*," he said, lowering his head into his hands. "But she'll never know me as her father, that opportunity is gone. Even though I walked away today, I'm not sure that's how I'll feel tomorrow."

He looked at Margaret, thinking how she had asked nothing of him, how little she revealed. He wanted to get at the truth of who she was. He wanted to ask her, *Who do you love?* And how she had come to grow so inured to the living. But he knew better. Closer inspection of her red polished lips, and the well-defended angles of her eyes, let him know that to expose her to these questions would be to put her in harm's way.

"And you," he said, lightly touching Margaret's wrist. "You can come to New York, and I'll take you to the worst neighborhoods, and you can find your stories of death and murder just the way you like it, and I'll do my best to protect you—if that's possible."

"Is it that obvious?" she smiled.

"*Sí*, all of it. You know you're on a collision course with disaster, it's only a matter of time. I'm afraid you'll be the last to know."

In between the lines, Tomás read the truth of Margaret's life: she had no man to hold her, no children for whom to brave a sense of morality, no world except the *Post*, which would pump her dry and put her out to pasture one day when she least expected it.

And yet he sensed she was the stronger of the two of them. By sheer force of will.

"Maybe now you'll think about returning to *periodismo*,

journalism," she said. "I can talk to my editor. You could start freelance and see how it feels, you could even try it from New York or New Jersey bureaus and wire it in. We won't be competing this time, I promise."

"*Sí, pero,* maybe. But still, there's something else."

"*Dime,* tell me," she said.

"There is still the question of what happened to my wife. *To Violeta.* I can't let myself see. When I try to look, I feel a numbness in my mind, no body, no face. I don't think I'll ever be able to tolerate not knowing what really happened."

"*Yo comprendo,* I understand. Some things defy the imagination," Margaret said dryly, stirring an invisible circle on the table with her fist. "It was like my parents. They could never fully explain, no matter how hard they tried, the devastation of having lost so much, no matter how well they thought they had put themselves back together. Nothing I could do was ever enough to make them remember who they were before it happened. But for you," she continued, adjusting the thin gold chain tangled around her neck, "it's enough to try to be there, to try to see. Wherever you look," she said, "Violeta will be there. I can assure you. I know," she said slowly and with great certainty, "she's never let you go."

43

They pulled up now in front of the terminal building, the ground silver-plated with slush, the concrete walk coursing with the weighted-down trappings of human pack mules, people heading home for Thanksgiving, the busiest travel day of the year. Margaret maneuvered through a sea of cars, double-parked and hovering, and found her way to the curb between a taxi and a Mercedes.

Tomás and Lee had limited themselves to carry-on luggage. Curbside check-in was relatively new. Within minutes, the line of fellow travelers grew in front of them like spontaneous generation.

"Wow," Lee said, "it's hard to believe people can get so worked up about giblets and gravy."

"I don't know how we did it," Margaret said, kneeling to put her hand on Lee's shoulder. "But we did it. Without you we would never have found Maria Teresa or managed to have such a great adventure. I'm so proud of you, Lee," she said, "so grateful." Her voice was trembling slightly as she struggled to keep it under control. She put her arms around him and was met with an odor of decay. She kissed his cheek and felt through to the bone.

Then she reached into her bag and removed the small present she had gotten as a good-bye gift. "Here, Lee," she said. "I had it made special."

Lee beamed, not knowing what to expect. He lifted the square of fabric above his head and shook it loose to find a white T-shirt inked with black letters spelling out *Agent 0013*.

"Look, Tomás!" Lee said excitedly, spinning around to show him.

"Consider it your diploma from Spy School," Margaret said, smiling. "Your honorary degree, for having graduated number-one in your class. Phi Beta Kappa-Bond in my book."

He lowered his arms and held the shirt in front of his chest, slightly embarrassed to see it was much too long. Then he looked at both of them, recalculating. "I do always get my man," he admitted proudly.

They were out of time. Tomás lifted their bags from the curb and slung them over his shoulder. "Better hurry now," he said.

Margaret knelt and hugged Lee.

"You better get going," Margaret said, eyeing the oncoming traffic, "or you'll miss your flight."

Lee's thoughts raced: *For every action there is an equal and opposite reaction. A body at rest stays at rest until it is disturbed by some other motion.* He didn't want anything to change.

And yet…to be *young* was out of the question.

He started to cry.

"Listen to me," Margaret said. "If I ever, I mean *ever,* have another mystery to solve, you're my man," she said. "I need to know I can count on you to be strong until then."

"If I ever need another good friend," Lee said to her, then stopped—not knowing how to finish the sentence.

"Never mind me," she said. "I've got work to do, and so do you. And Tomás also. You'll send me pictures of Cass and Patrick, no? And let me know how your check-up goes with Dr. Bream? And don't eat so much candy!"

Lee nodded a half-smile with bent, crooked teeth as Margaret gave him a final kiss.

It was one of the hardest things he had ever done, next to hearing the news of Kira's death and then having to endure the sadness of strangers at her funeral. Margaret had given him a lifetime inside a week, and now the porthole was closing like a softly falling waterfall. He hugged her one last time, his arms reaching only to her waist, then let her go by closing his eyes as tightly as possible, as though releasing a weightless butterfly.

⌒

Margaret hugged Tomás also. In the gray distance, she was already looking past them, already moving on. She got back into the car and slowly pulled away from the crowded airport.

Neither Tomás nor Lee said anything for a few long seconds.

"C'mon, Lee," Tomás said, taking him by the elbow. "We better find our gate."

They were airborne soon enough. The runways were cleared of melting snow, the plane full to capacity. The onboard terminology continued to impress Lee with its seaworthy vocabulary of *cabin, deck, crew.* They were seated in the exit row—Lee by the window, Tomás in the middle, flanked on his left by a heavy-set man whose shoes straddled the aisle. One false move against the exit door and Lee could send them hurtling into space like sudden astronauts, the oxygen sucked out of their faces, their bodies trailing like balloons.

It had been a much harder trip than Lee had been willing to admit. He had pushed himself in an effort to keep up, hiding his failing respiratory system from Tomás and Margaret as much as possible. But he knew that once Cass laid eyes on him, she'd know the truth.

Being up in the clouds set things temporarily adrift, leaving Lee's mind to wander. He watched a densely packed cloud formation shift abstractly from a humpback whale into a string of pearls and back again, and found himself thinking about the logic of things, and how it had become humanly possible to invent an abacus.

It would have been easy to rewrite Genesis from the Bible from the point of view of numbers, to subtract every human thing and leave Adam and Eve solely represented by odd and even integers, like two castaway numbers lounging nakedly on the number line without a care in the world. Who didn't want to hurt anyone, who wouldn't be tempted by an apple?

His idea to replace Adam and Eve with numbers worked only to a degree, Lee realized soon enough. Because the world wasn't limited to black and white. Other dimensions were possible, as were negative numbers and fractions of fractions.

Perhaps it was enough to see that not-knowing was its own answer, that good and evil existed in and of themselves and weren't necessarily connected to human actions.

But all of this distraction was just an excuse for the dreaded question that had been molting inside him for days and which now required an answer. Tomás's eyes were closed, but Lee knew he wasn't sleeping.

"Tomás," Lee said, tugging on his wrist. "Tomás," he repeated. "You'll still stay with us now, won't you, now that we're going home?"

⁓

It was a short flight. Lee's mind continued to spiral, Tomás having refused to answer. Lee knew Cass might fire Tomás on the spot once she heard the truth. He knew Tomás might choose to move to DC in order to be closer to Maria Teresa.

Stars were tiny suns, clouds a mixture of opposing gases. Orbits, elliptical. Mars drenched in a shade of red the color of rust, where oxygen was assumed to have been completely evaporated. To Lee, the facts of the world were indisputable. Time traveler that he was, stranded on the third planet from the sun.

Soon the landing gear dropped down from the hold beneath the wing, and the urban sprawl of New York City was visible in a series of tiny symmetrical Legos set in grids caulked with concrete and mud. The Statue of Liberty swimming girlishly in the harbor, then the slope of Newark cross-stitched along the bay.

Tomás had said almost nothing the whole flight home. He had kept his eyes closed but now felt the weight of Lee leaning against his shoulder.

In the beginning, when Tomás had first come to their apartment, he had only been interested in being paid cash under the table in order to get from month to month—to pay his rent, to buy a steak dinner and a bottle of scotch. If he'd had a wife, he would have gone home to her and complained about the pathetic child and his pathetic mother and the idea of humans living with a contraband pig in an apartment so close to the commuter rail you could have boarded a train at midnight in your sleep. And she would have comforted him and told him it was only temporary.

And now he was ashamed.

Lee had become his world. Together they existed on an island of letting go.

PART V

44

It had stormed in New York, too, heavier than in DC. Plows were out rearranging the white protective coloration of the snow, making Cass feel temporarily invisible as she tunneled inside the cavernous maze of Newark airport, built decades ago upon a swamp. She approached the terminal through the hectic traffic, newly electrified with holiday lights and the dolor of bells from the round red wishing pots of the Salvation Army. It was now official that, this being Thanksgiving, Christmas would shortly follow.

She scanned the front of the airport now, looking for her son as though sweeping a minefield with a Geiger counter. He would be small and sickly and hers alone; he would be loved with a fierceness that could shrink prehistory.

She had called ahead to learn the plane was on time. They had agreed to meet out front, not at the gate. The car's windshield wipers were working overtime to separate slush from ice, the airport crowded with last-minute travelers and businessmen come home to wives and families. She watched the polished black Lincoln town cars arrive in waves, their license plates stamped *Livery*.

Then she saw them. As lopsided as the legend of David and Goliath come to life, one very tall and one very small, irregularly married into a single shape. Her heart sank, realizing now that Lee was back safely, how reckless it had been to let him go.

Even from this distance, Cass sensed that something had permanently shifted. Lee looked as if he had aged a thousand years in a week—his eyes sunken into caves, his head held by tendons straining at the back of his neck. She had wanted more than anything to give him what he wanted, to make him happy—and now she began to realize just what that lapse in judgment had cost.

Despite her alarm, with one look at them standing side by side, Lee holding Tomás's hand, she could see Tomás had gained the camaraderie of her son.

"Lee," she called out. "Tomás, over here!"

She double-parked and killed the engine, got out and ran to him. He stared, blinking in the cold, his blue eyes sluggish twin lakes, his body skating toward the sound of her voice, not seeing her at first through cloudy cataracts.

She hugged him hard and lifted him in her arms.

"Hey, kiddo," she said. "So glad you're home."

"Mom!" he said, burying his face in her coat.

It was twenty-eight degrees, but beads of sweat lined her forehead. She wiped her face with the back of her hand. Then, not wanting to neglect Tomás, she reached for him also, offering him her cheek.

"I want to hear everything," she said, swinging Lee's backpack over her shoulder, steering them toward the car. "All about your trip and the monuments and George Washington and everything Ben Franklin. Sounds like it all went well, but I can't lie, I'm so glad you're back."

"Tomás," she said, whispering to him once Lee was buckled into the backseat and couldn't hear, "he looks terrible, he's down to nothing. I'm going to have to get him to Bream right away. Tonight even, if I can reach him. Why didn't you tell me?"

"Now wait a minute, Cass," Tomás started, but she held up her hand to silence him and made her way brusquely around to the driver's side. "Hold on," he said. "You've got to believe me, Lee's okay."

Cass couldn't look at him. She turned on the engine, wordlessly pulling away from the curb.

"Why didn't you bring Patrick, Cass?" Lee asked, once they were on their way. "I have to say I've missed him too," he said, stifling a cough with the back of his hand and shrinking deeply into the hood of his parka.

"That would have been too much, even for me," she breathed. "I would have had to make a stop at J. C. Penney and buy him a snowsuit. I sure hope you're okay back there, Lee. You sound like the abominable snowman. Sounds like you picked up a terrible cough and maybe a cold too," she said, shooting another hazardous look in Tomás's direction.

"Cass, you won't believe everything good that happened!" Lee exclaimed as they exited the airport and moved toward the Route 9 ramp.

"I can only imagine," she replied, thinking the worst.

"DC is amazing," Lee continued, having decided to break the news to her himself in order to save Tomás from the job of explaining. "It's magical, like Oz. Tomás and I did some serious detective work. We found Tomás's daughter, Maria Teresa. She's three and even smaller than me!"

"What? What are you talking about?" Cass said, her throat constricting, not sure she'd heard right. "I don't know anything about that. Are you sure you're not making something up, Lee? Tomás?" she said, turning to him. "Can you explain what he's talking about?"

"I will tell you everything," he said, swallowing hard, "when we get inside. I wanted to tell you sooner, but there wasn't a good time. The only thing I can say is that everything worked out. We did everything on Lee's list and more. You should be proud of your son. I know I am."

"You're the last person who needs to tell me to be proud of my son," Cass replied sharply, hoping Lee couldn't hear. "I know who he is and what he is better than anyone. You, of all people, don't have a clue. If you did, you would have taken better care of him."

They pulled up in front of the apartment building, where a pile of snow and debris had been ploughed into a tidy iceberg nearly barring the walkway. When she was a girl it had been the kind of thing Cass would have raced home from school to climb before the other neighborhood children, scrambling up to become king of the castle in a matter of seconds. But she looked at Lee, knowing all too well he was too fragile for that kind of game.

She cut the engine, and Tomás opened Lee's door, airlifting him up and out, onto the frozen sidewalk. Cass gripped Lee's hand, trying to determine how to best navigate the frozen stairs. She pressed her arm around his shoulders, feeling the winged scapula unfold as they started forward. No matter what awful sequence of events would follow, his first white baby shoes still sat bronzed and defiant and indestructible on the mantel, his milk teeth preserved in a velvet box, his toddler days a lick of memory—of when she had hauled him round and round the block to school in the little red Radio Flyer wagon, at four and five and six and at seven, in never-ending revolutions, his book bag bungee-corded across his lap.

In baby steps they crossed the slippery path to the front door, the ground sheathed in ice, the wrought-iron banister jagged with miniature stalactites, their wool gloves slipping along the rail. Tomás offered help, but Cass said, "No, no thanks, we can manage without you."

She unlocked the front door and guided Lee up the darkened stairs. Then she swung the door swung open, and the aroma of things sweet and savory cooking at once drifted out into the carpeted hallway.

"We made it," Cass said, trying to be cheerful. "Finally, we're home!"

She switched on the hall light and dropped her bag on the chair. "Here, I'll take that," she said to Lee, helping him slip his arms out of his coat.

"Shoes there," she ordered them both, pointing to the faded cherry-red carpet remnant she had picked up at a yard sale two summers ago and kept stored in the closet for just such an occasion. And she remembered in a sudden flush of emotion Lee's first day in the world, when it had snowed and they had driven home from the hospital in slow motion, Neil at the wheel, whiteness everywhere, breathtaking beyond belief—not knowing what was in store for them.

Lee abandoned his frozen appliquéd cowboy boots in a flash and stood grinning and barefoot, wiggling his toes.

"Ah, that's more like it," he said weakly. "They need to thaw."

"Nice boots," Cass said and closed the closet door. "How did you manage to get those?"

Patrick was within inches of them, standing in the shadow of the hallway wearing a silk bowtie, his cloven feet dainty as Merlin in tights.

Lee sank to the floor and buried his face in Patrick's neck, Eskimo-style. "Missed you, boy," he said.

Earlier that morning Cass had herded Patrick into the bathroom and turned on the shower in order to make him as germ-free as possible.

"Lee," Cass said, not wanting to let on how worried she was about how bad he looked, "now that you're home and you've said your hellos to Patrick, I'd like you to go lie down and rest for a bit. I'll be in to take your temperature and check your blood pressure in a few minutes. We'll have a lot of fun in a little while, but first things first. Go on, kiddo."

"Do what your mom says," Tomás chimed in, avoiding Cass's eyes. "I might not be in charge of you anymore, now that we're back, but I'm on your mother's side."

Lee looked quickly from Cass to Tomás and back again.

"Are you going to be here when I wake up, Tomás?" Lee asked. "You two aren't going to fight about what happened, are you? Cass, Tomás was my bodyguard. He didn't do anything wrong. I promise, Cass. Please don't fire him."

She stood, hands on her hips, struggling to control her temper. She was ready to throw Tomás out on his ear, out of their apartment and out of their lives. But she didn't want to upset Lee so quickly after they'd come back, and not on Thanksgiving.

"Everything is fine, sweetie," Cass said. "Tomás will be here when you wake up. We're sticking with our plan. Don't worry about that."

"Okay then," Lee said uncertainly, looking back and forth between the two of them one more time. "I could use a nap, especially if Patrick keeps me company. C'mon, boy."

Once Lee was gone, Cass ignored Tomás, who was still

standing awkwardly in the hallway with his coat on. She reached for the phone on the hall table and dialed Dr. Bream's emergency number, powered by sheer adrenaline. She knew he was spending Thanksgiving with his family somewhere on Long Island. The on-call nurse answered, someone whose voice she didn't recognize.

"Hello, this is Cass Adams," she said, trying to stay calm. "My son, Lee, is a patient of Dr. Bream's. His condition seems to have gotten worse over the last few days. I know it's a holiday, but if you could please page him immediately and let him know how important it is. We need to see him as soon as possible. If not today, then first thing tomorrow."

"Do you think he needs to be seen in the emergency room today?" the nurse asked. "Have you taken his temperature? Does he have chest pains or shortness of breath?"

"No." Cass thought for a minute, shaking her head. "Not really. The shortness of breath isn't new, and the cough isn't either, but he just seems sicker to me. He was on vacation for a few days under someone else's care and just got back home. I don't know what's wrong, but he looks much worse than before he left."

"I'll contact the doctor right away and try to set something up for tomorrow morning," the nurse said, "and I'll get back to you as soon as possible. In the meantime, if anything changes, you should go to your nearest emergency room."

Cass hung up and turned to Tomás, who was still standing in the shadows of the dimly lit hallway.

"Okay, Tomás," she said, her mind racing, "can you tell me what Lee was talking about? Was it his imagination or did something happen while you were away that you decided not to tell me? Whatever it is, he looks terrible, and you can be sure I will hold you accountable if anything bad happens to him. Now tell me. What's this about finding your daughter?"

Tomás hesitated, then started to explain. "I wouldn't blame you if you threw me out right now," he said. "It's true, I lied, but there's more to it than you might think. It wasn't meant to hurt anyone. Do you mind if we sit?" he said, gesturing to the living room sofa. "What Lee said is true, we had a wonderful time, we saw everything on his list, and he was really excited and happy. But there's more I need to tell you. When you first asked me to take Lee to DC and Philadelphia I didn't hesitate, but I didn't tell you everything either, because I couldn't, and because for better or worse, things all seemed to fall into place naturally."

Cass wrapped her arms around her waist, bracing herself for what would come next. She realized how little she had thought to ask Tomás about his past.

"I haven't told you very much about my life outside, my life before coming to the States," Tomás continued. "Now I'm afraid I'm going to have to. But keep in mind it all worked out. Lee was completely safe all the time."

By the time Tomás had told her the whole story, from how he and his pregnant wife had been arrested and sent to separate prisons in Buenos Aires, to trying to find Maria Teresa—including enlisting the help of Margaret and spending her money on a senseless bribe—Cass was not only speechless with disappointment but enraged at his ability to fool them. When Tomás had finished describing how they had recovered Maria Teresa, in a manner of sorts, and how they had driven all the way to Ocean City, Maryland, without her permission, she didn't even know if she had it in herself to feel sorry for him.

"So you see we went through all that trouble to find her, and she's never going to be mine anyway," Tomás said, slamming his fist on the armrest of the sofa.

"That's quite a story," Cass said, rising, but feeling off-balance. Her empathy for Tomás and his daughter ended when she imagined Lee and Tomás dangerously trudging through the streets of Washington and Philadelphia, Tomás having convinced Lee he was a real detective, selfishly dragging him into places he didn't belong. No wonder he looked so bedraggled.

"You two had yourselves quite an adventure," she said, hands on hips. "At Lee's expense, and mine. It was reckless of you, Tomás, really reckless and deceitful. You took advantage of us both. I should fire you on the spot," she said, eyeing his ashen face, his hands stuffed clumsily into his coat pockets. "And if I had been smart enough to make you sign a contract to take care of Lee ahead of time, you can be sure I'd be filing papers to sue you tomorrow. But then you have no real certification of any kind, do you? And nothing of value. I have no reason to believe any of your story. As it is, I can only blame myself for trusting you when I should have known better. It's amazing you brought Lee home in one piece."

And yet it was also true, she realized, looking into Tomás's deadened eyes, proofed by shame, that he had given Lee something she never could have—a companion, a friend.

"Cass, you must know how sorry I am," Tomás said. "You were right. I don't deserve to be here with you and Lee, but I also don't think what we did made Lee any worse. You have to believe I did my best to protect him. There was just one time we worried, when we got to the hotel in Philadelphia. But we gave him his heart medication and watched him so closely. Margaret and me. I wish you could have met her. She was sort of a mother to him while we were away. I'll pay you back whatever money I owe you. But just so you know, I think the trip may have meant almost as much to Lee as it did to me. He was really proud to have helped me find my daughter. And it was really because of him that we were able to find her."

"And what about your daughter, Tomás? Will you go back for her?"

"I'm afraid I can't answer that yet," he said. "I need to think about what's in her best interest. As you can see, I don't always use the best judgment."

"In some ways, I'm grateful to you," Cass said. "Lee seems happier than he's been in a long time. Kira's death was awful. There's no easy way to get over that. But am I the only one who sees what rough shape he's in? I'm his mother," she said. "His *mother*. And I don't think you can begin to imagine how upsetting all this is. It just feels like the world is closing in too fast. I can't do anything to stop it."

"Cass," Tomás said, "when I saw Maria Teresa, I wanted

more than anything to protect her. It was the first time I'd seen her, and without even knowing her it was such a powerful feeling. I know I'm not Lee's mother. Or his father either. But I must be something somewhere in between. We got very close. I would do anything for him. For Lee's sake and for what's left of our time together, can't we try to enjoy the rest of the day? All this work you've done, all these preparations," he said, moving into the kitchen, to where her cooking was in various stages and things were simmering in pots and pans on the stove. "Let's not let it go to waste. It's been a very long time since I shared a home-cooked meal with anyone. If it's okay, I'd like to stay."

"Maybe later I'll feel differently," Cass said. "Right now I'm extremely angry and disappointed, Tomás. I trusted you, and you let me down. I agree, we should go on with our day as planned. I'm up to my eyeballs in…well, wooden spoons and who knows what else, but there's a method to my madness. And there will be food on the table by the time we sit down. Keep an eye on Lee while I finish cooking, will you?"

"Sure thing," Tomás said. "I've never been much good in the kitchen. My wife used to say I…" He caught himself and stopped.

"Relax, Tomás," Cass said gently. "Can I make you some coffee? Or would you like something stronger?"

"I'm fine," he said. "Mind if I turn on the football game in a bit? Some big games today."

"Help yourself," Cass said, pointing to the remote on the coffee table. "The whole country's probably going blind doing the same thing."

☙

"How's the show doing, Cass?" Lee asked a little while later, having finished his nap and come into the kitchen wearing his Davy Crockett faux-coonskin cap, for what could only have been intended as comic relief. He had slept deeply for twenty minutes, nuzzled against Patrick, and emerged with more color in his cheeks. He helped himself to a piece of celery from amidst a colorful platter of crudités.

So much seemed to have changed in a week. Cass looked at his pale temples crosshatched with swollen blue veins, his sunken cheeks, as though life itself was withdrawing from him in spades. Had he been this gaunt last week, had she stopped noticing? He seemed exhausted—despite his cheerfulness. She could still take him to the ER tonight if things got worse.

"It's a historic day," Lee announced. "We should have a moment of silence for the pilgrims and for Plymouth Rock, and for Christopher Columbus who was so nearsighted he thought he had arrived in India."

"All in good time," Cass said, tugging on the tail of his hat affectionately. "We could use you at the theatre. You could be our haberdasher. And you *would* have to ask about the show," Cass sighed, wiping her hands on a dishtowel. "We closed last night to a standing ovation. And we're about to start rehearsing something new. No one really knows what it's about yet," she said, her eyes narrowing. "The producer wants to keep us in the dark until after the holidays. That's the beauty of off-off-Broadway. Hopefully it won't be something that requires too much melodrama and eyeliner. My hands aren't quite as steady as they used to be."

"Maybe it'll be something about Tarzan," Lee suggested. "Or Einstein or Mata Hari. Or James Bond. Did you know I've become an honorary spy?"

"Tomás started to tell me a little about your adventures—" Cass began.

"Tomás was like Superman and Batman and Shazam all in one," Lee broke in. "He would have stopped a speeding bullet for me. He would have done anything. You have to promise not to be mad at him."

"I would love your help, Lee, and yours, too, in a little while, Tomás," Cass called into the living room where Tomás had turned the TV on. "We'll get back to the details of your trip a little later. But right now, sir, do you mind putting your things away?" She pointed to his backpack where it sat marooned in the middle of the hallway. Reminding him—regardless of his ill health—that he wasn't immune to daily chores.

45

It was near noon by the time Lee had unpacked his clothes and put his treasures away in drawers and on shelves and began to feel at home again. As far as he could tell, everything in his room looked the same, from the neat fold of his blue-cotton bedspread to his army of plastic figures set up for the Battle of Gettysburg. Since meeting Alicia, Gettysburg was no longer the same.

Things in the kitchen were moving along nicely. While Cass resumed her preparations, Tomás put on his glasses and began flipping through the pages of the newspaper.

Lee came into the hallway and followed Tomás into the living room. "Do you think Margaret is having Thanksgiving?" he asked dreamily. "Do you think she's been invited anywhere?"

"I'm sure of it," Tomás answered. "I'm sure she's ordering somebody around even as we speak, in somebody else's kitchen, telling *them* what to do," he said with the smallest hint of sarcasm.

"I bet you're right," Lee said. "Margaret seems like the kind of person who could sit alone in her apartment for an entire week, and not miss anyone."

Tomás patted the sofa cushion next to him. "Come watch the game with me. Thanksgiving football is an American tradition. These people are crazy, it'll make a good show."

"No thanks," Lee said. "I'm not much of a sports fan."

It was Detroit versus Chicago. Lions versus Bears. Jeff Komlo, the QB for Detroit, controlled the ball and was strutting his stuff on the twenty-yard line.

"Touchdown!" Tomás got to his feet for the instant replay.

Lee continued to look at him blankly.

"Okay, whatever you say." Tomás held up his hands, sensing it was better to leave Lee alone.

❧

Meanwhile, Cass continued with the meal in the kitchen, her sleeves rolled. Already, in the last hour since hanging up her coat, she'd prepped and arranged three pots beginning to boil or sauté concurrently on the stove.

She pushed the loose strands of hair behind her ears and set to work on the turkey, crowning it with foil, leaving the legs and wings to brown evenly.

It was going on four o' clock. She donned the oven mitts and lowered the oven door, taking a stab at the stuffing, which loosened on schedule, away from the cavity. She withdrew the pie from the upper rack and set it on the stovetop to cool. Through the back porch window, the approaching darkness split the sky into pieces, like storm clouds descending upon the roof.

Then, she heard Lee's footsteps coming down the hallway.

It was now or never, Cass thought. She had to tell him.

"What's our ETE—estimated time of eating?" Lee asked jovially. He stood on a step stool, inspecting the pie. "*Mmm*," he exhaled aloud, "maybe we should start with dessert?"

"Another half hour if I had to guess," Cass checked her watch. "By the time everything's said and done."

"Thirty minutes," she called out to Tomás. "Thirty minutes before we eat."

❧

Then Cass turned to Lee, the burden of withheld information weighing heavily on her shoulders. "Lee," she began, "There's something important I need to tell you. I probably shouldn't have waited so long," she said. "A letter came while you were away. Here, I'll give it to you now. I didn't want to risk forwarding it."

Lee blinked, and wiped his glasses fogged over from moisture in the kitchen. The thick oversized letters of the return address slowly came to a standstill. He immediately recognized the handwriting as Kira's. But she was gone, wasn't she? She had been dead two weeks. He had seen her body on display at the funeral.

He looked up at her, confused.

"I don't understand, Cass. Kira's dead. How could she have written to me?" The small crimped edges of his mouth began to pucker.

"It came two days after you left. Forwarded by Kira's mom. I couldn't bear to tell you over the phone. I guess Kira had something more to say to you. I don't know how else to explain. I know you must miss her terribly."

Lee took the envelope, feeling deceived. "Why didn't you tell me immediately?" he shouted. "Maybe I could have done something, maybe there was something she wanted me to do."

He walked wordlessly down the hall to his room, Patrick at his heels, and locked the door. He stood on the step stool to switch off the overhead light and lay on his back in his bed and stared at the ceiling in the darkness. The fluorescent plastic solar system pasted there grew eerily luminous. He wished he could lose his center of gravity long enough to disappear.

Kira was calling to him from the dead, from some outside other place he had not wanted to be touched by yet, not wanted to believe was real. Above, the shapes of the planets arranged around the sun stayed fixed in their orbits, but Lee began to feel the sensation of walls closing in, the way they did in an old Superman episode he had watched on TV, in which Superman used x-ray vision to see through solid rock and search for Lois Lane, who had accidentally stumbled upon a pharaoh's tomb in an ancient Egyptian pyramid. Stop-motion photography was new. Lee had read an article about a man named Harold Edgerton at MIT whose invention of the stroboscope could capture individual splashes of milk on film, breaking down time.

If Lee stood perfectly still, someone could shoot an apple off his head, reinforcing the ideas of Newton, fixing him forever, despite the fact that everything hurt—his bones, his ears, his nose, even his breath, and his kneecaps that creaked with every step. He sighed, sloughing skins, feeling fear outright. He reached for her letter and began to read.

Dear Lee,

Hey, amigo. I got rings for both of us. I'm already wearing mine. It would have been nice to get married in Central Park near the Alice in Wonderland statue like we jokingly planned. I know we never really asked each other out loud. But you're the only one I would ever consider marrying. Ben Franklin had seventeen children and two wives. He became a father before he was twenty! No matter what, I'll wait for you.

Love,
Kira

Lee stopped reading and reached inside the envelope. At the bottom, scrunched into the corner, was something thin and round and made of metal—a gold paper clip twisted into a circle. Immediately he remembered the similar gold ring he had seen on her finger that day she lay in the open casket. He picked it up and put it on, remembering what he knew of the story of Romeo and Juliet. He immediately felt close to her again, almost as if she were in the room.

He slipped it onto the ring finger of his left hand, and remembered her lively face—her tutus and toe shoes, the way they'd tried to escape their parents in Central Park in order to find time alone, exploring Sheep's Head Meadow and listening to live music. How every day with her was more than he could have hoped for. And he remembered again that she was gone.

He was surrounded by shelves and shelves of American history memorabilia, documented facts—the replica of the first American flag sewn by Betsy Ross, the miniature vellum scroll of the Declaration of Independence, knowing from his detective books how you could falsify the age of documents with lemon juice and tea bags and a little bit of skill. The small faux-marble bust of Ben Franklin stood out, the man who had devoted himself to the written word, having courted the inventions of Gutenberg.

The impulse to write things down was what mattered; Lee

understood that now. Without words, he concluded, he would know nothing of the people who had inspired him.

He realized suddenly that he had underestimated Dr. Bream, who was on the right track after all, having encouraged him to keep the journal—without which he would have no drawing of Cocoa. And how the legal system, with its hierarchy of precedents, made sense finally, and how we had to learn from the actions of the past. And that the written word is far superior to the spoken, because it can be repeated over and over. So that the most important thing one can leave behind is evidence, evidence that one has lived the best life they could.

Tomorrow he would begin to rewrite his epitaph, based not on who he thought he was but on who he had become now that he had done some good in the world, now that he had helped Tomás find Maria Teresa. He knew from the time they left Philadelphia that he was far sicker than when they'd started, that his insides were deteriorating in ways so new and fast he couldn't keep up. He had decided not to tell anyone, he had willed himself to go on.

He reached down and boxed Patrick's large prehistoric earflaps between his palms, the texture leathery and thinned and seemingly related to elephants—and thought what a profound thing it was to have this creature in their midst. And he stared, wondering, into Patrick's brooding doomed eyes to where innocence lurked, blinded by love.

Lee came into the kitchen, where Cass was holding aloft an aluminum potato masher, poised to bring it down with force into the steaming pot of root vegetables, when he relieved her of it.

"Let me," he said. "It's my favorite part. And it's okay, Cass," Lee said, getting to the point ahead of her. "I didn't mean to get so mad. It was nice, a nice letter. I was just so shocked it was from Kira. It didn't make sense at first. I'm okay, I guess. It just made me miss her more. I was so sad she didn't get to come with us to DC, and that she didn't get to meet Margaret or Maria Teresa. If she had been there everything would have been perfect. She was so close, and she missed it all."

"Oh, hon," Cass said, moving closer. "Whatever she said to you, wherever she is, I know she misses you too. Life goes on though." She put her arm around him. "It has to. We're here together today, that's what matters. And this is going to be a fabulous Thanksgiving. Mash the hell out of these, will you? And when you're done with that, Lee, can you find the poultry string? I need to tie this baby up again," she said, tossing a dishtowel across her shoulder. "It's somewhere in the junk drawer over there, I'd imagine."

"Got it," Lee said, finding the poultry string, after fishing around in the overstuffed kitchen drawer. In the dining room Cass set the table for four—not three.

Lee took one look and guessed. "Do you mean what I think you mean?" he asked.

"Sure enough," she said, turning around, her cheeks flushed. "Sir Patrick will be joining us for dinner. Assuming he behaves. I don't think we have a choice," she said, donning the oven mitts. "He's as much a part of the family as any of us, don't you think?"

They could hear the roar of the crowd, signaling the end of the football game in the living room. Tomás was on his feet and cheering, when the quarterback threw a winning pass that was intercepted for a touchdown. Final score: Detroit Lions 20, Chicago Bears 0.

46

Near five, finally, everything was done and they were ready to sit down at the table.

"Can I get some help finishing the silverware in here?" Cass called out to both of them.

Tomás had switched off the game and was laying out cards on the coffee table for an after-dinner hand of poker. He set down the cards and surveyed the dining room table.

"This is nice, Cass," he said, scanning the overflowing table of delicious smelling food, the turkey dressed in short white paper go-go boots worthy of the Dallas Cowboys cheerleaders, the stuffing a mesa of savory cornbread delicately ferned with rosemary and sage. The table set with cloth napkins and silver.

Two unlit white tapers sat on either side of a bouquet of yellow roses and blue irises, a tribute to Cass's parents.

She was pleased they were all together, almost forgetting for a moment how angry she was.

"Well, it's a good occasion for an occasion. I just hope everything tastes good."

Lee took Tomás's hand. "C'mon, big guy, you can help me finish the silverware." And together they completed setting the table, though Lee couldn't remember which side was forks and which was spoons. There was something small and quietly enduring about how they worked so seamlessly together—a kind of intimacy Cass hadn't noticed between them before.

"I think we're ready," she said, her eyes shining, her hair pushed back behind her ears to reveal her delicately delineated jaw. She had done it, she had made everything she had planned, and so far nothing disastrous had happened.

She poured a glass of chardonnay for her and Tomás and a glass of sparkling cider for Lee and sat back in her chair, with a deep sigh of relief.

"Hold on, Cass," Lee exclaimed, attempting to settle Patrick once and for all at his new place at the table, working to tie a white cloth napkin beneath the pig's chin as a bib. As if on cue, Patrick began to lap water from his bowl, splashing the edge of the tablecloth, his rough pink hindquarters barely fitting on the hassock they had rolled in to replace the wooden chair, his nostrils free-associating in the moist exuberance of smells as if at a county fair.

Cass and Tomás sat opposite the two of them, laughing while Lee tried to mop the table with a napkin.

"C'mon now," Lee said. "Give him some credit. He's trying to be a person!"

"Every play needs a fool," Cass said. "In Shakespeare, and in Donne, and in all of the great works of literature. But Patrick is more than that, I can assure you. He's a prince among men. While you were gone, we became great friends."

It was good to be home. They joined hands for a moment of silence, Lee holding tight to Patrick's pink cloven-hoof included in prayer, as he momentarily stared straight ahead, sober as a Quaker.

Darkness had closed in during those last few minutes they'd bowed in silent prayer. Each one hoping for a miracle, Cass imagined.

"Tomás, do you mind lighting the candles?" she asked.

"Of course." He lit a match and leaned across her, almost but not quite touching her shoulder.

"To things borrowed and shared," Lee said, beginning a toast. "To the pilgrims," he said, "for getting lost and landing at Plymouth Rock. For planting corn. Without which, all this, our lives might be based on rice—or wheat—or graham crackers."

"Hear, hear," Tomás said, while he and Cass clicked glasses.

"And here's to the pilgrims for hunting wild turkey and not wild boar," Lee added. "Though let's face it," he said, covering the side of his mouth with the back of his hand, pretending to keep a secret, "I'm not exactly sure how long he'll last sitting on that stool."

Cass laid her fork on the edge of her plate and pressed forward on her elbows, deciding to try to clear the air. She tapped the blunt edge of her knife against her wine glass until it rang clear as a bell.

"Lee," she said, "Tomás has already told me the whole story. You don't have to worry, I'm not angry anymore, I'm not going to ask him to leave. Some of the things you did could really have landed you in a lot of trouble. And Tomás, as the adult, should have known better. I'm just glad you're both okay. As your mother, I'm responsible for your safety and your welfare. I wish you and Tomás had told me what was really going on. But now that part's over. The rest is between Tomás and me."

Lee looked down guiltily, lowering his eyes to where Patrick shifted his weight under the table.

"Cass," he said. "It was the best week of my life! Kira and I had planned everything for so long I really didn't want to go on living after she died. I didn't know what to do. But then, when Tomás needed my help, I started to feel better. It was amazing to try to think like a detective. And Margaret, I know you would have liked her. I walked the same streets where Ben Franklin conducted his lightning experiments with a key! I saw Edison's lightbulbs! I want to go back again. Next time with you, so I can show you myself. One thing I can tell you, though, the Liberty Bell is *way* too loud!" he said, pretending to cover his ears.

Cass listened, knowing on some small level that despite his disease, she was looking at something of a human miracle.

The meal was delicious, earning high marks for presentation as well as for flavor. They dug into the turkey, which was perfectly moist, the side dishes crisped and boiled to tender proportions.

"So you'll be back with us on Tuesday, of course?" Cass asked in a kind of peace offering to Tomás, as she held the platter of mashed potatoes before him. There was nothing else to do but call things settled for the time being. Tomorrow they would take Lee to see Dr. Bream, and hopefully get some reassurance.

Her eyes were shining, her cheeks flushed pink as the wine began to work its way through her bloodstream. The candles continued to burn, lazily flickering.

"I'll be leaving for work at eight as usual," Cass continued. "And you'll see, as it gets closer to Christmas around here, New York starts to feel a little bit like Las Vegas. We'll have to get a tree and decorations."

"*Sí*, of course," Tomás said, pushing his chair away from the table in order to stretch his legs.

Unbeknownst to Cass and Tomás, over dark meat and cranberry sauce, Lee had spent the entire evening under the spell of Kira's letter. He fingered the slim metal band on his left ring finger admiringly, marveling at how it glowed in the flickering candlelight. She had managed to reach him even from the dead.

"I better get dessert," Cass said, folding her napkin neatly, leaving them alone with their guilty conspiracy.

Dessert was a hit, though the servings were much too big. Lee struggled to take more than a few bites of pie—which Cass had generously dolloped with homemade whipped cream. She poured glasses of port for herself and for Tomás and set them on the sideboard to breathe.

"I'll clear," Lee volunteered, stumbling a bit as he tried to stand and gather what remaining dishes he could.

Cass noticed his unsteadiness and was afraid. She had to keep herself from getting out of her chair, in order to let him have the dignity of doing things on his own. She was counting down the hours until morning, when they'd be in Bream's office.

"Thanks, Lee," she said, "for remembering to be a gentleman."

"Here," Tomás said, "that should be my job. You both did all that work. I'll start the coffee."

Later, in the living room, after he and Cass had said their goodbyes to Tomás, Lee sat on the sofa alone, relieved that things would return to normal on Monday. He turned on the TV and stared, mesmerized, at the replay footage of the morning's Macy's Thanksgiving Day Parade—featuring appearances by the Goodyear Blimp and Felix the Cat and Mickey Mouse.

He was happy Cass wasn't too mad at Tomás—at least that's how it seemed. He planned to wear Kira's ring to sleep that night, whether or not anyone noticed. He was yawning as he watched the giant helium Mickey, tethered like a kite, hoisted up on strings. Then Charlie Brown and Linus followed suit, waving their hands in slow motion.

"Bedtime, sweetie." Cass was beside him. He was sleepy and cooperative and immersed in a deeper swell of feeling than any of them could begin to imagine. Cass walked him down the hall and into the bathroom, where he brushed his teeth and put on his pajamas, then got into bed.

"C'mon, Patrick." Lee signaled, snapping his fingers, and the big lug came ambling down the hallway and skated across the floorboards.

When Lee was safely tucked into bed, Cass leaned beside him, his head resting in her arms, the small bedside lamp dimmed to a nascent pearl. In the shadows, still visible, were the familiar first books of his childhood. The Golden Books, the early readers, the sentences built of monosyllabic words designed to karate-chop a young child's brain into hot pursuit of language. The *ge* and *de* and *sh* of letters defying intuition. The *ing* of *zing*. The *rrr* of *brrr*. Hutchinson-Gilford did nothing to impair Lee's intellect, and it had been easy and natural for him to learn to read.

How odd it was she'd found herself come home to the wisdom of fairy tales this night, in a wave of weakness in which nursery rhymes boiled down to good and evil, with little in between. She remembered them viscerally, in this dark-hearted hour, still wanting on some level to be the child with him—at odds, to be held, to be read to.

And now the oversized tome seemed to levitate toward her as though she were a guest at a séance, trying to reach out and recapture the underworld of lost love. *The Big Book of Mother Goose Rhymes* beckoned to her from the bottom shelf, its gold spine metallically lit, beside the pop-up picture books of *Alice in Wonderland* and *Pinocchio* and good old standbys of *Runaway Bunny* and *Good Night Moon.*

It seemed to rise and teleport itself into her hands, the long-necked goose on the cover illustration wearing glasses and a straw hat and high button shoes, as though she needed to borrow humanness in order to tell her anthropomorphic story convincingly. Inside, a series of unrealistic cryptic rhymes, distilled from all walks of life, releasing their set of human ills in a way strikingly similar to those released from Pandora's box.

Cass opened the book to the table of contents as if choosing a piece of chocolate akin to poison, knowing that the jewels of childhood had yielded nothing but disappointment, but that the music of the words lured her still. Stumbling as they did with their strange distorted origins of cobblestones and woods and caves and brick ovens—of candy houses and evil queens and trickery. Soups made from stone and gingerbread that could run on two feet. Monsters being eviscerated, hunted, eaten. In dark caves and wicked castles, and in armor that failed to do its job. In creatures bludgeoned by swords and bunioned with warts and wings, and magic transformations of ogres into princes. Beauty was wished for, confused with goodness.

Cass sat now, her arm around Lee's shoulders, his body heaving with frailty, hollow as a bird despite the weight of a hefty meal, as his snores rebounded in and out of his nasal passageways, gathering strength there.

"Rub a dub, dub, three men in a tub," she began, trembling a little. Her arm neatly tucked around his shoulders. His childhood had come and gone before he was old enough to really be afraid of anything. The grief she felt tonight was for herself also, selfish, uncontrollable.

By now she found the page she wanted.

"Little Boy Blue, come blow your horn," she began from memory. "The sheep are in the meadow, the cow's in the corn." And she remembered their early happiness together, every day a new beginning. "Where is the boy who looks after his sheep?" she asked, looking down at him, and then answering for herself as his heavy eyelids breathed and shuddered. "He's under a haystack, half asleep."

Beneath his navy flannel pajama shirt, the internal organs worked to corrode themselves, devoid of magic. No spells to break, no alter egos.

He was sound asleep.

She closed the book and lightly rubbed his forehead with her fingertips.

⁊

Afterward, Cass sat in a daze on the living room couch, the air salted like sand—the candles having long burned out—feeling capsized on a raft in a colorless land. It was then she realized she hadn't been herself in years. In the hollows of her wrists and the span of her ribs, in her hips that braked at ninety degrees, making her slave to the geometry of rising and moving, she had simulated a life far more mechanical than his.

She looked out the window toward the distant skyline, past the stark whiteness of snow that would soon be gone, giving way to the permutations of gray that most people lived by. How the color gray coddled and protected people's dreams with uncertainty, neither black nor white, but guarding against disappointment. More and more, New York had taken on the character of her hopes and her griefs. The city filigreed with the intricacies of survival and disaster, day after day posing the same human question. When she watched a street person on her way to or from work—nomadically attempting shelter between the width of dilapidated brick buildings, hair hived in a nest and swaddled in far too many layers of wool and polyester and cotton, body stench putrid as rotten eggs—she saw herself easily embroidered into that same pituitary axis of searching. An impulse as old as caves, mind-swept with grief and gut instinct.

Drawing was like that; you started with an inner flame that rose up inside from places you couldn't name.

And you went on.

Like all people who do one thing exceptionally well, her center of gravity was known to her.

When he was gone, she would have no choice but to start over, losing herself like a captive ghost to his ghost, speaking the Morse code of disappearances. The language of shadows would not be wasted on her.

47

Of all the deaths he had ever heard of, death by beard was the most impressive. It had happened to Austrian Hans Steininger in 1567 when he tripped on his unrolled four-feet-five-inch beard in the middle of the night—and broke his neck while attempting to escape a fire.

It was only 5:13 on the bedside clock. In the early morning hours, the room still laden with shadows, Lee lay adrift in bed and thought of all the strangest deaths he had ever heard of: There was death from holding in a pee, and death by conductor's cane, death by dessert, death by biting one's tongue. Death by baseball, and toilet, and robot, and helicopter blade. Death by bottle cap, and death by telling a joke, and death by body slam.

He lay in bed and held his breath, afraid to acknowledge even to himself that something in his body felt different this morning. As if the heavy trunk of a tree had heaved itself angrily against the length of his spine in his sleep, making him helpless to sit up and fight gravity.

Where the window glass met the shade, navy clouds scraped the fire escape like brushed steel slaughtering the sky. The ice-encrusted windowsill had barely begun to melt.

Patrick awoke, one ear folded down and one ear up, and stared at Lee through the gray flannel dawn like a prehistoric gnome, the flaxen hairs on his chin combed loosely into a beard. Cass was no doubt still asleep, exhausted after the colossal efforts of yesterday's undertaking, not to mention the confessions of his and Tomás's small—though innocent—conspiracy.

Lee lay there helpless, feeling what it was like to be his own man—for once not worrying, not waiting for her to come hurrying down the hall to wake him and say good morning.

He looked at the ring on the index finger of his left hand

and had an inner hush, a hope, remembering. Today might be the day. It was Friday after all, and they had made it home and through Thanksgiving. He had a weird tingling sensation in his legs that went straight to his chest and upper arm along the entire left side of his body. Air groaned inside his lungs, circling like a Ferris wheel, and he experienced an accompanying wave of nausea that came from being flung out far over the ocean.

"Here, boy," he said to Patrick, who clambered up lazily over the small blunt hill of covers for a brusque headlock. "Do you know I'm getting married soon?" he said, whispering into the parched pink face where the eyebrows lifted, listening in the dark. Patrick's head nodded omnisciently, bowing like a metronome, measuring all things the same.

Lee leaned his elbow against the pillow, attempting to sit up, and felt a wash of nausea swab his forehead, his temples throbbing. The flu maybe coming on. It was 5:32 now and stalling, time thickening to a honeyed standstill.

He thought of pancakes and maple syrup, how they soothe the brain. He knew that Cass would forgive Tomás, that she was incapable of staying angry for more than a few days, that things would be all right again. They might stay friends even—after… after he was gone. Only since Kira's letter did he realize there was a *now* and *then.*

Had it begun to happen? he thought in a panic that sank to his waist, entwined there like a snake. Was it happening now? Dr. Bream had, from the beginning, described to him the symptoms of the onset of a possible stroke or heart attack, sensations like these he now felt but were hard to keep track of. Blurred vision, the beginning of a headache, the edges of the room beginning to curve as though forced through a periscope. He tried to lift his head but couldn't fully manage it. His tongue starting to slacken in his jaw.

But he wasn't done! He reached for his notebook in a ferocious act of defiance and opened it to where he left off yesterday, remembering his promise to himself to revise his epitaph, to be worthy of Ben Franklin, to leave something behind.

He glanced at the list, now strangely slanted, of people and things that had come prematurely to unfortunate ends:

Geronimo

Sam Adams

Horseless carriages

Mary Queen of Scots

Monkeys as astronauts

Dracula

Blocks of ice being used to cool food before refrigerators

Gas lamps

Cleopatra

Penny candy…

He spread open the spine of the notebook on his lap and tried to breathe. Is this what it felt like? A slow disappearance in which one tries to hold on but keeps getting pulled involuntarily backward?

Did he owe anyone anything?

The act of leaving made him want to take stock of what was left undone. In all the world's words there were endless waiting pairs of nouns and verbs intent on actions waiting to happen. Did evil exist in its own right? Some people say the death penalty is immoral, that everyone is capable of rehabilitation. But in the natural selection of the world, it seemed only natural to him that some people would be dealt something less and others something more, inevitably leading them toward self-destruction. The way Hutchinson-Gilford claimed nothing personal against him, having simply exploded out of random DNA to arrive at his door.

Was it worth anything to be a good sport? All along he had tried to be. But today he felt different, felt anger well up in him for what he was afraid to lose, when what he wanted most was to live.

❦

The nerve endings in his legs tingled, racing unfamiliarly up his arm. He still had his appendix and his liver, though they felt as if they were shriveling by the minute. His heart now coming to a standstill. The first successful human heart transplant had taken place in 1967 in Cape Town, South Africa, by a dashing young surgeon named Christiaan Barnard who had earlier practiced the procedure on dogs, poor things. After all the expense and hubbub in the news, the patient had survived for only eighteen days.

What was a beginning and what was an end? Did you have to be exceptionally good at anything to feel your life had been worthwhile? Ben Franklin, by his own admission, had been terrible at arithmetic. And what was Dr. Bream's ulterior motive for helping victims of progeria? Did he think that by studying the accelerated death of others he could discover the fountain of youth? And did Rodin's *Thinker* really think anything?

Lee had a vague memory of Cass reading to him the night before, laying her hand on his forehead where she had comforted him, as always. She was his one true person in life who had helped pilot him through everything. And now he was going to let her down.

A good death, like a good kill, he realized, was preceded by what the Native Americans considered to be an apology.

So now he reopened the journal on his lap and propped himself up on the pillow one last time, in order to scrawl what words he could:

I wanted to be more... he began simply, feeling the heat grow inside his cheeks, crowding his brain.

I wanted to be more and do more and say more...

Adults always say, don't grow up too fast, but in my case I didn't have a choice...

I used to think that leaving a mark on the world meant having to say something grand and melodramatic like, Off with their heads! like the Queen of Hearts in Alice in Wonderland, *or having a dessert named after you as in the case with Napoleon. Or having a bat cave or a secret compartment in one's ring like the Flash.*

He paused for a second to take a sip of water, knowing how

in the end it all came down to chance, like games of War and Go Fish and unexpected snowstorms that leave people stranded in faraway places for days on end, and records that skipped, stalled in the same dusty track over and over.

He was scared and breathing unevenly, feeling a kind of prescience about what lay ahead, about the letting go that was already in progress. A thin pale ribbon of words was working its way through his brain, trailing like smoke. He could see them leaving him behind even as he formed them, like rough outlines of snores or individual breaths exhaled—trying to keep pace with their overriding intention to slow and fade.

The recessional of thoughts reached him now, retreating through his bones—past marrow, past indignity—as the individual words shed their meanings along the way in a bric-a-brac of dismantling code, like Alpha-Bits swirling in a foggy bowl of milk—the fatigue of which was overwhelming.

With the journal open on his lap, he realized how all things in life are by definition unfinished…

And now I lay me down to sleep, he thought, his head softly merging with the contours of the pillow, his thoughts jumbling, trying to relax into a new, compellingly persuasive order that persisted outside him, as he joined the company of historians and thinkers, artists, and men of letters: Shakespeare and Ptolemy and Newton, friends he'd made in books, Mary Queen of Scots and the Pied Piper of Hamelin. George Washington. Popeye. Pluto. Alice, who was both too large and too small. Little Jack Horner, who stuck his thumb in the pie and got caught. And the three blind mice, their tails notwithstanding. Footsteps down the hall and crusts of bread given by strangers to fat pigeons carousing in alleyways. Cass's love of painting and takeout Chinese. And Tomás's need to find his wife and daughter. And Margaret, who was not nearly as tough as she thought she was. And Maria Teresa, who he still hoped would know him one day. His father, Neil, who he wished had given him a second chance… He had heard he had a new family—he hoped they were suitably normal.

And Kira, who awakened in him a feeling and a future he didn't know he had. He dove towards her now, headfirst—out of air and time and the hopes for something better finally in his future. And for Ben Franklin, who was like an honorary father, having shown him the ways of time and humor and how to cope with the bum hand that life had dealt him.

And one more thing he thought, his mind blurting ahead of himself, barreling forward for a few vast wild seconds of cogency, recovering control. Whoever is reading this, Cass most likely, please bury me with a compass, because in the end I have to believe we're all travelers. And please don't forget my bifocals. And remember that love is only two letters short of *evolve,* which is what I intend to do. At some point or another. So you may be seeing me. Sometime. Somewhere. And please take care of Patrick, who will miss me most of all. The poor dumb beast is more sentimental than all of us.

He sensed he was getting closer to finding where Kira and Violeta had disappeared.

And as far as an official epitaph, I would just like to finish with the following: *I make no apologies for what I am. If I could have managed it, I would have been more. I would have dared it all to begin again.*

And now I've come up with my own riddle:

What is never the same twice?

The answer is TIME.

48

Cass had overslept. It was nine-thirty when she made her way out of the covers, sat up, went to the window, and opened the shade. A yellow taxi was just turning the corner. Across the street, a girl, maybe twelve, in a red parka, was pulling a younger child dressed in blue on a sled. From those three colors she could mix a palette that could describe every color and surface in the universe.

The floor was cold under her feet as she tied her robe around her waist and made her way down the hall where Lee was still asleep, the dark floorboards creaking in the cold, expanding under her weight. The pale ocher squares of light through the living room hallway were oblique and concave.

She paused outside Lee's door for a moment, not knowing what she'd find.

She opened it now slowly and went inside. At the far edges of his bed, he was still asleep, his cheek turned askew on the pillow, the ceiling dark as if pumped with dense clouds. She knelt and touched his forehead, where she realized now that he was neither awake, nor disappeared—but gone.

She put her arms around him, lifted his small head and shoulders in her arms, his eyes still the blue-gray color of the Atlantic, open in defiance but unable to see—while her own feelings raged. She had a fleeting, irrational thought that if she pulled open the window curtain and slowly introduced the winter light she might reawaken him, like the finale to a magic act in which one is cut in half or impaled by swords. At the last minute reversing the outcome with a round of applause. But it wasn't so. Not today. Not here.

It was a scene she had never rehearsed, despite the time she'd had to prepare. She wanted more than anything to do something defiant, tactile. To put her hands in clay, to touch, to feel. She wanted the opportunity to begin again. And she began to break down at the impossibility of it all, and for all that had gone wrong and all that had gone right, and how little control she'd had over any of it. Her beautiful boy was gone.

Now she lifted him in her arms, whole—feeling the small, small, small of his orderly bones connected in a line, like a masterpiece of vertebrae, capable of sitting quietly upon her shoulder.

On his outstretched hand she spied the semicircle of gold arced across his ring finger. Kira's letter still lying on the night table, the envelope flap left open—the revelation of a promise she didn't need to read in order to understand. How he must have felt encouraged to be moving on to something.

"My love," she said aloud, knowing he couldn't hear her, carrying him toward the blind light of the window. Across her lap, his eyes still open. And still he was unafraid, wanting to protect what remained—the missing earlobes, the beaked nose, that which resembled a prehistoric bird more than a child. At last she was able to ask herself freely: *How had they managed it, coping day to day?*

Patrick bumped up against her knee now, wanted to be petted, his tear ducts snagged with mucus, blinking in the unknowability of the moment, the same as any other day.

"It's okay, boy," she said, gently.

What tears there were would wait until things were taken care of. She sat in the dark with him for a few long minutes, still holding him to her with great restraint, knowing this would be the last time she would have alone with him before everything changed.

She dialed Tomás. "It's happened," she said. "Lee's gone." And she heard him quietly break into sobs. Then she dialed Dr. Bream, whose answering machine came on, and she was overcome momentarily by the loose floating digits of her parents' old phone number resurfacing in her brain, like fragments of recovered code still circulating.

She sat on Lee's bed and waited. She considered herself lucky to have been given the privilege of being his mother. It was her destiny in this life, but might have been something very different in another. She had been made aware at all times of life's dangers and of forgiveness, though it was hardest to forgive herself most of all.

Every day, she had awakened and stood and braved the knowledge that she was standing ever so briefly on a circle of land that could shift beneath her feet at any moment, the way the continents had shifted over the ages, leaving adrift Antarctica and Australia. The architecture of the city was made of light and would continue that way through its shifting future of wild successes and dismantling failures. That was New York. The city had been her muse and salvation, leading them through the years like a miner's lamp through every sordid darkness. Ben Franklin had been there, too, guiding them with invention.

❧

Tomás was at the door now, waiting to be let in. She closed Lee's door, and Patrick followed her slowly down the hall to meet him, her whole body trembling, not knowing what it would be like from this day forward.

There was nothing to ask. No one to thank. The cold planes of the apartment stood alone in their simplicity, like doors to a future she couldn't know where would lead.

He was never hers. He was always hers. She had learned from the theatre that illusion was everything.

In the broad strokes of heat that create a life, piece by piece in scraps of black and white or in dots of color, naked and incomplete, misjudging distance over time, he had made his way from childhood to old age within a fraction of a lifetime—always happy, never grieving—and for that she would be eternally grateful.

She would lay her son to rest and go to work or take a trip, and she would always, always, always lie awake at night guarding the open space between them.

ACKNOWLEDGMENTS

This book would not exist without the help of the women in my writing group. Linda Levin-Scherz, thank you for your unwavering support, wisdom, and love. Julie Thacker, likewise, you made me feel my characters were in the room.

Enormous thanks to my readers: Kirstin Valdez Quade, Chris Castellani, Dawn Tripp, Anna Solomon, Pam Painter, Rachel Weaver, Caroline Leavitt, Lauren Grodstein.

Thanks to Joshua Rubenstein at Amnesty International, who introduced me to the group of former prisoners of conscience who changed my world and made me aware of human rights abuses across the globe. A chance encounter with a boy who had progeria at Camp Sunshine in Sebago, Maine, introduced me to the disease. I never knew his name, but his presence stayed with me. So much more has been learned about progeria since the time in which this book is set. For further information, visit the Progeria Research Foundation progeriaresearch.org

To my teachers and friends, not all of whom are still with us: Michael Harper, Jack Hawkes, Barth Suretsky, Paul Golubiewski, Pamela Wade, Elaine Weingarten, Alice Hackett, Rebecca Boyd, Mark O'Connell, Teri Keough. In different ways you supported me and I'm grateful.

Huge thanks to Jaynie Royal at Regal House, whose encouragement, patience, and stamina brought this book from manuscript to the finish line. And to everyone else at Regal who took the necessary steps to make this book happen.

Thank you to Clarise Snyder for walking me through English to Spanish translations.

And in loving memory of my mother, Blanche Weingarten Gordon Camson, Carol Gordon, and Janis Johnson.

And to my family—my husband Phil Johnson, and my sons Ben and Jack—who watched me slowly create this story over time and applauded me along the way.